HANOI SPRING

LIZ HARRIS

HEYWOOD PRESS

'But we stopped so that I could look at my house. We've been stopping in the same place every day for the past two weeks, not thinking how dangerous it must be. If we'd driven straight on to the drive—'

'No one will blame you for an accident I caused,' he repeated firmly. 'I should have been paying attention to what was happening on the road, and I wasn't.'

The chauffeur moved to the back of the car, and bent down to look at the bumper.

'There are a few scratches on the back bumper, but nothing serious, Madame,' he told Lucette, straightening up. He glanced at the bumper that was touching hers.

'Your front bumper is scratched, Monsieur,' he said. 'But neither car has any dents in the bodywork.'

'You must allow me to have your bumper replaced,' the man told Lucette, his hand still lightly under her elbow. 'If you'll permit me to see you into your house, I can explain to your husband what happened, and we can talk about how best to arrange for the work to be done. I know a place not far from here that'll do it.'

Feeling a little steadier, she looked properly at the stranger for the first time.

He was a handsome man, well built, with dark brown hair. She guessed he was about ten years older than she was —about thirty or thirty-one, so a couple of years older than Philippe. The eyes that were looking at her with genuine concern were a piercing grey in his lightly tanned face.

She shook her head. 'He won't be home, I'm afraid. He's one of the administrative staff of the Résident Supérieur so he'll be at the Résidence.'

'Then perhaps you'll allow me to see you into the house, Madame? You're somewhat pale, and I wouldn't feel comfortable leaving you to go in alone, especially as all this was my fault.' With his free hand, he indicated the two cars standing bumper to bumper.

He turned back to her. 'I'd better introduce myself. My name is Gaston Laroche, and I'm one of the many diplomatic attachés you'll find in Hanoi. What I suggest I do is take you inside, and leave my card with you. Your husband will then know how to contact me about the bumper.'

She gave him a wan smile. 'I do feel a little shaken, I must admit, and I wouldn't mind something reviving. Perhaps you would care to join me for some refreshment? This is bound to have been a shock for you, too.'

He gave a slight bow. 'It's very kind of you, Madame. You're right, it was. And, yes, a short break before I continue on my way would be the sensible thing to do.'

And angling himself towards the gate in the iron railings, he started gently propelling her towards the short drive that led up to her house.

'So, GASTON?'

The police chief supervising Gaston leaned back in his chair in the small, undistinguished building on the southern edge of the Old Quarter that housed a branch of the French Sûreté Générale, and folded his hands across his ample stomach. 'From the expression on your face when you came in, I imagine this morning went according to plan.'

Gaston laughed. 'It's that obvious, is it, Emile? Yes, I can truly say it did. Watching her routine over the past week certainly paid off. A tap that was just sufficient for her to feel a little shaky and in need of support, and a few scratches on the bumper, but not enough to bankrupt the Sûreté.'

'I take it you were invited into the house?'

'Indeed, I was. We had brandy for our nerves, followed by sweetened tea.'

'What's the wife like?'

'It's too soon to be able to answer that. But Lucette, as she asked me to call her, seems like any young woman of about twenty-one or twenty-two, who's had a somewhat sheltered upbringing. She's looking forward to getting to know Hanoi's range of restaurants, and the many cafés with live music. From the short amount of time I spent with her, I'd say she's a typical newlywed, who clearly adores her husband, and who doesn't have a single political bone in her body.'

'I assume you didn't get to meet the husband?'

Gaston shook his head. 'No, I didn't. I watched him leave this morning to make sure he'd be at work. I wouldn't have wanted him taking over before I'd achieved my goal. As it is, I've made her acquaintance, and got her trust, if that's the right word.'

'That's a start, anyway.'

Gaston grinned at him. 'Oh, I went somewhat further than that. The brandy settled Lucette sufficiently for us to talk a little about Hanoi, and for her to mention that her husband was one of those supervising the smooth-running of the Hoa Lo Prison. I was naturally greatly impressed to learn that her husband held so important a post.'

The police chief chuckled. 'I'm sure you were.'

'I insisted that she and her husband permit me to show my regret for the accident by taking them to dinner at the Hôtel Métropole on Saturday.'

'Now that could bankrupt the Sûreté,' Emile said with a smile.

Gaston laughed. 'They'd be delighted to go, she told me. They weren't doing anything—they hadn't been there long enough to have built up a circle of friends—and she'd seen the advertisements for the hotel on the trams, and had heard it was excellent from Monsieur Bouvier, the man her husband assists. And she knew her husband was keen to go, too. It means that I'll be meeting Philippe Delon in a couple of days.'

'You *have* done well,' the chief said in satisfaction.

'And there's one more thing,' Gaston added with a smile. 'The Bouviers will be joining us on Saturday.'

The chief sat up sharply and stared at Gaston in amazement. 'I don't believe it! Just how did you arrange that?'

'By assuring Lucette before I left that she was still very pale—fortunately, she didn't have a mirror to hand or she would have seen that her colour was fully restored and that she was looking remarkably pretty, in fact—and by saying that she should have someone with her other than the servants. I asked if she'd a friend nearby. She said that the Bouviers lived in the house next to theirs, and I suggested that her maid go across for Madame Bouvier.'

The chief burst out laughing, and shook his head.

'Minutes later, Simonne Bouvier was rushing into the house, the picture of concern. As I got up, I made a great thing of saying that I'd be in touch before Saturday about our dinner at the Métropole. Madame Bouvier visibly pricked up her ears, expressed great envy of Lucette, and before you could say successful ploy, I'd invited her and her husband to join us. It was my way of thanking her, I explained, for coming to the support of Madame Delon in her hour of need, a need for which I'd been responsible.'

The chief laughed again. 'Well done, Gaston. To get all that out of a scratch on the bumper was, indeed, a triumph! I don't know how you did it.'

Gaston gave him a dry smile. 'You can do anything when

you've mastered the inanity of the small talk favoured by your peers.'

'All I can say is, France did well to send you to us. Via Africa, of course,' Emile added, and laughed again. He paused. 'You're sound on the Côte d'Ivoire, I take it?'

Gaston smiled. 'I've done my homework so well that I'm actually beginning to believe I've been there.'

'Good. This could work. If you can worm your way into Marc Bouvier's circle of friends, you'll have a strong chance of finding out whether or not he's smuggling papers out of the prison and generally supporting terrorist activity. And if he *is* guilty, you'll be well placed to discover the person helping him inside the prison, and also the person to whom he passes the information. We need to find out the delivery chain.'

'That's the idea. First of all, I intend to get an invitation to take a look at the prison from the inside.'

'From what I've seen of you, I'm sure you'll succeed. If you come here tomorrow morning, you'll meet the operatives you can call on for help. You'll be told how to get hold of them. I know you prefer working alone, but there're bound to be occasions when you need more people on the case.'

'If that's what you want, fine.'

Emile nodded. 'It is. Whoever's responsible must be stopped. Take the time you need, but get it right. The prison's become a school for terrorists, thanks to the news-papers circulating among the inmates. And the papers being smuggled out of the prison are encouraging anti-French feeling among the local population.'

Gaston nodded.

'We've uncovered one or two arms' dumps,' Emile continued, 'and rumour has it that the garrison troops have been infiltrated. It's clear they're planning an uprising, but all our intelligence can tell us is that the terrorists are organised in cells of fifteen to twenty people. It's just not good enough.'

Gaston leaned forward. 'Believe me. I'll find out for certain if Bouvier *is* responsible, and if he isn't, I'll discover who is. Whoever it is, they're going to learn that France won't tolerate any betrayal of the colonial administration. If Bouvier's guilty, he'll pay the highest price. And so will anyone else involved.'

2

The *Hôtel Métropole*
Saturday evening

THE CHANDELIERS in the restaurant Le Beaulieu sparkled above a room full of tables, each covered by a crisp white cloth and encircled by mahogany-framed chairs upholstered in plush red velvet. On every table, white bone china gleamed and silverware settings and crystal glasses dazzled in the glittering light.

With the violet of her eyes enhanced by her lilac silk dress and matching silk gloves of elbow-length, Lucette gazed around her as she unknotted the silver stole from around her shoulders and let it fall over the back of her chair.

Her gaze met Simonne's, and they smiled at each other.

'It's beautiful here, Monsieur Laroche,' Lucette said, turning to Gaston, who was sitting on her right. 'It's even lovelier than I'd heard. It's very kind of you to invite us this evening.'

'Lucette's right, sir,' Philippe said. 'It's most generous of you.'

'Not at all,' Gaston said smoothly. 'It's going to be very pleasant for me to have an evening in such good company. And it would give me even more pleasure if all of you were to call me Gaston. After all, I hope we're going to be friends.'

Marc Bouvier nodded. 'Agreed. We're Marc and Simonne. Philippe and Lucette are correct about this being most generous of you.' He raised his eyebrows questioningly at Gaston. 'But I'm not quite sure what Simonne and I have done to deserve our seats at the table.'

'Put it down to my feeling of guilt,' Gaston said with a disarming smile. He took a piece of crusty white baguette from the platter the waiter was offering around the table, and put it on the plate beside him. 'Owing to my careless-ness, Lucette was very shaken, and your wife was an instant comfort to her. I'd been feeling extremely bad, having been so clearly at fault, that it was a great relief to see the improvement in Lucette, and I'm delighted to be able to show my gratitude to your wife this evening.'

Marc inclined his head.

'Lucette said that you were a diplomatic attaché, Gaston,' Philippe remarked. 'In what field, may I ask?'

Gaston smiled. 'I think general dogsbody probably best describes my field.' They all laughed. 'I was recently trans-ferred here from Africa owing to a shortage of diplomats in Vietnam at the moment. Apparently, a number of governors, officials, and general bureaucrats are going to be arriving from France over the next few months, and they'll need to be taken around. I'm sure, though, that over time, I shall become more than just a highly paid tourist guide. I hope so, anyway.'

'I take it you haven't seen the colonial edict forbidding us to use the name Vietnam,' Philippe said with a nervous glance at Marc. 'With each of the three parts of the colony being administered separately, Tonkin in the north, Annam along the central coast and Cochinchine in the south, there's no such thing as a national identity.'

Marc laughed. 'Relax, Philippe. You should hear the local people on the subject! The Annamese people established their nation two thousand years before we French arrived,' he said cheerfully. 'They called it Nam Viet. Many years after that, one of their emperors called it Viet Nam. I'm sure that ease of expression and reality can, on occasions, be allowed to override strict accuracy of terminology. So long as we use the correct form in official documents, I think we can be relaxed when we speak among ourselves.'

Gaston smiled at Marc. 'I agree.'

'So you've been to Africa, have you, Gaston? Whereabouts?' Simonne asked.

'The Côte d'Ivoire. On the south coast of West Africa.'

'How wonderful to have travelled as much as you've done,' she said, a tinge of envy in her voice. 'Papa, too, was in the colonial administration, and he and Maman hoped they'd be sent to lots of different countries.'

'And were they?' Gaston asked.

'Not exactly,' she said with a laugh. 'His first posting was Saigon, which is where I was born. And when I was two, he was transferred to Hanoi. That's as far as he got. Maman kept on telling him to ask for a transfer, but he liked Hanoi and didn't want to leave. When I was younger, I was glad about that as I wouldn't have wanted to go to a different school—I was happy at Lycée Albert Sarraut. But now I rather wish I'd been to some other places, too.'

'Where would you like to have gone?' Gaston asked with a smile.

'Top of my list was Paris. I'd love to have gone there.' She paused. 'Papa died a year ago, not long after Marc and I were married. Maman didn't want to stay here without him, so she went back to Paris. It's where she was born and she'd written regularly over the years to her few relatives there, so she had people to go to.'

'I'm sorry to hear that, Simonne,' Gaston said. 'I imagine the loss of your parents is still raw.'

'It is,' she said quietly. 'I really miss them. Especially Papa. He was a wonderful man.'

'What about you, Philippe?' Gaston asked, turning to him. 'Is this your first visit to the colony?'

Philippe nodded. 'That's right. Until about two months ago, not long after Lucette and I were married, we'd both assumed we'd be in Paris for the rest of my working years. But the administration had other ideas, and here we are.' He smiled across the table at Lucette. 'But as long as we're together, I don't really mind where we are.'

'And I can say the same,' she said, blushing.

'And you, Marc?' Gaston asked. 'Is Hanoi your only such posting?'

Marc shook his head. 'No. I've only been here for two years. Before that, I was in Cochinchine for four years, based in its capital, Saigon. I liked the city a lot. It reminded me of Paris with the same sort of beautiful villas, grand public buildings and wide, tree-lined boulevards. You ought to get there if you can, Gaston.'

'I certainly will,' Gaston said. 'You make it sound worth the effort.'

'I didn't realise you'd been in Saigon for as long as that, Marc,' Philippe said in surprise. 'Save me working it out, were you there at the same time as Simonne's father?'

Marc shook his head. 'No, he'd already gone north. We met when I was transferred to Hanoi. We both had offices in the Résidence Supérieure, and I still do.'

'Me, too!' Gaston exclaimed. 'They've assigned me a small office, but I've not really started using it yet. I imagine we'll bump into each other when I do.'

Marc smiled. 'I'm sure we will. It's how I met Antoine, Simonne's father. Gradually, we got into the habit of having coffee and croissants together each morning. I think it's true to say that over the months we became good friends. At least, when I asked for the hand in marriage of his lovely daughter, he instantly came up with the right answer.'

He smiled at Simonne.

She laughed in embarrassment. 'One thing I'm sure of,' she said quickly, 'is no matter how lovely Saigon might be, the Saigon shops can't be as excellent as the shops in Hanoi. Nothing could come near Les Grands Magasins Réunis. It's like entering another world.' She looked across the table at Lucette. 'We must go there together before too long, Lucette. And also to Chez Dolly, which I like, too. That's a bit cheaper.'

They paused in their conversation as the waiter handed menus around the table.

'Whatever we choose,' Gaston remarked, opening his menu, 'I'm sure it'll be excellent. The chef has a considerable reputation, and I understand that their cellar is second to none.'

A few minutes later, they'd all chosen grilled shrimp under crushed garlic, lime juice and freshly ground pepper, followed by flambéed lobster bisque with Cognac, and a soufflé glacé Grand Marnier for dessert.

'Since we're having the same, and it's fish for both courses, the choice of wine will be easy,' Gaston said, taking the wine menu from the waiter. 'Do you all want wine, or would anyone prefer something different?'

'I think we'd all be happy with wine, wouldn't we?' Marc said, glancing at the others.

There was a murmur of assent.

'Well then, to start with, we'll have a couple of bottles of the Grand vin Château Couhins,' Gaston told the wine waiter. 'We'll select a dessert wine later.' He closed the menu and returned it to the waiter.

'I was interested in what you said about being in Africa, Gaston,' Marc said, reaching for the butter. 'What role did you play there, if I may ask? Presumably, you weren't a tourist guide.'

They all laughed.

'Indeed, no, far from it. I was looking at the structure of prisons—my background is in engineering. But while I was there, I saw how they punished those who'd been captured while acting against French interests. It's hard to believe, I know, but some of the very people who'll benefit most from our mission civilisatrice were actually trying to subvert it. They had to be stopped, and in a way that deterred anyone else from attempting the same thing. We're here to help them, after all.'

'Absolutely!' Philippe exclaimed. 'A civilised nation has a duty to help backward nations. Without the roads, schools and hospitals we've been building, and the telegraph, and the railway, too, that's under construction, the colony would remain undeveloped and impoverished.'

'Quite so,' Marc murmured.

'Hoa Lo Prison is one of Marc's areas of responsibility, and I'm helping him with it,' Philippe continued enthusiastically. 'I'm one of the supervisors.'

'That rings a bell. I seem to recall Lucette mentioning that on the morning of the accident,' Gaston exclaimed, 'but I'd forgotten. So we're both in the prison business, are we? Well, I never.' He shook his head. 'But I imagine that the structure of Hoa Lo, and its practices, are quite different from those in the Côte d'Ivoire.'

'There's only one way to find out,' Philippe said warmly. 'You must allow me to show you around.' He hesitated, and glanced at Marc. 'That's all right, Marc, isn't it?'

Marc looked at Philippe in amusement. 'Of course, it is.'

'It's a very kind offer, Philippe, but I wouldn't want to interrupt your workday. I imagine you already have more to do than there're sufficient hours in which to do it.'

'Not at all. It would be my pleasure,' Philippe said with a smile.

'Well, thank you, then. I must admit, it's something I'd be very interested in doing. My office is on the upper storey of the Résidence so you could contact me there to arrange a time.'

Philippe nodded. 'I'll do that.'

Gaston sat back and smiled around the table. 'I know I should regret the accident I caused, but on the contrary, I'm glad it happened. The damage to the bumpers can be easily fixed, and it's resulted in me meeting people with whom I feel I could become friends. Why, there might even be the odd occasion when I have company on a Wednesday evening in Café Barnard.'

'Where's that?' Lucette asked.

Gaston turned to her. 'Opposite le Petit Lac, near the cathedral. They have live music on Wednesday and

Saturday evenings. It's also a good place for morning coffee.'

'Simonne and I know it, of course,' Marc said. 'I don't know why, but we haven't been there for a while. I believe they've now got a very good pianist.'

'They have. He's excellent,' Gaston said. 'The standard of the music is always high, so they invariably get a good turnout. And because the ambiance reminds us of Paris, there's always a sense of nostalgia at the end of the evening.'

'We must go again soon, don't you think, Marc?' Simonne said.

Gaston smiled. 'Then the next time I go, I'll keep an eye open for you.'

'I should make it two eyes, Gaston,' Philippe intervened. 'Judging by the look Lucette's just given me, we too will be going there.'

THE NIGHT WAS balmy and the air still.

Side by side, Lucette and Philippe sat on the verandah outside the dining room, their faces pale in the light of the moon, a brandy for each on the small bamboo table that stood between them.

Completely relaxed, they sat in a companionable silence, enjoying the powerful fragrance that rose from the mass of flowers in the garden, their rich aromas intensified by the swift fall of dusk followed by the rapid cooling of the air.

As the moon climbed higher in the night sky, the shadows cast by the cluster of banyan and tamarind trees at the rear of the garden shortened, and from the depths of the darkening bushes and ferns that filled the area between the lawn and the trees, came the high-pitched whine of invisible cicadas and the buzz of the myriad insects that thrived in the light of the moon.

The late-evening noises of the town drifted towards them over their red-tiled roof: accordion music from various cafés; the strains of a piano; the hooting of cars; people shouting; people singing; people laughing; doors closing.

'The best of both worlds,' Philippe said in quiet satisfaction. 'We're very lucky.'

He held out his hand, and Lucette took it.

'We certainly are,' she said with a smile. 'And we're fortunate, too, that in no time at all, we've met some lovely people. And now we can add Gaston to them. He's such a pleasant, easy-going man.'

3

Café Barnard
Monday, over a week later

FROM THEIR SEATS at one of the round marble-topped tables on the pavement in front of the café, Lucette and Simonne, both wearing a sleeveless floral dress and a cloche, stared across to the jade-green lake that glistened behind the straggling line of flower sellers on the opposite side of the road.

'You can see why Gaston likes this place,' Simonne remarked as an accordion sounded behind them in the depths of the café. 'It's really pleasant here, and it isn't as hectic as when you get right into the Old Quarter.'

Lucette glanced in both directions along the road that separated them from the lake.

Cars were hooting in warning whenever they approached a pousse-pousse pulled by a coolie, most of whom were wearing a shirt that hung open above cloth shorts. Without glancing back, the coolies swerved effort-lessly out of the way of the cars.

Bicyclists going in both directions wove a path around the coolies, avoiding the cars too, and the occasional horse-drawn cart laden with people sitting under a square canvas roof.

A number of solitary men and women, each in a conical straw hat, and wearing a dark tunic over dark baggy trousers, were making their way along both sides of the road, a wide pole spanning their shoulders of most, from each end of which hung a basket with items for sale.

'It seems lively enough to me,' she said.

Moving easily among the pavement tables, waiters in white shirts and white trousers, their trays held aloft, shooed away coolies who pulled up their pousse-pousse in front of the café, let their passenger step off, and then lingered on in the hope of finding another customer.

The waiters were quick to move, too, when street sellers tried to insinuate themselves between the tables, offering their wares to the café's customers.

'Philippe and I came here on Saturday evening,' Lucette added. 'Gaston was right about the music and the ambiance. We loved it, and we'll certainly come again. Probably not on a Wednesday evening, though, because of Philippe's work.'

'Did you see Gaston?' Simonne asked.

Lucette shook her head. 'No. I don't think he was here. It was really crowded, but I think we'd have seen him or he would have seen us and come across.'

'If you want company next time you decide to come here, let me know and Marc and I will join you.'

'I'll do that,' Lucette said with a smile. She looked around her. 'It's nice here in the morning, too. We're so lucky, being able to sit here like this and enjoy such a view, while the men are working.'

'If you think it's lovely now, wait till June and July when the flame trees flower. They're absolutely glorious. Marc and I used to come here when we were courting. We'd sit on a bench by the water, and because of all the trees around the lake, it felt quite private, even though my maid was only a short distance behind me, her eyes fixed beadily on us. And you should see it at sunset. Memories, memories,' Simonne said with a happy sigh.

'You said you hadn't been here for a long time. Where've you been going instead?'

'Occasionally to Au Printemps, which is a salon de thé on Rue Paul Bert. I go there after I've been to Chez Dolly. And also after going to Maison Josephine, which sells beautiful lingerie. But to be honest, I rarely went out for coffee.'

'Why not?' Lucette asked in surprise.

'It wasn't that I didn't want to—it was that I didn't have anyone to go with. The wife of Philippe's predecessor, who lived where you do, was much older than I am, and very serious-minded, so not really much fun to be with.'

'But you went to school here, so what about your school friends?'

Simonne shrugged. 'I've two or three friends who live a little to the north of the Petit Lac, on the other side of the Old Quarter, and I used to meet them up there on occasions. But they're not yet married, so it's not that simple any longer. Either they have to be chaperoned, or I must go to their house and be their chaperone, which is uncomfortable for us all. And it feels a little wrong as we're all the same age.'

Lucette pulled a face. 'It must do.'

'At some point, we'll go to the Old Quarter together.

That's where the natives live. It's a bit unsavoury there, but it's an excellent place for shopping.'

'Can they speak French?'

'A lot of them know a little French, especially the traders as they have to be able to understand what we want. The area's called the Thirty-Six Streets, but there are far more than that. All the shops in a street sell the same sort of item, and the streets are named after whatever that is, so it's easy to find what you want.'

'What do you mean?'

'Well, if you need silk, for example, you just walk down Rue de la Soie. Every shop in the street sells silk, apart from one or two tailors, but they make silk clothes. And silverware is sold in all the shops in Rue d'Argent.'

Simonne paused as the waiter put the coffees they'd ordered in front of them, and a plate of small macarons in the centre of the table.

'In what way is it unsavoury?' Lucette asked.

'It's filthy, and the natives have truly disgusting habits. I'd never go there other than to shop, or to cross through it to meet my friends,' Simonne continued, stirring her coffee. 'It's totally different from around here. Our area is lovely. Like this café. I'm glad Gaston reminded us of it, and I'm so glad that it's you and Philippe who moved next door.'

'Me, too,' Lucette said, reaching across to take a pink macaron. 'In a short space of time, you and Marc have become good friends. And Gaston seems really nice. He's not the only one who's pleased that his car hit mine last week—Philippe and I are, too. He's good company, and we both really enjoyed the Saturday evening with him.'

'Me, too. And so did Marc. Did you sort out the car?'

'Yes. Just before leaving the Métropole, Gaston suggested that he arrange for someone to come from Garage Boillot.

He said they'd collect the car at a time that suited us, change the bumper in their workshop, and then return the car. He didn't want us to be inconvenienced.'

'That's very thoughtful of him.'

Lucette nodded. 'Yes, it is. I'm sure Madame Fousseret would have liked to have found fault, but she couldn't.'

'Housekeepers often try to run the house as *they* want, not as their employers want. She's been there a while so I'm not surprised she wants to rule the roost.'

'That's putting it mildly! Whenever I ask her to do something, which I try to avoid as she makes me feel as if I'm imposing, she moves her lips in such a way that I'm convinced I've said something I shouldn't. To my horror, a couple of times I've heard myself asking for confirmation that my request met with her approval,' she added with a giggle.

Simonne laughed. 'My Madame Mercier's not much better. They must have gone to the same school for housekeepers. Mai's all right, though, isn't she? Marc thought she'd be ideal for you and Philippe.'

'He's right. She's very sweet. And although she's quite young, she seems really competent. I'm very grateful to Marc.'

'Your predecessor's maid would've been most unsuitable. She was quite old and set in her ways, and they were the ways for someone of *her* age, not yours. She'd intended to stay on, but Marc arranged for her to be given what he called a financial reward for her hard work, and she was able to stop working and return to her village. It's turned out very well for everyone.'

'Was she métisse, too?'

Simonne shook her head. 'No. Unlike Mai, she was fully Vietnamese. Mai's father must've been fair-skinned. Probably American or English. Or even French, I suppose. I'm sure you know that she used to work for my parents. I asked her once about her father, but Papa overheard me. He told me off for attempting to discuss Mai's parentage with her, and I was forbidden to do so again.'

'Whoever her father was, she's very pretty, and her French is excellent.'

'If I remember rightly, unusually for villagers, she already spoke a little French when she started working for Papa. But since then, she's really improved. Maman would've encouraged her to do so. She'd have wanted to make sure that Mai understood her instructions.'

'I know you told Gaston that you missed your father, but you must miss your mother, too.'

Simonne shrugged her shoulders. 'I'd like to say I do, but in truth, I was much closer to Papa. Anyway,' she said with sudden briskness, 'let's have one more macaron, and when we've finished our coffee, let's walk around the Petit Lac.'

'I'd like that.'

'As you can see, the bridge is bright red,' Simonne said, pointing vaguely towards the bridge. 'It's quite striking. And there's a little coral pagoda on an island in the centre of the lake, but you can't really see it from here. It's only about thirty minutes to walk around the whole lake. We ought to take advantage of it still being comfortable enough to walk. Just wait till it gets more humid!'

'The timing's perfect,' Lucette said with a smile. 'Mai was going to check our clothes this morning to see if anything needed repair. I'll be happy not to go back until all signs of her industry are gone, and there's nothing to make me feel guilty about enjoying being waited upon in such a way.'

· · ·

STANDING in the laundry room on the right-hand corner at the back of the house, waiting patiently for the silence of night to enfold the building, Mai folded with deliberate slowness the clothes she'd just ironed, having brought them in earlier from the outside drying area.

Mme. Fousseret had been the first, as always, to go to her quarters on the uppermost floor, and would have already been asleep for some time. Cook had gone up to his room not long afterwards.

Although M. Delon had returned from the Résidence looking exhausted, Mme. Delon had bubbled to him all evening about the lovely morning she'd spent with Mme Bouvier, and the things she'd seen, and the book she was reading. Thankfully, she'd eventually seemed to tire, and had let her poor husband go up to bed. And the lack of chatter coming from their bedroom suggested that both had fallen asleep.

She placed the final garment on the pile with the other clothes, and went quietly through the scullery to the kitchen and out into the hall. She went to the foot of the staircase, and stood and listened.

Silence.

Finally, she murmured under her breath, and she returned to the kitchen, took the torch she kept concealed at the back of one of the lower drawers, and removed the package she'd secreted beneath the clothes she'd pressed.

Holding the torch and the package close to her stomach, she went back through the scullery, stepped out into the velvet darkness that shrouded the garden, and swiftly closed the door behind her.

In the absence of moon or stars, night had moulded the deep green undergrowth at the back of the garden into a solid mass of black.

It was just how she liked it to be whenever she had a message or a parcel to deliver, and she ran lightly forward into the unrelieved darkness, in which every stone and leaf was visible in her mind.

Then she heard a twig snap.

She stopped abruptly.

Her heart leapt in terror, and she listened hard.

Should she go back to the house, she wondered in panic, or should she continue to the tamarind tree. If she turned back and didn't go to the tree, and there was a message in the hollow at the base of the trunk, she wouldn't see it.

Worse still, someone else might find it.

And she had a package to leave for Vinh to collect.

But suppose she'd been found out? Suppose they all had?

She put her hand to her mouth and pressed back her fear.

4

———————

Mai strained harder to hear any further sounds.

But there was nothing.

It had probably been a flying fox foraging in the undergrowth, or a snake slithering away, she thought, reassuring herself. Whatever it had been, it was unlikely to have been a person or people—they'd have identified themselves by now.

Forcing herself to relax, she resumed walking quickly across the soft, spongy earth towards the largest of the ancient tamarind trees, which stood just inside the railings at the back of the garden.

When she reached the tree, she switched on the torch she'd been given for such a purpose, bent down and shone the beam into the hollow at the base of the gnarled trunk.

The hollow being empty of anything that could harm her, and there being no message from Vinh, she pushed the package into the gap, switched off the torch, and moved slightly back.

Her eyes by now accustomed to the dark, she peered through the shadows beyond the railings in the fervent hope that Vinh might choose that very moment to see if there was anything for him.

If he did, she'd move swiftly forward so that he could slide his arms between the railings and bring her close to him. And they'd stand like that for as long as they dared, each holding the other tightly.

How she ached for him!

She couldn't wait to feel his arms around her again.

She could pinpoint with precision the moment when she'd first begun to feel that way about Vinh because it hadn't always been thus.

He was born in the same village as she, but a year earlier. Like her, he'd gone to a nearby school set up by a group of French missionaries. They'd been friends there, just as they had with all the other children, but there'd been nothing special in the way that they'd felt about each other.

As they'd got older, he'd seemed to distance himself from all of the children, including her, and after he'd left school, he was seldom seen in the village.

She'd heard rumours that he'd joined a terrorist group that was hoping to force the French to leave Vietnam, but she hadn't known whether or not it was true. And she hadn't been particularly interested in knowing, either.

After all, he wasn't a part of her life.

And he was even less so when, two years earlier, when she was fourteen, she'd been sent from her village to live in Hanoi.

This had been arranged by her French father.

After her mother had left Hanoi and moved back to the village, her father had gone quite often to visit her mother and to see her. He had known that she didn't want to stay in the village, but longed to go to Hanoi, and he'd made that possible.

She'd been confident that whatever job she'd be able to find in Hanoi, it had to be better than weaving rugs, which was what her mother did all week long. And it would have been her destiny, too, had she stayed in the village.

On the occasions she'd had to join the village women and weave alongside them in order to help them meet a pressing order, she'd found the work hard, boring and very tiring. Her mother had assured her that it would get easier with practice, but she'd been distraught at the idea of spending her life in such a way.

So, being sent to Hanoi, and being given a position in the house of a French administrator, as had happened, had been infinitely to her preference.

For the first year and a half of the two years she'd been in Hanoi, working for M. Joubert, Mme. Bouvier's father, she hadn't seen Vinh, and nor had she given him a moment's thought.

But he'd come to work in the Jouberts' garden one day, being one of a succession of temporary gardeners.

She'd been in the kitchen at the time, and hearing a knock on the back door, she'd opened it. They'd taken one look at each other, liked what they'd seen, and in no time at all, they'd fallen in love.

At first, the most that either could hope for was an occasional glimpse of the other when she performed any tasks that took her into the garden.

But their chances of meeting had greatly improved when Vinh had asked her on the day before a permanent gardener took over at the Jouberts, if she'd help him and his friends by passing on to him anything M. Joubert might give her. She could put any such items into a box concealed on the other side of the railings at the back of the Jouberts' garden.

Why couldn't M. Joubert put the messages into the box himself, she'd asked.

His presence in that part of the garden would be much more noticeable than would Mai's, and could arouse suspicion, Vinh had explained.

They'd had to move the box from its original place as, unlike the temporary gardeners, the new gardener wasn't a revolutionary fighter. He was someone taken on by Mme. Joubert, who'd been recommended to her by a friend who was returning to France.

In its old position, the box, which had been easy to access by M. Joubert, would have been discovered by the new gardener. In its changed location, it would be safe from detection, but it would be harder for M. Joubert to get to it.

Couldn't Vinh become the permanent gardener, she'd asked.

To which he'd replied that he was far too important to the cause to be tied down in such a way.

Feeling as she did about Vinh, she was ready to do anything that would enable her to continue seeing him, and she'd agreed.

There'd been the occasional week without any messages to pass on, but usually there'd be at least one in the week, and when she'd checked the box late at night, or put something in it for him to collect, which she'd frequently had occasion to do, she'd always hung around for a short time afterwards, hoping to see Vinh arrive.

If after a while he hadn't come, she'd have to return to the house, and slip back the following morning to check that he'd been to the tree. If he hadn't done so by the morning of her day off, she knew to take any messages to the revolutionaries' house in the Old Quarter.

She was always pleased when that happened as Vinh would sometimes be there.

The system worked very well.

But then, M. Joubert had died. She'd been extremely upset as she'd liked him enormously.

And she'd been alarmed, too, that she might not be able to continue seeing Vinh. His revolutionary work was taking an increasing amount of his time, and she'd been forbidden to go to the headquarters without good reason as every visit increased the risk of discovery by the Sûreté.

Her alarm was heightened when Mme. Joubert decided to return to France.

Her spirits had lifted, however, when M. Bouvier, a friend of M. Joubert, had sent her to work for M. Delon, the French administrator who'd moved into the house next door to M. et Mme. Bouvier, and she'd been suddenly hopeful that she and Vinh might find a way of continuing to meet.

They did.

Apparently, M. Bouvier was sympathetic to their cause, as M. Joubert had been, and he intended to pass on messages just as M. Joubert had done.

The box in the bushes was transferred to the Delons' garden, and was concealed among the glossy green plants close to the side gate separating the Bouvier and Delon gardens.

The profusion of plants in that area grew in such density, and in so natural a manner, that a gardener would never need to tend it.

There was an old tamarind tree at the back of the Delons' garden, which had a hollow low in its thick trunk, and she was told to transfer any messages from the box to that hollow.

So far, it had all gone very smoothly, and in the short

period of time that she'd been working for M. Delon, she'd had several messages to conceal in the tree, and had been able to enjoy an occasional few moments with Vinh.

Those fleeting minutes in the dark, pressed against the railings, feeling Vinh's arms around her, were the best she could hope for until the French were gone.

But when that day came, she and Vinh would marry.

There'd be no need for her mother to ask the matchmaker to find her a husband, nor for any astrologer to advise about auspicious dates. She and Vinh loved each other and were going to get married. And that was that.

Until then, though, she'd continue passing on messages, and would remain on her guard.

As Vinh often reminded her, if the French were to suspect her of helping his group, she'd be locked up in Hoa Lo Prison, and both of them knew enough about the treatment of the revolutionaries held there, to be fearful about her fate should that happen.

She would never slip up by being over-confident, she regularly assured him. No one would ever discover what she was doing. Of that she was sure.

AFTER WHAT SEEMED like hours of staring up at the ceiling, Lucette abandoned her futile attempts at getting to sleep. She slipped out of bed, crossed over to the window and started to open the shutters, thinking that the sight of a world veiled in darkness and at rest, might help her to fall asleep.

As she did so, she glanced down into the garden.

She caught her breath in sudden surprise, and stopped mid-action.

From the corner of the house, a sliver of amber light shot across the garden. It vanished in a trice.

But not before she'd seen Mai.

Inching back, she watched Mai run towards the rear of the garden and be swallowed up by night.

Instinctively, she glanced over her shoulder at Philippe to tell him about Mai, but he was fast asleep.

He'd realised that she'd wanted to tell him about her day, and had been lovely enough to listen patiently to her throughout their dinner, but as soon as they'd finished their meal, he'd suggested that they skip their brandy that evening and go straight up to bed.

It would be cruel to disturb him, she decided, and she turned back to the window and peeped through the gap between the half-open shutters.

But it was too dark to see anything.

So why was Mai, who should be in bed, given the early start to her day, out in the garden at such an hour, she wondered, frowning.

Of course, it could be something harmless, she mused.

Mai could be meeting a beau, for example. She was of an age, after all, to be thinking about men. But the way she'd been moving—almost furtively was how she'd describe it— and the fact that she'd seemed to be carrying something, made her think that this wasn't a lovers' tryst.

Impatient to know more, she stared towards the back of the garden, willing Mai to return.

After about twenty minutes, just as she was wondering whether to go back to bed, she saw Mai step out of the darkness. She was walking quickly towards the kitchen, glancing frequently around her. But this time, she wasn't carrying anything.

A moment later, a shard of light again streaked across the garden, and then both the light and Mai disappeared.

Mai had looked downcast, she thought, and nervous about being seen.

She stared out at the garden for a moment or two longer, and then closed the shutters very quietly, locked them and turned to face the bedroom.

She probably ought to tell Philippe when he woke up, she thought, leaning back against the wooden window frame. But he was so busy at the moment. He had so much to learn and so many things to do, and this was probably nothing at all, so perhaps it would be a kindness not to bother him.

After all, what could she tell him apart from the fact that Mai had gone out into the garden at night, and then come back?

And actually, it might be quite fun for her to try to find out what was going on.

She had plenty of time to do so, but Philippe didn't. And she, not Philippe, was in the house with Mai for most of the day, so she was better placed to watch her.

That's what she'd do, she decided as she climbed back into bed. She'd keep an eye on Mai without it being obvious, and if she discovered anything Philippe should know, that would be the time to tell him.

5

The following day
The beginning of June

GASTON SAT at his desk in the Résidence, as he had done the whole of the day before, waiting for the visit from Philippe or Marc or both of them, that he was confident would take place before the end of the week.

He hoped very much that they'd stop by his office that day. Although he had a pile of information to wade through in order to equip himself with what he'd need to know about the city, he intensely disliked being forced to sit behind a desk for any length of time.

In preparation for their arrival, he'd spread out some papers in front of him to make it appear as if he was working hard on a visit to Hanoi by highly placed officials, which was due to take place in about six weeks' time.

Its ostensible focus was to demonstrate the efficiency of

the colonial administration. Its reality was to give him something to appear to be doing.

Each of the visiting officials was attached to the Sûreté, and wouldn't demand the in-depth knowledge of a genuine visitor. Nevertheless, he didn't intend to take any chances, and he was learning everything there was to know about each of the stops on the group's itinerary, the last of which would be the Hoa Lo Prison.

Preparing himself in such a way was partly because it was in his nature to research fully every task he undertook, but also because he was mindful that Philippe, new to Hanoi and eager to learn all he could about the city, might decide to go out on a visit with the fake officials.

In fact, it might be an idea to suggest to Philippe that he join them.

The more genuine occasions on which he met Delon and Bouvier, and the more varied the circumstances in which he did so, the more likely it was that their burgeoning friendship would develop into something stronger.

Of the two men, it was more important that he got close to Philippe.

If he was going to discover anything untoward, the weak link would be Philippe. Marc had been there too long to allow anything revealing to slip out.

So having Philippe with them when they toured the local places of interest, particularly the prison, would be a very good idea.

He could make a point of calling on Philippe to air his knowledge in front of the officials as they moved around the areas they'd be shown. Allowing Philippe to shine during the sham visit, and to feel important, was bound to help their friendship grow.

It was when people felt truly relaxed in the company of each other, in the way that friends did, and trusted each other, that defences were lowered and truths revealed.

Fortunately, there were few people who'd made the choice he had—which was to shut himself off from others, and to trust no one but himself.

For that, he was thankful. Had there been more people like him, his job would have been very much harder.

With a heavy sigh, he picked up his pen, and reached across the desk to his map of Hanoi and a plan of the prison.

There was a knock at the door.

Thank God, he thought. At last!

'Come in,' he called.

The door opened and Marc entered, followed by Philippe.

'Welcome!' he exclaimed. Rising slightly from his seat, he indicated the two chairs facing his desk. 'Take a seat, do,' he said, sitting back down.

'We're not interrupting you, I hope,' Marc said as they sat down.

'Not at all! On the contrary, it's a pleasant surprise,' he said cheerfully. 'I'm assuming, of course, that you aren't here to request a tour of the Pagode des Corbeaux. Built in ten hundred and seventy, it's dedicated to Confucius, the temple layout being similar to that of the temple at Qufu, the birthplace of Confucius. The structure of the internal courtyards is of particular scholarly interest.'

All three laughed.

'Not exactly,' Marc said. 'Though you make such a visit sound almost irresistible. No, it's that Philippe and I have just been having coffee and croissants in the café a little way along on the other side of the boulevard. We seem to have got into the habit of doing this in the same way that Antoine and I used to—not every day, but quite often. We thought we'd ask if you wanted to join us tomorrow, rather than breakfast alone.'

Gaston leaned back in his chair and smiled broadly. 'That's very kind of you. I'd be delighted to do that.'

Marc nodded. 'We'd enjoy having your company.' He hesitated. 'I hope you don't think we've jumped to conclusions in an inappropriate way, but after the Métropole, we rather thought you might be on your own at the breakfast table,' he said with a trace of awkwardness.

'It's not in the least inappropriate. And you're right, it's just me, I'm afraid. There used to be someone, but that was a number of years ago, and despite being on the lookout since then, I've never found anyone who came near to taking her place. There are advantages to being on one's own, of course,' he added with a half-smile. 'Such as not having to endure a detailed account of one's wife's every meeting with her friends—'

'You must have been hiding in my cupboard last night!' Philippe exclaimed. 'Lucette was full of her morning with Simonne. She recounted it second by second.'

Gaston laughed. 'I suspect that I could have been hiding in any number of homes last night and have heard the same sort of conversation, or listened to the minutiae of problems with the staff. But to be serious, it's over meals that one most misses company, and I'd be pleased to join you.'

'That's decided, then.' Marc nodded towards the papers on Gaston's desk. 'What's with the Pagode des Corbeaux? Are you preparing for an imminent visit from overseas?'

'Yes, if you consider six weeks to be imminent. I haven't been here that long myself, so I've a lot of work ahead of me.'

'I see you've got a map of the prison,' Marc said. 'I take it that's on your list of places to show them.'

'It certainly is. Assuming it's all right with you and Philippe, that is. Methods of punishment are high on the list of the officials' interests. I thought that it could be our last stop on the tour. I was even wondering if Philippe might be able to accompany us. They'd benefit from his knowledge.'

'It's early days,' Philippe said. 'I don't yet know that much.'

Gaston smiled. 'But you know more than they do.'

Marc nodded. 'That'd be fine, Gaston. It's the sort of thing I'd leave to Philippe, anyway.' He turned to Philippe. 'It'll be good practice for you, Philippe. It'll be your first time with such a group, but it certainly won't be your last. Can I leave you to liaise with Gaston?'

Philippe smiled broadly. 'Of course. In fact, if you like, Gaston, I've got to go to the prison this afternoon, and if you've nothing on, you could come, too. I imagine you'll want to decide in advance what to show the visitors.'

'That's an inspired idea, Philippe. I'd like that very much, and I've nothing on that can't wait.'

He leaned back in his chair and smiled in satisfaction.

COLUMNS of late afternoon light sliced through the wooden shutters into the small room in the southern tip of the Old Quarter.

Gaston and Emile sat across the desk from each other, a snifter of brandy in front of each, motes of dry dust dancing in the air above them.

'So, you're satisfied with how it went today, are you?' Emile asked. 'I must say, I'm impressed by how far you appear to have got in so short a time.'

'It's more than just appearing to have got—I would say I'm most definitely further than we'd expected me to be at this stage.'

Emile nodded. 'I'll give you that. Did Bouvier go to the prison with you? You said that you thought he might.'

Gaston stretched out his legs. 'No, he left it to Philippe. But that was better.'

Emile raised his eyebrows. 'I don't follow that. It's Bouvier we need to watch, not Delon. Delon's only been in Hanoi a few weeks, but the anti-French activity in the prison has been going on for much longer than that. Delon obviously can't be involved, and he's too new to know anything.'

'Exactly,' Gaston said with a grin. 'And because he doesn't know anything, he won't be aware of what he must hide. It means that he's far more likely than Bouvier to reveal something significant.'

Emile laughed. 'I should know by now not to doubt anything you plan to do. You've clearly got this in hand.' He swirled his brandy in the snifter. 'Well, then,' he said, 'what about today? Did Delon let anything helpful drop?'

Gaston thought for a moment. 'Not as such. Today was useful. Not because of anything Philippe said, but for what I can now rule out.'

'Such as?'

'Well, the walls around the prison are thick and solidly built. And as they're topped with sharp broken glass and wired with a high-voltage electric grid, it would be impossible to escape that way.'

Emile grunted.

'And getting anything over the wall would also be impossible. Added to that, guards patrol the narrow corridors between the walls and the barracks, and with watch towers in all four corners of the prison, the guards can observe the inner and outer parts of the prison.'

'You see!' Emile held out his hands in a gesture of anger and despair. 'Given the level of security, you can understand our frustration that propaganda's still getting out! We're certain that one of the Party cells is behind the hand-written journals, such as *Red Prison* and *Prisoners' Life*, but we can't locate it. And we can't find how the newspapers are getting out of the prison. They're doing this under our noses, and getting away with it!'

'But not for much longer,' Gaston said soothingly.

'I hope not!' Emile said, glowering. 'D'you know, the inmates are even running classes in politics, reading and writing? They've made pens out of tropical almond branches, nibs out of Antigone flower buds, and chalk out of half-baked bricks and charcoal. The literate teach the illiterate by writing on the floor. Thanks to our techniques of persuasion, we know all this, but we can't seem to stop it.'

He pounded his desk in anger.

'We're sure that Bouvier brings in the material they need, but we have to tread warily with an official that senior,' Emile went on, shaking his head in frustration.

'He must have inside help,' he continued. 'If we could discover who that is, and also the source of newspaper production, and the line of distribution outside the prison, both to the villages and to the garrison, we could stop the flow of propaganda. And we have to, Gaston. There's trouble building.'

'I don't yet know how they're doing it, but rest assured,' Gaston said calmly, 'I'll find out. Today was about eliminating ways in which the papers or prisoners could get out. I've ruled out the wall and the windows—there're only a few very small windows near the roof of the barracks. And with inmates fettered and shackled, some with the section of a ladder over their heads that increases their width, we can rule out any escape down the narrow alleys or sewers, or newspapers and messages accessing the outside world in such a way.'

'Which means?'

'Which means that the propaganda must be walking out of the prison door. Which brings us back to Bouvier.'

'We could have him stopped and searched,' Emile volunteered.

Gaston smiled. 'I imagine that I'm in Hanoi because you don't want to do that. You realise that you'd get Bouvier, but not the rest of the chain. And you'd like them all, I'm sure.'

Emile slumped back and scowled.

STEPPING out of the house used by the Sûreté for meetings with their undercover agents and informers, Gaston took a deep breath of the jasmine-scented air, and decided that having started the day cooped up in his office, and then having spent much of the afternoon in the depressing, over-crowded prison, followed by the feedback session with Emile, he'd return to his house on foot.

Enjoying the freshness of the night air, he skirted the top of the Petit Lac and made his way to Rue Henri Rivière. Reaching the boulevard, he strolled down towards Rue Bonheur, where he lived, passing first the Résidence, and then the Bouvier house, which was on the other side of the road, and next to it, Philippe's.

When he reached a point opposite the two houses, he stood for a moment or two and stared across the road. Then on an impulse, he crossed over, went up to the railings in front of Philippe's house, and studied the layout of his house and garden.

To the left of the house, there was a narrow track running along the outside of the railings. On the other side of the track, a line of trees stood between Philippe's house and his neighbour's.

To the right of Philippe's house, there were railings between his house and Marc's, but no narrow track or trees.

He went up to the railings on the right-hand side, and with his gaze, followed them to the back of the garden where they met a horizontal line of railings that ran along the back of Philippe's garden and Marc's.

There must be a side gate in the railings, he realised, or Simonne would never have reached Lucette as quickly as she had on the day of the accident. There didn't appear to be any break in the line of railings along the back of the two houses so there'd have been no access that way.

Since the house was in darkness, the hour being late, and the night sky starless, he might as well have a quick look around the perimeter of the Delons' house, he decided. And taking a small torch from his pocket, he went to the narrow track on the left of the house and started walking quietly up the track.

He'd almost reached the back of the house when a beam of light shot across the far corner of the garden, and vanished.

He stopped abruptly, slipped into the trees to his left, and crouched down. Someone must have opened a door to go into the garden, or to return to the house, and it'd be interesting to know who that was.

His eyes accustoming themselves to the darkness, he stared towards the back of the house.

And then he heard the sound of a door opening.

It was so slight that had the hearer being anyone other than someone whose senses were always alert, it could have been missed.

There must be two people moving around, he thought in amazement.

Squinting through the darkness, he saw a silhouette creeping forward towards the dense mass of black foliage at the rear of the garden.

Surely that's Lucette, he exclaimed inwardly.

His instinct was to stand up at once and call to her, but he forced himself to stay low on the ground, and not move.

And then he heard another sound.

And so did she.

Swiftly, she turned and ran to the side of the house closest to him. Flattening herself against the wall, she peered once or twice round the corner of the house, each time hastily drawing back.

She obviously wanted to see what was happening in the garden, but not herself be seen. What would she do next, he wondered, his gaze fixed on her.

Out of the corner of his eye, he saw another brief flash of light. Then he heard a door close.

Cursing to himself at not being far enough forward, he bent low and ran as quietly as he could through the trees to a point from which he could see the back of the house, but he was too late.

All was once again in darkness. The person she'd been watching had clearly gone back into the house.

Angry at himself for his lapse of attention, he stayed where he was, hidden by ferns and leaves, and watched Lucette.

After a few moments, she inched cautiously forward,

checked that the garden was empty, and then ran along to a door in the centre of the house.

Caught in the light from the door she'd opened, she stood on the threshold, a slender figure in her pale night-dress and negligée, listening apparently for noise from within, and then she stepped inside and closed the door behind her.

He stood upright and stared at the house. Not much had the power to surprise him these days, he thought, but what he'd seen moments ago had done just that.

There was only one possible explanation for Lucette's action.

The Delons hadn't been in Hanoi long enough to be involved in subterfuge, had that been their inclination, which was unlikely. So Lucette must have come upon something, or overheard a conversation, that had made her suspect someone in her household of wrongdoing.

She must have been spying on that person, seeking confirmation of what she thought she'd heard or seen.

In the light of this, he must consider the possibility that someone in the Delon household might be the next link in the chain that began with Marc Bouvier and whoever was helping him in the prison.

It meant that he must widen his circle of interest to include Philippe and Lucette.

And Lucette, as the person best placed to uncover any hidden intrigue in her home, or next door, for that matter, through her friendship with Simonne, and as someone who'd already seen something suspicious, was now of particular interest.

He'd let her continue her amateur spying, unaware that she'd been seen that night, but from now on, he'd be watching her.

And waiting.

Waiting for the day that would come, he was sure, when she'd need to unburden herself to someone. And that someone was going to be him because by then, she'd be looking at him with eyes that held considerably more than friendship.

That sort of closeness with Lucette hadn't been his original intention, but it was now.

6

C *afé des Arts*
   The following day

THE SUN GLITTERED between the leaves of the tamarind trees
that lined the boulevard. Gaining in strength as it inched higher
into the clear blue sky, it bleached the pavements and roadway.

Protected from the glare of the sun by a canvas awning
that covered the tables outside the café, Gaston stared with
pleasure at the plate in front of him.

'When you said coffee and croissants, I didn't expect to
be able to get an omelette, too,' he said, picking up his fork.

Marc indicated for the waiter to bring them more coffee,
sat back and smiled broadly.

'You'll find omelettes on most café menus these days,
along with baguettes and croissants. And that's not all.
Food's now fried in butter, and you can get cauliflowers,
courgettes, pâté and potatoes. And those are only some of

the items we've introduced to the colony. The people here have a lot to thank us for.'

He paused while the waiter refilled their cups. 'So, tell me, Gaston, how did Hoa Lo compare with similar prisons in Africa?'

Gaston smiled. 'I can only talk about the Côte d'Ivoire. Hoa Lo's stronger and more secure. It seems to have been excellently planned in terms of its layout and security, and to be efficiently run by administrators and jailers who know what they're doing. And I'll make sure that I'm never invited to take up residence there.'

All three laughed.

'No, I found it extremely interesting,' he went on. 'And I'm very grateful to Philippe for giving me so much of his time. At the end of my tour of the place, we discussed what best to show the visitors.'

'And what did you decide?'

'To show them the hospital and guardhouse, the work-shops where they're making textiles and leather products, and one of the seven houses in which prisoners are detained. Also, they'll expect to see one of the cells for dangerous prisoners.'

Marc nodded. 'It's a good plan.' He grinned at him. 'And I agree with what you've omitted—it would be better not to show them the guillotine. They know it's our method of execution for extreme offenders, but they don't need to see it.'

Gaston smiled. 'Those were our thoughts, too. I'll draft something for the officials to take away with them at the end of their visit. Obviously, I'll run it past Philippe first. In fact, I could show you the draft on Friday morning, Philippe, after the garage has returned your car. I thought to stop by, anyway, as I'd like to check that the work has been done to your satisfaction.'

'They're bringing the car back mid-morning. If you come at about that time, you're sure to catch me. We could have coffee while I glance at the draft,' Philippe said, taking off his solar *topi* and fanning his face with it before putting it on the chair next to him.

'Talking of paying visits, Gaston,' Marc said. 'Philippe and Lucette are coming to lunch after St. Joseph's on Sunday. Simonne and I wondered if you'd like to come, too. If you don't want the church part first, you could turn up at the house at noon.'

'I'll be going to Mass, too, and I'd be very happy to join you afterwards. Thank you.'

'You'll have to come to us the next time,' Philippe said. 'By then, Lucette should have plucked up sufficient courage to inform Madame Fousseret that there'll be guests for lunch.'

Gaston grinned. 'You make Madame Fousseret sound a veritable martinet. I feel quite sorry for Lucette, if that's the case.'

'In all fairness to the housekeeper, it's probably partly Lucette's fault,' Philippe said ruefully. 'It's just that she was fairly new to running a house when we moved here. Madame Fousseret wasn't, and she doesn't make it easy for Lucette. Deliberately, I'd say. With the result that poor Lucette is quite daunted at the thought of asking her to do anything.'

'What about Mai? I hope Lucette finds her biddable,' Marc said with a trace of anxiety.

'She does. Mai's delightful. She and Lucette get on very well. Mai goes out of her way to be helpful and to make

Lucette feel at ease, but she never forgets her place. We're very grateful to you for sending her to us.'

'That's a relief,' Marc said. 'You had me worried for a moment.'

'Where did you find Mai, Marc?' Gaston asked, finishing the last of his omelette.

'I didn't—Simonne's father did. I think someone recommended her when he was looking for help in the house. She comes from a village not far from Hanoi, and I think she still visits her mother. And she's got family in the Old Quarter, too, I believe.'

Philippe nodded. 'She has. She told Lucette so.'

'Anyway,' Marc continued, 'Madame Joubert's return to France coincided with Philippe's arrival, and as Mai was much more suitable for a young couple than the dour woman who'd worked for my last aide, she was the obvious choice for Lucette.'

Gaston picked up his coffee cup. 'She's a lucky girl to work close enough to her home to be able to return there regularly. And quite unusual to want to do so,' he added. 'Of course, its attraction may take the form of a young man, although I hope for Lucette's sake that it doesn't.'

'I echo that,' Philippe said fervently.

'Whereabouts d'you live, Gaston?' Marc asked, taking a drink of coffee.

'I've a place on Rue Bonheur. It's not as grand as your houses, but it serves me well enough. The domestic staff are quietly efficient, and the cook is excellent. You must come to dinner one evening, and see if I'm telling the truth.'

Marc and Philippe murmured their gratitude, but said that it wasn't necessary for him to go to that trouble.

Gaston laughed. 'Your denial wasn't particularly convincing. It'll be my pleasure. And you'll be able to admire not only the skill of my cook, but also my office. As I expect you've done, I've made myself an office so that I don't need to go into the Résidence every day.'

Philippe nodded. 'Me, too. I followed Marc's example and set a room aside. It'll be useful to have somewhere to work over weekends if it's a particularly busy time.'

'Once again, we're of the same mind,' Gaston said, smiling. 'Fortunately, whether I'm in the Résidence or at home, I'll be close enough to join you for breakfast.'

He took a croissant from the basket in the centre of the table, and reached across for the butter. 'Do your wives ever join you for breakfast here?' he asked.

'No, thank heavens!' Marc exclaimed.

All three laughed again.

'Simonne's still in bed when we leave in the morning,' Marc went on. 'Also, they know that Philippe and I often discuss work over breakfast, and that we see it as part of our working day.'

'You must tell me any time you want to talk privately. I wouldn't take offence,' Gaston said quickly. 'Heaven forbid that I come between two men and their work!'

'Don't worry. I doubt that there'd be many occasions when a matter was so urgent that it couldn't wait,' Marc said.

'And just because Lucette and Simonne don't come here for breakfast,' Philippe said cheerfully, 'it doesn't mean that they go without. They're going to Café Barnard this morning, in fact, and I'm sure they'll have coffee there. And if not croissants, they'll have some gâteaux. It'll be the second time they've been there this week. You've started something there, Gaston.'

'Is that so? Then I think I should ask Café Barnard for a commission,' he said in amusement, dribbling honey on to his croissant. 'And what do they do for the rest of the day?'

'I don't know about generally,' Marc said, 'but after her siesta today, Simonne will be visiting friends in the Old Quarter. When she was telling Lucette about them a little while ago, she felt quite guilty that she hadn't seen them for some time, and she's remedying that. I don't think Lucette's going with her, though.'

'She isn't,' Philippe said. 'Simonne invited her, but it's getting hotter and more humid each day, and as Lucette's not used to the humidity, she decided to stay in the cool of the house this afternoon. She's going with Simonne next time, but they'll go early in the morning.'

'Aren't you bothered by the humidity?' Gaston asked, glancing at Philippe. 'You can't be used to it, either. It's at its worst late afternoon, so aren't you tempted to be back at the house by then, like Lucette?'

'Not really. The Résidence walls are thick enough to keep it cool inside, and if you've work to do, you take it in your stride.'

Marc pushed his empty plate back from him. 'Nevertheless, Philippe, Gaston's got a point. When the heat's at its height, if you can do your work at home, you must do so.'

'Thanks, Marc. I need to be at the Résidence this afternoon, but I'll keep that in mind for the future.'

'Well, that was most enjoyable. Both the breakfast, and the company,' Gaston said, screwing up his serviette and dropping it on to his empty plate. 'I'll certainly join you again, if I may, but now, most regretfully, I think I ought to be moving.'

He turned, caught the waiter's eye and raised his finger.

· · ·

WITH THE AFTERNOON heat beating down on him, Gaston turned through the wrought-iron gates and headed along the drive to Philippe's house.

On either side of the drive, the hydrangea bushes were perfuming the air with the delicate fragrance from their heavy white blooms.

Reaching the front door, he removed from his pocket an outline of the proposed tour, and also a draft of the leaflet he intended to hand to the officials after their visit to the prison, which, despite his earlier words to Marc and Philippe, he'd prepared the day before.

He rapped on the door with the brass knocker, and took a step back.

As he stared at the green front door, waiting, his mind went back to his childhood in the Vendée, to another house with a green door, the house in which his life had begun.

7

T*he Vendée*
    Some years earlier

YOU COULDN'T DO anything about the way you started your life, but you could insulate yourself from other people, and show them that because you didn't care what they thought, they couldn't hurt you.

He'd learnt that as soon as he'd reached the age of reason.

There hadn't been a child in the public elementary school in the Vendée that he'd attended from the age of six, who hadn't heard that when he'd been less than a day old, he'd been dumped in a wicker basket outside the green front door of one of the few artisans left in the area who made the traditional bourrine houses found in the marshlands of the Vendée.

As a result, there was nothing unusual about him

finding a wicker basket on his school desk, or a drawing of one.

Such baskets were common, and just as there was no way of knowing from the basket which woman had given birth to him, he had no way of knowing which malicious classmate had decided to taunt him that day.

He'd solved the problem by disliking them all, by treating them all with an open contempt, and by keeping his distance as much as he could.

And by working as hard as he could to show them that no matter the shameful way he'd come into the world, he was sharper and cleverer than they'd ever be.

He was grateful to the artisan and his wife, René and Marie, who had taken him in, rather than handing him over to the local priest, who'd have placed him in an orphanage, but he wasn't blind to the reason they'd done so.

As the woman who'd discarded him must have known, the couple were childless, and as the man got older, he'd increasingly need help with constructing the bourrines he'd been asked to build.

And the young man they'd taken in, had allowed to grow up in their home, to eat the food they'd put on his plate and wear the clothes they'd given him, would provide that help.

And from a very early age, René had started to teach him the basics.

Not that he'd minded.

He was fascinated, in fact, by the way in which the artisan drew only upon local resources for the construction of the houses, which were usually just one large room with a chimney, especially as, with the area being a huge expanse of marshland, there wasn't much timber available.

What might have been an insurmountable problem to

some people wasn't to René, who was single-minded in his approach to solving any perceived obstacle.

The walls were built with a mixture of earth and water that had been made into a paste. Sand was added to prevent any cracks from appearing as it dried, and the whole lot was mixed with straw to bind it.

The wall was laid directly on to the ground without any sort of foundation, and a frame of elm, willow, or sometimes poplar, was placed against the wall. The roof was then covered with reeds.

It was very cleverly done, he used to think as he watched the artisan in admiration.

When he was very young, the whole construction took René about a month. But as the man grew older, it took longer, and increasingly he had to give René a hand so that the bourrine was ready at the agreed time.

He was glad to be able to help—he owed that to René and Marie, who, although they hadn't bestowed much affection on him, had given him a home—and as there was no school on Thursdays, which allowed those who wanted to attend religious services to do so, he started working on the bourrines every Thursday morning, and also part of the weekend.

But not during the Thursday afternoon.

He'd recognised from a very early age that if he was going to be the best at what he chose to do, he'd need to study hard, and do more than the minimum. And his schoolteacher, discerning both his ability and his drive, had aided him by providing books that were more advanced than those given to the others in the class.

His schooling was assured until he was thirteen, but the artisan had made it clear that when he turned thirteen, and attending school was no longer compulsory, he'd have to leave school and work with him full-time.

But he'd had no intention of finishing his education at such an early age, and thus being restricted in the choices he could make in his life. He was far too ambitious for that.

His heart was set on going to one of the grandes écoles, which specialised in science and engineering.

The schoolteacher had explained that grandes écoles admitted students according to their national ranking in highly competitive written and oral exams.

Anyone could register for those exams, but to be successful, it was almost always necessary to have attended preparatory classes for two or three years before sitting the exams.

With the help of his schoolteacher, he'd embarked upon the preparatory work.

As the time he was going to have to leave school drew near, the teacher told him that he would like to continue helping him, but that he'd normally be paid for undertaking such a programme of study.

It was obvious to both Gaston and the teacher that René would never pay Gaston sufficient in wages for him to be able to afford such lessons. And both had hoped that something miraculous would occur that would enable Gaston to continue studying with the teacher.

To his great despair, when he'd reached thirteen, René had made it clear that if he didn't help him full-time, he must leave the place he'd known as home since he'd been one day old.

He'd kicked the front door in anger and disappointment.

But he hadn't had anywhere else to go, so he'd had to agree to leave school and help. He'd insisted, though, that he must have time to study, with or without the teacher. And René had reluctantly agreed.

And then the longed-for miracle had occurred.

The miracle took the shape of a girl of Gaston's age, who came from a distant Vendéen village.

The girl had been quite unwell and had missed much of the past year's schooling. She was now fully recovered and her parents were anxious for her to have extra teaching so that she'd be at the same level as her peers when she started at the lycée.

They would be paying the teacher for his tuition, and he'd managed to work it that they were under the impression that they'd be paying a slightly reduced fee because she'd be sharing the classes with a boy who was preparing for the entry exams for a grande école.

That spoke well of the boy's application and intelligence, the girl's parents had obviously thought, and they'd accepted the arrangement.

Gaston hadn't yet met the girl, but he assumed that when he did, he wouldn't regard her any more highly than the children he'd encountered in the elementary school.

He hadn't for one minute missed any of them, having never been close to any. They'd treated him with a mixture of contempt and fear. He'd treated them with disdain. His only interest in them had been to study how they talked to each other, and how they behaved together, for he'd realised instinctively that those were skills he might one day need.

But he'd been mistaken about the regard he'd feel for the girl, whose name was Adèle.

At first, he'd virtually ignored her, resenting, if he were honest with himself, the fact that he had to share his lessons with her.

But gradually, her quiet ways and gentle nature, had

made him start noticing her, and they began to exchange a few words at the beginning and end of each session, discussing the work they'd been doing, which was of genuine interest to both of them.

Before long, their conversation had taken on a more conversational tone, and when she'd asked about his family, he'd hesitated for only a moment before telling her that he'd been taken in by a couple, and given a home by them.

When he'd done so, he'd paused, waiting for her to heap upon him the contempt he'd been shown by his former classmates.

But nothing like that had happened.

All he'd seen was dark brown eyes looking at him with sympathy and concern.

It explained, she told him, why he never mentioned his parents or his home.

It must have been so difficult for him, she'd said quietly, not to know anything about his parentage and where he came from, and not being able to see in himself the same features that he could see in the faces of his parents and family. Even though the people who'd taken him in must have been good people to have done so, he must have felt so alone at times.

She'd understood in a way that no one had ever done.

Tears had sprung to his eyes, and for the first time in his life, he'd felt emotional towards another human being.

From that moment on, in the long break for lunch, with the tang of the sea strong in the air, they'd walked side by side through the flat marshland near the teacher's dwelling, and among the labyrinth of canals and locks that controlled the amount of sea water allowed into the land, and she'd introduced him to a world that he'd never noticed before.

For the first time, he'd paused in the day to take note of

the ducks, herons, kingfishers, egrets and storks that haunted the marshes. And she'd made him stop and look at the damselflies and butterflies that formed a flickering arch above the beach grass and tamarisk bushes.

His interest had so developed that one day, when he saw in the water next to him an elusive otter, he'd grabbed Adèle in uncontrolled excitement, and hugged her tightly.

Realising what he'd done, he'd stood where he was, aware of her heart beating next to his, and didn't move.

Nor did she.

Then, looking down into the face that was gazing up at him, he saw in her eyes the same feeling that was flowing through him, and lowering his head, he kissed her.

With a shy smile, he drew apart, took hold of her hand, and together they continued walking along the white sand path, each repeatedly turning to smile at the other.

He didn't have to tell her that he loved her, as he was sure she knew it. Just as he knew that she loved him. Both of them wanted spend the rest of their life together.

And by the time the examinations approached, they'd started talking about the future.

In all the time they'd been friends, he'd never suggested taking her to the house where he lived. It was no more than a roof over his head. It had never felt like a proper home.

What he would have with Adèle would be a real home, and he hadn't wanted her to see where he lived for fear that, no matter what he'd said about his future ambitions, she might think that this was the sort of place in which she'd have to live when they married.

It was Adèle who'd raised the subject of them going to each other's home.

She'd explained with a blush that she'd played down the fact that they'd been walking out together, knowing her parents would express alarm at her being alone with a man. But if they were going to share a life in the future, and she hoped they were, she thought that perhaps, introducing himself as her fellow student, about whom they'd known, he should start calling upon her.

And she should visit his home with her parents.

To go there without her parents would be unseemly, she told him.

His heart had sunk. But he'd felt obliged to agree with her suggestion.

The artisan had been most surprised, and not at all thrilled, at the idea of meeting Adèle and her parents. But he'd reluctantly agreed that they could join him and his wife for their afternoon tea of bread and jam, grunting that he'd have nothing to say that would interest them.

And he'd been right.

The meeting was a disaster.

He and Adèle had sat side by side and cringed as her parents had made an effort at conversation, but found their questions met with monosyllabic replies. They couldn't drink their tea and leave fast enough, and René and Marie had made no attempt to hide the fact that they couldn't wait for them to go.

Acutely embarrassed, he'd whispered to Adèle that they'd meet at the teacher's the next day.

When he arrived there the following morning, his heart leapt as he saw Adèle through the small pale-blue shuttered window. At least, she hadn't withdrawn from him, he thought in relief, and his steps had hastened as he approached the house.

As he reached the front door, the teacher stepped outside.

Gently, he'd moved Gaston to one side, and apologised that he was going to be unable to continue teaching him.

Adèle's parents had given him an ultimatum—either he stopped teaching Gaston when Adèle was there, or they'd remove their daughter. As he couldn't afford to lose the income that Adèle brought in, he'd have to ask Gaston not to come back, and never again to attempt to speak to Adèle.

He'd only leave, he told the teacher, his face ashen, if Adèle came out and told him herself that she didn't want to see him again. And he'd planted his feet firmly on the ground, folded his arms, and waited.

The teacher had obviously realised that he wasn't going to get rid of Gaston until he'd spoken to Adèle, and a few minutes later, she'd appeared in the doorway.

The teacher had gone inside, leaving them to talk alone.

Gaston's arms fell to his sides, and he stepped forward.

He loved her, he told her. And he was sure she loved him. That was all that mattered.

René and Marie weren't his real family, and he was very different from them. He wanted the same things as she did, and as he intended to take the exams whatever happened, and was hopeful of attaining a scholarship to a grande école, and after that, to an école supérieure, he knew he'd be able to offer her the sort of future she deserved.

Her parents would come round, he was sure, when they saw his academic success.

She'd heard him out.

But his words had fallen on deaf ears.

It wasn't only her parents who'd been unable to see beyond the rough-hewn furniture that had crowded the single-roomed bourrine, he'd realised. Adèle hadn't been able to see beyond it, either.

From the start, she told him, she'd assumed that the man and woman who'd taken him in were paying for the classes they were sharing. The teacher had implied as much. She'd thought, therefore, that they must have had sufficient money to do so.

And the importance they placed on education had indicated a cultural background that if not on a par with that of her parents, wouldn't be too far below it.

She liked him enormously, she'd explained, and if circumstances had been different, they could have had a future together. But just as he was ambitious, so was she, and she agreed with her parents that at her young age, it would be foolhardy to deny herself the chance to meet someone with the right background, with whom she'd be guaranteed to have the life she wanted.

Marrying well was important to her, just as it was to her parents, she confessed, more so than she'd realised until the moment she'd seen how Gaston lived.

And it was also important, she added, that her parents knew how much she appreciated everything they were doing for her. They were making sure that she was well educated for a girl, knowing that it would improve her chance of a good marriage.

She couldn't throw this away. And she didn't want to.

He'd listened to her betrayal of all his hopes, and he'd turned and walked away.

She was no better than the rest, he'd thought in bitterness and pain.

But he'd learnt his lesson. Never again would he allow another person to get close enough to hurt him in such a way.

He'd already achieved a great deal by his own endeavours, relying upon his brains and determination, and he knew he was cleverer than the people he used to sit alongside.

But that wasn't all that he'd gained from the past few years.

By listening to the exchanges between his peers in the elementary school, and by talking with Adèle, he'd learnt to speak their language.

And one day, he swore to himself, he'd have a job where he was paid to go after people who were wronging others, and see that they were punished.

And he didn't need anyone to help him do so.

There were worse things than being alone.

8

Gaston didn't have long to wait before a grey-haired woman opened the door, her thin face etched with responsibility.

'Yes, Monsieur?' she asked questioningly, and she patted the bun at the nape of her neck.

He raised his panama hat and smiled. 'It's Madame Fousseret, isn't it? We met a couple of weeks ago, after I accidentally hit Madame Delon's car.'

She nodded. 'I remember.' Her mouth set in a grim line.

He smiled again. 'I've something for Monsieur Delon. From what he said this morning, I've reason to think he might be at home now.'

'He isn't,' she said bluntly.

Since nothing more was forthcoming, he moved slightly forward. 'Then if I may, I'll leave these for him,' he said, speaking a shade or two more loudly. He indicated the papers he was holding. 'But first, I'll need to write a covering note in explanation. If it wouldn't inconvenience you too much, perhaps I could use the hall table to do so?'

Without waiting for an answer, he stepped over the

threshold and on to the tiled hall floor, thrust his panama hat into her surprised hands, and went towards the small table that stood on the other side of a tall fern.

As he approached the table, he took out his pen and made a show of searching in his pockets for a piece of paper.

'Gaston!' he heard Lucette exclaim from just behind him. 'I thought I heard your voice.'

He turned and saw her standing in the doorway, smiling in obvious pleasure at seeing him. Her violet eyes, framed with long dark lashes, were filled with genuine warmth.

There were worse ways of finding out what one needed to know, he thought wryly. Much worse.

'What a lovely surprise,' she said. 'But why are you standing out here? You must come into the salon and sit with me.' She turned to the housekeeper. 'I'm sure Monsieur Laroche would welcome some refreshment, Madame Fousseret. Would you bring us tea, please? Or would you prefer something else, Gaston? Whisky, perhaps, or a glass of wine?'

'Tea would be perfect,' he said.

His smile of thanks embraced both Lucette and Mme. Fousseret.

Mme. Fousseret's expression was stony.

'This way,' Lucette said, and she led the way back into the salon.

He followed her into the high-ceilinged room and across the hardwood floor to an arrangement of chairs.

She down on a directoire chair upholstered in sage green velvet, which was next to a small occasional table, its mother-of-pearl inlay iridescent on the dark wood. An open book lay on the table. Smiling, she indicated that he should take the similar chair opposite hers.

'This is very kind of you,' he said. 'I hope it's not too much of an interruption in your day.'

'It isn't,' she said. 'In fact, it's lovely to have company. Simonne's visiting friends. I could have gone with her, but the heat's so oppressive in the afternoon these days that I didn't want to.'

'You'll get used to it,' he said, his voice warm with sympathy. 'Simonne's known it all her life, so it's different for her. But the temperature in here is very pleasant.'

Both glanced up at the large-bladed ceiling fans that were humming rhythmically above them.

'Simonne also told me I'd adjust to the heat,' she said, looking back at him. 'Philippe's obviously working, so I was actually feeling a little lonely, if you want to know the truth.' She laughed in embarrassment.

'What about Mai? Is it her day off?'

'No, she's off on Saturdays. Philippe tries to be home on Saturday afternoons, so I'm happy for Mai to be out that day. If we're going anywhere in the evening, she'll put my clothes out before she leaves, but I'm quite capable of dressing myself and doing my hair. At the moment, she's upstairs, repairing one of my dresses. So, I really was alone.'

'Then I'm glad I arrived when I did,' he said smiling. 'I came here because there's something I need to show Philippe before I have it typed up, and I thought he'd be back by now.'

'He isn't usually home this early.'

'I know that used to be the case. But over breakfast this morning, we were talking about the humidity, and Marc told Philippe he must leave early whenever his work permitted.'

Lucette sighed with despair. 'That's kind of Marc, but Philippe will never do that. He's far too conscientious. When he started, he was told his hours, and he'll stick to them. He finishes lunch at half past twelve, has a siesta in his office till half past two, and always comes home at half past seven.'

'Then he's a stronger man than I,' he said warmly. 'If I had someone as lovely as you, waiting at home for me, I'd go home the moment I could.'

Lucette blushed, and shifted in her chair. 'A comment like that puts me in an awkward position. If I say thank you, it'll sound as if I think I deserve your extravagant compliment, and that will make me come across as very conceited. But if I don't say thank you, it'll make me appear very rude. So you can see, I'm in a quandary.' Glancing at him, she bit her lip.

He grinned at her. 'I'm curious to see how you resolve it.'

'So am I,' she said, and she giggled.

The door opened and Mme. Fousseret entered, pushing a trolley. On the top tier, there was a silver tea set and an array of china, cutlery and napkins. A cake stand with a selection of afternoon cakes stood on the lower tier.

'If you'd be kind enough to leave the trolley, Madame Fousseret, we'll serve ourselves. Thank you.'

'As you wish, Madame.' Mme. Fousseret's voice dripped disapproval. With a slight inclination of her head, she left the salon.

'Would you prefer your tea with lemon or milk?' Lucette asked, getting up and going across to the trolley. She picked up the teapot.

'With lemon, please,' he said, and she started pouring the tea. 'Saved by the teapot, you could say,' he added cheerfully, loosening his narrow black tie and undoing the top button on his white shirt. 'Now I shall never know your response.'

She looked across at him and smiled. 'Yes, that worked out well, didn't it? We can move on to another topic. By the way, you can take off your jacket, if you wish,' she added as she put a cup of tea on the table next to him, and a plate.

She picked up the cake stand and offered him the selection of cakes. 'I know your jacket's light in weight, but it's still a warm afternoon, and I shan't think you disrespectful.'

'In that case,' he said, and when he'd taken a cake, he took off his jacket and rolled up his shirtsleeves as far as his elbows.

When they both had a cup of tea and a cake on the table next to their chair, Lucette sat back down.

'Is it a silly question to ask if there's anything I can do for you?' she asked.

'Perhaps you ought to be more specific in your question,' he murmured in undisguised amusement. 'I wouldn't want to put you to the blush again.'

She went red, and burst out laughing.

'I meant, is there a message you'd like me to give Philippe?'

He indicated the papers on the table next to his cup. 'Those are for him to check,' he said, picking up his cup. 'They're about the prison visit.'

'He told me you were going to be showing some people around.'

'That's right. Their visit's quite an important one—not just to the prison, but to everywhere else, too. While they want to see our achievements in Hanoi, they're also here to find out why we aren't making more money than we are. America's economic woes have had a disastrous effect in Europe, and foreign trade has dried up. Not unreasonably, therefore, Paris is looking to the colonies to boost its income, and they want us to do better.'

She frowned. 'I didn't realise we were doing badly.'

He smiled. 'We're not. Yes, the rural economy's

depressed because we've been forced to tax the peasants quite highly in order to pay for the construction of public works, such as the railway from Hanoi to Saigon. But in the end, ease of transport from one end of the country to the other will benefit French and Vietnamese alike, and the rural economy will pick up.'

Her brow cleared. 'I can see that.'

'Also, although the peasants might not like it, we've kept a tight control on the cost of the labour we use, and this will further improve the economy. And our monopoly on alcohol, salt and the opium trade means that they're producing good revenue for us, too. So don't worry, Lucette, Paris will soon be more than satisfied with what we send them, and the guests will report back that in every way possible here, we're promoting the economic interests of France.'

She sat back in her chair. 'Thank you, Gaston,' she said quietly.

He glanced at her, surprised at the tremor of genuine gratitude in her voice. 'I'm glad that helped,' he said.

Feeling suddenly awkward, he picked up his cake.

She nodded. 'It did. But perhaps not in the way you think I mean. What you told me was interesting, of course, but that you took the trouble to explain the situation matters to me even more than what you said.'

His forehead creased in puzzlement. 'I'm afraid I don't quite understand.'

'You spoke to me as I assume you would to a man. You didn't take one look at me and think I'm a silly young woman with an empty head, and I'd never understand anything about the economy. And you didn't fob me off by saying that I need not worry, that there'll always be sufficient money for me to have coffee with friends.'

He stared at her in open surprise. 'I've never thought of

you as a silly young woman, Lucette. It's true that I think of
you as beautiful, but I know that it's possible for a beautiful
young woman to have a brain and also be interested in the
world around her.'

'Most of the men I've met don't think that way,' she said,
a pink haze spreading across her cheeks.

'Then it's surely the same as saying that if a man's good-
looking, he can't have a brain. That can't be true, though.
Your Philippe is a handsome man, but he wouldn't have
risen to the position he's in if he wasn't extremely
intelligent.'

Her face lit up. 'I've never thought about it like that! But,
yes, you're right, Philippe's both good-looking and very
clever. One characteristic doesn't rule out the other.'

'We're agreed, then: brains and beauty can go hand in
hand. And that's why I'm hoping that you and Philippe will
be present at a small reception I want to hold in the Résidence before the visitors leave. I'll run it past Marc first, of
course, as technically he'll be the host, but I'd like you and
Simonne to be there, as well as your husbands.'

'How enjoyable that sounds.'

'I hope it will be. I thought it would be a good opportunity for the visitors to ask any last questions before they
leave for Saigon, and for us to ensure that their last memories will be of the beauty there is in Hanoi.'

She looked at him in exaggerated exasperation. 'You're
not talking about women's looks again, are you? I thought
we'd moved on from that.'

He held up his hands in protest. 'And so we have. I'm
thinking in particular of the splendid architecture in the
city. But as for women's faces, the last place they'll have
visited before leaving Hanoi will be the prison. Even
Madame Fousseret would be a beautiful sight after that!'

She burst out laughing.

Grinning, he rose to his feet, slipping into his jacket as he did so. 'I'd better be on my way. I'll leave the papers for Philippe. Perhaps you'd draw his attention to them.'

'I will,' she said, standing up and smoothing down the skirt of her dress. 'Thank you for coming, Gaston. I've really enjoyed talking to you. Philippe needs a break from anything to do with work when he gets home, so I don't like to ask him about his day. But in truth, I'd very much like to hear about the sort of things he's been doing. It would be interesting to know.'

Gaston paused and gazed down at her. 'You must ask him, Lucette,' he said gently. 'You're his wife, not a servant, and not a woman he pays to warm his bed. If you encourage him to feel that he can talk about his work, you'll develop an even greater closeness than you have now.'

'D'you think so?'

He smiled. 'I do. You told me not long after I got here this afternoon that you'd been feeling lonely. Well, a man who feels he can't share the things that are most important to him, as a man's work is to him, is a man who could also feel very alone. We neither of us would want that for Philippe, would we?'

She looked up at him with eyes that were moist. 'I've never thought about it like that, but you're right. That's what I'll do. Thank you, Gaston, for being so wise, and so thoughtful about Philippe. I'm so glad we met you.'

He grinned at her. 'Now it's my turn to feel embarrassed. I suggest you ring and ask Madame Fousseret to see me out before I go an unmanly scarlet.'

She opened her mouth to speak, but he put his finger to her lips.

'If you're going to say that you'll see me out yourself, it'd

be better not to do so. We shall do things by the manual of
social etiquette, which means that Madame Fousseret must
show me to the door. If we don't stick to form, she might
take to hiding behind the door, or in the linen basket, trying
to catch you being a naughty girl.'

'She'd waste a lot of time, in that case,' she said lightly.
'And boredom and backache would be her rewards.'

Both laughed.

'Nevertheless, I think we'll call for her. And I shall
increase the space between us,' he added.

He took a couple of steps back, tightening his tie as he
did so.

She rang the bell on the table next to her chair, and
stood with her hands folded primly in front of her.

'Philippe knows that I'll be here on Friday morning to
check on the car,' he said. 'If I don't see you then, I'll see you
at Marc and Simonne's on Sunday. I, too, have been invited
to lunch.'

Before she could reply, they heard the door open.

'I'll make a point of seeing Marc tomorrow about the
reception,' he went on. 'Don't forget those papers for
Philippe. But tell him there's no rush.'

Mme. Fousseret came into the room. 'Yes, Madame
Delon?'

'Please see Monsieur Laroche to the door,' Lucette
instructed.

'Certainly, Madame. This way, Monsieur Laroche.' Mme.
Fousseret turned towards the door.

Gaston exchanged a glance of amusement with Lucette,
and then followed Mme. Fousseret into the hall. He took his
hat from her, and put it on as he went out through the door
she was holding open.

The moment he was outside, he heard the door close firmly behind him.

THE AROMA from the hydrangea blossoms was at its height as he walked back along the drive, a satisfaction on his face at the success of his visit.

His intention had been to get closer to Lucette, and in the last hour or so, he'd achieved that, he was sure.

But not exactly in the way he'd planned, he thought wryly.

The form of closeness that had been in his mind at the start of his visit had been the kind where their heads would eventually lie side by side on a pillow. In moments of ecstasy, secrets fall from lips, and that was what he'd aimed at achieving.

But it had been very clear from the outset that Lucette didn't enjoy being paid compliments, and was not of a flirtatious nature. And being newly married, she was still dewy-eyed about her husband. That short amount of time he'd spent with her had been long enough to show him the unlikeliness of the closeness he'd envisioned.

He wouldn't totally abandon his original intention, however, as he'd sensed a response to him deep within her —one that she herself wouldn't have recognised, and wouldn't have welcomed if she had. But because of that response, he would keep his original intention at the back of his mind in case of emergencies.

But he shouldn't forget that there were different sorts of closeness.

To his great surprise, it was the outcome of what he'd told her that afternoon, not his compliments, that had set them on a path that could end in a friendship based on mutual respect, rather than one based on physical attraction.

In her rejection of him, Adèle had shown him that women wanted to feel safe and protected by a man. Before that afternoon, though, it hadn't occurred to him to think of Lucette in such terms.

But if she were caught up in something about which she was uncertain, or if she suspected she'd happened upon wrongdoing, and with Philippe so busy she didn't want to bother him with her possibly pointless concerns, she could be feeling confused, and even unsafe.

If so, to whom would she turn for guidance and reassurance, but to a friend in whom she trusted.

And it looked as if that friend could be him.

He knew from the night he'd seen Lucette outside her house that she was deeply suspicious about something she'd come across or overheard. It was hard to believe that this could involve Philippe, or the woman who went in daily to clean, or the kitchen-maid, or the chauffeur-gardener, all of whom left for their own homes at the end of the day.

That left their cook and Mme. Fousseret.

And Mai.

Mai, who'd been placed in the Delons' house by Marc Bouvier, was the most likely of the three.

Since she would almost certainly assist on the Friday morning when they assembled to look at the repaired car, it would give him a valuable chance to watch her closely.

And Lucette, too, would almost certainly be there on Friday, so he'd have an opportunity to build on his achievements that afternoon.

He could tell that she'd enjoyed his visit, and as she didn't yet know many people, a reason for her feeling lonely, it would be highly surprising if she were elsewhere on the Friday morning.

At least, he hoped his reasoning was correct.

Reaching the end of the drive, he paused and on an impulse, turned to look back at the house.

His gaze met Lucette's.

She was standing at the salon window, staring at him. He raised his hand and waved. But she stepped quickly out of sight.

A smile on his face, he turned back to the road.

Yes, she'd definitely be there on Friday.

9

T*he Delon house*
    Friday morning

THE BLACK PEUGEOT gleamed on the drive, surrounded by Philippe and Lucette, Marc and Simonne, and Gaston, a champagne flute in their hand as they'd laughingly admired the new rear bumper.

Two open bottles of champagne, a white napkin around each neck, were embedded in a floor-standing ice bucket next to the front door. And just inside the hall, Mme. Fousseret stood waiting lest she was needed.

'I know it's somewhat early in the day for champagne,' Philippe said with a broad smile, 'but the car's been done to an excellent standard, without any inconvenience to us, and we should toast that. Plus, it's also worth toasting again the fact that the accident resulted in us meeting you, Gaston. To the car, and to you.'

He raised his glass in salute, and the others did likewise.

'It was kind of them to collect the car, and return it when it was done. I didn't know garages did that, not when the car could be driven,' Lucette remarked.

'That's part of Gaston's magic, I rather think,' Marc said with a smile. 'Not every garage would have been so obliging. You obviously have a way with words, Gaston.'

'I'd like to say that you're right, and to take full credit for the garage's obligingness, but in all honesty, I can't. There's something more powerful than words,' Gaston said.

'Which is?' Simonne asked.

Grinning, Gaston rubbed his thumb and index finger together.

'Oh, money! Of course!' she exclaimed.

They all laughed.

'The truth is, there's nothing you can't get done, and in the way you want, provided you know how to go about it,' Gaston added, and he took a sip of his champagne.

Marc looked appreciatively at his glass of champagne. 'Fortunately, Philippe and I have a fairly easy day ahead of us,' he said, 'since we've begun it in such a pleasant way. We're going to the prison this afternoon, but it won't be very demanding. All metal and glass equipment is imported from France, of course, and must be strictly checked before being used for construction. There's just been a new consignment of locks and hinges, and we're overseeing the people checking it. All I'll be doing is showing Philippe what to look out for.'

'Such as?' Lucette asked as Philippe moved round the group, topping up everyone's glass.

Marc shrugged. 'We make sure that the required glass plates are crystal without bubbles, and that the bricks have fully absorbed water before being used. That sort of thing. With construction standards as high as ours, no one could ever break into the prison, or out of it. Not even an ant.'

'I see. Thank you.'

Gaston gave a low whistle. 'Your attention to detail is most impressive. I'll make sure our visitors appreciate it.' He raised his champagne flute to his lips again. 'Darn!' he exclaimed, and gave a slight jump.

Holding his arms out wide, his glass tilting slightly in his right hand, he glanced down at his white jacket where a patch of damp was spreading across the lapel.

'I seem to have missed my mouth. And no,' he added quickly, a note of amusement coming into his voice. 'Don't make the obvious comment about my mouth being too big to miss!'

They laughed.

Lucette hastily gave her glass to Philippe, and hurried round the car to Gaston.

'We must wipe that at once, Gaston, or it'll leave some discolouration. It'll only be slight, but it'll be visible, never-theless.'

'I'm so sorry,' Gaston said, looking around in apology. 'Having just put a full stop to the first accident that involved me, there's now a second.'

'Don't worry. It could have happened to anyone,' Lucette said. 'Come on. Let me take you inside.'

As she went into the house, Mme. Fousseret stepped forward.

'Ah, Madame Fousseret! Would you take Monsieur Laroche through to the kitchen and ask Mai to stop what-ever she's doing and clean the jacket?'

'Of course, Madame Delon.'

Lucette turned back to Gaston. 'Come out again when Mai's finished, Gaston. It'll dry in the sun in minutes.'

He nodded. 'I appreciate your quick thinking, Lucette.'

Giving him a sympathetic smile, she went back out to the drive.

'This way, Monsieur,' Mme. Fousseret said, her voice frosty, and she began walking along the hall.

He glanced swiftly at the room to the right of the entrance, on the opposite side of the hall from the salon. The door was open, and he saw that the back wall was lined with bookshelves. In the centre of the room, a large rosewood table was strewn with papers.

So that's Philippe's office, he thought as he followed Mme. Fousseret past the foot of the staircase to the kitchen leading off the far right-hand corner of the hall.

As he entered the kitchen behind the housekeeper, he saw a petite Vietnamese girl coming into the kitchen through a back door.

Aha, he exclaimed inwardly in satisfaction. Spilling the champagne had paid off.

The Vietnamese girl stopped abruptly when she saw them, and a look of alarm swept across her face.

Interesting, he thought.

But the alarm was momentary, and the double-lidded dark brown eyes that stared at him seconds later were expressionless.

He gave her a polite smile.

'If you remove your jacket, Monsieur, Mai will remove any stain,' Mme. Fousseret said. 'I suggest you wait here as it won't take long. I'll go back to Monsieur Delon in case I'm needed. If you'll excuse me.' And she went back into the hall.

He handed Mai his jacket. 'The stain is champagne, if that helps. While you're doing that, I think I'll take some air.'

'Certainly, Monsieur.'

Thrusting his hands into his trouser pockets, he went across the kitchen and through the door by which Mai had come in. Finding himself in the scullery, he walked through it to the laundry room.

The beam of light that he and Lucette had seen that evening had definitely come from the kitchen area, he confirmed as he strolled with studied casualness into the garden.

The other door that opened out into the garden, presumably from the dining room, was too centrally placed to have been the source of the light. That would be the doorway through which Lucette had entered the garden.

He glanced at the iron railings on his right, which separated Philippe's house from Marc's, and, as he'd expected, he saw a side gate, which would facilitate contact between the two houses.

And the dense cluster of rhododendron bushes that grew by the railings in the area next to the gate could easily conceal a box for messages, if messages were, indeed, being passed between the houses.

That was something to explore one day, but only when he could do so unseen, he resolved as he headed across the lawn towards the rear of the garden.

Beyond the lawn, there was an abundance of deep green leaves and heavily fringed ferns, interspersed with a number of brightly coloured flowers and a profusion of deep pink peach blossom—patches of brilliance in the sun-dappled shade thrown out by the several spreading banyan and tamarind trees at the back of the garden.

Reaching the edge of the lawn, he made a point of seeming to admire the white flowers of the glossy-leaved wild gardenia that bordered the grass, and of inhaling their strong perfume that scented the air.

Then he moved further forward, into the shadows.

The iron railings came into sight—an unbroken line along the rear of the Delon and Bouvier gardens. A large tamarind tree stood just inside the railings, its thick gnarled trunk proclaiming its age.

Just the sort of tree to have a hollow in which messages could be left, he thought.

He felt a sudden excitement, and his pace quickened.

'Monsieur,' he heard Mai call sharply from behind him.

Damn, he exclaimed inwardly, and he stopped at once.

Arranging his lips in a smile of gratitude, he turned towards her and waded back through the greenery to the lawn.

'That was admirably quick,' he said when he reached her. She held out his jacket, and he allowed her to help him into it. 'I can tell you've managed to remove all trace of champagne,' he added, glancing down at the damp patch on the white lapel. 'Thank you.'

'It was my pleasure, Monsieur,' she said, unsmiling. 'If you come with me now, I'll take you back to Monsieur Delon.'

And she walked forward, checking frequently behind her to make sure that he was following her.

As they went along the hall, past the table and the standing fern, he glanced sideways at Philippe's office.

The door was still ajar.

But Mai kept walking, and he did, too.

They reached the front door, and went through the doorway on to the drive. Just in front of him, Mme. Fousseret was exchanging a few words with Philippe.

Mai stopped.

He turned to thank her again for her efforts with his jacket, but she was staring past him.

Without it being obvious, he turned back and followed her gaze.

She was looking at Marc Bouvier. He was standing behind Simonne, who was engaged in conversation with Lucette.

As he watched, Marc put his glass to his lips, and then gazed casually around the group.

Just for a moment, Marc's eyes lingered on Mai. If he hadn't been watching closely, Gaston realised, he would've missed Marc giving her an imperceptible nod.

He looked back at Mai. She was smiling slightly as she turned to go back into the house.

Well, that's one link in the chain confirmed, he thought in satisfaction as he went across to Philippe. 'Mai's done an excellent job on my jacket,' he told him cheerfully.

Philippe grinned. 'It's obviously safe, then, to offer you more champagne. After all, should there be another accident, we now know that Mai can fix it.'

Laughing, Philippe went across to the ice bucket.

While he waited for Philippe to bring him his drink, he glanced at Lucette. Ostensibly she was listening to Simonne, but her gaze was actually on the house, and she was frowning slightly.

He turned fractionally and saw that Mai, clearly visible through the open front door, was rearranging the fronds of the giant fern that stood between the hall table and Philippe's office.

So that's what caught Lucette's eye, he thought.

Could she think that Mai was planning to slip into Philippe's office, he wondered.

Surely not.

Had she seriously harboured any suspicion that something on Philippe's desk might be of interest to Mai, she would have alerted Philippe to the fact.

And for Mai to have shown such an interest would have been so highly suspect that Lucette was unlikely to have allowed her to remain in their employment.

So it couldn't be that.

Yet there was clearly something about Mai that intrigued her, and that something must be the reason why she'd been watching Mai that night, assuming that Mai had, indeed, been the other person in the garden.

He looked back at Lucette, but she was now concentrating on her conversation with Simonne.

Would he have been aware that for all Lucette's animation that morning, she'd been preoccupied with something else for part of the time, he mused, if he hadn't witnessed her nocturnal activity.

He didn't know. Probably not, if he were being honest with himself.

But he could see it very clearly now, and he'd put any money on it that she was planning to watch the back of the house that evening.

And when she did, unknown to her, she wouldn't be alone. He'd be watching, too.

But he wouldn't be watching from the same position as before—he'd be among the bushes behind the houses, a position from which he could move in several directions with ease, should that be necessary, and whence he'd be able to observe anyone who approached the railings and trees at the back of the Delons' garden.

That person would be the next link in the chain.

And if the moon were bright enough, he might also be able to see as far as the side gate between the two gardens.

There was a strong likelihood, this being the eve of Mai's day off, and given Bouvier's nod to her that morning, that Bouvier might have left a message for her to pass on. It meant that under the cover of darkness, she might check the box, and if so, he'd discover its location.

His operatives would thereafter watch the house at night, and follow whoever collected any messages from the tree. And Mai would be shadowed on her day off. Thus they'd discover the terrorists' headquarters and printing press, and the terrorists themselves.

But he had no intention of apprehending them at this stage as it would be counter-productive to do so.

It would be of more value to see where that person went. They needed to identify not only the terrorists in the Old Quarter, but also their contacts in the outlying villages. Only when these were known, would the Sûreté move in.

As he took his champagne flute from Philippe, he felt the thrill of a chase closing in.

'Cheers!' he said, raising his glass, and this time he didn't miss his mouth.

10

L *ate that evening*

IT FELT to Lucette as if she'd been hours in the unlit dining room, peering into the moonlit darkness between the slats in the window shutters.

The moment she'd been confident that Philippe was sleeping deeply, she'd slipped out of bed, wrapped a shawl around her shoulders, taken her torch from the drawer in her bedside table, put on her sturdiest sandals and run silently down the stairs and into the dining room.

She was determined that as soon as Mai went through the kitchen door into the garden—and she was certain that Mai would do so that night—she'd open the French windows, and nudge apart the shutters, which she'd unlocked before she'd gone upstairs with Philippe.

She'd then squeeze through the smallest possible gap, and follow Mai into the garden, keeping well behind her.

Since that morning, she hadn't been able to forget Mai's interest in what was happening on the drive.

When Mai had emerged from the house with Gaston, she'd looked right past her, and past Marc, who was behind her, and she'd stared fixedly down the drive.

It had been as if she was expecting to see someone coming along it.

And she'd been clearly reluctant to return to her duties after helping with Gaston's jacket. All the while she'd been going through the motions of rearranging the fern, her attention had actually been on the drive.

The more she'd thought about it, the more she'd come round to thinking that Mai must have a beau, and had been hoping to see him that morning.

And if she was right in that belief, it was a matter of concern.

If Mai had thought, as she'd seemed to do, that her beau might have turned up that morning while she and Philippe were entertaining friends, and have come along the drive, he must be someone who felt entitled to use the front door, not the back, and that had made her both curious and anxious.

After all, it wasn't too preposterous to think that Mai, an extremely pretty girl, had caught the attention of one of the administration's officials.

Indeed, Mai, herself, was the result of a relationship between a Vietnamese woman and a non-Vietnamese man, who had probably been French.

Her purpose that evening, therefore, was to see the person whom Mai had been meeting, and now that the moon had finally come out, she should be able to do so.

She'd be unlikely to recognise the man, not having been long in Hanoi, but there'd be social occasions for the French officials and wives in the Résidence, such as Gaston's proposed reception, and if she saw the man at such a function, she'd be able to find out his name.

Only when she knew who he was, would she know if this was something she should tell Philippe.

Leaning further forward, she strained to see through the darkness

HIDDEN among the bushes outside the railings, Gaston waited.

Slowly, the sun sank into the horizon, and swathes of crimson and orange blazed across the sky, followed by a wall of deep purple shadow, which climbed inexorably upwards, smothering everything in its path, and thickening into an unrelieved darkness.

And then, as if on cue, a bone-white crescent moon slid forth from the canopy of night, and touched with silver the tips of the bushes and trees that encircled him.

Thank goodness for the moon, he thought. And for the stars that were emerging one by one.

For a moment or two, he'd been worried that he might not be able to see what happened that night, assuming that something did, as to use his torch would have drawn attention to his presence. But with the moon on his side, and in a strong vantage point, he felt his anxiety evaporate.

The moonlight would probably be a relief to Lucette, too, who must have had the same concern as he.

He'd been in his position for several minutes before he'd seen her.

At first, he'd wondered if she'd watch the garden from her bedroom window, but not so. It was the dining room shutters that had suddenly opened, with Lucette appearing in the space between them.

She'd adjusted their position to leave a narrow gap only, and had then stepped back into the room, and settled herself where she could see the garden in front of her.

He frowned.

She was obviously intending to follow Mai, but if she did so in a clumsy manner, it could alert Mai to her presence, and Mai would surely, in such an event, return to the house at once.

Earlier in the day, he'd realised the risk to his mission that Lucette posed.

There'd still been time enough to have tried to deflect her from her plan, but to have attempted to do so was risky, and he'd decided that it was better not to do so.

He hoped that he hadn't made a mistake.

From his position, he was able to watch both the side gate and the largest tamarind tree. But Lucette, he realised, was limited to what she could see through the gap in the shutters, and would be unable to see the gate.

It meant that if it came to a choice between following through on something that happened at both the gate and the tree, he could safely stay with the gate, knowing that Lucette had her eye on the tree.

If that happened, he was sure that in the next few days, he'd be able to find out from her what she'd seen, and to do so without arousing her suspicions.

And he shouldn't forget that there was almost certainly something inside the house that had aroused her suspicions, but he had yet to learn what had first alerted her to Mai's intrigue, and to discover if she was aware of Marc's involvement.

As it was important to find out the answers to those questions, as well as to pursue anything that might happen that night, he must make a point of getting some time alone with her again as soon as possible, and of encouraging her to confide in him.

He settled further into the seat he'd made himself.

He'd be seeing Lucette at the Bouviers' lunch on Sunday, so he needed to work out before then when they could meet and for reason. He could then take her aside during the lunch, and propose whatever he'd decided.

There was a faint click from the area of the side gate—the sound of a metal latch rising and falling.

He sat up sharply, and stared towards the house.

Leaves rustled.

The kitchen door opened, and Mai appeared, framed for an instant by the beam from the kitchen. Then she extinguished the light, closed the door behind her, and ran up to the cluster of rhododendron bushes.

A tall figure stepped from the shadows on the other side of the gate.

Marc Bouvier.

So he'd come in person that night, and hadn't left a package in the concealed box, he thought in annoyance. He'd wanted to find its location.

He watched as Marc handed Mai a parcel over the gate, and then stood talking with Mai for a moment or two. Finally, she nodded, turned and went back into the house.

And Marc returned to his house.

He waited till he was certain that Mai wasn't going to appear again, and then he stood up. His presence concealed by a tree, he stared towards the dining room.

Lucette, too, had risen. She was standing in the long narrow gap between the full-length shutters, staring out into the dark garden.

Then she, too, seemed to realise that nothing else would

be happening that night, and with a dejected air, she pulled the shutters together.

LYING ON HER BACK, her eyes wide open, listening to Philippe's gentle breathing next to her, Lucette thought back to the events of the past hour or so.

She'd been certain that Mai would be going out to meet her beau, and she'd been very keen to see the man, especially if he was French.

If he were French, she'd decided, she would ask Philippe to question Mai as to the man's identity.

Once they knew who he was, they could find out if he was married.

If he was, the friendship must be brought to an immediate end.

Mai, who lived in their house, who was still very young, was her responsibility and Philippe's. It would be wrong of them to turn a blind eye to a situation that could end up in Mai having no choice but to be in the same position as Mai's mother had been many years earlier.

If the Frenchman were unmarried, Philippe would have to establish his intentions.

But even if he was single, the outcome for Mai could be the same as if he was married.

Too many Vietnamese women had been deserted by their French beaux and left to bring up a métis child on their own. Being free to marry didn't guarantee a willingness to marry, but Mai might be too innocent to know that.

But not only did she not see the man, she thought in despair, she didn't even see Mai!

Instead of staying in her bedroom, she'd settled herself in the dining room, assuming that Mai would run across the lawn as she'd done before. Knowing that Mai would be in her line of vision, she'd intended to creep outside as soon as she saw her and follow her to the railings.

But this time, Mai hadn't done that—she'd exited the kitchen door as before, but had stayed on that side of the house.

Although she'd seen a speck of light in the kitchen area, she'd not been able to see the people outside. She wasn't high enough off the ground to see the whole garden, and her position was too central.

Of course, it might not even have been Mai who'd opened the kitchen door and closed it a few minutes later, she speculated. Cook could have done so, though that was unlikely. Or even Mme. Fousseret.

Realistically, though, it must have been Mai.

The briefness of the moment suggested that it could have something to do with the following day, which was Mai's day off. Rather than leave a message that she might not find in time, her beau could have taken a risk and come quietly up the garden that evening to let her know where and when they could meet.

That would make sense, she thought, and it would account for the short amount of time that she was outside the house.

And in that case, since she'd nothing planned for the following day, and she knew that Philippe had work to do, she would follow Mai.

She wouldn't go on her bicycle, though—she'd take a pousse-pousse. She'd make sure that the pousse-pousse stayed well back, while keeping Mai in sight, and should Mai turn at all, the coolie would screen her from view.

At the very least, the place to which she followed Mai

would give her a strong indication as to whether Mai's beau was French or Vietnamese.

Her lips curving into a smile, she closed her eyes.

SINCE MARC HAD GIVEN Mai a package, and Mai had taken it with her into the house, rather than depositing it in a secret hiding place, and since she was off on the following day, it was a safe assumption, Gaston had concluded, that Mai intended to deliver the package herself the following morning.

At least, he hoped he was right.

If he wasn't, he'd have had a very late night for nothing, he thought wryly.

With a package to deliver, it was a fair bet that Mai's destination the following morning would be the terrorists' house, the location of which they'd yet to discover, but which they'd long known was in one of the maze of streets that characterised the Old Quarter. But now, at last, they could be about to learn its whereabouts.

It was essential, therefore, that Mai was followed from the moment she left the Delons' house.

He would dearly have loved to have been the person who followed her, but he didn't dare risk it.

She'd seen him so clearly that morning that she'd instantly recognise him if she saw him again, and there was a reasonable chance of that happening as he'd stand out in the narrow cobblestoned streets in the way that a Vietnamese wouldn't.

Even if he changed out of his customary double-breasted linen suit and white panama hat, his features were unmistakably French, and also the way he carried himself, and if Mai didn't see him, one of the people watching the area around the headquarters might.

If that happened, Mai would be instantly intercepted by one of the terrorists, and told to go in a different direction. Furthermore, if they realised she'd been followed, she and her fellow terrorists would be on their guard at all times.

And so, too, would Marc.

Marc wasn't stupid, and if he was told that Mai had been followed, having someone so new to his circle of friends would instantly arouse his suspicions, and he'd be dropped at once. All of his efforts at establishing a friendship would have been wasted.

Reluctantly, therefore, before going back to his house, despite the lateness of the hour, he'd gone straight to the home of one of Emile's operatives and arranged for him to follow Mai the next day.

So that he didn't miss her, the operative was instructed to be outside the Delon residence at the break of day, and to be prepared for the fact that Mai would almost certainly be on her bicycle.

The operative hadn't been best pleased at being disturbed after he'd gone to bed, and then at being told to be at a house in Rue Henri Rivière at the crack of dawn.

That was his job, Gaston had reminded him tetchily, and he'd be well rewarded.

He'd told the operative to report at the end of the day to Emile's office on the southern tip of the Old Quarter, where he, too, would be waiting.

As he put his key in the lock, he felt an impatience for the new day to begin, and for the information that he hoped it would bring.

11

The early morning air was still raw when Mai, in a long-sleeved dark top over loose white trousers, cycled out of the drive and headed north in the direction of the Old Quarter.

The package was in the metal basket on the front of the bicycle, concealed beneath a bag of milk cakes, which she intended to claim, if stopped, were made for her uncle.

By the time she reached the Old Quarter, the lanes were already teeming with life.

Vietnamese men and women of every age were ambling along dusty streets strewn with garbage, most wearing a cone-shape hat of plaited palm leaves, and a large number carrying a bamboo pole across their shoulders.

Bare-chested men sitting cross-legged on the kerb were selling oranges from large baskets. While behind them, men and women sat on low stools before open-fronted shops, their wares displayed on the shop's tables behind them.

At the back of the shop, skilled craftsmen could be seen making the items for sale.

Carts and large-wheeled pousse-pousse clattered noisily

over the cobbles, and every so often, a cloud of dust rose from a motor car, the hooter of which added to the cacophony of sound in the streets.

In the market area, fruit and vegetables had been piled into baskets shaded by parasols, and brightly coloured spices had been heaped in separate mounds on tables.

On the ground between the poultry stalls, caged chickens struggled noisily to free themselves, their squawking adding to the general mêlée.

Despite the earliness of the hour, the air above the narrow streets was already redolent with the scent of ginger, spices, garlic, boiled noodles, onions, peppermint oil, and the sweat of bodies that jostled each other in the burgeoning heat of the day.

Every so often, a pungent aroma of incense rose from one of the small red and gold temples that nestled between the shops, their red paint peeling, and hovered above the small brightly coloured building.

At intervals, narrow flagged alleyways led off the streets. At the end of each alley, there was a proliferation of small rooms and tiny houses in which the natives lived.

As the day burgeoned, families emerged from their cramped homes and settled on low stools placed on either side of the entrance to the alleyway.

Children ran in and out of the alleyways and up and down the streets, older children often carrying a younger child on their back, while bare-bottomed infants toddled aimlessly in the street, a soft toy frequently clutched in their arms.

It was towards one of those alleyways that Mai was heading.

As she cycled along, the sun already hot on her back, she glanced around her every so often, searching for any nearby Citroens or Peugeots, which she'd been told were the preferred cars of the Sûreté, or for any signs at all of being pursued.

But there were none.

There were only the pousse-pousse pullers who populated the streets of Hanoi, and the men on bicycles, hunching over their handlebars as they dodged the people and vehicles in their path.

Reaching the alleyway that had been her destination, she propped the bicycle against the wall, took the package and cakes from her basket, and hurried along the dark passage to the small house at the end on the right.

Moments later, an elderly Vietnamese man with blackened teeth and a grey wispy beard gave an exclamation of annoyance as he came to a stop outside a shop a little further on from the alleyway.

Stiff in his movements, he leaned the bicycle against the wall, crouched down beside the wheel, and with an imperceptible turn of his wrist, removed the cap from the valve.

Straightening up into the slightly bent posture that befitted his age, he exclaimed again, and indicated the flat tyre to no one in particular.

Slowed by his apparently arthritic limbs, he began the laborious process of removing the pump, attaching its head to the valve and blowing air into the tyre.

'MAI LEFT on her bicycle some time ago,' Mme. Fousseret told Lucette in a tone of surprise when Lucette asked at breakfast if Mai could be sent to her. 'It's Mai's day off,' the housekeeper reminded her. 'Is there anything *I* can do for you, Madame?'

'Thank you, Madame Fousseret, but there's no need,' she

said. 'I was just wondering if Mai would be going to the Old Quarter today, and if so, there was something she could have got for me. But as Madame Bouvier and I will probably be going there in the next couple of weeks, there's no urgency about this.'

She smiled in dismissal.

How annoying, she thought, irritated with herself, as the dining room door closed behind Mme. Fousseret.

She should have got up earlier.

Instead, tired after her late night, she'd allowed herself to drift back into sleep after Philippe had left for the Résidence. Despite it being Saturday, he wouldn't be back until the afternoon.

She'd nothing planned till the evening, when she and Philippe had decided to go again to Café Barnard, so it would have been fun to have shadowed Mai, just like a real spy.

But now it was too late, she thought dejectedly.

She took a croissant, and pulled the butter across to her.

If the following Saturday were as free of commitments in the day as this, she'd make sure that she got up early and followed Mai, she told herself firmly. It would give her something to do till Philippe got home, if nothing else.

'So Emile, we now know where Mai deposits the stuff that Marc gives her,' Gaston said. He glanced at the elderly Vietnamese. 'And you're sure she didn't suspect you of following her?'

'Completely sure,' the man with blackened teeth and a grey wispy beard, who was standing upright against the wall, confirmed. 'There was no sign at all of her being suspicious. She looked back a few times, as one would expect, but she didn't double back on herself, suddenly dart down an alley, or do anything at all to suggest that she thought she was being followed.'

'Well done,' Emile told the man, and he held out an envelope to him. 'We'll be in contact again soon, I'm sure, but that will be all for now.'

He waited for the man to take the money and leave the room, and then he glanced across his desk at Gaston. 'I suggest we go into the house and apprehend the terrorists, and then go for Mai and Bouvier afterwards. Would you agree?'

'No, I wouldn't,' Gaston said. 'Mai could be replaced without difficulty. It wouldn't be quite as easy to find someone to take on Bouvier's role, but I'm sure they'd find someone in the prison to do so. There's not much that the right amount of money can't buy.'

Emile scowled. 'I suppose you're right.'

'And arresting Mai and Bouvier wouldn't break the line of distribution, which is what we need to do. We must capture everyone involved, which means the people who do the printing, those who take the papers to the outlying villages, and those in the villages who receive the papers and distribute them.'

'But wouldn't we find the printers when we raided the headquarters?'

Gaston smiled ruefully. 'I very much doubt we'd find anyone or anything. The moment our cars appeared, a lookout we'd failed to spot would give the warning, and the terrorists would dive through the cellars into the network of alleyways, each one following a foolproof escape route planned for just such an occasion. By the time we'd identified their house and entered it, all trace of them would be gone.'

Emile frowned. 'So what do we do?'

'Well, we don't alert them to the fact we know about Mai and Bouvier, for a start,' Gaston said. 'If they knew that, they'd close that line of distribution, start another, and we'd be back to square one. No, we wait.'

'For what?' Emile asked, in visible impatience.

'To find out two things. Namely, who collects the messages that I'm convinced Mai leaves in a tree in the Delons' garden, and the names of the terrorists who deliver the propaganda to the outlying villages.'

'And how do we do that?'

'We watch the back of the Delons' house, and we keep a round-the-clock surveillance on the entrance to the alley-way. It'd be too risky to attempt to find out which was their house, so we must focus on all the people coming and going.'

'But you won't know whether they're conspirators or just people who live in one of the other houses there.'

'If we watch who comes and goes, and at what times, we'll deduce a pattern,' Gaston said firmly. 'From that, we'll identify those who aren't involved, and those who are. We'll follow the people delivering the propaganda, and see who receives it. When we know the villages involved, and the traitors in those villages, we can co-ordinate the capture of them all, and that includes Bouvier and Mai.'

Emile nodded. 'That makes sense, I suppose,' he said gruffly. 'All right, we'll do it your way. It's what you're here for, after all.'

12

S *unday*

'YOU CAN SEE why it's often called the Great Cathedral,' Gaston said, moving across to Lucette, who'd just come out of the high-arched entrance to St. Joseph's Cathedral and was surreptitiously trying to ease her cornflower blue cotton dress away from her damp body as she stood in front of the building, looking around her.

'The domes, and two bell towers,' he continued with gravity of tone, 'show the architects imitating the Gothic style and design of our beloved Notre Dame de Paris. As do the colourful glazing and religious paintings. But these also show a degree of simplification in terms of the decorative elements. The cathedral itself is built of brick and plastered with concrete.'

She clapped her hands in delight. 'Bravo, Gaston! Full

marks to you. The visitors are going to be extremely impressed. As am I.'

He grinned at her. 'It wasn't too pompous, was it?'

'It was hugely pompous,' she said, laughing, 'but they'll love it. Don't change a thing. You came across as being extremely knowledgeable, and that's what they'll want to hear.'

He bowed his head in acknowledgement.

She lifted her straw cloche, pushed some loose strands of hair away from her face and tucked them into the loose coil she'd wound on top of her head.

'I'm sorry to be fiddling with my hair,' she said, putting her hat back on to her head. 'But because my hair's quite long, it sticks to my face when it's hot and damp like this.'

'Does it?' he said smoothly. 'I didn't notice.'

'Liar.' She laughed again.

'Well, maybe it was a teeny lie,' he said with a smile. 'But what's not a lie is that whether or not you've got hair on your face, you look charming.'

'I look hot and sticky, Gaston, and you know it. But thank you for trying to make me feel better. So tell me, did you describe the cathedral's architecture because you thought my empty head needed to be filled with facts, or were you taking advantage of being in one of the locations your guests will visit, and rehearsing?'

'Neither,' he said with a smile. 'I saw that Marc and Philippe had been dragged off by colleagues for a discussion so intense that they'll be gasping for a drink long before we get to Marc's house, and that Simonne's talking to a frightfully boring woman with a face like a horse. I thought, therefore, that to avoid an attack on my ears and my eyes, I'd come across and engage you in conversation.'

She giggled. 'Once again, you leave me nervous about what to say. I'd hate my shallow chatter to be an attack, as you put it, on your ears. But after that wonderful summary of St. Joseph's architectural style, I'm ashamed that I've have nothing as lofty in my head with which to follow it—only trivia.'

'After a late Saturday night, trivia's exactly what I need.'

'What did you do last night that made it such a late night?' A haze of red spread across her cheeks. 'Ouch! I shouldn't have asked. If it involves a woman friend, please let's talk about the weather instead.'

'You'll be pleased to know that I can spare us both from a tedious exchange about the discomfort occasioned by the increasing humidity and heat—though the heat of the day is to some extent compensated by the freshness of the nights—as it doesn't involve any member of the fair sex. No, I was playing cards with a few reprobates from the Résidence.'

'I hope you won.'

'Put it this way,' he said with a smile, 'when I meet Marc and Philippe for breakfast next week, I'll be able to afford a croissant with my morning coffee. And I might even go as far as treating each of them to a pastry, too.'

'Then the late night was definitely worth it.'

'I think I'd have to agree,' he said. He hesitated. 'Tell me to mind my own business, Lucette, but you've seemed a little distracted, even worried, the last couple of times I've seen you. And during the homily just now, you seemed to be miles away. I suspect that you weren't, however, meditating on the priest's words.'

She looked at him in surprise. 'I didn't realise I was giving that impression. It's true that my mind was wandering during the homily, but my only conscious thought was that I wished he'd stop talking and sit down, and let us get to our lunch with Simonne and Marc.'

They both laughed.

'I'm glad you're coming, too,' she added.

He smiled at her. 'Let's stretch our legs,' he said, and they started strolling down Rue de la Mission. When they reached a wooden bench in the small triangle of green at the bottom of the short street, Gaston sat down. 'They're now sufficiently stretched, I'd say,' he remarked, and he indicated that she sit next to him.

'A little while ago,' he began, 'when I came to your house looking for Philippe, we got talking. You were reluctant, you told me, to talk to Philippe about his work. I encouraged you to do so. I'm going to say the same thing again. If there's something bothering you, and I believe there is, you should tell someone. And your husband is the obvious person to tell.'

'It's kind of you to be concerned, Gaston, but it really isn't important. And I'd hate to burden Philippe with something that doesn't matter, especially at a time when he's still finding his way at work.'

'Then perhaps you could tell someone else—someone who's a friend. I'd suggest Simonne, but as she's married to Philippe's boss, it might be wiser not to risk her saying something you'd rather she didn't to Marc in a moment of forgetfulness.'

She nodded. 'Yes, that would be a mistake.'

'But if you don't talk to someone, Philippe could become anxious about you. Just as I can see that there's something worrying you, so, too, will Philippe. He loves you and this would distress him. I'm sure you wouldn't want to cause him anxiety, particularly when you say it's not really important.'

She stared at him in alarm.

Grey eyes filed with warmth and concern stared back at her.

'As they say, a problem shared is a problem halved. I'm always here, Lucette,' he said quietly. 'As your friend, I want what's best for you. I think you need peace of mind. If you tell me what's bothering you, I'll see if I can help you to find that peace of mind. It would be of benefit to Philippe as well as to you.'

'It *would* be a huge relief to talk to someone,' she said, a slight tremor in her voice. 'I think I've magnified things out of all proportion. And really, it's so unimportant.'

'Why don't you let me decide that,' he soothed.

She turned slightly towards him. 'All right. If you really don't mind.'

'You two look very serious,' Philippe said coming up to them, and sitting on the other side of Lucette.

At the same moment, an identical bolt of frustration and disappointment shot though both Gaston and Lucette.

'You were busy talking,' she said, swallowing her regret that it was now impossible to lessen her worries by sharing them with Gaston. 'We didn't want to disturb you.'

Recovering his poise, Gaston forced a grin to his face. 'Lucette's very kindly refraining from telling you that I shamelessly used this morning as an opportunity to rehearse some of the things I plan to tell the group about the cathedral.'

'And very good he was, too,' Lucette said, smiling in gratitude at Gaston. 'I really didn't mind, Gaston. It was interesting. You should tell Philippe.'

Philippe raised his hand in feigned protestation 'I won't ask you to repeat it, Gaston, as I'm thinking of joining you for some of the tours, and the cathedral's one of them. As we come here on Sundays, we ought to know something about its history and architecture.'

'Lucette will be inwardly thanking you that she doesn't have to sit through it all again,' Gaston said cheerfully.

They laughed.

'Shall we get going, then?' Philippe suggested. 'Marc and Simonne have already set off, and they said to come as soon as we want. I don't know about you, but I'm hungry and the heat's made me quite thirsty.'

Gaston was just the person to give her advice, Lucette decided, standing up and tucking her arm into Philippe's. He was obviously intelligent man, and he seemed to understand people, and as soon as there was another occasion on which she could have a quiet word with him, she'd do so.

'WELL, what did you think of today?' Marc asked Simonne as he lay in bed, gazing up at the ceiling, his hands behind his head.

She turned her head on the pillow to look at him. 'I thought it went well. Didn't you?'

He slid his arm around her shoulders. 'I most definitely did,' he said, and he kissed her shoulder. 'You're a wonderful hostess, Simonne. You always know the right menu to give Cook, and you invariably put everyone at their ease by knowing exactly the thing to say, and you're unsurpassed in keeping a conversation going.' He kissed her shoulder again.

She giggled. 'It's Papa's shoulder you should really be kissing. It was Papa, not Maman, who taught me how functions should be organised, and he was the one who insisted that I never reply to a question with a one-word answer, as that would shut down the conversation.'

'Much as I liked Antoine, and grateful as I am that he consented to our marriage, I'd have shrunk from kissing his shoulder and would still have sought yours,' he said, and he kissed her shoulder again, and then the top of her forehead.

She nestled against his chest. 'I do like Philippe and Lucette, don't you? And Gaston, too. He's great company.'

Marc nodded. 'All three are.' He glanced down at her. 'So what were you and Lucette talking about?'

'About Gaston's idea of holding a formal reception at the Résidence at the end of each group of visitors. Lucette, too, thought it sounded excellent. She's looking forward to meeting more of Philippe's colleagues.'

'She's not looking to replace him so early in their marriage, I hope,' Marc said in feigned concern. 'Philippe's a good man.'

'If she is, she hasn't told me,' Simonne said, giggling. 'No, she just wants to make some more friends. She said she doesn't want me to feel responsible for all of her social activities, which she's afraid I might think if she doesn't know anyone else.'

'She's got a point. But I can't see Gaston's receptions leading to Lucette increasing her body of friends.'

'Not on their own they wouldn't, but your colleagues have wives. She'd see the same wives at the different receptions, and at other venues, and some might become friends. And we're doing something else, too.'

He gave a theatrical sigh. 'Right. What are you planning?'

'Lucette's going to join Club French. I've been remiss in keeping her to myself, and not taking her there before now. But it's time she met all of the French community, and that's the best place to do so. Just about all the French wives go there. Mostly for the social activities, I suppose, but there's tennis, too, and golf and croquet. We thought we'd go there next Wednesday and enrol her.' She paused. 'What do you think?'

'I think it's a good idea,' he said smiling. 'You always enjoy it when you go, even though you say some of the wives can be quite catty, and I'm sure she'll enjoy it, too.'

She looked up at him curiously. 'I can tell you're genuinely enthusiastic about the idea. I can also tell that you're a lot less keen on Gaston's idea of a reception. Why?'

He tightened his arm around her. 'To be honest, I think it's unnecessary. He's planned something interesting for every day of their visit, and a small group reception at the end of their stay would be more than sufficient. There's no need to make a big thing of it.'

'Well, as far as I'm concerned, the more formal receptions we have, the better. It's lovely to have a reason to dress up.'

'Now why didn't I think of that?' he said, a smile in his voice.

Simonne laughed.

'At least, planning receptions will give him something to do in the gaps between visitors,' he went on. 'I don't know how else he'll fill the time.'

'He said there were going to be lots of visitors in the coming year. I suppose that the information he'll need to know, and working out the itineraries, will keep him busy.'

'That's true, and that may well be all he's here to do. Nevertheless, he's an intelligent man, who's clearly a highly paid official, who's been assigned an office. It would be unusual for such a person to do no more than guide visitors around a city.'

She sat up and looked down at him, frowning. 'What are you saying?'

He smiled up at her. 'I don't really know, and I'm happy

to leave it at that. But what I do know is that neither of us seems particularly sleepy at the moment, so it might be an idea if I went downstairs and found where Madame Mercier put the dessert wine we opened at the end of lunch, but didn't finish, and brought it up here with two glasses.'

She ran her hand down his arm. 'That sounds a lovely idea,' she murmured, and she lay back.

With a smile, he threw back the cover and got up.

13

Lucette lay in bed with Philippe's arm around her. He glanced down at the dark hair tumbling over her shoulders.

'So you had a good time today, did you?' he asked.

'Yes, I did,' she said happily. She looked up at his face. 'The priest's homily could have been shorter by twenty minutes, though,' she added, her eyes laughing.

'It was only about twenty minutes all together,' he said in surprise.

'Exactly.' Giggling, she snuggled closer to him. 'But the lunch at Marc and Simonne's was really pleasant. I was bound to enjoy today, though, whatever we did,' she added, her voice muffled against his chest, 'because we spent the day together. I don't see enough of you these days.'

'That's what worries me,' he said.

Hearing the anxiety in his voice, she glanced up at him. 'I didn't mean it as a criticism. I know how hard you have to work. And Marc's the same, too. It just makes every minute we have together more precious. I love you so much.'

He rolled on to his side and stared down into her face.

'And I love you, too, ma belle Lucette,' he said, his voice shaking with emotion. 'I love you more than I can say.'

Then he lowered his lips slowly to hers, and kissed her.

He lifted his head and looked down at her again, with love in his eyes. 'The day I met you was the luckiest day of my life. But I'd hate to think that by marrying me, you'd subjected yourself to a life of loneliness and boredom. It's different for me. My day's full and flies by, and everything I do is so interesting—it's not just prisons I deal with, you know. But I feel guilty that you might not have enough to occupy yourself.'

He brushed her hair gently from her face with his fingers. She stilled his hand with hers, raised her free hand to his face, and trailed her fingertips lovingly down his cheek.

'Dear Philippe. I've more than enough to fill my day. And every week brings something new. This week, it's going to be Club French. Simonne's taking me there on Wednesday, and I'm going to join. We arranged it at lunch today. Apparently, nearly all of the French wives belong.'

'I wondered what the two of you were talking about so intently.'

'And that gives me an excuse to go shopping on Thursday,' she continued. 'I left my tennis dress in France, so Simonne and I are having breakfast at Café Barnard on Thursday morning, and then going to Les Grands Magasins Réunis. I keep hearing about the store, and how wonderful it is, but I haven't been there yet.'

'Well, you're obviously going to have a good week. You've no idea how pleased I am. And relieved, too, I must confess.'

She smiled up at him. 'If anything, I'm the one who should feel guilty. I'm having a lovely time, but you're working so hard. So, I order you not to worry about me.'

'All right, I won't.' He settled down next to her, and put his arm around her shoulders. 'We're lucky, aren't we, living next door to Marc and Simonne. Marc's the ideal boss, and you and Simonne get on very well. You like her, don't you?'

Lucette nodded. 'I wasn't sure if I would at first as she's very rigid, if that's the right word. Everything's right or wrong—there's nothing in between. But I realise now that it's because she's had a colonial upbringing, and there's a set way of doing everything here.'

Philippe laughed. 'That's an understatement!'

'Also, she can be rather nasty about the Vietnamese,' Lucette went on. 'But she was here a couple of years ago when we French were faced with terrorist uprisings, and she told me how frightening it was. So it's not really surprising that she feels as she does. But at heart she's very kind, and I do like her.'

'That's good, then,' he said. 'It was a good day, wasn't it? We didn't stop talking,' he murmured sleepily, his arm still loosely around her. 'First after Mass and then over lunch. And I drank a fair bit, too. I feel just about ready for sleep. What about you?'

'I will in a minute,' she said, 'but I'm quite thirsty. Stupidly, I forgot to bring up any water. I think I'll go down and get a glass. Can I bring you something, too?'

He shook his head. 'I'm fine, thanks.'

She leaned back over him, kissed him lightly on the lips, slipped out of the bed, and picked up her torch and negligée. Crossing the room as she put the negligée on, she went out on to the landing and down the stairs.

As she rounded the foot of the stairs, she was surprised to see a beam of light sliding from under the kitchen door.

She hesitated, and then crept silently along the hall, and past the dining room door to the kitchen. She eased the kitchen door slightly open, pressed back against the hall wall, and listened hard.

There was no one inside the kitchen, but she could hear people talking in the garden. She couldn't tell who they were, though.

There was no way she could go back to her bedroom without trying to see who they were.

Crouching low, she crept into the kitchen, confident that despite the light being on in the kitchen, the scullery and laundry room were both in darkness and would hide her from sight.

Her heart beating fast, she reached the open door leading to the scullery, crept inside the scullery, and sat with her back against one of the cupboards.

There were two people outside, she was sure—a man and a woman.

Could this be Mai and her beau, she wondered.

Biting her lip, she glanced at the laundry room door. It was open, but the half-glazed door leading from it to the garden was closed.

Her heart beat fast. She might never have a better chance of seeing the man, and it was only right that she try to do so, as Mai was effectively in her protection.

Taking a deep breath, she inched forward into the laundry room, keeping close to the tiled floor, and crouched down behind the bamboo linen basket.

She could now hear the voices more clearly. The woman was definitely Mai.

Frustrated, she couldn't hear either properly, but they were talking in French, she was sure. The cadence of their sentences was French, not Vietnamese, and so, too, was the pitch of the man's voice.

So Mai's beau was a Frenchman, not a Vietnamese, she

thought in great disappointment, and a wave of sorrow for Mai swept through her. Most Frenchmen wanted a native woman for one reason only, and no matter what they might tell the woman, that reason wasn't marriage.

Of course, she could be wrong.

Some Frenchmen must have genuinely loved their Vietnamese woman. But it wasn't easy to take such a woman back to France, and she'd heard that many had been left behind when the man's appointment in Hanoi had come to an end.

And their métis children, too, children to whom she'd heard Frenchmen cruelly refer as poules-canards—chicken-ducks—neither one thing nor the other.

If only she could see what the man looked like. His appearance might give her an idea as to the nature of his interest in Mai.

Moving into a kneeling position, she raised herself slightly, trying to see through the glass panel into the garden. To her annoyance, Mai's back was blocking her view of the man.

Then she heard Mai laugh.

She peered closer to the window in excitement. Mai had a habit of bending slightly when she laughed, and of putting her hand in front of her mouth to stifle her giggles.

If Mai now lowered her head in such a way, she might see the man's face.

She saw Mai put her hand in front of her mouth and start to hunch her shoulders over her fingers. At the same moment, the man moved back, out of her line of vision.

Oh, no, she cried inwardly in despair.

The man said something to Mai, who nodded, and then began to turn back to the house.

The man must be leaving, and Mai would be back in the

kitchen in a matter of moments, she thought in a panic. She must get back to her room at once, and forget about water.

Keeping her head well down, she sped as quickly as she could through the kitchen, out into the hall and along to the staircase. As she was putting her foot on the first of the stairs, she heard the scullery door close, and footsteps cross the kitchen.

She ran up the stairs to the landing, her heart racing.

Pausing momentarily outside her bedroom door, she tried to catch her breath. Then she opened the door, went quietly inside, slipped off her negligée and climbed back into bed, relieved to see that Philippe was asleep.

Lying on her back, she stared up at the ceiling, her heart still beating fast.

Mai was a sweet young girl, and she couldn't bear the thought of anyone taking advantage of her.

It was true that Mai had seemed happy to be with the man, but she was of an age to believe any declarations of true love, and any promises about a future together. And because she felt safe in the man's love, she wouldn't be thinking as far ahead as to what would happen if she became pregnant.

For Mai's own good, therefore, the relationship must end. Something that had begun as mild curiosity on her part, had turned into a steely determination to protect Mai from herself.

To do that, she would have to find out the name of the man.

And this she would only discover by following Mai.

On the following Saturday, when Mai set off for wherever she was going, she wouldn't be lying in bed—she'd be concealed among the street traffic behind Mai.

14

T*he following Friday*

LUCETTE SAT on a wooden bench beside the water, in the dappled sunlight that filtered through the fern-like leaves of the tall flamboyant trees that surrounded the lake. She stared at the view in pleasure.

Ruffled by the light breeze, the surface of the Petit Lac glistened pink and gold, and across the lake, the tiny coral pagoda, which stood on a small rock known as the Island of the Turtle, glowed red in the strengthening sun.

Before they'd left Paris, she'd read the legend about the lake, called by the natives Ho Hoan Kiem, the Lake of the Restored Sword. She'd been entranced by the story, and as she sat there, she was amused to find herself willing the jade dragon to rise again from the water. Even though, if it did so, it could mean bad news for France.

Many years ago, a jade dragon that slept in the depths of

lake, she'd read, was believed to have transformed itself into a magical sword.

A fisherman casting his net from the shore caught the gleaming sword. Amazed, he'd taken it home and stood it in the corner of his cottage.

Not long afterwards, when the general in charge of the Viet forces happened to stop at the fisherman's home, he saw the sword and marvelled at it.

A few days later, when the general was travelling through a forest, he was struck by a strange brightness at the top of a banyan tree. Climbing up, he found a shining sheath. Remembering the sword he'd seen in the fisher-man's hut, he went back and found that the sword fitted the sheath.

With the miraculous sword in his hand, he'd raised a huge peasant army, and had repelled an invasion from the Ming-ruled China. And that was the beginning of a glorious era for the Viet people, during which the general was their emperor.

About a decade later, the emperor was boating on the lake, and a golden turtle rose to the surface of the water and asked the emperor to return the sword that had been entrusted to him.

The sword leapt out of its sheath, exploded in a blaze of light, and once again took the form of the jade dragon.

With a mighty roar, the dragon plunged into the depths of the deep green water. At that very moment, a coral pagoda materialised on an island rock in the lake.

Given the legend, she thought, it was no wonder that the lake was revered by the natives, who believed that the jade dragon still slept in the shadowy depths, waiting for the time when once again it would break through the water's surface as a mighty sword, which someone would grasp, and with it lead the Vietnamese to freedom.

At that point in time, it would be freedom from the French, she thought wryly.

Before they'd come to Hanoi, she'd been warned that they'd find some hostility towards the French. But as the uprisings in the past couple of years had been put down, she was sure that in the peace the colony now enjoyed, the Vietnamese would come to appreciate all they were doing for them, and would be grateful. And the jade dragon need never reappear.

She glanced towards the northern shore of the lake, to Jade Island on which stood the Temple of Jade Mountain, and to the ornamental arched wooden bridge that led from the shore to the island.

The bridge, painted a deep vermillion, shone brilliant red in the late morning sun. Its name translated into Perch of the Morning Sunlight, and it was easy to see why.

She leaned back against the bench, and smiled to herself.

She liked the atmospheric way in which the Vietnamese described the places around them. It had so much more charm than Simonne's explanations.

When she'd mentioned the dragon legend to Simonne, Simonne had told her that six thousand years earlier, Hanoi had been a huge swamp populated by crocodiles, and that one of those crocodiles had probably given rise to the belief in a dragon.

She preferred the Vietnamese version.

Yes, it had been a really enjoyable morning, she thought.

Returning to Les Grands Magasins Réunis that morning had been a good idea. There was so much to see there that she'd barely scratched the surface the day before when she'd gone there with Simonne, and she'd wanted to go back and wander around the different departments by herself, which she'd done and which she'd thoroughly enjoyed.

And she was even more pleased that she'd gone there on her own.

With Simonne tied up that morning with the dress-maker, it had been an opportunity to show Simonne that she was quite capable of going out in Hanoi by herself, and not only when she was being driven by her chauffeur.

The two of them had been to Café Barnard on the Wednesday for breakfast, and had then gone on to Club French, where Simonne had introduced her to a number of people she hadn't met before. And then yesterday, they'd gone together to the store, and Simonne had helped her to choose two outfits for tennis, and a couple of dresses suit-able for a midday lunch at the club.

She'd no reason to think that Simonne minded doing so many things with her, but had she been Simonne, she might have begun to be a little concerned that she could be expected to include her neighbour every time she went out in the week. And if so, Simonne could start to regret that she and Philippe had moved there.

But by going out on her own that morning, albeit to the familiar territory of Café Barnard, where she'd enjoyed a cup of coffee and a scone at one of the pavement tables, she'd shown Simonne, without putting it into words, that she was quite capable of standing on her own two feet.

Their friendship would be the stronger for that, she thought.

She looked up at the patches of clear blue sky visible between the leaves. It was another hot afternoon, but it was less humid than on occasions, and there was no sign of the heavy bouts of rain that had started to fall on most days, so she would take advantage of the weather and go as far as the ornamental bridge, and then get a pousse-pousse to take her back home.

She got up from the bench, strolled past an age-old willow that was dipping the tips of its slender leaves into the glittering water, and started walking up the path between the lake and Boulevard Francis Garnier.

MAI FINISHED FOLDING the last of the clothes, and sighed in relief.

Thankfully, as she'd had no interruptions, both M. and Mme. Delon being out, and with Mme. Fousseret busy issuing instructions to the cleaning girl, she'd been able to race through all of her tasks for the morning, and could now leave.

She was actually free for a whole day and a half!

Still unable to believe her luck, she ran upstairs to her room at the top of the house.

She couldn't remember the last time she'd been given an afternoon free on a day that wasn't her official day off, but Mme. Delon had been quite clear the day before when she'd told her how pleased she was with her work, that if she'd like to take the Friday afternoon off, she could do so.

As she'd listened to Mme. Delon, she'd been suddenly overwhelmed by a kindness rarely shown to her people by the French, and she'd felt quite emotional as she'd expressed her gratitude.

Mme. Delon had told her that she shouldn't expect an extra free afternoon every week, and she'd assured her that she wouldn't. But if she worked extra hard in the coming weeks, there was a chance that she might be given a few more free Friday afternoons. It was something to strive for.

She'd known exactly how to use the time, and the minute that Mme. Delon had dismissed her, she'd hastily scribbled a few lines for Vinh, and under the pretence of looking for any coriander growing at the back of the garden, she'd slipped the note into the hollow at the base of the tamarind tree.

The first thing that morning, she'd checked the hollow, and it was empty. So he'd discovered her note in time to meet her that afternoon outside Garage Boillot.

She'd suggested meeting outside Garage Boillot as she'd felt it wiser for him not to be seen near the house. And it was well placed for going to the Old Quarter, and also for heading south to her mother's village, if they decided to go there.

Feeling in the mood to celebrate her unexpected night away from the house, she selected her best bright red silk *ao dai*, knowing that the high-necked dress clung to her figure in a way that showed off her slenderness and tiny waist, and that the narrow side-split skirt moved flatteringly over the white silk trousers she always wore with it.

When she'd fastened the *ao dai*, she slipped into her wooden sandals, pulled her long dark hair back from her face, and secured it at the nape of her neck with a plain tortoiseshell clip. Then she put a few personal items into a small bag, picked up her conical hat, and left the house in elation, heading on foot for Garage Boillot.

Vinh wasn't yet there when she arrived, so she stood back against the shop wall and waited.

She didn't have long to wait. A few minutes later, a horse-drawn cart stopped in front of her, and Vinh jumped down. She ran up to him, beaming.

For a long moment, each stared at the other without moving, and then he took her in his arms and drew her gently to him. Her cheek rested against his, and their breaths mingled.

Feeling his chest hard against hers, she trembled.

'My enchanted lotus,' he whispered into her hair, and then he drew back.

'And I love you, too, Vinh,' she said.

Again her cheek rested against his, and they stayed motionless for a moment.

Then Vinh grabbed her hand, led her to the cart and helped her up into the back. Sitting side by side under the canvas awning, they smiled at each other as the driver urged the horses up Boulevard Francis Garnier.

As she made her way up the lakeside path, loving the bright colours of the dresses worn by the Vietnamese girls who passed her by, Lucette glanced down at her sage-green cotton dress, which was the same colour as her cloche hat and gloves. She, too, was going to wear brightly coloured clothes at times, she decided. She was too conservative in her taste.

Cue for another visit to Les Grands Magasins Réunis, she thought with an inward smile.

Reaching the bridge, she turned on to it, walked as far as the middle, and stopped.

Leaning against the parapet, she stared over the side at the mass of red and white lotus flowers that bobbed on the gleaming jade-green water below. It wasn't hard to imagine a dragon asleep in the depths, she thought in amusement.

This was a lovely way of ending her very enjoyable morning, she decided, but with the heat of the afternoon sun now more intense, and her dress beginning to stick damply to her, it was time to go home.

A short while later, she was leaning back in the padded seat of a pousse-pousse.

Staring beyond the aged coolie with grey hair springing in wisps from beneath the sweat-drenched turban wrapped around his head, she glanced idly at the passengers coming towards her, some in covered carts, some being pulled in a pousse-pousse.

There was a sudden lurch, and she was jolted forward as her pousse-pousse coolie swerved to one side to accommodate a horse-drawn cart approaching them.

Grabbing both sides of the pousse-pousse, she stared at the cart.

Her eyes were instantly drawn to the brilliant red of the *ao dai* worn by a woman in the cart, who was smiling at the man next to her. She looked up at the woman's face.

It was Mai.

She sat upright in surprise, and stared at the man next to Mai, against whose cheek Mai had put hers.

He was Vietnamese.

Not French.

But she'd heard him talking in French. She was sure she had.

What was going on, she thought in bewilderment, as the cart passed them by.

Frowning deeply, she sat back in her seat.

AN ELDERLY VIETNAMESE man with blackened teeth and a wispy grey beard, who was cycling a short distance behind the horse-drawn cart and keeping pace with it, saw the

French woman in a pousse-pousse coming towards him, glance at the people in the cart, and give a sudden start.

He saw the surprise on her face as she sat up and stared at the cart.

He'd instantly recognised the French woman as Mme. Delon. He'd watched her house on Rue Henri Rivière often enough.

And he'd recognised both of the Vietnamese.

It wasn't the first time he'd shadowed the woman he knew to be Mai.

As soon as she'd set off on foot that afternoon, he'd realised that she was unlikely to be planning to visit her mother, as she sometimes did. Her mother's village lay to the south-west of Hanoi, and it would be too far to go on foot.

And after she'd climbed into the cart, he'd seen that they were heading to the north of the lake, almost certainly to the Old Quarter.

And he knew the Vietnamese man to be Nguyen Tan Vinh.

By watching the alleyway to which Mai had led them, Sûreté operatives had identified Vinh as being a regular to the terrorists' house, and they'd seen him with Mai.

It had been believed, therefore, that Vinh could be Mai's contact. But now, having seen the two of them kiss when they'd met, and again on the cart, it could be that he was no more than her beau.

Of course, he could be both.

But why had the Frenchwoman been so surprised at seeing Mai with Vinh, he wondered as he cycled behind the cart into the first of the Thirty-Six Streets, for surprise had been the emotion that had first registered on her face, followed closely by extreme puzzlement.

Her maid wouldn't have left the house without her permission, so merely seeing the maid could hardly have caused such a reaction.

One thing was certain, M. Laroche was going to be extremely interested in knowing that Mme. Delon had appeared to be seriously disquieted about something connected with Mai and Vinh.

And from past experience, he was pretty sure that M. Laroche would make every effort to find out the reason behind it.

15

_____

L *ater that day*

LUCETTE AND SIMONNE sat opposite each other at the white wrought-iron table on the paved back terrace of Simonne's house, shaded from the late afternoon sun by a large green umbrella, and surrounded by a variety of greenery and large stone pots filled with bright yellow chrysanthemums.

A cake stand in the centre of the table was laden with a selection of finger sandwiches, small scones with jam and clotted cream, and pastel-coloured pastries. Beside each of them was a plate, a silver cake fork, a white napkin and a glass of citron pressé.

'I'm so glad you came over,' Simonne told Lucette, helping herself to a scone. 'I'd been wondering what you were doing today, but thought I'd look too nosy if I came across and asked. Did you go anywhere nice?'

'I most certainly did,' Lucette said. And gleefully she began to tell Simonne about her day.

When she reached the point where she'd picked up a pousse-pousse to bring her home, she'd been about to mention seeing Mai with a native man. But something within her made her pause, and she closed her mouth, the words unsaid.

But she didn't really know why she'd stopped when she had.

After all, seeing Mai with a man was relatively unimportant. At most, it might be a matter of some slight interest to Simonne, but no more than that.

But this instinctive holding back about something so trivial troubled her, and while Simonne was describing her visit to the dressmaker, and detailing the material and style of dress she'd chosen, she found herself asking why she'd consciously refrained from telling her about Mai.

The answer came to her in a rush. And it was all too clear, she thought with a rueful inner smile—she was embarrassed to do so.

During her first days in Hanoi, Simonne had told her that she must always take a strong line with the servants or they'd cheat her one way or another.

Yet here she was, giving her maid an afternoon off for no reason other than that she thought it would be a treat for the girl to have a little extra time to herself, and perhaps to see her mother.

She knew Simonne well enough by now to realise that she'd be horrified at what she'd done, and might think her weak.

She'd once remarked to Simonne that the way in which some of the French used to cuff their coolies round the head, and, even worse, beat them for nothing, was extremely upsetting.

But Simonne had merely shrugged, and told her that controlling the peasants was of the utmost importance for the colonists' safety, and that this was a way of doing so, and then she'd gone on to a different subject.

So Simonne would not be sympathetic to the idea that a servant should be given a little extra free time on occasions.

And she was fairly sure that if Simonne had known that Mai had a beau, whether he was a native or French, she would have told Marc about him, and both of them would have advised her to dismiss Mai.

She could just hear Simonne patiently explaining that having a beau would distract Mai from her duties, and that as Mai would probably end up with child, when she'd have to be sent away, anyway, she should be sacked before that happened.

But she liked Mai and would be sorry to have to replace her. The risk of finding herself with a maid who turned out to be a younger version of Mme. Fousseret wasn't one she wanted to take. The very thought made her shudder.

So it was wiser that she'd withheld that information.

As she took a madeleine from the cake stand, she decided to say something to Mai, though, about her Vietnamese beau, as she ought to know that if she became pregnant, they'd have to let her go.

Feeling better now that she'd talked herself through the situation, and more than a little relieved that after the full day she'd had, she wouldn't have to get up early the next morning to follow Mai, since Mai would be elsewhere, she agreed with Simonne's suggestion that they go to the French Club on the Monday.

And she picked up her madeleine and bit into it.

· · ·

So, Gaston thought, stepping out into a night air saturated with the fragrance of mimosa and frangipani, and settling into his favourite rattan chair on the small verandah at the back of his house. So Lucette had been very surprised to see her maid with the terrorist, Vinh, had she?

He put his glass of bourbon on the table next to him, and leaned back, deep in thought.

Of course, Lucette wouldn't know the man was a terrorist.

Or would she?

Could this be connected with her skulking around outside her house that evening?

Surely not.

If she'd had any reason to think the man a threat to their safety, which she knew all terrorists to be, she would surely have told Philippe, and he would have gone straight to Marc.

If their suspicions were right about Vinh, Marc would know that the man was part of the chain of delivery, and before he'd reported Vinh to the Résident, he'd have got a warning to him, telling him to stay out of sight or even to leave the area.

That Vinh was still in the vicinity, and visibly so, was proof that Lucette hadn't spoken to Philippe.

So what could it be that had so surprised her, he wondered.

She'd have known that her maid was free that afternoon, so it couldn't be that. Mai would never have jeopardised her position by leaving the house without permission.

Apart from the fact that Mai seemed fond of Lucette, she'd recognise the importance of the terrorist work in which she was engaged, and ensure that she didn't give the Delons any cause to fire her.

Given all that, it must have been seeing that Mai had a beau that was the surprise, he decided.

The sight of Mai being affectionate with a man, which was how the operative had described Mai's behaviour when he'd reported back to him and Emile, might make Lucette afraid that her maid, whom she clearly liked, might be thinking of marrying, and if so, possibly leaving her employment. And if Mai became pregnant, she'd almost certainly have to leave the job.

Almost certainly, but not definitely, Lucette might think.

In such a circumstance, Lucette might be tempted to allow the affection she felt for Mai to prevail, and to tell Philippe that she'd like to keep Mai in her employment.

But Philippe would never agree to that, he was sure.

And nor would he listen to Marc in this. Marc would be appalled at the idea of losing the person after him in the chain, who lived next door, and he'd try to persuade Philippe to keep Mai. But in this, he, too, would fail.

The weight of the disapproval expressed by Philippe's colleagues would be more powerful than any argument Marc could come up with, and more persuasive than Lucette's entreaties.

Philippe, from what he'd seen of him, was like nearly every other young man who, filled with pride and excitement about his first overseas posting, unfailingly conformed to the standards expected of him.

Retaining in his household a pregnant métisse maid wouldn't sit well with Philippe's colleagues, and he'd be told to dismiss her.

He was intelligent enough to realise that if he didn't comply with their wishes, his soft attitude towards the Vietnamese might be seen as suspect, and furthermore, his colleagues might even think that Philippe himself had fathered the child.

In a situation, therefore, where there was a risk of Mai ending up pregnant, Philippe would almost certainly want to avoid that, and would sack the girl. And deep down, Lucette would know that, and it could be why she didn't tell Philippe that Mai had a beau.

So the knowledge that Mai had a male friend could account for Lucette's surprise at what she'd seen, followed by signs of displeasure.

Of course, all that was a matter of guesswork, and he could be entirely wrong, he thought as he reached for his bourbon. There really was only one way of finding out for sure, and that was to try to wheedle the reason out of Lucette.

The problem was, he could really only do that if she was alone.

But catching her by herself would be virtually impossible.

He could hardly do as he'd done before—go to her house on the pretence that he expected Philippe to be at home. And to have a conversation of any depth outside St. Joseph's had proved on more than one occasion to be impossible.

He could always try to separate her from the others on one pretext or another when they all met up together, but there was a risk of him coming across as too heavy-handed, and thus alienating her. And also of arousing some curiosity, if not suspicion, in the others.

And to make things even more difficult, the so-called officials would be arriving on Monday week, so he was going to be tied up with matters relating to the visit for a substantial amount of the following two weeks.

So it was essential to find an occasion to talk to Lucette before their arrival.

If he left it till after the officials' visit, whatever it was that had bothered her about seeing Mai with Vinh would have been tempered by the passage of time.

And by then it would be virtually impossible to find a subtle way in which to induce her to volunteer the reason for her concern.

It must be Lucette who introduced the subject as he mustn't in any way let her know that she'd been seen and reported upon.

He took a drink of his bourbon, and looked around the garden.

His mind was blank.

Unfortunately, he couldn't think of anything more inspired than approaching her about something to do with the reception. So that's what it would have to be, he decided.

And if he did that, he couldn't really avoid involving Simonne, too.

And perhaps he could use Mai, too, he thought, as an idea began to take shape in his mind.

He now knew for certain that Marc's contact was Mai, and Mai's contact was most likely Vinh. Any doubt about that had been swept away by the knowledge of the closeness between Mai and Vinh.

Emile's operatives were following the people who left the terrorists' alley, and they were building up a body of information about the villages to which the newspapers were delivered, and about the way in which they were getting the propaganda and newspapers into the garrison, too.

But although they were making good progress, it was a slow business, with many deliberate red herrings engineered by the terrorists, who'd obviously been told to assume at all times that they were being followed.

And the other thing it wasn't doing was shedding light on any other French officials who might be involved. The whole thing was so widespread that it was highly unlikely that Marc was the only official involved, and they needed the names of the others, too, that Marc might have recruited.

They also needed to know his contact inside the prison.

If he could get Mai into the reception, he and the visiting officials could surreptitiously watch her to see if any of the permanent staff gave themselves away by a look or a word that showed they knew her. If they did, they'd have taken a giant step closer to discovering the rest of the traitors among their own people.

Mai would have to be one of the waitresses at the reception.

It wasn't customary to use non-Résidence personnel for such an occasion, but nor was it unknown to do so in the event of a shortage of available staff.

And since it wouldn't be difficult to arrange for two of the Résidence waitresses to be booked in advance for a dinner elsewhere on the day of the reception, there was most definitely going to be a lack of staff on that occasion. And where else to turn to for help but to your friends?

Those friends, of course, would be Simonne and Lucette.

He'd have to ask Simonne, as well as Lucette, if she'd lend him her maid, Tan, to act as a waitress that evening. If he'd asked for Mai only, Marc might have been suspicious.

Yes, he thought, finishing his bourbon, that could work.

While he didn't expect to get a great deal from the reception, apart from the pleasure of seeing Lucette again, a pleasure he was somewhat surprised that he felt, he was pretty sure he'd achieve something.

And everything was worth having, no matter how small. Indeed, it was out of a small acorn that the giant oak tree grew.

16

---

*C*afé Barnard
    The following Wednesday

'A WEEK TODAY, and Gaston's group will be here in Hanoi, starting their visit,' Lucette remarked, sipping her coffee.

Simonne opened her mouth to comment, but a seller, festooned in silk scarves, appeared at the side of their table, placed himself in the gap between their chairs, and grinned hopefully.

She raised her hand to wave him away, but before she could do so, he must have seen the waiter fast approaching, as he stepped swiftly back on to the roadway, and hurried out of their line of vision.

'They never give up,' Simonne murmured. She took a small tarte aux noix from the plate in the centre of the table, and pushed the plate closer to Lucette. 'Has Philippe been involved in any of the preparations for the prison visit?' she asked, biting into the pastry. 'After all, he'll be accompanying Gaston and his group.'

Lucette shook her head. 'Not really. Gaston's told him what time they'll be getting there, and how long the tour will last, but he's worked on the details himself. Philippe thinks he's overjoyed at having something to do at last. At least, that's the impression he gives when they have breakfast together.'

'I'm sure that's right,' Simonne said. She paused. 'Don't you think it strange that such an intelligent man,' she went on, 'who's obviously paid a lot, doesn't have a more demanding role in the administration?'

'I've not really thought about it,' Lucette said in surprise. 'But I suppose that's the way it is with large organisations, especially when they're spread apart. The government in Paris can't possibly know the details about what's happening in faraway places like the Résidence in Hanoi. After all, this isn't the only colony.'

Simonne nodded. 'That's true.'

'And also, Gaston, himself, said that he doesn't expect to be taking visitors around indefinitely. When they get more attachés, he'll move on to other things.'

'That makes sense. It was just something Marc said a few days ago.'

'I thought he liked Gaston. Doesn't he?' Lucette asked.

'Oh, yes. Very much.'

'Did I hear my name mentioned?' Gaston's voice reached them from the kerb.

Both looked instantly at the road in front of the café, and saw Gaston stepping down from a pousse-pousse. He gave the coolie a few piastres, waved him away, and came across to their table.

'Gaston!' Simonne exclaimed. 'What a surprise! Do sit down.'

'I will, thank you,' he said, taking off his hat and sitting on the chair closest to him. 'And I'll have a coffee, too, if you'll allow me to spend a few minutes with you. I saw you as I was going past, and couldn't resist taking the liberty of joining you.'

'You did exactly what you should have done,' Simonne said happily.

'May I get you both another coffee, or something else perhaps?' he suggested, looking from one to the other.

They told him that neither wanted anything, so he signalled to a waiter, ordered a coffee and sat back.

'Funnily enough, we were just saying that your first visitors will be arriving very soon,' Lucette told him.

'How gratifying to know that I'm never far from your thoughts.' His amused gaze lingered momentarily on Lucette, and then widened to include Simonne.

Lucette felt herself blush. She pushed the plate of small tartes aux noix towards him. 'Please, do help yourself,' she said, and then she picked up her drink and took a sip.

He pushed the plate back into the centre of the table. 'I won't, thank you all the same. It's not long since I had breakfast.'

'How lucky you saw us when you were passing,' Simonne remarked when the waiter had finished pouring a coffee for Gaston. 'Lucky for us, anyway,' she added with a laugh.

'There wasn't that much luck involved,' he said, grinning at her. 'I've just had breakfast with Marc and Philippe, and they said you might be here. I was watching as I went past, just in case you *were* here, as I've something to ask you.'

'The men know we've been coming regularly since you

reminded us that the place existed,' Simonne said with a warm smile. 'We like it very much. But what did you want to ask?'

'I could use some help.'

Lucette and Simonne exchanged a look of surprise.

'What sort of help?' Lucette asked.

'I was wondering if you'd each lend me your maid.'

They exchanged another look of surprise.

'Why d'you want them, Gaston?' Lucette asked.

'To be waitresses. The reception's got to be more lavish than I'd originally intended as some of the officials appear to have important contacts in the world of trade.'

'How exciting,' Simonne said gleefully.

'I agree. But annoyingly, two of the Résidence waitresses, whom I'd been counting upon, are tied up with a dinner elsewhere that very evening. It leaves me two short. Since both of you will be there—at least, I hope you will—I thought you might both release your maid for the evening. But don't worry if it'd cause problems,' he added quickly. 'I can always ask someone else. I thought I'd start with you, though.'

Lucette raised her eyebrows at Simonne, who gave a slight nod.

'You're welcome to have Mai,' Lucette said, turning back to Gaston.

'And also Tan,' Simonne said. 'I know that Marc and Philippe intend to go there ahead of us, just to see if there's anything they can do, and they can take Tan and Mai with them. We'll follow a little later.'

Gaston nodded. 'I'm very grateful to you. Next week, then, I'll give Marc and Philippe a Résidence uniform to take home for each of the girls.'

He took a sip of his coffee, and sat back again. 'So,' he

said, embracing both in his smile, 'the two of you are now a familiar sight in the café, are you?'

'We do like it here,' Simonne said, 'and we've been coming most Wednesdays, as well as other times too.'

'How fortunate that both of you enjoy coming here,' he remarked. 'It's always better to have a companion when you go for coffee. I doubt you'd enjoy it so much if you were on your own.'

'That's not so,' Lucette said quickly. 'We do things by ourself, too, you know. Only the other day, I came here by myself for a coffee. I missed having Simonne to talk to—' she smiled at Simonne '—but I had a book to read, and the lovely view to look at, and it was most enjoyable.'

'It sounds it,' he said warmly. 'And did you do anything special after that?'

'Indeed, I did,' she said lightly. 'I walked up the path at the side of the lake, and when I reached the bridge, I walked as far as the middle.'

'You should go all the way round the lake some day. It makes for a very pleasant walk. Provided it's not too humid,' he added.

She pulled a face. 'I hate the humidity. I don't think I'll ever get used to it. But I *have* done the walk—Simonne and I went together. But that was before it had got so humid.'

'I'm sure you'll soon acclimatise. Look at Simonne.' He indicated her with his hand. 'She's French through and through, but she functions well in the humidity.'

'You make me sound like a car or some other machine,' Simonne remarked with feigned indignation.

He laughed. 'Then we'll forget Simonne, and look only at the way in which the natives work in the heat. Your maids, for example.'

'They certainly seem to manage,' Lucette said, 'though I

don't know how. They work very hard all week, whatever the weather.'

'But they don't work *all* week, do they? They get time off, don't they?'

'Yes, but not much. They get one day off in the week.' She felt herself colour slightly, remembering the extra time she'd given Mai.

Gaston gave an appreciative nod. 'I'd say that's very generous.'

She looked at him in amazement. 'D'you think so? I thought it very little, considering how much they have to do and what a long day they work.'

'I'm sure your maids have no complaints,' he said, including Simonne in his glance. 'We've helped the natives so much that they must be glad to have a chance of showing their appreciation. I'm sure they'd far rather work in a French home than eke out a meagre living in a small village with a husband and numerous children, which would certainly be the fate of many, were it not for us.'

Lucette finished her coffee.

'I hope you're right, Gaston,' Simonne said. 'I'm very satisfied with Tan's work. Mind you, I should be. I was the one who trained her,' she added with a giggle. 'And I'd be very sorry if she started walking out on her free day with a beau. She might want to marry him and leave me, and then where would I be?'

She gestured with open palms her helplessness were that to become the situation.

'So you'd dismiss her if she got married?' Lucette asked.

'Of course, I would. A maid's loyalty must be solely to the family that employs her. She might have to alter her day off occasionally, for example, if the family needed her to do so, and if she was married, she might resent the change to her routine. And also, there'd always be the risk of a child. A pregnant maid couldn't work in the way expected of her. No, any suggestion of Tan marrying, and she'd have to be sacked.'

'What would you do if the man she was seeing was French?' Lucette asked with a forced lightness of voice.

Gaston leaned forward and helped himself to a tarte aux noix.

'I'd sack her at once!' Simonne exclaimed, staring at Lucette in horror. 'That would almost be worse. It would be a completely unsuitable relationship. No maid of mine will ever be someone's concubine while they're working for me. She would be out of the door before you could say trollop! Don't you agree?'

Lucette nodded vigorously. 'Absolutely. But I'm sure Mai would never get into such a situation.'

Biting her lip, she picked up her cup, put it to her lips and then put it back on the saucer. 'I didn't realise I'd finished my drink,' she explained, seeing Gaston's eyebrows raise questioningly.

'That's easily sorted. Let's have another coffee,' he said smoothly. 'Simonne, you'll have one, too, won't you?'

'I will, thank you. I'm glad you don't have to rush off, Gaston. I wanted to ask you about the degree of formality of the reception. Lucette will want to know, too. That's right, isn't it, Lucette? She's as trivial as I am, Gaston,' Simonne added with a laugh.

Lucette gave Gaston a wan smile. 'Thank you, Gaston. Another coffee would be lovely.'

LUCETTE COVERED IT WELL, Gaston thought as he stepped off the pousse-pousse outside the Résidence.

He went through the wrought-iron gates, up the wide terrace of canopied marble steps, through the arched entrance, above which fluttered a French tricolore, and into the pale ochre building.

But not well enough for him to miss the implication of what she'd said.

At some point, she'd obviously had reason to think that Mai was in a relationship with a Frenchman, and not a Vietnamese.

That would account for her surprise at seeing with whom Mai was sitting in the wagon that day, and also her displeasure. There was more likelihood of her maid getting married and having to leave her if her beau was a native.

Thinking that Mai's beau might be French, in which case he'd be unlikely to be a serious suitor, could explain why Lucette had been outside her house, in her night-clothes, late that night.

She could have been trying to catch Mai with the man in order to confirm that she was correct in her belief, and to know, if possible, the status of the man.

Once she knew who he was, she'd have to take the appropriate action. And her awareness of that could have been of concern to her as she was inexperienced in handling staff, and might not have known what to do. That could account for the aura of anxiety that had at times surrounded her.

But the expression on her face that morning had shown that she'd realised her mistake.

So what had made Lucette think that Mai's beau was French, he wondered as he headed upstairs.

It could only be because she'd heard them talking to each other, he decided as he pushed open the door and went into his office.

And what was interesting to him was her failure to recognise the man's voice.

She'd have recognised Marc, so it couldn't have been him. It meant that the Frenchman Lucette had heard could be another link in the delivery chain.

Obviously, the man didn't have to be associated with the terrorists' cause, but with Mai regularly in touch with Vinh, and with her receiving and passing on information from Marc, she was entrenched in the world of the terrorists, and it was more than likely that this was how she'd met him.

In the past few weeks, the operatives had been increasingly picking up rumours circulating the Old Quarter that an uprising and a prison breakout were in the planning.

The Frenchman could be connected with that, and it was essential, therefore, to identify him as soon as possible.

It couldn't have been more fortuitous that in two weeks' time, a number of senior officials in the administration would be present at his reception in the Résidence, and so would Mai.

And just maybe, the Frenchman Lucette must have heard in the garden would give himself away.

There'd be many eyes watching Mai, so if the man betrayed himself, they'd be sure to see it.

And unlike Lucette, he'd know exactly what to do when the man's identity was revealed.

17

The *Résidence*
Friday, two weeks later

As the guests arrived at the Résidence for the reception, they were met by a member of the Résident's staff, who saw them into the grand salon.

The room was resplendent in the light thrown down by the sparkling chandeliers on to crystal glasses that glistened, and on to mahogany tables and frames that shone, and on to the potted palms that stood on the polished wood floor, encircling the room with a mesh of glossy fronds that gleamed brilliant green in the glittering light.

And it was alive with colour.

While the administration officials were identically dressed in black trousers and a white dinner jacket cut away at the waist, their wives, elegant in dresses made of silk, satin or chiffon, many of which were backless and sleeveless and fitted at the waist through the hips, whence they fell elegantly to mid-calf or the floor, were a riot of colour.

Varieties of green abounded—jade green, celadon, olive and sage—alongside pale gold, earthy tans, ivory, blues of every hue, silvered almond, every shade of purple, and the occasional streak of crimson or black.

'It looks really wonderful, Gaston,' Lucette said, her eyes shining as she gazed around the salon. 'But I thought it was to be only a small, modest reception at the end of the visit. If this is modest, I can't imagine what lavish must be like,' she said turning back to him with an amused smile.

'You know how it is,' he said ruefully. 'You start out with a little idea, in this case that we all to come together before the visitors leave. And then a colleague latches on to the idea. He spots the economic potential of making a fuss of the guests, and before you know it, the modest reception has escalated into this.' He gestured around him.

'Well, it's lovely,' she said, taking a glass of chilled champagne from the silver tray offered her by a waiter clad in a white top over loose white trousers.

The waiter offered Gaston a glass, but he waved it away.

'Aren't you drinking this evening?' she asked in surprise.

'Not until I've said the necessary few words,' he told her as the waiter moved across to another group.

'So you're speaking tonight, are you? What fun! I look forward to it,' she said with a smile. Then she looked around the room. 'I wonder where Mai and Tan are.'

She stared at the several waiters weaving a path between the guests, and at the handful of waitresses, each in a black dress with a white collar, and a starched white apron tied with a bow behind her waist, but she couldn't see Mai.

She caught a glimpse of Tan, though. She was carrying a tray of glasses on the other side of the salon.

'I can see Tan,' she said, turning back to Gaston. 'You've done so well tonight, Gaston. It's really lovely,' she repeated.

'And so are you, Lucette,' Gaston said quietly. 'You're truly a vision in that lilac chiffon.'

She made as if to speak.

He held up his hand. 'You can relax—I'm stopping there,' he said with a laugh. 'I know you don't like compliments. But I felt I had to put into words what everyone who sees you will be thinking. Philippe is a lucky man.'

'All I know is that I'm very lucky to have him,' she said.

'Yes, you are. And having said that, I must now rescue your husband from the visiting officials. They were enormously impressed by everything in the prison, and when I last saw him, they were besieging him. So if you'll excuse me, I'll leave you to Simonne, who appears to be heading this way.'

With a slight bow, he moved away.

'Isn't it glorious?' Simonne said as she reached Lucette. 'Gaston must be thrilled.'

'I think he is, despite it being larger and more glamorous than he'd wanted.'

Simonne laughed. 'I'm sure that this was his plan all along. Gaston doesn't do small and discreet. No, this is Gaston through and through. And what's more, I'm sure he'll make a speech.'

Lucette giggled. 'He's going to.'

'Where is he now?' Simonne looked around.

'He's gone to extract Philippe from the grip of the visiting officials.'

Marc appeared at Simonne's side.

When he'd put into his pocket the small black leather pouch in which he kept the keys to his car and the office, he helped himself to two flutes of champagne from a waiter standing just by him. He handed one to Simonne.

'If you're ready for another glass, Lucette, you can take this,' he said, holding out the other. 'If there's a toast, you'll need something to drink. I can get another.'

'Thank you,' she said. She finished her champagne, gave her empty glass to the waiter, and took the glass that Marc was offering.

'So you, too, assumed that Gaston would make a speech, Marc. It hadn't occurred to me that he would.' She glanced to where Gaston and Philippe were standing, surrounded by guests.

Marc grinned. 'Of course. He'll want his presence felt by all, if I know Gaston.'

'Then I must go slowly with the champagne as I don't want to blur my senses. At least, not until I've heard him speak,' she added with a giggle.

'Talking of champagne, I see that Mai's over there with the visitors,' Marc said. 'And very importantly, she's got a tray of champagne. Excuse me while I grab a glass for myself,' he said, and he hastened across to Mai.

Lucette's gaze followed Marc to Mai, who must have heard Marc approaching, as she turned her back on the visiting officials and held out her tray to him. He made a short remark to her, at which she nodded, and then he took a glass from her tray.

Returning to Simonne's side, he raised his champagne flute. 'Santé!'

'What were you talking to Mai about?' Lucette asked.

'I asked if she was enjoying the evening. She said she was, or rather she nodded that fact.'

'Well, she could hardly say she wasn't,' Simonne

retorted. 'That would be seen as a criticism of Lucette for sending her here.'

Mark shook his head in mock wonder. 'The minds of you ladies are beyond me. To read so much into so little.' He shook his head again.

Simonne opened her mouth to comment further, but the lively buzz in the room was starting to subside.

They noticed that Gaston had stepped slightly away from the group he'd been with.

When the salon was quiet, he cleared his throat.

Simonne exchanged an amused glance with Lucette.

'As I think most of you know,' Gaston began, 'this was the first group of visitors I've had the pleasure of introducing to Hanoi. I haven't been here long myself, but I've been here long enough to marvel at the work that France is doing here in Tonkin, and in the rest of Indochine, too, I'm sure. And I'm delighted to have had the chance to share what I've seen with others.'

There was a murmur of assent throughout the salon.

'Everywhere you look in Hanoi, there's evidence of France's great civilising mission, a mission underpinned by a high moral purpose. I'm sure we all hope that our visitors, who are about to leave us—' smiling, he inclined his head towards a group of the visitors '—have found their time here interesting and fruitful, and we wish them a very pleasant stay in Annam and Cochinchine.'

He took a step back, and polite clapping broke out.

Several of the visitors approached him as the air again filled with laughter, and guests once more moved around the room, forming in groups that every few minutes, broke up and reformed with other guests.

Disentangling himself from the people around him,

Philippe went across to Lucette, Simonne and Marc, and put his arm around Lucette's shoulders.

'It was a good speech by Gaston, wasn't it?' he remarked.

'Yes, it was. And it was just the right length,' she said.

'How did the prison visit go?' Marc asked him.

'Very well, I think. They seemed genuinely interested. Mind you, Gaston had everything prepared to the minutest detail. He's clearly not a man to leave things to chance. He's also very generous.'

'As we've been lucky enough to find out,' Simonne remarked.

'I don't mean as in taking us to the Métropole, but in the way he allowed me to shine at the prison, if I can put it that way. You know what I mean, though. He always pushed me forward, and made sure they'd registered my name, which means I might be mentioned in any reports they send.'

Marc nodded. 'That's a good trait for a man. Visibility like that could enhance your career.'

'Champagne, Monsieur Delon?'

Philippe glanced to his side and saw Mai.

'Thank you, Mai, I will,' he said, taking a glass. 'So how's it going?'

'Very well, Monsieur. I hope Monsieur Laroche is pleased with our work.'

'I'm sure he will be,' Marc said.

'Do you know where Tan is, Mai? I haven't seen her for a while,' Simonne asked.

'She's in the kitchen, helping with the canapés,' Mai said, and she pointed towards a far door in the wall behind a long table covered with a pristine white cloth on which were set out champagne flutes, and silver ice buckets in which bottles of champagne had been embedded.

As she spoke, the door opened and a line of waiters emerged from the kitchen, a silver platter of canapés in each of their hands. They put one of the platters on the long table, and holding the other, they started to circulate among the guests.

'You'll excuse me, please,' Mai said, and she went across the salon and into the kitchen.

'I expect we'll soon have Gaston's company,' Marc remarked. 'I caught his eye a moment ago when he was looking across at us, and he indicated he'd join us as soon as he could escape.'

'He must be exhausted,' Simonne said. 'It's been a long week or so for him, not to mention all the preparation beforehand. That said, now that he's done it once, it'll be easier on the next occasion.'

Philippe nodded. 'You're right about it being tiring. I joined the visits to the Opera House and the Supreme Court, and believe me, a lot of work had gone into each visit. Gaston was asked some tricky questions, but he could answer absolutely everything. I was quite impressed, I must say. You should ask him to give you a shortened tour of the city, Lucette. Marc and Simonne have lived here for years, so they'll already know its history, but we don't.'

'I'll keep it in mind, but I imagine he'll have had enough of tours for quite a while.'

She glanced across the salon towards Gaston. Their eyes met. Both smiled briefly, and turned away.

'Why don't I take you across to meet some of the people I work with, Lucette?' Philippe suggested. 'You've met very few of my colleagues as yet, and what better time to meet some more?'

'If you don't mind, I'll come with you,' Simonne said

quickly. 'I'd like to say hello to some of the wives we've been meeting in Club French. I can tell that Marc's about to go off and talk about work with someone.'

Marc muttered something indeterminable.

'Most of the other wives are older than we are,' Simonne went on, 'but one or two are quite pleasant. If you like, Lucette, we could suggest they join us for coffee in Café Barnard one morning.'

As she and Simonne followed Philippe across the room, Lucette looked around to see if Mai had come back into the salon, but there was no sign of her.

She wished Mai would hurry up and return.

She still wasn't ruling out there being a Frenchman in Mai's life. She was certain that Mai had been talking French that evening, and not Vietnamese.

If one of the men there went across to Mai and spoke to her in a way that seemed more personal than just asking for a drink or a canapé, Mai's response might reveal a degree of familiarity. If so, she could ask Philippe or Marc to identify him.

But the kitchen door remained closed.

Frowning, she hurried to catch up with Philippe and Simonne.

'A VERY IMPRESSIVE SPEECH, GASTON,' murmured one of the visiting officials who'd come up to Gaston when he'd finished his speech. 'Just the right note to strike.'

'And thankfully short, I'm sure you were about to add.'

'There's that, too,' the sham official agreed with a smile. 'It didn't keep people from moving around for long. And your timing was perfect. Bouvier had finished talking to the girl before you started speaking. Congratulations.'

'And I should congratulate you all on asking your set questions at exactly the right time during the visits. Not surprisingly, they allowed me to display the depth of my knowledge.'

Both laughed.

'As for the timing with Bouvier, it was pure chance, of course,' Gaston went on, with amusement in his voice. 'It had nothing to do with the fact that I was watching him, and waiting till he'd clearly finished what he'd intended to say. So what *did* he say?'

'It was short and to the point. He told the girl that they were very pleased with her work and Tan's, and that there was no need for them to have an early morning.'

'I see,' Gaston said slowly. 'It's Mai's free day tomorrow, so whether or not she gets up early is of no account to the Delons, and even less so to Bouvier. Mentioning Tan would merely have been a cover. That means he'd thought that there'd be something for her to deliver tomorrow, but now there isn't.'

'I agree. Something on the domestic front wouldn't have aroused suspicion had it been overheard.'

'And no one else has approached her at all?'

The operative shook his head. 'No one. And when Bouvier was elsewhere, I was deliberatively crude and suggestive in some of my comments to the girl, and loudly so, and very free with my hands. Had she got an admirer here, or even a fellow conspirator, he would've stepped in for sure.'

'Then we can probably assume that Bouvier's the only one here tonight who's in league with the terrorists. And from what he said, there's no point in watching Mai tonight or tomorrow.'

'It's not much of a result for the work and money that

went into this, is it?' the operative remarked, glancing around the grand salon.

'It's enough of a return to be able to rule out anyone in the immediate permanent staff. All the possible candidates are here tonight—I made sure of that by personally inviting them—and no one's attempted to speak to Mai.'

'But their wives are with them so they wouldn't!'

He grinned at the operative. 'My experience has shown me that a small thing like that would never deter an amorous Frenchman from making some contact, however slight, with his lover. Or stop a traitor, inebriated by his own cleverness, from showing off. The added danger would excite him, and spur him into action. So what didn't happen tonight is as important as what did.'

'I'll bow to your superior knowledge.'

'Continue keeping a close watch till the end of the reception, won't you? It won't be for much longer. I'll wind it up as soon as I can. In fact,' he added, 'you could tell some of the others to start leaving now, and that would signal to everyone that it was time to go.'

'Of course,' the operative said. He raised his voice. 'It's been most productive, and most fruitful. And I'm very grateful, Gaston, as I'm sure we all are, to you and your staff for the informative visits you arranged for us.'

He and Gaston assumed an expression of gravity, and shook hands.

THE SUMMER EVENING was still and balmy.

'Did you enjoy tonight?' Philippe asked, as they sat side by side on their verandah, each with a cup of coffee beside them, gazing up at the night birds that sang above the trees, dark silhouettes against a night sky pinpointed with sparkling lights.

'Yes, very much,' Lucette said.

'I'm glad of that.' Philippe paused. 'I did wonder. I noticed you frowning on one occasion.'

'That's because I had a slight headache,' she said quickly. 'But it's gone now.'

He leaned across to her, took her hand in his, and kissed the back of her hand, and then released her hand. 'You must always tell me if you're not feeling well,' he said. 'We would have left earlier if I'd known.'

'I do so love you, Philippe, you know, and one of the reasons is that you're so kind. I didn't say anything because I knew what caused it, so it wasn't a worry.' She shifted in her chair to face him. 'So what did *you* think of the evening?'

'I thought it excellent. I thoroughly enjoyed meeting my colleagues in a more social environment. Although we were all in our place of work, so to speak, everything was much more relaxed. And you seemed to be getting on well with the wives.'

'They were really pleasant. I'd met some of them before at Club French, and I told a couple of them that I'd meet them there next week and we'd play a game of tennis. In addition to having a good old gossip, of course,' she added with a laugh. 'But I thought that now I've got a tennis dress, I really ought to wear it and hit a ball over the net from time to time, rather than just talk about getting some exercise while having coffee and macarons with Simonne.'

'You don't need to do anything you don't want. You're perfect as you are.'

She laughed. 'Flattery will get you everywhere.'

'It's the truth. A number of my colleagues told me this

evening how lucky I was. But I knew that. I'm aware of it every time I look at you.'

He took her hand in his again, and sat back in his chair, staring at the dragonflies darting to and fro in front of the verandah, their iridescent wings agleam in the darkness of night.

'Yes, Gaston did well this evening,' he went on. 'It was an impressive end to the visit, and even more so as it was done in haste. Apparently, more senior people turned up than he'd originally expected.'

'What did Marc say about it?'

'He, too, thought it well done, but that it was more extravagant than it needed to be. He hopes that Gaston doesn't intend such a performance—his word, not mine— every time a group of officials leaves.'

She hesitated. 'Marc's a little funny about Gaston, don't you think? It's not just thinking a formal reception unnecessary, which casts a bit of a slur on Gaston, but Simonne told me the other day that Marc thought it very strange that someone as clever as Gaston, and as highly paid, would be no more than a guide.'

'But that's not his permanent job. And anyway, he's a little more than an ordinary guide. Thanks to him, the visit looks as if it'll bring some economic advantages for Hanoi. And it'll certainly please the Paris government, which is no bad thing.'

'That's more or less what I told Simonne. I thought the evening lovely.'

'It was, and so were you,' he said, his voice breaking with emotion.

They leaned towards each other, and their lips met.

'I know it's still a little early, but it's been a long day, with a lot of champagne. Shall we turn in?' he asked.

'I'm not in the least bit tired,' she said with a giggle. 'But yes.'

18

She'd been right about not feeling tired, Lucette thought as she lay in bed, listening to Philippe's steady breathing.

From the moment Philippe had zipped up her evening dress and they'd left their house for the reception, to the moment that they'd returned to their bedroom where, bathed in the silvery moonlight that fell through the shutters, she'd let her dress fall from her shoulders and stood in her silken slip in front of Philippe, the evening had been one of sheer exhilaration, and she couldn't have felt further from sleep than she did at that moment.

She rolled over on to a piece of cool sheet, and closed her eyes.

If she tried hard enough, and refused to allow herself to re-live any of the highlights of the evening, she might just drop off.

She squeezed her eyes even more tightly shut and tried not to hear the eerie cries of the birds outside that were flapping in the dark of night.

How funny, she thought as she lay motionless, her eyes shut.

The first time she'd seen Mai in the garden at night, she'd been by herself, running towards the back of the garden. She'd been carrying a package with her, now she thought of it, but she hadn't on her return.

And on another occasion, she'd heard her go outside again, and had seen the beam of light from the kitchen. She hadn't heard Mai speak to anyone, so she must have been alone that time, too.

But why would she go by herself into the dark mass of foliage at the rear of the garden, stay too short a time for it to be a meaningful assignation, and then return?

There were railings along the back of the garden, so she wouldn't have been able to go out through the back, and no one would have been able to enter the garden that way.

So why had she gone there on more than one occasion, and what had she done with the package?

She opened her eyes.

Mai would never tell her, she was sure, so there was really only one way to find out.

Philippe was fast asleep, and Mai would be, too.

Mai had been pale with exhaustion when they'd got home, and had gone straight up to her room. She wouldn't be going outside that night. And Mme. Fousseret and Cook had long been in their beds.

So as she was nowhere near ready to sleep, and was the only person awake, there'd be no better time for her to go to the back of the garden to see what could have drawn Mai there.

She shivered at the thought.

There was something frightening about the idea of walking into a dark mass of leaves and plants, unable to see clearly where you were about to put your feet, especially as snakes were nocturnal.

Could she do this, she wondered.

Yes, she could, she told herself firmly. If Mai could, so could she.

She would just have to find the right balance between making sufficient noise and vibrations which, she'd been told, would cause any nearby reptiles to slide away, but not so much that she was heard from the house.

She got out of the bed as quietly as possible, took her torch from the drawer and grabbed her negligée from the chair. Then she crept into her dressing room, picked up her leather-soled pumps, and clutching everything in her arms, headed for the bedroom door.

When she was out on the landing, she closed the door carefully behind her, slipped into her pumps and negligée, and holding the torch, hurried down the stairs and along the hall to the kitchen.

She crossed to the corner of the kitchen, and went through the scullery and laundry room to the back door. Pushing the door open, she peered outside and listened hard.

The only sounds to be heard were the sounds of night.

She stepped out into the garden, closed the door quietly behind her, and ran lightly to the far edge of the lawn.

Everything between her and the back railings looked black and forbidding.

She hesitated, and wiped her hands on her negligée.

Then she took a deep breath, pushed back her rising nervousness, switched on her torch and started walking along the near-invisible track through the foliage that led to the railings.

With every step, she stamped her feet firmly on the ground.

A few moments later, two or three tall trees loomed up in front of her and she saw behind them, the railings that enclosed the garden.

Her steps faltered, and she stood there, uncertain what to do next.

Then, shining her torch on either side of the path, she looked to see if there was perhaps a small shrine to a Vietnamese god, such as were frequently seen by the roadside, or anything else that might have drawn Mai to that spot.

But there was nothing. Only trees and plants.

She moved closer to the railings.

And heard footsteps coming towards her.

She stopped in a panic.

Her heart pounding, she switched off her torch, and promptly crouched down behind the cluster of giant ferns at her side.

Peering cautiously between the fronds of the ferns, she saw a dark shape approach the aged tamarind tree to her right.

The shape switched on a torch, and bent down by the tree trunk.

And she saw his face.

He was Vietnamese.

What's more, she was sure it was the young man who'd been with Mai in the wagon.

So her beau *was* Vietnamese, she thought in relief, watching him shine the beam of light into a hollow at the base of the tree, and feel around the inside.

Then he withdrew his hand and stood up, staring towards the house.

She crouched even lower, trying not to breathe.

He stayed like that for several minutes, as if hoping that Mai would appear. And then, his shoulders slumping, he turned away, went slowly towards the dense growth of trees behind him, and was lost in the darkness whence he'd come.

When she was confident that he wasn't coming back, she rose from her hiding place, switched on the torch again, and went up to the tamarind tree. Bending down, she looked at the clearly defined hollow.

So that was how he and Mai communicated, she thought, straightening up.

An exchange of messages, and maybe a quick word on Friday night about arrangements for the following day, when Mai was free.

But Gaston's reception that evening would have thrown everything off-kilter.

Mai would probably have told her beau about the reception, but he could have been hoping that she'd be able to meet him as usual, nevertheless, and had gone to the rendezvous.

After all, why else would he have been there?

Remembering to stamp her feet on the hard earth, she made her way back to the lawn, and hurried into the house.

She poured herself a glass of water in the kitchen, and carried it upstairs, thereby giving herself a reason for going downstairs, should Philippe have woken up in her absence and wondered where she was.

Reaching their room, she crept inside, returned her pumps to the dressing room, threw her negligée over the chair, put the torch back in its drawer and the water on top of the bedside table, and climbed into bed.

She glanced across at Philippe. He was still deep in sleep.

Turning away, she stared at the ceiling, her heart racing from the excitement of the night.

Of the two options, she thought, a Vietnamese and a Frenchman, the former was so much better because he and Mai were equals.

But if they truly loved each other—and it looked as if they did—there was a chance of Mai becoming pregnant and having to leave. And that was something she really didn't want.

A wave of guilt shot through her.

She liked Mai very much and should be thinking of Mai's happiness, not her own. She was being selfish.

But she did genuinely feel responsible for Mai.

The ideal thing would be to talk to Mai's mother, but her mother would probably have forgotten the French she once knew, and since she couldn't speak Vietnamese, such a delicate conversation would be impossible.

Moreover, Mai might resent the fact that she had, in effect, been spied upon.

What she must do, therefore, was try to persuade Mai to open up to her.

For a start, she could show an interest in where Mai went on her day off, and perhaps even suggest that she go with Mai on occasion.

If Mai began to see her as not only an employer, but also as a friend, then she might bring up the subject of the man she loved, and perhaps even ask for advice.

What her advice would be, she wasn't sure. Nor even if she'd give any.

At most, if she were able to win Mai's trust, she could acquaint her with the implications of her situation, and what might happen if she didn't exercise the utmost caution. After that, it would be up to Mai to decide what to do. That was something no one else should try to tell her.

Settling down, she resolved to ask Mai the following morning if she could accompany her to wherever she was going.

Mme. Fousseret would have left for the market by then, so she wouldn't hear her employer make a request that would have appalled her. And Philippe was sure to have already left for the Résidence, so he wouldn't be around to object, either.

Of course, if he knew the reason why she wanted to befriend Mai, he might consider that to be the right thing to do. But as he didn't, it was better not to involve him, at least not for a little longer.

And as she'd nothing planned for the day, going with Mai might actually be interesting.

After all, although they were living in Vietnam, they were living as they would've done in France, and all of their friends were French. The only Vietnamese they encountered were their servants, waiters, street sellers, pousse-pousse coolies and the like.

Thinking about it, she had no idea how the natives lived, and it would be fascinating to find out.

Her final thought as she drifted into sleep was that in addition to broadening her knowledge, the following day would bring her the satisfaction of knowing that she was taking the first step towards protecting Mai.

19

T*he following morning*

IMPATIENT TO HEAR Mai's footsteps on the stairs, Lucette stared at the book on her lap with unseeing eyes.

She'd had her breakfast and would be able to leave the house within minutes. Her bicycle was propped outside the front door, and she had sufficient piastres in her purse to pay for anything she and Mai might need.

Finally, she heard Mai coming downstairs.

She rose quickly and went out into the hall.

Mai had reached the bottom stair. She was wearing an unadorned high-necked brown *ao dai* over white silk trousers, her long hair held back at the nape of her neck with a simple clip.

'Mai,' she said with a smile. 'I wonder if I might have a quick word. Don't worry,' she added quickly, 'I know it's your day off and I won't keep you long. Do come and sit down.'

She turned and went back into the salon, followed by Mai. Sitting down, she indicated that Mai should sit opposite her.

'I feel more comfortable if I stand, Madame,' Mai told her.

Her face anxious, Mai started fingering the rim of the hat she was carrying.

Lucette gave an awkward laugh. 'Of course. As you wish.' She paused. 'Did you enjoy yesterday evening, or did we work you too hard for that to be possible?' She gave another awkward laugh.

'I enjoyed it, Madame. The room was very beautiful. Most of the people were very kind.'

'I'm glad to hear it. I imagine that Monsieur Laroche was very pleased with you all. He should have been.'

'He was very kind, thank you.'

'That's good.' She cleared her throat. 'Actually, while I wanted to hear how you found the evening, Mai, it's not the main reason I asked you to step in here.'

She smiled reassuringly at Mai.

'I've done so because it's occurred to me that I seem to meet only French people, but never any Vietnamese. I think that's such a shame.' She smiled again. 'I was wondering, therefore, if you'd mind if I came along with you today. I'd like to meet your friends, and your family if you're visiting them. Would that be all right?'

Mai stayed at her in undisguised dismay.

She vigorously shook her head. 'No, Madame. I'm sorry, but this would not be all right. I'm sorry,' she repeated. Then she closed her mouth and looked down at her black velvet shoes.

'Obviously, I'm not going to force you to let me come,' Lucette said, her voice reflecting her discomfort. 'And if I've given offence, I'm sorry.'

Locking her fingers together, she clasped her hands in her lap.

'But I'm curious, Mai, as to why you're so against the idea. I thought we got on well together, and that you might like me to meet your family. And that perhaps they would like to meet me, the person you work for.'

'You don't understand,' Mai said bluntly, her gaze still on her shoes.

'What don't I understand?' she asked gently. 'I'd really like to know.'

Mai shrugged her shoulders.

'Look at me, Mai, please.'

Mai raised her eyes.

'There's nothing you could say that would make me angry, I promise you. I just want to know why you feel as you do. So, tell me, please.'

Mai took a small step forward. Her face ashen, she raised her eyes to Lucette.

'You people think Vietnamese people are not like white people. You think we're all lazy, good-for-nothing people. We know you feel that—you show it every time you push us aside, or you beat us for nothing. Every time you do something that takes our dignity from us. But we're not like that.'

A shock wave ran through Lucette. 'I'm sure you're not,' she managed to say.

'We are good, hard-working people,' Mai said, ignoring her. 'So Vietnamese people don't like the French people, or the Americans or the English. We work for you because we have no choice—you've stolen our land from us. But that doesn't mean we want to be friends with you. We don't.'

She felt a sudden, overwhelming sense of distress, and a lump came to her throat.

'But some Vietnamese are friendly with the French, and work *with* them, not *for* them,' she said, her voice shaking.

'They're collaborators,' Mai said, in icy contempt. 'We despise them.'

'I can understand that. But surely you know enough about me, Mai, to know that I'd never be friends with anyone who treated others badly,' she said, trying not to cry. 'And I'd never maltreat anyone myself.'

Mai stared at her in disbelief. Then she gave a harsh laugh. 'But you already have such friends, Madame,' she retorted. 'Monsieur Delon is a supervisor in a prison which treats my people with cruelty, with brutality. He sees this and he does nothing.'

Her face went even paler, and she stared at Lucette in utter panic.

'I was not thinking what I was saying,' Mai said, her voice betraying her sudden fear. 'I'm not criticising Monsieur Delon, Madame. He's not responsible for the system. I'm saying only that the system is cruel to the Vietnamese.'

'I understand,' Lucette said quietly.

'I'm very grateful to be working for you and Monsieur Delon. I know you're good people, and I'm fortunate to be treated with kindness,' she went on quickly, her words tumbling out in a rush. 'If you were a Vietnamese woman, I should be very happy to be your friend. But you're not.'

Lucette nodded slowly. 'Well, all I can say is, I'm sorry. I'm sorry that a friendship between us is impossible, and I'm sorry about the reason why. But you've made me understand why this is, so thank you. And I should like you to know that even though I'm French—' she gave Mai a watery smile '—

you can always come to me if you have any worries, or if there's anything with which you need help.'

'Thank you, Madame.' Mai visibly hesitated.

'What is it, Mai?' she asked.

'Please, do not repeat what I said about Monsieur Delon and the prison. He's always very kind to me. It's not his fault.'

'I won't say a word,' she said. 'You may go now. Have a lovely day, Mai.'

Mai inclined her head, turned and left the room.

THERE WAS a knock at the salon door.

Lucette glanced at her watch. It was more than an hour since Mai had gone out. She'd been gazing at her book with unseeing eyes for most of that time, she realised.

'Come in,' she called.

Mme. Fousseret appeared in the doorway. 'Monsieur Laroche is here. He wishes to speak with you,' she said, her voice disapproving.

'Show him in, please.' She smoothed down the skirt of her pink cotton dress as she stood up.

'How lovely to see you, Gaston,' she said as he came in, his hand behind his back.

'Do sit down,' he told her. 'It's not my intention to disturb you.'

'You're not. You couldn't have come at a better time, in fact. I was feeling a little low and seeing you has already raised my spirits.'

'How very flattering,' he said cheerfully, and he went across to her and placed a striking red rose on the table next to her.

Then he took the chair opposite her.

'Some refreshment for us both, please,' Lucette called to Mme. Fousseret, who was still in the doorway, and she sat back in her chair, picked up the rose, sniffed it and smiled at Gaston.

'The scent is heavenly, Gaston. Thank you. I'm not sure, though, what I've done to deserve my rose.'

'I've just given Simonne a similar rose. As I told her, I'm very grateful that you lent me your maids yesterday. They were a great help.'

She sniffed the rose again, and then put it back on the table. 'It's beautiful, but really there was no need to do this.'

'I know. But I wanted to, anyway.' He sat back and surveyed her. 'So you're feeling a little low, are you? I suggest that I make polite conversation about the weather and my preference for roses over orchids until Madame Fousseret has brought in our coffee, and then you tell me what's bothering you. I shall, of course, come up with the perfect solution.'

She giggled. 'No one would ever accuse you of lacking self-confidence, Gaston,' she said.

'I should hope they wouldn't,' he said with mock indignation. 'So how are you getting on with the humidity, Lucette?'

WHEN AN UNSMILING MME. Fousseret had wheeled in a trolley with coffee, and a platter of lemon almondines and small strawberry gâteaux, and had seen that each had a cup of coffee and a cake, she left them.

Gaston put his plate on the table next to him, and leaned forward, his knees apart and his hands clasped between his knees.

'Let me help you, Lucette,' he said quietly. 'What is it that's worrying you?'

She took a deep breath and told him of her proposal to Mai that morning, and Mai's response.

'I felt rather hurt, if you want to know,' she concluded. 'We've been very kind to Mai and I was shocked that she should speak so about the French. After all, *we're* French. She must realise that there are good and bad in every race, but I was included with the bad. It was a little upsetting. And, to be honest, I'd been quite looking forward to seeing how the Vietnamese live.'

'Was there any particular reason why you thought of doing this now?' he asked.

She opened her mouth to tell him about Mai and the Vietnamese youth, but stopped herself.

Instinct told her that there was a risk—a very slight one, but a risk nonetheless—that Gaston, clearly quite high up in the administration, despite the work he was doing at present, could feel that for Mai to have a divided loyalty was unacceptable, and he might tell her to solve the problem by dismissing her.

She'd hate to have to get rid of Mai, but she'd also hate to ignore openly the advice given to her by such a good friend, advice she'd solicited.

'I don't really know,' she said slowly. 'Perhaps it was seeing Mai and Tan being moved around in a way that suited us, but maybe not them, that made me start thinking about how they might live if they weren't working for us. And then Mai having the day off today... I can hear how feeble that sounds...' Her voice trailed off.

'No, it doesn't,' he said warmly. 'I completely understand. But I think that Mai might have told you only a part of the truth.'

'What d'you mean?' she asked in surprise.

'*You* don't think in terms of inferiors and superiors, Lucette, but the natives do because that's the reality for them. Even though they're benefiting from us being here, we're still their rulers and they must do as we say. This means that they must always show the respect of an inferior to a superior.'

'I didn't think of that.' She stared at him, wide-eyed.

He smiled at her. 'But you wouldn't. You just wanted her to see you as a friend. But think about it from Mai's point of view. If you'd gone out with her today, every native she'd met, whoever they were, would have had to defer to you and show you obeisance. As would Mai throughout the day.'

Lucette bit her lip.

'She would have had a ghastly day off,' Gaston went on, 'and you wouldn't have seen how they really lived because she'd have had to be careful about what she showed you. Mai wouldn't have told you that this was her reason, as it would have sounded as if she resented having to show you respect, and I'm sure she doesn't—she'll know the good person you are.'

Lucette beamed at Gaston. 'Thank you,' she said. 'You've made me feel so much better. Silly as it sounds, I'd been feeling as if she'd rejected me. No one likes that.' She laughed in embarrassment. 'But now I see that it's just the situation in which we find ourselves.'

'Exactly,' he said. 'It isn't at all personal.'

He took a sip of his coffee and sat back. 'So what are you and your ever-working husband planning to do for the rest of the weekend?'

. . .

It would have been interesting to have been told the whole reason why Lucette had chosen that precise moment to make such a request of Mai, Gaston mused as he walked down the drive to Rue Henri Rivière.

He'd been told the truth, he was sure. But only a part of it, he was equally sure.

It was that she'd hesitated before telling him why she'd chosen that particular day. It was only a momentary pause, but it was sufficient for him to realise that she was wondering whether to hold something back, or whether to tell the whole truth.

And she'd decided to hold back that something.

It could relate only to the reception or to something that had happened afterwards at the house.

As Marc had let Mai know that there was nothing to be delivered that week, Mai was unlikely to have left the house after she'd returned home, so that rather threw things back to the reception.

But he and the others had been watching her all evening. They would have seen anything suspicious in her behaviour, or in that of those in her vicinity, but there'd been nothing.

And there were no Vietnamese at the reception, apart from the servants, so there was nothing obvious to account for Lucette's sudden interest in Vietnamese life.

Maybe she'd told him the full reason, he thought as he went out through the wrought-iron gates. But somehow he didn't think she had.

He smiled ruefully to himself. Women were reputed to be unable to keep anything to themselves. What a shame that he seemed to have encountered the one woman who was proving an exception to the rule.

20

L*ater that day*

SHADED by the widespread arms of a banyan tree, Mai lay back on the grass and gazed up at the clear blue sky that she glimpsed in the gaps between between the large, leathery leaves that clothed the branches.

'On a day like today, when it's hot and the air's both heavy and damp, but it isn't raining, this is the perfect place to come,' she told Vinh, who was stretched out beside her. 'I was cool on the bicycle as we cycled so fast to get here, and now that we're here, I still feel cool as there's a breeze from the water.'

'I'd like to feel cool, too,' Vinh murmured, rolling over on to his side and staring down at her, 'but funnily, I always feel hot when I'm with you, Mai, whatever the weather. You do that to me.' He inched closer to her.

Giggling, she pushed him gently back, and sat up and stared at the small lake that lay in front them.

Sunlight was painting with gold the surface of the water and outlining the tiny green island that stood at its centre. And every so often, a large fish jumped from the dark green depths, sending out ripples that widened until they finally disappeared.

Two swans flew low across the lake, skimming its surface, their wings flapping.

And then her view was blocked by an iridescent green and blue peacock that strutted between her and the lake.

Pausing in front of her, it proudly unfurled its magnificent train, spotted with metallic green and blue eyes. For a long moment, it stood motionless, its gossamer tail fanning out behind it.

Then emitting a piercing cry, it folded its train and continued on its way.

'I love it here,' she said, lying back down on the grass. She turned her head to look at Vinh. 'Are we going to the island today?'

'I'm afraid it's bit late,' he replied. 'And it looks as if it's going to rain before too long.'

'I can't wait for September and the dry season,' she said, with a trace of irritation. 'I know everything dries up very quickly, but the frequent downpours are annoying.'

'True,' he said. He turned his head to look at her. 'Since we're not going to the island, you've got time to tell me what you've been thinking about all morning. When we're together, I want you to be thinking only of me, as I think only of you.'

She glanced at him. 'I always think only of you when we're together,' she said with a coquettish smile. 'And I think of you even when I'm not with you. I love you, Vinh.'

She stretched out her arm and trailed her fingers down his chest.

He took hold of her hand and kissed her fingers, one by one.

Then he rolled on to his side again and propped himself up on his elbow.

'I love you, Mai,' he said, looking down at her. 'That's how I know when something's bothering you. Did anything happen at the reception last night? Did you see or hear anything that made you think we'd been found out?' He stared into her face in anxiety. 'I'd hoped to see you after the reception, and I went to the tree, but you weren't there.'

She put her hand lightly to his cheek, and smiled up at him.

'It's nothing like that. The reception was fine. I was tired when I returned, and I didn't have any messages for you, so I didn't go out. You knew about the reception, so I didn't expect you to be there. And I knew I'd see you today.'

'So what's on your mind, Mai? Something is, I can tell.'

'It's nothing much. It's just something Madame Delon asked me this morning.'

'Well?' he prompted.

And she told him about Lucette's request. 'She says she wants to meet my family and friends and see how we live,' she finished by saying. 'But I don't really believe this.'

He lay back on the grass.

'She's a good employer, isn't she?' he asked after a few minutes.

She nodded. 'Yes.'

'And she treats you with more consideration than Madame Bouvier treats Tan, doesn't she?'

'That's right.'

'So she could mean what she said, couldn't she?'

'I suppose so. It's just that it's a strange thing to say. She must know we can't be friends. Friends are equal with each other. But she and I are obviously not equal. It makes me wonder why she asked.'

He sat up and looked down at her, his forehead creasing. 'Are you afraid that the Sûreté has asked her to get close to you? But why would they want her to do that?'

'When you say it like that, it does sound unlikely,' she said slowly.

'But if you truly think that's a possibility,' he went on, 'you must think that the police suspect you of being a revolutionary. If so, they could take you to Hoa Lo at any time.' He bit the inside of his cheek. 'You've got me worried now, Mai.'

She sat up, put her arm around him and rested her head against his shoulder. 'I didn't mean to, Vinh. I think I'm just being silly. As you say, Madame Delon has always been kind to me. She gave me extra free time when she didn't have to, didn't she? Tan's never been given such a thing. No, the more I think about it, the more I think she meant what she said. She just didn't realise how impossible it was.'

He nodded. 'I'm sure that's right. But all the same, I think you should tell Monsieur Bouvier about it. We've always agreed within the group that if any one of us feels a thing instinctively, or has a slight suspicion but no proof, they must tell the others about their fear. It would put us all on an even higher alert. Our lives are at stake, after all.'

They exchanged anxious glances. Sitting quietly side by side, they held hands.

'Let's go back to my place,' he said at last. 'If we leave now, we'll be there before it rains again.'

They stood up.

For a long moment, each gazed at the other, their faces close, their cheeks almost touching. His breath, scented with musky spice, was hot on her face, bathing her with love.

Shivering with longing, she moved nearer to him.

He cupped her face in his hands, and stared down into her dark heavy-lidded eyes. Speckles of sun fell like liquid gold on to her face, and wonderingly, he touched with his fingertips her smooth skin, and her lips.

'I want you to be my wife, Mai, more than anything,' he said, his voice hoarse. 'As soon as the uprising's over, we'll marry, leave here and go south.'

She looked up at him pleadingly, her hand on his chest. 'Can't we go sooner? What Madame Delon said this morning has frightened me.'

He shook his head. 'No, we can't. We'd be turning our backs on the cause we believe in, and we can't do that. There's nothing more important than freeing our country from the French.'

'I know that,' she sad quickly.

'And there's no real reason to think we've been discovered. We're always careful, aren't we? We always assume that we're being followed and we regularly vary the routes we take. Just as you and I are always careful, my lovely Mai, when we show our love for each other, much as I wish it wasn't necessary.'

He raised his hand and ran his fingers through her hair till he reached the grip that fastened her hair at the nape of her neck. Then, very gently, he traced the curve of her neck with his fingers.

Prickles ran down her spine, and she moaned in pleasure.

'Let's get back as quickly as we can,' he said, and they turned and hurried across to their bicycles.

AT THE STROKE OF MIDNIGHT, Vinh stood with his arm around Mai, both of them staring across Rue Henri Rivière to the Delons' house.

'You must find a way of getting Monsieur Bouvier to meet you tomorrow night, or as soon after that as you can,' he told her. 'You must tell him about Madame Delon. I'm sure he'll agree that there was nothing behind it but genuine interest, but nevertheless, he should know what she asked. After all, he's at risk, too. Can you do that?'

'I think so. Monsieur et Madame Bouvier are coming to lunch with Monsieur et Madame Delon tomorrow after their church. Madame Delon told me they were going to gossip about the reception. She said it'd be easier to do so without Monsieur Laroche, so he's not been invited.'

'There you are!' he exclaimed triumphantly, and he hugged her tightly. 'That she spoke to you in such a way proves that she sees you as a friend—at least, as close a friend as a servant can be. Can you imagine Madame Bouvier confiding in Tan in such a way?'

Her face broke out into a broad smile. 'No, I can't. You're right, Vinh. How clever you are! You've made me feel so much better.'

He grinned. 'I'm pleased. But you'll still tell Monsieur Bouvier as soon as you can, won't you?'

'I promise.'

He ran his fingers down her cheek. 'Goodnight then, Mai. Sleep well.'

Their cheeks met, and then with a little wave, she

turned, checked that nothing was coming along the road, and then ran lightly across to the other side.

Standing in the shadows beneath the tamarind trees that lined the road, she waved again at him, and then hurried towards the drive.

Moments later, she'd been swallowed up by the darkness that shrouded the house, and was lost from his sight.

21

S *unday afternoon*

RAIN FELL in sheets from the large grey pillows of cloud that hung low in the sombre sky, flattening the grass, transforming the hard earth into mud, drenching the flowers and leaves, and silencing the insects.

Sliding in rivulets down the tiled roof, rainwater collected in large beads beneath the eaves, and dropped thence to the ground in glistening vertical lines that veiled all the windows in the house.

With each strong gust of wind, the shutters rattled.

Sitting in one of the armchairs in the salon, Lucette glanced towards the windows.

'I'd been going to suggest having coffee and brandy on the verandah,' she said ruefully, 'but I rather think not. It'll have to be in here.'

'Good decision,' Simonne said with a smile. 'It won't last

long—these showers never do. But it'll take a little time for the garden and verandah to dry out, and for the vapour that rises from the wet ground to settle. It'll all be fine by the evening.'

'A coffee and brandy would be the perfect end to a lovely meal, wherever we have it,' Marc said, 'so thank you. As for the rain, that's the way it is, this time of year. At least, it won't be as humid for a while, and between the showers, the air will smell of flowers, wet grass and fresh earth. All good aromas.'

'But this is a little more than a shower, isn't it?' Philippe remarked in surprise. 'The rain's really quite violent.'

'If you'd lived close to the coast, such as in Da Nang or Hoi An, you'd know what storms are like. The coast there gets the full force of the monsoon rains. We're protected here, being inland. Saigon's inland, too, but I believe it gets more rainy weather than we do. Perhaps you don't notice it quite as much there, though.'

'Whenever I hear you mention Saigon, Marc, it's always in a very positive way. It sounds as if you prefer Saigon to Hanoi. Do you?' Lucette asked.

Marc thought for a moment. 'I suppose, in some ways, yes. Business matters take centre stage in Saigon, and the city abounds with vitality, energy and an unbridled enthusiasm. Hanoi is a calmer, more leisurely city, more stately perhaps, and more reflective. I can see why at the beginning of the century, the man in charge, Paul Doumer, picked Hanoi to be the capital city, not Saigon.'

'But surely he'd have wanted the livelier city?' Lucette said in surprise.

'You'd think so, but no. Hanoi was hardly a city at that time. It was a blank canvas, and perfect for Doumer's vision. He wanted to create something new, something modern, something French. And that's what he did. But with a part of the city only. We were outnumbered by the Vietnamese, so there was only ever going to be a part of the city that would feel French. And that's where the money was spent.'

'I can't imagine that any city could be livelier than Hanoi,' Lucette said in wonder.

Marc nodded. 'The pace in Hanoi has picked up considerably since Doumer's time.'

'That's an interesting comparison of cities, Marc,' Philippe said. 'I hope Lucette and I get the chance to prove the truth of it, or otherwise, before we're sent back to France.'

'You certainly should visit Saigon at some point if you can. But being purely selfish, I hope it's no more than a visit, and that you're not transferred there. We'd be sorry to lose you.'

'We certainly would,' Simonne said fervently.

'When you were in Saigon, did you travel to other places?' Lucette asked. 'To nearby villages, for example?'

'Occasionally. I think I told you my work took me to the Mekong Delta. The river's prone to flooding, and many of the houses there are built on stilts. They often have a prepared upper storey with beds and food and so on, in case the ground floor's flooded and the family has to live upstairs for a while.'

'How interesting!' Lucette exclaimed.

He smiled at her. 'I, too, found it interesting. Despite the flooding, families frequently have stone tombs in their garden, and you see graveyards in rice paddies—people are buried in the place where they lived.'

'I suppose that makes sense in a way,' Lucette said.

'And ancestor worship is very important to them. Every family, no matter how poor, has a shrine to their ancestors in their home, or at the very least, an altar in their sitting room. Some houses even have a door for ancestors to use. There are three doors. The middle is for ancestors. Women use the door to the left of it, and men go through the door on the right.'

'You've never told me any of that before,' Simonne said accusingly.

'You've never asked,' Marc replied.

'Did you actually go into their homes,' Lucette asked, 'and see how they lived?'

Marc shook his head. 'Not really, no. In Hue, I went into the homes of some of the wealthy Vietnamese who're in business with us, but I don't think that's what you mean.'

'I was thinking of ordinary people.'

Marc nodded. 'That's what I thought. But as with Saigon, you ought to go to Hue if you ever have a chance. It's a very special place. At the heart of Hue, there's a citadel surrounded by a moat that's fed by water from the aptly named Perfume River. The imperial family lives in the citadel. There's an area inside it called the Purple Forbidden City, which is reserved exclusively for their use.'

'It sounds fascinating,' Lucette said, her eyes shining. 'I'd love to go there. Wouldn't you, Simonne?'

'To be honest, not particularly. I don't remember Saigon as I was too young, and I'm not sure if I ever went to Hue. But I've no real desire to go back to the area again. I love Hanoi, despite the rain, and I'm quite content to stay here. Unless I get the chance to go to Paris, of course,' she added with a laugh.

'Aren't you curious about how the Vietnamese live?' Lucette asked her.

Simonne shook her head. 'Actually, no. I don't feel any interest in the lives of the people we rule, who are our servants or who pull us in pousse-pousse or serve us in cafés.'

'They weren't always ruled by us,' Marc said mildly.

'But they are now. Whenever I go across the Old Quarter, I pass the places where they live—in narrow alleys, for example, which stink of drains, and countless other horrible things. And I've seen bare-bottomed children urinating in the gutter, and doing even worse than that.' She shuddered. 'And they throw rubbish and household waste into the street. That's all I need to know about their lives, thank you.'

'Perhaps one day you'll show some understanding of why things are as they are,' Marc said quietly.

There was a momentary silence.

'Don't forget our coffees, Lucette,' Philippe said quickly.

Her hand flew to her mouth. 'Oops, I'm sorry.' She rang the small brass bell at her side. 'Are we all having a brandy with our coffee?'

There was a murmur of assent as Mme. Fousseret came into the room.

Lucette asked her to bring in the drinks, and Mme. Fousseret left.

'I think we exhausted the topic of the reception during lunch,' Simonne said brightly. 'And we seem to have said all there is to say about the natives.' She turned towards Lucette. 'Yesterday, Gaston kindly dropped off a rose to say thank you for lending him Tan, but there wasn't really time to talk as he had a lot to do. I expect you got a rose, too, didn't you?'

'That's right. He came in for a minute or two, but like you, we didn't really talk. I didn't see him at church today, but to be honest, I didn't look—we were too anxious to get back before the rain.'

'He won't have been there,' Philippe said. 'He had to

have breakfast with the group as they're leaving tomorrow. I doubt we'll see him before Tuesday, if as early as that.'

The door opened, and Mme. Fousseret entered with a trolley of coffees, four empty snifters, a bottle of cognac and a plate of petits fours.

Lucette indicated that Mme. Fousseret should leave them.

But Mme. Fousseret took a slight step forward. 'If you'll excuse me, Madame, Mai asked me to give this to Monsieur Bouvier.'

She put her hand in the pocket of her black dress and brought out a small leather item.

'Why, that's my pouch!' Marc exclaimed.

'Apparently, you dropped this at the reception on Friday, Monsieur,' Mme. Fousseret told Marc. 'Mai found it when she was leaving the salon. But it was her day off yesterday, and the silly girl forgot to take it across to you. If she'd been thinking clearly, she could've left it in your house earlier this morning when she went across to return something to Tan. As it is, she's asked me to give it to you now.'

She put the small black leather pouch on the table next to him.

He looked at it in surprise, which swiftly gave way to relief.

'How fortunate she found it, and before I'd even noticed it was missing!' he exclaimed. 'I've had it a long time and I'm embarrassingly attached to it.' He smiled at Mme. Fousseret. 'Would you thank Mai for me, please?'

Mme. Fousseret nodded, and left the room.

'How strange,' Simonne said. 'I could've sworn I saw it on the hall table last night, where you always put it.'

'And I would've assumed I'd put it there, too. But obviously not so. I must've dropped it when I took out my key.

Because I always leave it in the same place, half the time I'm not aware of what I'm doing. Or not doing,' he added with a laugh. 'How lucky that it was Mai who found it. She'll have seen me with it, so she'd know it was mine. I must look after it better in future.'

Smiling around the table, he picked up the pouch and put it into his pocket.

As MME. Fousseret went back into the kitchen, Mai paused in her efforts to remove a stain on the dress that Lucette had worn on Friday evening, and glanced towards the housekeeper.

'If ever that happens again,' Mme. Fousseret scolded, 'you must be sure to return the item to the owner at once. I know it was your day off yesterday, but you could've given it to me before you went out, and I'd have returned it to Monsieur Bouvier. You wouldn't want to be suspected of stealing, would you?'

'No, Madame. I'm afraid I forgot about it yesterday. But if anything like that ever happens again, I'll give it back at once,' Mai murmured, and returned to her task.

M. Bouvier would realise that she'd put a message inside the pouch, she thought in satisfaction.

He'd almost certainly read it before he went home, and if he was unable to meet her outside the kitchen door on the Monday night, as she'd suggested, he'd be sure to find a way of letting her know before he and Mme. Bouvier left.

She felt quite pleased with herself that she'd picked the following evening to tell him, and not that evening. After a day at work, M. Delon always fell into a heavy sleep soon after getting to bed, whereas on Sundays, he and Mme.

Delon were in the habit of talking in bed for some time after going upstairs.

Monday would be much better.

A few minutes later, she heard the distant sound of someone opening the salon door. She stopped scrubbing, and listened.

She heard M. Bouvier's voice. He seemed to be making a joke as he came out into the hall—at least, they all laughed so she assumed that he'd said something amusing—and then she heard the door close behind him, followed by footsteps heading for the water closet.

Smiling inwardly, she returned to her work.

22

C*afé Barnard
Monday*

'I'M REALLY glad you popped round and suggested we took advantage of an hour or two without rain,' Lucette said, stirring her coffee. 'I was in the mood for a coffee with a friend.'

'So was I. But, to be honest, there was also another reason why I came round.' Simonne shifted her position in her chair. 'It's about yesterday,' she began. 'Marc and I really enjoyed our lunch with you, by the way.'

'And so did we. You must come again before too long.'

'It's your turn to come to us next time. Assuming Philippe doesn't mind meeting Marc so frequently out of work, that is. He might want a break from him.'

'I'm sure he doesn't. He really likes Marc, and so do I. Not only is he pleasant, but he's also very interesting.'

Simonne cleared her throat. 'It's about that,' she said.

Lucette looked at her in surprise. 'What d'you mean?'

'It's just that Marc said I came across as a little hard and unsympathetic yesterday. You know, my comments about the natives and how they lived. And the things I said about the Old Quarter.'

'I didn't think that. And I'm sure Philippe didn't, either, or he'd have told me. I just thought that Marc and you'd had different experiences in the past, and as a result, didn't see things in the same way.'

'That's true.'

'Not everyone has to think the same as everyone else. It's better to be honest, than pretend to feel something you don't. So you don't have to worry, Simonne—I like you as much today as I did before yesterday's lunch.'

Simonne wiped her forehead in mock relief. 'Thank goodness for that. And you know that although I've no interest in visiting any of the homes in the Old Quarter, I willingly go there I need anything from the shops, so I can't think that badly of the area. And I go through it to get to my school friends' houses.'

'And you're fair to Tan. You don't treat her badly. If you did, she would've told Mai, and I'm sure Mai would've told me.'

'Yes,' Simonne said slowly. 'Yes, that's true. I treat her very well. She could never complain about me as an employer.'

'There you are, then,' Lucette said with a smile. 'I imagine your father was a good employer, too, and you'll have learnt it from him.'

'He was a kind man, much kinder than I am.' She hesitated. 'When I think about it, I never actually heard him say anything nasty about the Vietnamese or their homes. I've an awful feeling that if he'd heard me yesterday, he would've been appalled.' She grimaced.

'What about your mother?'

Simonne laughed. 'That was my mother talking yesterday. She could be scathing about the natives. I wasn't at all surprised she went back to France as soon as she could.'

'Was she equally hard on people like Mai, who had a white father?'

Simonne laughed again. 'Even harder, if you can believe it. She saw their mothers as tainted. The woman had lured the man into her bed with her magic, she would say, and deliberately got pregnant to ensnare him. And she'd see the product of the liaison as being equally tainted. I don't know about sins of the father, but in Mai's case, she would have carried the weight of the sins of her mother, as well.'

'D'you think that, too?'

Simonne was silent for a moment. 'I've never thought about it before. But in a way, I suppose I do. I don't mean about magic and all that,' she added hurriedly. 'And I wouldn't describe the husband as guiltless, but, yes, I do criticise the woman. She may not have encouraged him, but she certainly made it possible for the husband to cheat on his wife.'

Lucette frowned slightly. 'But she might not have had a choice. She could have been forced to do as the man wanted. She could have had to give in, or leave the job and live in poverty.'

'I suppose that's true.'

'And none of it would be the fault of the métis children, would it?'

'Of course it wouldn't. But the sight of a face that's both Vietnamese and white would remind me that someone's husband betrayed his wife. I'm glad that Tan is Vietnamese through and through. In fact, I don't think I'd have employed her if she hadn't been.' She paused, and gave Lucette a rueful smile. 'I imagine you feel differently.'

'I do, but you were brought up here and I wasn't. That must make a difference.' She took a small tarte aux fraises from the plate in the middle of the table. 'We're neglecting these lovely pastries by talking so much. And strawberry tarts are my favourite.'

Simonne laughed. 'You really are a diplomat's wife,' she said in amusement. 'That was a very skilful change of subject.'

Lucette giggled. 'Well, I was aware that time was moving on, and we haven't yet mentioned Gaston. No meeting would be complete without a reference to him. I meant to ask Marc yesterday if he'd had time to talk to Gaston's visitors before they left.'

'He exchanged a few words with some of them at the reception, but apparently they weren't that forthcoming. They seemed to prefer to keep to themselves, and didn't volunteer anything.'

'That's what Philippe found, too. Although he said they were very warm and friendly at the end of the prison visit.'

'I wonder if Gaston's got the dates for the next group yet,' Simonne said, taking a strawberry tart. 'Perhaps we should come here again on Wednesday before going to Club French. Gaston's stopped by before on a Wednesday on the off chance we'd be here, and he might do so again. If he's got a new group coming, or been assigned something different, he'll be keen to tell us. And if he hasn't, he'll be bored and want to pass the time of day.'

'That's a good thing about Gaston, he's so predictable.'

· · ·

GASTON GLANCED at the clock on the corner of Emile's desk. It showed two o'clock in the afternoon.

'I trust I didn't disturb your siesta, Emile,' he said smoothly. 'But I wouldn't want to be seen in the Old Quarter today, and it was a pretty safe bet that I wouldn't be if I came at this time.'

'I'm sure you're right, Gaston,' Emile said, rubbing the sleep from his eyes. 'You seem to have been right about everything else so far. So what next, now that your visiting officials have gone?'

He leaned forward and picked up a half-empty bottle of brandy. He held it out towards Gaston, but Gaston shook his head.

'No, thanks,' he said. 'One thing you can be sure of, it won't be another such group. I wouldn't want to go through all that again, nor to organise any more receptions. And there's no need to. I think I've succeeded in establishing a valid reason for my presence.'

Emile nodded. 'I'm sure you have.'

'I'm confident that Mai's only contact is Bouvier, and we now know almost every link of the delivery chains. Unfortunately, though, we still need the names of one or two village contacts. And also his contact in the prison.'

'When will you get them?'

Gaston shrugged. 'The prison contact won't be difficult to identify. We'll pick an inmate who'd know and exert some pressure on him. As for the village contacts, I don't know. It's a slow process.'

'Surely it doesn't have to be that slow!' Emile said, filling his glass.

'Believe me, it does. It's difficult to follow a person in the countryside, and even more so into a village. There are several operatives on each person, with one taking over from another during the length of their route. But they have to discover the route before they can get into place, and they can't do that till there's a delivery. But when we know who they all are, we'll move in on the group, and bring in Bouvier and Mai, as well.'

'In the meantime, what next?'

Gaston grinned. 'Next, I'll be asked to write a voluminous report that makes it necessary for me to spend more time in the Old Quarter.'

Emile raised his eyebrows. 'About what?'

'Ostensibly, I'll be looking into the possible reconstruction of parts of the Old Quarter. If you recall, I have an engineering background.'

'And in reality?'

'I'll be trying to discover all I can about the people delivering to the villages where we don't yet know the contact. It'll give me a reason to move around in the Old Quarter, and one that will make me welcomed by the natives.'

Emile grunted.

'That, plus the fact that when the weather's unsettled as it is at present, people are careless in their haste to get out of the rain, and will be less focused on whether or not they're being followed. It means that with luck, I won't get as far as writing any actual report.'

'And what're you going to do about your newly established friends?'

Gaston smiled. 'The same as I've been doing all along—continue with the breakfasts, lunches, and so on. If I suddenly drew back from them, it would put Bouvier on his guard. I've seen the way he already looks at me at times, and I'm not sure he doesn't think I'm too good to be true, for want of a better expression.'

'I'd be surprised if that wasn't the case. You've appeared

out of nowhere, and in a trice, you and they are all but inseparable. He's an intelligent man, who's engaged in an act of treason that could cost him his life. He's bound to be readily suspicious.'

Gaston nodded. 'Hence I'll be true to the character I've created. I'll drop by Café Barnard on Wednesday morning, provided it isn't raining too heavily, and see if Lucette and Simonne are there. If they are, I'll invite them and their husbands to dinner at my house next weekend.'

'Well, let's hope you get a result before too long, Gaston. We've given you all the time you need, but there's got to be a limit.'

'I'm aware of that,' he said, standing up. 'The net's closing in.'

SHE'D ENJOYED meeting Simonne that morning, and she was pleased that Simonne had said what she had, Lucette thought as she lay in bed, waiting for sleep.

She hadn't been consciously thinking about what Simonne had said the day before, but it had been at the back of her mind, she'd realised as soon as Simonne had raised the subject.

But if she'd been harbouring some slight unacknowledged disappointment in Simonne, her explanation that morning had completely dispelled it.

No one could say for certain what their attitude would have been had they been brought up in Hanoi, and by a mother like Simonne's. She certainly couldn't, so she wasn't going to give it another minute's thought.

She turned on her side, and closed her eyes.

Could she hear talking, she wondered a moment later.

She opened her eyes, raised her head slightly and listened hard.

Yes, there was definitely someone in the garden on the kitchen side of the house, where Mai had met her beau before—two people, in fact.

This was her opportunity to find out for certain whether Mai's beau came from Tonkin or France, and she wasn't going to waste it.

The last time she'd heard them together, she'd been so anxious not to be seen that she'd left it too late to see the man.

She wouldn't be making the same mistake again, she decided as she slid out of bed. Grabbing her negligée and slippers, she ran lightly to the door.

When she entered the kitchen, she instantly crouched down as she didn't want to be seen before it was too late for the man to vanish, and crept towards the scullery.

Pausing at the entrance to the laundry room, she listened.

No, she wasn't mistaken—there *were* two people. One was Mai and the other was definitely French. So it wasn't the man with whom she'd seen Mai be so affectionate.

How strange, she thought, inching forward.

Just about all of Philippe's colleagues had been at Gaston's reception on Friday, and not one of them had gone near Mai, even though a rather unpleasant member of the visiting officials had overstepped the mark a few times with behaviour towards her that verged on being lascivious.

Frenchmen were gallant, and had Mai's French lover been there, he would surely have found a subtle way to intervene.

So it must be someone else. A businessman, maybe. If

so, she need not fear that unmasking the man would cause trouble for Philippe at work.

She strained hard, trying to make out any words.

To her alarm, a change in the man's tone of voice suggested that he was about to leave.

Bending even lower, she slipped into the laundry area, and then, at the same moment as she stood upright, she pushed open the door that led to the garden, and found herself facing the man.

'Oh, no!' she cried in horror. 'It can't be you, it just can't!'

The blood draining from her face, she took a step back, her hands pressed against her mouth, her eyes filling with tears.

Then she spun round.

Marc reached for her arm, but she pulled away from his grasp, and ran back into the house.

23

---

he following day

A T LAST, Lucette thought, as Philippe left for the Résidence. For the first time since she'd seen Marc with Mai, she felt herself relax, but only slightly.

Having lain awake all night, wondering whether to tell Philippe, whether to tell Simonne, wondering if she could bring the liaison to an end without either Simonne or Philippe finding out about it, she was nowhere near being able to answer any of her questions.

Fortunately, she hadn't yet seen Mai that morning. She knew she wasn't ready to face her.

She stood up, went out of the dining room and into the salon, and sat down in her armchair. Thank goodness she wasn't seeing Simonne till the following day, she thought in a mixture of relief and exhaustion. By then, she should have decided what to say to her, if anything.

She looked miserably around the room.

If only Gaston were there.

He would have been the person from whom to seek advice. He was friendly with Marc, and would perhaps understand him better than she did. And as he didn't work with Marc, he could be freer than Philippe in what he said.

It certainly wouldn't be right to tell Philippe at the moment—not till she'd had time to digest what she'd seen.

And thinking about it, perhaps it was just as well that she couldn't consult Gaston, either, about this.

If Marc would assure her that he'd end the liaison at once, the fewer who knew about it the better. And that included Gaston.

Gaston had always liked Marc, but it would be difficult for him, as it would be for anyone who knew about Marc betraying Simonne, ever to look at Marc in the same way again.

And more than anything, she wanted things to go back to the way they were, or rather, to the way she'd thought they were.

Not that they ever could.

Even if she decided to keep everything between Marc and her, there was Mai.

A wave of anguish swept through her.

She'd have to dismiss Mai.

But Mai was an excellent maid, and she liked her a lot. And none of this would have been Mai's fault. She must have been forced into the affair. Mai's heart had been captured by a young Vietnamese man. She'd seen that for herself.

But Mai would have to go.

She'd have no choice.

Letting Mai carry on living in the house next to Marc's

would have been putting before Marc a daily temptation that could prove too great to resist, and that would prolong an unwanted situation for Mai, and the wrong being done to Simonne.

She stood up and went across to the window that looked out towards Rue Henri Rivière.

The hydrangea, luminous in the bright morning sun, made the thought of a short stroll an attractive one, especially as it was some time before the heat and humidity would peak.

Yes, a walk would clear her head, and help her to work out when and where she could speak to Marc without Simonne or Philippe knowing.

And also what she would say to Mai.

There was a knock on the salon door, and the door opened. Mme. Fousseret stood in the doorway, an expression of profound disapproval on her face.

'Monsieur Bouvier is here to speak with you, Madame. He apologises for coming at so early an hour, but he has a busy day ahead.'

Her heart started racing.

'Please, show him in,' she said, fighting to steady her voice.

She thought frantically.

'I wonder if you'd do something for me, Madame Fousseret,' she said as the housekeeper returned to the salon with Marc behind her.

'Of course, Madame.'

'I'd intended to take Mai to the tailor this morning to have another work dress made. But I've a headache, and I'd be grateful if you'd go with her in my place. I was going to the tailor we used before. If you set off now, you'll be there and back before the intense heat of day, and the rains. Mai can leave whatever she's doing until she gets back.'

'As you wish, Madame,' Mme. Fousseret said frostily. And she went out, leaving the door open behind her.

Lucette went to her chair and sat down again. Unbidden, Marc took the chair opposite her. Neither said a word until they heard Mme. Fousseret and Mai leave the house.

'Thank you, Lucette,' he said quietly. 'That was quick thinking.'

'It was born out of necessity. I'd hate Madame Fousseret to know what you've been doing. And Cook's at the market, so he'll be gone for a while longer.'

'I haven't been doing what you think.'

'You mean, cheating on poor Simonne,' she hissed through clenched teeth, a red spot of anger on each of her pale cheeks. 'And with my maid, who's not in a position to deny you. That's why you gave her to me, is it? To make it easy to carry on with her. You bastard!'

He started to stand, and then sat heavily down again. 'You've got it wrong, Lucette. Very wrong, indeed. There's nothing between Mai and me. There never has been. I love Simonne.'

'I'm sure that's what you'd like us all to think. But this isn't the first time I've heard you in the garden with Mai. And I've seen her go outside late at night on other occasions, too.'

He gestured despair with his hands. 'She and I are friends. But it's no more than that. I swear to you.'

'I'm not blind,' she snapped, her back ramrod straight. 'I know what I saw for myself. And I know that I wouldn't be able to live with myself if I let Simonne remain in ignorance. Unless you promise me that it'll never happen again, and make me believe that you mean it, I'll tell her tomorrow.

And I'm obviously going to have to dismiss Mai, much as I'll hate doing so.'

'You couldn't be more wrong in what you're thinking,' Marc said, his voice shaking. 'Please, Lucette. You'll hurt Simonne for no reason.'

'If you know what I'm thinking,' she said, her eyes flashing, 'you'll know that I'm thinking a man in your position, who admits to a friendship with a maid, who's years younger, from a different culture, one of a people subservient to us, is friendly with her for one thing only.' Her voice dripped contempt. 'I'm not stupid, Monsieur Bouvier.'

'I know you're not, Lucette, but you're mistaken. Dangerously so.'

Her laughter was brittle. 'The only danger is to you, and to Mai. She'll have to find another post, and Simonne will probably decide to leave you. A cheating husband is like a leopard—he never changes his spots. You hear all the time of men betraying their wives, being forgiven, and then committing the same sin again.'

'Please, let me explain,' he begged.

'I don't want an explanation, nor any of the sordid details. The only thing that'll stop me telling Simonne is if you assure me that this thing with Mai ends now. Sacking her alone wouldn't end things—you could still carry on with her, even if she went back to her village. It isn't that far away. No, you must promise me, in a way that I believe you, that you'll never see her again.'

'I can't,' he said looking down at the floor.

She audibly drew in her breath.

'I can't because, although there's no relationship between us, I have to see her again.'

She frowned, bewildered. 'I don't understand.'

He looked up at her, his hands clasped in front of him, his knuckles white. 'I need an assurance first, Lucette, that you'll tell no one what I'm about to say, and then I'll have to trust you to be true to your word.'

She bit her lower lip.

'If I satisfy you that there's nothing sexual between Mai and me, will you promise that you'll keep what I tell you to yourself?' He leaned slightly forward. 'It's urgent that you do so. If you don't, you'll endanger both of our families, as well as Mai and others, too.'

A frisson of fear ran through her.

'You're frightening me, Marc,' she said, fingering her bead necklace.

'Will you promise me that?' he repeated.

'I can't,' she said at last. 'I don't know what you're going to say. You say you'll trust me to stick to my word, well you'll have to trust me to do what I think is right.'

He sat back and stared at her. 'I suppose I've no choice.'

She stared at him in defiance. 'That's right, you haven't.'

'I think, when I've explained, you'll understand why you mustn't tell anyone else. In effect, my life will be in your hands.'

She gave an awkward laugh. 'Don't you think you're being a little over dramatic?'

'No, I don't. Not at all,' he said quietly. 'But to make sense of what I'm about to tell you, I need to go back in time. Back to my years in Saigon, in fact.'

'Did you meet Mai in Saigon?' she exclaimed.

'No, of course not,' he said impatiently. 'She'd have been a child. Forget about Mai for the moment. During my four years in Saigon, I was working on matters related to natural rubber and rice, and I frequently went to the south of Saigon. Through the construction of irrigation works,

chiefly in the Mekong Delta, the area of land devoted
to the cultivation of rice has quadrupled in the past forty
years.'

'I don't see what that's got to do with anything.'

'You will. Rubber is helping to make the colony rich, and
the exports of rubber and rice are vital to the French economy. But they've been achieved at the expense of the lives of
the Vietnamese. When I was there, I saw for myself the
hardship they're suffering.'

'Why shouldn't we profit from being here? Philippe said
our civilising mission is really helping the poor.'

Marc made a noise of dismissal.

'It isn't,' he said bluntly. 'The so-called mission is just a
façade. We're here for profit. Years ago, merchant adven-
turers and soldiers who wanted land and power persuaded
Paris to support them. Britain had colonies, they said, so
France should have a colony, too, or it would be left behind.
And that became Indochine.'

'Is that so bad?'

'Yes, if there's no real interest in developing Vietnam,
except where it benefits us. We need resources, raw mate-
rials and cheap labour to keep costs down, and the Vietnamese must supply that.'

She shook her head. 'I don't believe you. I know
Philippe. He's not like that. He's kind and caring.'

'He's subject to pressure, as we all are.'

'I just don't believe it,' she repeated.

'Open your eyes, Lucette. Ask Mai, if you want. Millions
of Vietnamese are forced to work for long hours and little
pay, and are subject to high taxation. Land that's been
tended by their ancestors for generations has been stolen.
Many have had to take jobs on the rubber and tea planta-
tions we own, where conditions are desperate. Malnutrition,

dysentery and malaria are rife. It's not uncommon for several workers to die in a single day.'

'That's very one-sided. What about the school system we introduced?'

'Its effect is exaggerated. It's not of benefit to many children. Most receive some basic elementary education, but few get the chance of a higher education.'

'And the railroad and projects like that?'

'Of more benefit to us than the Vietnamese, but paid for by the Vietnamese through high taxation.'

She sat silent for a moment or two.

'Where does Mai fit into all this? We seem to have come a long way from me seeing you alone with her,' she said at last.

'Not really, we haven't,' he said. 'Over the years, I came to feel a tremendous sympathy for the natives, and disgust at how we were treating them. And for a long time now, I've been helping them.'

She frowned. 'In what way?'

'By bringing things out of the prison, and taking items in, too. I'm helping them to produce newspapers that educate those in the prison and those outside.'

She stared at him, her eyes wide open. 'You're helping terrorists? That's what you're saying, isn't it?'

'I'm helping people who want to be treated fairly and to live in dignity.'

She put her hand to her mouth. 'And what does Simonne think about all this?'

'She's no idea what I'm doing.'

'And Mai?'

'I pass everything on to her. She conceals it at the back of your garden, where it's found by the next person in the chain.'

He paused. 'That's the truth, Lucette. I don't know what else I can say. If you don't believe me and decide to tell Simonne, you could be destroying our marriage for what's a lie. I love Simonne very much, and I would never betray her. I just pray that you believe me.'

She nodded slowly. 'I do.'

'Thank you.' He sank back in his chair, relief on his face.

'I believe you because Philippe once mentioned the high taxation needed to build the railway, which is close to something you said, and because of what Mai said to me recently. And because I saw her with a young Vietnamese man, whom she clearly adored.'

She looked around the room. Her gaze returned to Marc.

'Why did you and Mai meet last night?'

'Because of you,' he said with a half-smile. 'She wondered if there was any significance in you asking to go out with her on her free day. She thought you might suspect something.'

'I see. Why don't you tell Simonne what you're doing?'

'To be honest, I'm not sure how she'd react. You've heard her on the subject of the natives. She's been brought up surrounded by colonial life, and you could say that she'd almost been indoctrinated. But not by her father. He was a good man, and he felt anger on behalf of the Vietnamese.'

'You're probably right about Simonne.'

'Also, the less she knows, the safer she'll be.' He edged slightly forward. 'And the same can be said of you, Lucette.' His voice took on a note of urgency. 'Unless you decide to go to the Sûreté and turn me in, which would mean certain death for Mai and me, you'd be wiser to forget what I've told you.'

'That's easy for you to say,' she said bitterly. 'But I can't forget what I now know. I wish I could.'

He cleared his throat. 'You should be aware that if you *did* decide to report us, there's always—' He stopped abruptly.

'What were you going to say?'

'I'm so sorry, Lucette,' he said, his face stricken, 'but there'd always be a risk that despite you reporting us, they'd think that without you knowing, Philippe was involved, too, and they might take him in.'

Her face went ashen.

'So what are you going to do? I need to know, Lucette. Tell me, I beg of you—please.'

24

Lucette stood up.

Marc immediately rose to his feet, and took a few steps towards her.

'What are you going to do?' he repeated, with fear on his face.

'You've put me in an impossible position,' she said, her voice shaking, 'and I'm very frightened, for both Philippe and for me.'

'I'm so sorry, Lucette. Believe me, I understand what you're feeling. But forgive me, I must ask you again. What're you going to do about Simonne?' he asked, his breathing ragged.

'I believe what you said about Mai, so there's nothing to tell her.'

His shoulders slumped in relief.

'And what about the things I've been doing?' he asked.

'Your treason, you mean?' she said bitterly, her face deathly pale. 'If you were to be caught, so would Mai, and possibly Philippe. You say you love Simonne, but she, too, could come under suspicion. Because of that, I've no alternative but to keep quiet about your activities.'

'I feel I have to try to right something that's very wrong...' His voice trailed off.

'And that's part of my dilemma. I can see you truly believe in your cause. And I suspect that if I asked you to stop, you wouldn't. You might assure me you would, but you'd still carry on passing messages.'

'I can't answer that,' he said slowly.

'I can. So I'm caught in a web, aren't I? I'm trapped into turning a blind eye to treason. How can I do otherwise? I couldn't live with myself if I was responsible for Philippe being imprisoned.' A sob caught in her throat. 'I could never do anything that might hurt him, I love him so much.'

'I do understand. Don't you think it doesn't hurt every day, trying to square what I'm doing with my conscience as a Frenchman?'

'But you've chosen to be in that position. I haven't,' she cried.

'That's true,' he said quietly. 'And I can't expect you to understand why I've done so, or to believe that, despite everything, I still love France. I just think we've lost sight of values we should be holding dear.'

'To be honest, from some of the things I've seen in the streets, to some extent, I *do* understand. But I believe you're wrong to engage in treason.'

'I hate it that I have to.' He took a step forward. 'And I hate it that you've been put in such a difficult position.'

She moved back.

'But you must promise,' she went on, 'that you will never, in any way, involve Philippe. And you must have minimum contact with Mai in the future. Leave the message where you usually do, but don't stay to speak with her. If you agree to this, I'll try to carry on as if nothing has happened.'

'I promise.'

'But if I ever, for one minute, think you've gone back on that promise—'

'I understand.'

'Then you can see yourself out,' she snapped, and she turned and went across to the window.

A moment later, she heard the kitchen door close behind him.

She pushed the shutters wider apart, stared out of the window and let the warmth of the sun wash over her.

The songs of a multitude of invisible cicadas wrapped around her, and in front of her, a profusion of bright yellow butterflies danced around the hydrangea bushes, mesmerising her.

Was there anything she could have said, or done, that might have persuaded Marc to desist from activities that put them all at risk, she agonised.

But by the time that Mme. Fousseret and Mai returned, she'd still not been able to think of anything further she could have said.

As soon as she heard them come back into the house, she went swiftly across to her writing desk in the corner of the room, picked up a pen and a piece of paper, waited a few minutes and then rang for Mme. Fousseret.

She explained to the housekeeper that there were some things she'd like Mai to do for her, but as she was too busy to talk to Mai for the moment, she would have to do so after lunch.

She asked, therefore, that Mme. Fousseret tell Mai to come to her after lunch, before she went up for her siesta.

There was no need for Mme. Fousseret to delay going

for her afternoon rest, she added. She must go up at the same time as usual.

Then she returned to her chair, and sat thinking.

She loved their house and the life they'd been building in Hanoi. It was a place where she and Philippe could have been so happy. But everything was now tainted, and would never be the same again.

A part of her would always be waiting for Marc to be caught, because caught he would be, she was sure. And she'd live in perpetual fear about who else would be taken with him and Mai into Hoa Lo.

And as she sat there, she realised what she'd have to do.

However much she'd have ridiculed any idea of leaving Hanoi had someone mentioned it two days earlier, as soon as they'd completed a year there, she must ask Philippe to request a transfer.

They could ask to be returned to Paris, perhaps.

She drew in a deep breath. The appeal of going home, to a place where they'd be safe, suddenly seemed overwhelming, and her heartbeat quickened with longing.

Frustratingly, they wouldn't be able to move before the year was out as it would be harmful to Philippe's career to do so. Even after a full year, it would be frowned upon by some.

But it would be worth more than a few frowns to ensure that Philippe stayed safe.

Oh, if only he'd been placed with someone other than Marc!

But he hadn't.

And leave Hanoi they must, although it wasn't going to be easy.

It wouldn't be easy to persuade Philippe to move, or for him to find a post elsewhere that he'd like as much as his current placement, nor to walk away from Simonne, knowing that she was leaving her in a dangerous situation.

Poor Simonne.

She'd come to like her enormously, despite the attitudes that Simonne had sometimes expressed, and she was fearful for her safety.

She looked around the salon in despair.

And there was also Mai to consider.

What was she going to say to Mai?

Whatever it was, she must decide soon. Lunch wasn't far off, and afterwards, Mai would be coming to the salon—assuming she hadn't secretly run away by then, terrified about what Lucette might think of her.

Her lunch thankfully over, during which she'd been pleased to see that Mai was still there, although Mai's gaze had been averted throughout, she returned to the salon, sat down and rang the bell.

When Mme. Fousseret entered the salon, she told her that she was ready to speak with Mai, and asked her to send Mai in at once.

Moments later, a timorous knock sounded on the door.

'Come in,' she called, and Mai came into the room.

'Close the door behind you,' she told Mai, 'and sit down.' She indicated the chair opposite hers.

Mai closed the door, hesitated a moment, and then went and sat down.

Lucette pointed towards the door. Mai turned her head, glanced at the door, and then looked back at Lucette, questioningly.

Lucette put her finger to her lips.

Mai nodded her understanding, and her eyes downcast, her hands in her lap, she waited.

A few moments later, they heard heavy footsteps climbing the stairs, followed soon after by lighter footsteps. Two doors closed, one after the other, and a moment later, all was silent upstairs.

'We can assume that Cook and Madame Fousseret will be in their rooms for some time,' she said coldly, 'so you and I can talk freely, Mai.'

'Yes, Madame,' Mai whispered, studying the area of floor in front of her.

'You should know that Monsieur Bouvier has told me everything. I know that you're both part of a terrorist chain.'

Mai raised her head and stared her in the eye. 'It's to bring freedom to my people,' she said defiantly.

Lucette looked at her thoughtfully. 'But you're French—at least I assume your father was French—as well as Vietnamese,' she said at last. 'Doesn't it bother you that you're betraying your French heritage?'

'I'm Vietnamese, not French,' Mai said bluntly. 'The French have no interest in the métis. We're an embarrassment to them. My father was a good Frenchman, though, and he used to visit my mother and me, and try to help our village. He would be proud of what I'm doing. And that's important to me.'

'I understand.' Lucette paused. 'I realise that you and Monsieur Bouvier are risking your lives by your actions, but it's not just *your* lives you're risking, is it? You're risking the lives of my husband and me, and also of Madame Bouvier.' She paused. 'Do you think it's fair to endanger us in such a way?'

'No, it isn't, Madame. But in a fight for freedom, you can't think like that. In the end, what matters more than a few lives is that our country is free, and our people can live without fear. We would rather not hurt those who aren't involved, but in a war, this happens.' Mai hesitated. 'Are you going to report us?'

She shook her head.

'No, I'm not. I feel it would be even more dangerous for Monsieur Delon and me if I went to the police, innocent though we are, than to say nothing. The police could suspect us of being involved, and it would be hard to prove that we weren't.'

Mai visibly relaxed a little.

'At the very least,' Lucette continued, 'my husband's career would be damaged. You might think our lives and our happiness don't matter, but I think they do.'

'I do, too, Madame,' Mai said, looking up quickly. 'I would hate anything to happen to you or Monsieur Delon. I meant only that in a fight, people get hurt, even if this is not what you want.'

'I see.'

She stood up, and Mai stood up, too.

'I've told Monsieur Bouvier that the contact between you must be minimal, and that Monsieur Delon must never be involved. I don't ever want to hear or see anything that reminds me of what you're doing.'

Mai bowed her head. 'I understand.'

'And if I suspect for one minute that you've put my husband at risk, I'll go straight to the Sûreté. Is that clear?'

'Yes, Madame. Thank you.'

'One final word. There are several people in this household. If *I've* found out what you're doing, others might eventually do so, too. Perhaps you should bear that in mind and not go to the tamarind tree unless it's absolutely essential to do so. You may go now.'

Mai gave a slight bow, and left the salon.

IT ALL FELT SUDDENLY MUCH MORE real, Mai thought, as she made her way up the stairs to her room, and much more dangerous. And a sense of foreboding lodged deep within her.

She had to see Vinh as soon as possible, and tell him what had happened.

In spite of what Mme. Delon had said, she'd wait at the end of the garden that night until he came, no matter how long it took.

25

L *ater that night*

LUCETTE LAY ON HER BACK, her head turned towards Philippe.

Tired though she was, and distressed as she felt by what had happened that day, and also by some of the sights she'd seen that afternoon when she'd asked Tuan to drive her around the Old Quarter—the day had shown her how much she loved Philippe, and how she'd do anything to protect him.

She stretched out her hand and lightly touched his cheek, being careful not to wake him.

'I love you, Philippe,' she whispered. 'I love you more than life itself.'

She lay there a moment, staring at his sleeping form, a smile hovering on her lips. Then she withdrew her arm, turned on her side, and curled up facing the window, her back to Philippe.

She ought to get to sleep, she knew, but fragments of her conversations with Marc and Mai kept running through her mind, rendering sleep impossible.

It was also, she realised, irritated with herself, that she'd rather fallen into the nightly habit of listening for Mai.

And now, much as she wanted to shut down her mind, she couldn't.

She knew that it was possible that Marc would meet with Mai that evening.

If she were either of them, she'd want to know what the other had been told by her, and while she was confident after Marc's assurances that they would stop meeting at night unless it was absolutely necessary, it wouldn't be unreasonable for them to want a brief talk that evening.

And Mai was certain to want to speak to her beau.

So if she understood why they might meet that night, why would she listen for them?

Well, she wouldn't.

But she did.

The sound from below was so slight that had she not been on the alert, despite her best endeavours, she would have missed it.

She slipped out of bed, ran to the window, and glanced down at the garden. A beam of light illuminated the area in front of the kitchen door. And then it was gone.

Pressing closer to the glass, she glimpsed Mai running diagonally towards the back of the garden.

She turned away, her heart pounding.

She already knew far more than she wanted, and she didn't want to know anything more. One thing was absolutely certain—she was never again going to get out of bed at night to stare at the garden below.

She moved away from the window, climbed back into bed, snuggled up to Philippe and firmly closed her eyes.

MAI REACHED her arms through the railings and pulled Vinh closer to her.

'I'm so glad you came tonight, Vinh. I couldn't wait to tell you what happened today,' she whispered. 'Madame Delon knows about Monsieur Bouvier and the messages, and I've been so afraid. But from the moment I saw you, I was no longer afraid.'

'That's not good, Mai. You must be fearful at all times, even when you're with me,' he said, his voice urgent. 'When we stop being afraid, we become careless.'

'I'll always be cautious. I promise.' Their faces pressing against the hard railings, their arms around each other, Mai told Vinh what had happened.

'What are you going to do, now that Madame knows about us?' she asked when she'd finished. She moved back a little, and gazed up at him with anxiety.

'I'll go to the headquarters tomorrow and tell them. We can't abandon the plans we've worked so hard on, but perhaps we can make everything happen sooner. It'd be wise to do that, if possible. As soon as one person from outside the group knows, others find out. That's the way things go.'

'And what about us?' she ventured. 'Does that mean we'll be able to marry sooner than we thought?'

'It does.' With a broad smile, he took hold of each of her hands. He raised her right hand to his lips, and kissed it, and then her left hand.

'I love you, my Mai,' he said quietly. 'I'm counting the minutes until you're my wife.'

Then he dropped her hands, stared at her long and hard, took a step back, and disappeared into the darkness behind him.

FINALLY, Marc thought in relief as he heard Simonne's regular breathing.

He'd been waiting all day for a moment in which to reflect upon the events of the past couple of days, but up to that point, there hadn't been a single such moment.

It had been an enormously busy day at work, which had included an appointment at the garrison, and as soon as he'd got in that evening, Simonne had regaled him with ideas for future dinner parties.

He'd had nothing to add, and had said so, but that hadn't deterred her from running through a seemingly endless list of possible themes.

He gazed up at the ceiling.

Now that he had time to think, he was aware that he felt a degree of anxiety at someone else knowing what he was doing, but not the level of anxiety he'd have expected. Quite simply, he trusted Lucette.

He could do so because he could see how much she loved Philippe, and he knew that she'd never do anything that had the potential to harm him.

He'd have liked to have met up with Mai that night, to have reassured her about Lucette, and also to hear if Lucette had told Mai anything different from what she'd told him.

But it would have been risking Lucette's wrath to have done so, since she'd insisted that he keep his distance from Mai.

And anyway, he probably would have waited by the gate in vain.

He hadn't arranged to meet Mai that evening, and with everything that had happened, she was bound to have assumed that he'd be lying low for a while, and wouldn't be there.

And lying low was what he would do.

He'd pass on the messages as always, but the only physical contact he'd have with Mai would be when it was urgent that he do so.

Just as Lucette was concerned about Philippe, he was concerned about Simonne.

The day's events had jolted him into facing the situation he'd brought about, in a way he hadn't done for longer than he could recall.

Simonne was an excellent wife and she deserved better from him than to be put at unnecessary risk. And in future, he was going to be scrupulous about ensuring that he didn't do so.

Turning on to his side, he stared at Simonne. A wave of love for her engulfed him.

He moved closer to her, kissed her lightly on the cheek, and then inched back, his eyes still on her face.

'I know I'm taking a chance,' he whispered to her. 'But it doesn't mean that I don't love you, because I do. I really do.'

GASTON LAY IN HIS BED, his eyes wide open.

So what was going on, he wondered. The comings and goings at the two houses had been quite unusual for the past three days.

Because he hadn't been able to think of anything else to

do at that time, he'd assigned operatives to watch the two houses for the rest of the week.

The men on duty on Sunday had reported that Mai had run across to the Bouviers' house early on the Sunday morning, and had returned soon after. There was nothing significant in that, however—Mai might have had something to give back to Tan.

After church, which he'd avoided that week, knowing that they'd expect him to be tied up with the visitors, the Bouviers had gone back to the Delons for lunch. Eventually, they'd left for their home. There was nothing of interest in that.

The operatives on duty in the day on Monday had nothing to report, either. Lucette and Simonne had gone out for coffee. Once again, they'd been to Café Bernard.

He'd been tempted to call off the operatives, thinking it was beginning to look like a waste of money, but something —he knew not what—had caused him to refrain from doing so.

Indeed, he'd even reminded them to keep an eye on the back of the Delons' house, as well as the front.

And he was extremely pleased that he'd left things as they were—the report from the operatives about Monday evening had been most interesting.

From his vantage point at the back of the garden, one of the operatives had seen Mai and Bouvier talking to each other outside the kitchen late on Monday night.

To the operative's surprise, Lucette had suddenly appeared at the kitchen door. She had immediately rushed back into the house. Bouvier had tried to stop her, but failed.

And then the following morning, just after Philippe had

left for the Résidence, which he'd done at his usual time, Marc Bouvier had called upon Lucette.

A few minutes later, the housekeeper, her face furious, had left the house accompanied by Mai, who was noticeably pale.

Marc had clearly timed his arrival to avoid bumping into Philippe. And to judge from the expression on their faces, the housekeeper and Mai hadn't known that they'd immediately have to exit the house.

Now that was unusual.

After a length of time, Marc had returned to his house, and the operative had seen Lucette standing at the window, appearing distressed.

Soon after that, Mai and the housekeeper had returned.

Thinking that nothing else was likely to happen that day, the operative had settled down beneath one of the tamarind trees from which the house could be seen, only to hear the sound of a car door slamming.

Hastily scrambling up, he crouched close to the trunk of the tree, and saw that Lucette was getting into the back of her car. A moment later, the chauffeur started to drive towards the road.

On the spur of the moment, he decided to follow Lucette, rather than remain outside the house, and he climbed on to his bicycle, attached his basket to the handlebars and pedalled after the car.

She'd gone to the Old Quarter, he'd later reported, and had asked the chauffeur to stop on several occasions. Each time, she'd stared out of the car window at something that was happening in the street.

As far as the operative had been able to tell, it was when people were throwing rubbish into gutters, or children were using the gutters as a lavatory.

She'd then been driven back to her house, and a little while after that, Philippe had returned.

He rolled on to his back.

So Lucette was interested in the Old Quarter, was she—the source of much of the terrorist action against the administration. And not long before going there, she'd spent time alone with Marc.

He didn't know what could have led to her sudden interest in the area, nor if it had anything to do with Marc, but he was going to try very hard to find out.

Starting the following morning.

He'd most definitely be at Café Barnard at a time when the women were likely to be there. The invitation to dinner at his house could wait. The most pressing thing now was to know what had happened between Bouvier and Lucette, and for that, he'd need to get Lucette alone.

And he had an idea how to do that.

He'd have had to be completely obtuse not to have realised that Marc was suspicious of him—he'd seen it in Marc's face, and had heard it in words that weren't spoken—so his new project was going to sound more worthy of his abilities.

It had been his intention to tell Marc and Philippe about it at one of their breakfasts later that week. But the way things were turning out, he might be telling their wives first.

The following morning, in fact, if they were at the café.

And when he did so, he'd slightly change his focus from what he'd told Emile.

Given the operative's report, it wouldn't be enough to talk about the reconstruction of the Old Quarter—it needed to be more specific.

Examining the possibility of installing more septic tanks in the area, and looking into potential improvements to the drainage system, would be better, being more precise.

And what a coincidence—it just so happened that it would touch upon an interest that Lucette had shown that afternoon!

He couldn't resist a triumphant laugh.

With a little thought, he could probably find a way of enlisting her help. If they were working together, an even greater closeness between them would inevitably develop, and who knew what might happen then?

Perhaps the idea of a betrayal of secrets from a head on the pillow next to him wasn't as fanciful as it had at one point seemed.

Roll on the following morning, was his final thought before he fell asleep.

26

Café Barnard
Wednesday morning

'HAPPILY, the weather seems to be improving,' Lucette said as they sat at their favourite table on the pavement in front of the café.

'I'm glad it is. It wouldn't have been much fun in the rain.' Simonne glanced at Lucette. 'Are you all right, Lucette?' she asked hesitantly, running her finger around the rim of her coffee cup. 'It's just that Philippe told Marc he was a little worried about you, that you seemed peaky.'

'That's men for you! I'm fine, thanks. I was just a bit tired. And maybe it was all a little anti-climactic after the reception. Not your lunch with us, of course,' she added hastily. 'We really enjoyed that.'

'I see. And that's all it is, is it?' Simonne said, and she giggled.

Lucette tilted her head questioningly. 'What do'you mean?'

'I was wondering whether to start knitting.'

Lucette frowned at her in bewilderment.

'I was wondering if we'd soon be hearing the patter of tiny feet, of course.' Simonne giggled again.

Lucette's face cleared, and she laughed. 'You're spared any knitting, Simonne. At least for the moment, you are. It's certainly not that. I wouldn't mind if it were, but it's not.'

'That's a shame! It wouldn't have occurred to the men as a possibility, but when Marc used the word peaky, I did wonder.'

'No, it was just tiredness. I'm still finding the humidity somewhat difficult. It saps every bit of energy.'

'There should be less humidity from now on. I hope so, anyway.'

'And what exactly are you ladies hoping for?'

'Gaston!' they exclaimed in unison.

All three laughed.

'If I may?' he asked, pointing to the chair between them. Without waiting for an answer, he sat down.

The waiter approached the table, and Gaston ordered a coffee for himself, a plate of coconut cakes, and another coffee for Lucette and Simonne.

'I didn't ask if you wanted another cup,' he told them, 'as I knew you would. You'll have been talking since you arrived, and your throats will be horribly dry by now.'

'How d'you know we haven't just got here?' Lucette asked.

'Because all the cakes have gone,' he said, grinning at her. 'You take one, while murmuring that you really shouldn't. You eat it slowly, and then eye the rest of the cakes longingly, but not saying anything. Then you suddenly announce that you'll have just one more, and you won't eat pudding that evening. And thus you progress at a stately pace until the plate is empty, as it is now.'

'You know us too well,' she said, laughing.

'So, how are you, Gaston?' Simonne asked.

'I could say that I'm all the better for seeing you, but that would sound cheesy, wouldn't it, so I won't,' he said as the waiter poured their coffees.

'Your restraint is admirable,' Lucette remarked in amusement.

Gaston looked at her, and smiled. 'It is, isn't it.'

Feeling herself go pink, she looked quickly at her coffee. 'What are your plans,' she asked, 'now that the visitors have gone? Is there another group arriving soon?'

'So many questions,' he said, smiling.

He picked up the plate of cakes and offered it to Lucette, but she waved it away. He then offered it to Simonne, who took one.

'No more groups, I'm happy to say,' he said, returning the plate to the centre of the table. 'At least, not for a while. But I've been assigned another project, which is slightly different from the last.'

He took a sip of his coffee.

'That said, when the next group arrives, I may have to pause in my project to deal with them. But I'm rather hoping for a good stretch of time before I'm interrupted as the task sounds interesting.'

He sat back and smiled at them.

Lucette clapped her hands. 'Full marks for a tantalising introduction,' she said.

Simonne laughed. 'All that's missing is a drum roll.'

He grinned at them both. 'It's good to know that one's efforts are appreciated.'

'And what are you going to be doing?' Lucette asked. 'Or is there a second stage to the introduction before we get to the main event?'

He laughed. 'No, there's no second stage. The project's probably best described by my saying that I'm going to be immersed in septic tanks.'

Lucette and Simonne exchanged glances.

'What does that mean?' Simonne asked.

'That I've been asked to look into sanitation in the Old Quarter. Septic tanks have always lain at the heart of our colonisation of the city, but something's gone awry in the native area, and I'm looking at what can be done to improve the system.'

'Why you?' Lucette asked. 'This is very different from being a tourist guide.'

'That was only because of the shortage of attachés, and it's why I may be called upon again. But my background is in engineering, and this is more suited to my qualifications.'

'That makes sense,' Simonne said. 'Marc couldn't understand why you had such a lowly task. Oops, sorry! That was very badly expressed,' she added quickly. 'I didn't mean lowly, as such. I meant to say that it was something that didn't appear to draw upon all your abilities.'

'It *was* lowly, Simonne,' he said smoothly, 'but I appreciate your effort at extricating yourself from the mess of your terminology. Although, in the light of my newest undertaking, extricating oneself from a mess of words stimulates a more attractive picture than extricating oneself from the mess I'll be encountering. Heaven forbid it ever comes to that!'

They all laughed.

'This is such a coincidence, Gaston!' Lucette exclaimed, staring at him in amazement. 'Yesterday, I had the chauffeur drive me around the Old Quarter, and I saw how the gutters were regularly used in ways that hadn't been intended—you must know what I mean.' She blushed. 'And I thought that for all the life and activity there, it's a neglected area. Simonne, too, has commented on this in the past, haven't you, Simonne?'

Simonne nodded. 'That's right.'

'How interesting.' His smile embraced them both. 'Well hopefully, I'll be able to help bring the native quarter closer to the standards of the area in which we French live.'

'That's a very worthwhile aim, Gaston,' Lucette said. 'If there's anything Marc and Philippe can do to help, you'll ask them, won't you?'

'Rest assured, I definitely will. And also,' he said, reaching for a coconut cake, 'there may be something the two of you can do to help.'

'What do you mean?' Simonne asked, her voice taking on a hint of nervousness.

'I'd obviously avoid asking you to go anywhere too distasteful, if you take my meaning,' he said. 'But there'll be information a woman can get from another woman, that the other woman would never share with a man, and I'm wondering if you'd be willing to come out a few times with me, to see what we can find out.'

'I see,' Simonne murmured, and she glanced at Lucette.

'I'd like to get a clear picture, for example, of the woman's daily routine, which includes cooking, washing dishes, washing clothes, how the family wash themselves, and also how and where they relieve themselves.'

Simonne paled. 'I'm not sure I'd be much good at that,' she said weakly.

He looked at Lucette. 'I realise it's a lot to ask. And you wouldn't be paid.'

'I'd like to help,' Lucette said. 'We're lucky to live where we do. And I'd like to see things improving for others less fortunate.'

Simonne pulled a face. 'I feel so ashamed,' she said. 'You're a much better person that I am, Lucette. It's just the thought of what we might see when we went down those smelly alleys—' she shuddered in horror '—it makes me feel quite sick.'

'It's fine. Believe me, I understand, Simonne.' He turned to Lucette.

'That's very kind of you, Lucette.' He hesitated. 'I was planning to take a short drive around the Old Quarter later this afternoon, just to get an idea of the best way to approach my research. I don't know if you'd care to join me. You'd be home before Philippe returned, so there'd be no danger of him not finding his slippers by the door when he walked in.'

She laughed. 'Forget the slippers. A gin gimlet, more like. Yes, that would be fine, Gaston. I think I'm going to find this very interesting.'

RELAXING ON THE VERANDAH, they watched the sun fall behind the trees and the sky became a blazing canopy of crimson and burnished gold.

Dark birds, wheeling in groups above the tall trees, were stark against the blazing sky.

'It's a glorious evening,' Lucette said, sighing with pleasure as her gaze dropped from the sky to a tangled display of lustrous roses, vibrant splashes of colour among the thick green shadows thrown out by the ancient trees.

'I'm glad we decided to sit here for a while before going

into dinner. I've come to love these evenings out here together.'

She put her head back and inhaled the heightened aroma from a myriad flowers.

'I wonder why we never see the cicadas, but continually hear them,' she murmured. 'It's very strange.'

Philippe turned to look at her. 'I'm pleased to say that you look brighter this evening than on the last two days,' he said.

She smiled at him. 'I feel brighter. I had a really interesting day today.'

'You were meeting Simonne, weren't you?'

'That's right. And yes, we went to Café Barnard again.' She laughed. 'We go there so often now that I'm surprised they haven't allocated a table for our sole use. But that's not what was so good about the day—it was that Gaston joined us.'

He glanced at her sharply, and then looked quickly away. 'So that's why he didn't have breakfast with Marc and me. You and Simonne will have been a prettier sight across the table.'

'Flatterer!' She reached across and squeezed his arm affectionately. 'But no, it wasn't that. In a way, it was work for him. I didn't see it at the time, but it occurred to me when we got home this evening.'

'Were you and Simonne out all day?' he asked in surprise.

'No, we got back well before lunch. But after my siesta, Gaston came by in his car and we went for a short drive in the Old Quarter.'

He frowned. 'Couldn't you have asked Tuan to drive you there or taken a pousse-pousse? Presumably, Gaston's still got work to do.'

'But it *was* work. He's not yet told you, but he's been given a fascinating project, that's very worthwhile. And I'm going to help him.'

She explained to Philippe what Gaston had said that morning, and how they'd driven around the native area in the afternoon, with Gaston stopping every so often to make some notes.

They'd decided whereabouts to begin his survey, and he'd told her he was going to get the plans for the sewage system in the Old Quarter. He intended to approach the task systematically.

Philippe stared ahead in silence.

'Aren't you glad that Gaston thinks I can help him?' she asked after a few minutes.

'He's an engineer—you're not. I'm not quite sure in what way you could help.'

'By talking to the women about their daily routine, and asking how they manage with washing, and so on. They're more likely to open up to me than to a man. It'll tell Gaston what he must address.'

'I would have thought that fairly obvious. You need only drive once through the native quarter to see what the people need—they need proper sanitation.'

'And Gaston's going to find the best way of giving it to them. He wants to build on what's already there, rather than tear it down and start again. That's what he said.'

'I'm sure he did,' he said coldly.

She looked at him in surprise. 'I'm picking up that you don't think this a good idea. Surely, you can't be saying that we should ignore the suffering of the natives who live there, and think only of ourselves? Or are you?'

'Don't be ridiculous! Of course I'm not. If their lot can be improved, I'm all for it.'

'Then what's the matter?' she asked tersely. 'D'you think I'm a brainless woman, who's no use for anything more demanding than supervising the efficient housekeeper running the household?'

'I think you're deluded, not brainless. He's flattered you, and you've fallen for it.'

'For what reason exactly?' She glared at him.

He turned to her. 'When you're not scowling at me, you're really lovely, Lucette. You're young, beautiful, slender and full of vitality. What hot-blooded Frenchman wouldn't want to get you alone in his car?'

She laughed scornfully. 'Gaston's not like that. He's never made any attempt to indicate that he sees me as anything other than your wife. And what's more, he asked Simonne, too. It's just that she didn't want to do it. You seem to be the only one who can't see that there can be more to a woman than what immediately hits the eye.'

She stood up.

'I've suddenly lost my appetite. Please, make my apologies to Cook and Madame Fousseret. I won't be having any dinner this evening.'

27

T *he following day*

PHILIPPE LED the way into the café, and sat down at the nearest table, his back to the road. Marc took the seat opposite him. Philippe raised his finger to summon a waiter.

'Are you having breakfast or just coffee?' Philippe asked as the waiter came across to their table.

'Omelette, baguette and coffee,' Marc told the waiter.

Philippe gave the same order for himself, and then sat back, tapping the table.

'I've never seen you so forceful,' Marc said, looking at Philippe with amused curiosity, 'and I'm wondering what's behind it. One minute I was working in the office, and the next you were dragging me out. Not that I'm complaining—I was ready for a break. But I doubt this is just about hunger and thirst.'

Philippe nodded. 'It isn't.'

Marc raised his eyebrows. 'So?'

'Let's get some coffee into us first,' he said as the waiter approached them.

The waiter put a coffee in front of each of them, and left.

Philippe picked up his spoon, stirred his coffee, and then took a sip.

'Is this a guessing game?' Marc asked. 'Or are you going to tell me what's bothering you? Because something certainly is.'

Philippe looked up at Marc, strain visible in his eyes. 'I think Gaston might be interested in Lucette. And I'm afraid she might not realise it.'

Marc gave a dismissive laugh. 'Never! It's clear that he likes her, but I've never seen so much as a single flirtatious glance from him to her. You must be mistaken.' He paused. 'I take it that's why you didn't want us to collect him on the way here.'

'It is.'

'So what's put such an idea into your head?'

Philippe recounted the conversation with Lucette the evening before. 'It all ended on a bad note, and we didn't even speak to each other this morning,' he finished.

'Then I suggest you take the rest of the day off, get Lucette some flowers, go home and tell her what an idiot you were, and that of course you trust her.'

'Gaston's the one I don't trust.'

'If I were you, I wouldn't put it quite like that to Lucette. You're implying that you think she could be swayed by a few charming words.'

'The trouble is, I'm not sure that I don't think that,' Philippe said miserably. 'You've got to admit he's good looking, full of confidence, and has bags of personal charm.'

'And so have you, Philippe. Don't do yourself down.

Lucette obviously adores you. Whatever you do, don't let her think you believe she might give in to Gaston.' He glanced above Philippe's shoulder and swiftly straightened up. 'You'd better take yourself in hand,' he hissed, 'and quickly. Gaston's heading straight for us.'

'Good morning, gentlemen,' Gaston said, reaching the table. He pulled up a chair and sat down. 'I'll have whatever they've ordered, and a coffee right now, please,' he told the waiter who'd appeared at his side.

'What a pleasant surprise!' Philippe remarked, and he managed a smile. 'We assumed you'd be down in the Old Quarter, your nose in the sewers.'

Gaston threw back his head and laughed. 'You've been talking to Lucette,' he said cheerfully. 'I knew I should've told you first. Women can rarely keep a thing to themselves. Not that I asked her to—there's no reason for secrecy. But I'd wanted to tell you myself about my new project.'

'We've not been here long,' Marc said, 'so Philippe hasn't had time to go into any detail.'

'I couldn't, anyway,' Philippe said. 'Lucette didn't really say much. Just that she was helping you.'

'So what are you doing exactly?' Marc asked curiously. 'And in what way is Lucette able to help? Is it perhaps something that Simonne could do, too?'

Gaston pulled a despairing face. 'I asked them both—it's what I wanted. But Simonne disliked the idea of going to the places we'd have to visit, so she turned me down.'

'Is it that you're meant to be coming up with ideas for improving their sewage system?' Philippe asked as the waiter brought their breakfast to the table.

They stopped talking until he'd put their food in front of them, refilled their cups and had left the table.

'That's right. And the sooner I produce some plans, the better.'

'Everyone knows that the sewage system in the native area is far too small and too rudimentary for so many people,' Philippe said bluntly. 'But the system's been like that since the turn of the century, so why the sudden urgency?'

Gaston smiled at them in satisfaction. 'Because there's now some money for this. Isn't that always the reason why long-overdue action suddenly happens? You've got to admit, in our area, we've got an elaborate, complex system with running water and lavatories.'

'Of course, we have,' Philippe said, his food untouched.

'And we've built wide, tree-lined boulevards to give us ventilation and protection from the sun. None of that's true in the native area.'

'And you're going to change that overnight, are you?' Philippe asked.

'No, but we're making a start. We can't, in all fairness, leave things as they are for much longer. In the rainy season, waste runs into the river, and the sewers backflow and foul the streets in the native quarter. I hope I'm not putting you off your omelette, Marc,' Gaston added, grinning.

Marc laughed. 'It's a tribute to the chef that you're not.'

'I've been asked to see what can be done to improve the situation. There'll need to be more septic tanks, I'm sure, but the question is where to put them.'

'It sounds quite complicated,' Philippe said, picking up his fork.

Gaston nodded. 'It is. But we owe it to the natives. After all, when we tore down their wood and thatch homes to build an area for ourselves, we encouraged them to move into the Thirty-Six Streets. But then we spent all of the available money on our area, not theirs. Effectively, we caused the problems they now face, so it's up to us to put it right.'

'It's clearly something that needs sorting,' Philippe said slowly. 'But where does Lucette fit in?'

'I need to find out exactly how the residents live in the Old Quarter, which means questioning the women. It's basic to determining where to install new tanks. But I think the native women wouldn't be open with me in the way they would with Lucette and Simonne.'

'You could be right about that,' Marc said.

'I'm sure I am. If *I* approached them, they'd be frightened that they were doing something wrong, and they'd tell me what they thought I wanted to hear. I believe that Lucette, with her gentle manner and genuine interest, could persuade them to tell her the truth. And Simonne, too, had she wanted to do it.'

Marc glanced at Philippe and raised his eyebrows.

'That makes sense, I suppose,' Philippe said.

'Of course, not all the natives will speak French,' Gaston went on, tearing off a piece of baguette. 'If it's a problem to find enough who do, I'll take an interpreter with us. I'll get a native, of course. But the more help I get the better,' he added, 'and if Simonne changes her mind, Marc, I'd love to have her along.'

Marc sat back and smiled at Gaston. 'I'd like to be able to say that she probably will, but I think it unlikely. We all know Simonne's opinions about the Old Quarter. She goes to the north of it to see her friends, and she goes there when she needs to buy something. But her nose is wrinkled in distaste from the minute she enters the area until the minute she leaves. I don't think you'd get much from a native woman if she saw Simonne approaching her, holding her nose.'

The three of them laughed.

'Another coffee?' Gaston offered.

IT WAS possible that it was, indeed, harmless, Philippe thought grudgingly as they crossed the road on their way back to the Résidence.

What Gaston had said actually did make sense. He'd heard colleagues who'd been there longer complaining about the sewers emptying waste into the Fleuve Rouge, and that could hardly be a healthy situation for the river and for those who used its water.

And what he'd said about Simonne had the ring of truth, too. He didn't doubt that she'd have instantly turned down his request for help.

On several occasions, he'd heard her negative comments about the Old Quarter. And Lucette had relayed to him some of the things Simonne had said, too.

And Gaston had seemed genuinely disappointed not to have Simonne's help.

He'd make his apologies to Lucette as soon as he got home. She needed to know that he trusted her. And he'd take Marc's advice and send out a secretary in search of a bouquet of flowers, which he'd give her as soon as he saw her.

All the same, it wouldn't hurt to keep a close eye on what she and Gaston were doing, he decided, climbing the steps to the entrance.

AT TIMES, it was almost impossible to believe that two such intelligent, educated people could be so easily taken in, Gaston thought as he walked up the steps between Philippe and Marc, but thank goodness they could. It made his job so much easier.

Of course, he had no need of Lucette.

And he would have been utterly horrified to have had Simonne tagging along as well, as that would have defeated the purpose of taking Lucette.

That Marc and Philippe could actually believe he needed Lucette's help beggared belief.

By the following morning, he'd have the plans for the sewage system beneath the Old Quarter. And given that he'd thoroughly familiarised himself with the geology of the area for fear that he'd be asked searching questions the next time he saw the two men—he laughed inwardly, the questioning couldn't have been more gentle and less penetrating—he'd effectively have all he needed to take it from there by himself.

So no, he didn't need Lucette's input.

But that didn't mean that he wasn't going to ask her to go with him every day for the next couple of weeks, because he certainly was.

Trying hard to keep a straight face, he went through the door that Marc was holding open for him.

Marc looked at Gaston's back as he let the door close behind him.

It had all sounded highly plausible, and from the fact that Philippe was clearly more relaxed, he had taken what Gaston had said at face value.

He himself, though, had once or twice been tempted to probe a little deeper, to ask some questions that would have called for a depth of knowledge about the terrain. But he'd held himself in check, and they'd asked Gaston virtually nothing.

Rather, they'd just let him talk.

To have questioned Gaston too deeply could have been counter-productive.

He didn't have a shred of doubt about Gaston being able to answer anything put to him, but in forcing him to display his knowledge, he might have alerted Gaston to the fact that he wasn't automatically being taken in by everything Gaston told them.

He'd had a slight feeling of disquiet about Gaston for a while now, but he didn't really know why.

It was no more than a hunch, and it probably meant nothing, but he was so aware of the risks he was taking daily that he was inevitably suspicious of everything new.

And Gaston hadn't actually been in their lives for very long—it just felt as if he had.

And now he would be spending a lot of time with Lucette, and in the Old Quarter, too, where the revolutionaries had their headquarters, and that was a definite cause for concern.

Lucette knew the truth about him and Mai. One wrong word, one casual remark by her, and he could end up in Hoa Lo.

Of course, Gaston seeking Lucette's help might not mean anything at all, and be no more than a coincidence, but only a fool would totally ignore it.

And it was also possible that Philippe's suspicions were correct, and Gaston had an amorous interest in Lucette.

She was certainly a very pretty woman. Philippe worked a long day, and often on Saturdays, too, and Lucette could be feeling a little neglected.

She didn't yet have a child to occupy her, and the attentions of Gaston, were he to adopt a flirtatious manner towards her when Philippe wasn't around, might be well received.

So, he thought, watching Gaston head for his office, he'd keep an eye on him.

And it would be a wise precaution for the revolutionaries to move their headquarters to a different part of the Old Quarter. He'd suggest that.

They'd been at that house for long enough.

There were bound to be people watching the area, determined to establish the source of the newspapers circulating in the local villages, and of the anti-French propaganda that appeared regularly, posted to pillars and walls. And at some point, the activity around the house could arouse suspicion.

He'd leave a message to that effect for Mai that evening.

28

A week and a half later
Friday

'So ALL IN ALL, it's been a thoroughly irritating week,' Gaston told Emile. He folded his arms and scowled.

'I don't believe I've ever seen you look so beaten, Gaston,' Emile said.

'I'm not beaten!' Gaston snapped, straightening up. 'I'm frustrated. That's all. There's nothing I can't sort out, but it's annoying to have to do so.'

'So what're you going to do? Will you continue taking the woman out with you every day?'

'Of course. In fact, that part of the plan is working out very satisfactorily. She's always been perfectly friendly towards me, if perhaps a little on her guard at first. But she's now much more relaxed, and could be close to confiding in me.'

'You've done well there, then.'

Gaston nodded. 'So it seems. I have to admit, though, that her husband may be unwittingly helping me. Firstly, he's made it clear by his manner that despite what he says, he doesn't trust her to be alone with me, and that's really upset her. He's being a complete idiot by antagonising a woman who clearly loves him.'

'And secondly?'

He smiled. 'He's part of the administration that's responsible for the situation in the native quarter. However unintentionally it's come about, conditions there are very poor, and we've been ignoring it for years. Obviously, he isn't personally responsible—he's not even been here for a year—but it wasn't too difficult to suggest a collective guilt, of which he's a part. And with me hinting strongly that I'm the one who's pushing for action, not Philippe, I'm afraid that poor Philippe is some way behind in the popularity stakes.'

Emile chuckled. 'So what's been irritating about the week? It sounds to me as if everything's well on track.'

Gaston shifted his position. 'Apart from the fact that I've someone with me all day, so I don't get a break from the role I'm playing, which can be a strain, this past week's been marked by a total silence from my operatives.'

Emile sat up. 'Why's that?'

'Because the idiots took a deplorable amount of time to realise that the revolutionaries are no longer using the house we identified. With no one going in or out of the alley, there was no one to follow, and it took them far too long to account for it. I wasn't told that they'd moved headquarters till Monday, can you believe it? We've lost all that valuable time.'

'I see,' Emile said slowly. 'Why d'you think they've moved?'

Gaston shrugged. 'Headquarters like that are continually

being changed. Think of the number of people who come and go throughout the week—far more than for a normal home, which could arouse the neighbours' suspicion, and they'd be aware of that. What I don't think it means, having given it a lot of thought, is that they suspect we know about them.'

'I hope you're right,' Emile said, sounding less than convinced.

'I am,' he said firmly. 'So the next thing is to find out the new address. It was Mai who took us to their headquarters last time, and I'm counting on her to lead us there again.'

'It's her day off tomorrow, Gaston. If she doesn't go there, we've lost another week.'

'She'll go there, Emile. Trust me.'

PHILIPPE AND LUCETTE sat side by side on the verandah, neither of them saying a word.

The only sounds to be heard were the continuous clicking of crickets, along with the familiar fanfare from the insects of the night, and the distant strains of people, traffic and music that rose from the cafés and boulevards that had yet to go to sleep.

Gradually, the crimson sky took on a deep purple hue. A light breeze stirred the air, rustling the leaves, and wisps of cloud scudded across the ivory face of the moon.

'We've sat out here every night of the week,' Philippe said quietly, breaking the silence between them, 'politely asking questions of each other about our day's activities. Communicating with each other, a person might say, but at the same time, not communicating.'

Lucette turned to look at him. 'Is that a riddle?' she asked.

He shook his head. 'Unfortunately not. It's a fact.'

She turned back to the view, and for several moments, neither spoke.

'I don't know what you want me to say,' she said at last. 'I always ask what you've been doing in the day, and you usually tell me. That's communication, isn't it?'

'Is it? I sometimes think I could save you some effort if I just gave you my calendar for the day,' he said, a trace of bitterness in his tone. 'Then you could read the details for yourself, and there'd be no need to ask me.'

'If I did that,' she said coldly, 'what conversation would we have at the end of the day? And as you've just implied, communication is important.'

He raised his eyebrows. 'Do you call it conversation, or communication, you asking as a matter of routine what I've done and me telling you?'

'That would be very one-sided if that's all it were. But you ask me what *I've* done in the day. And I tell you.'

'Of course I ask you. I'm interested in knowing the answer,' he said.

'But not in the way you should be!' she exclaimed. She turned in her chair to face him. 'Whatever you ask, Philippe, however the question is phrased, whether it's about what I've seen, whether it's if I've spoken to any native women that day, whether it's if we've come up with any suggestions for improvements yet, you're actually asking one question only. It's there in your voice, in your face. And it's insulting.'

'And what exactly is that question?' he asked, colouring.

'What's going on between Gaston and me? That's what you're really asking.'

'Well, do you blame me?' he exclaimed. 'He's a good-looking man, full of charm and confidence. When you've seen him, you look so happy and so alive. What do you expect me to think?'

'I expect you to be pleased that your wife is enjoying having something more to do in the day than just meeting a friend for coffee or going shopping or going to Club French,' she snapped. 'Don't get me wrong, I like having coffee with Simonne, and I like going shopping or whatever we do, but that doesn't mean to say that I don't want any more in my life than that.'

'There must be other things you could do.'

'Maybe there are. I don't know. But what Gaston is doing is interesting, and very worthwhile. You should have seen the shock on his face when he saw the way the natives live— really saw, not just glanced at in passing. I don't think he'd realised before how truly bad they are. I'm just glad he thinks I can help.'

'I see,' he said tersely.

She hesitated. 'I hope you're not asking me to stop helping him. To do so would be saying that you don't trust me.'

'Would it be so very bad to ask, Lucette? You're my wife.'

'Yes, it would. Trust is at the heart of a marriage. If you don't trust me, what does that say about us?'

'I don't want to answer that, and I won't.' He finished his brandy, and hesitated. 'Have you thought about how it must look to other people? What my colleagues and friends might think, you being alone on a regular basis with a man who's not your husband?'

She caught her breath.

'And have you thought about what people might think about me? They could think I'm weak, too scared to stand up to a man who could be wrecking my marriage. Just because you no longer need a chaperone, it doesn't mean that it's wise to engage in behaviour a chaperone would've condemned.'

The colour drained from her face. 'To be honest, I hadn't thought about that.'

'Then I'd like you to start thinking now about the points I've made. And I'll give you something else to think about. Can you honestly say that your attitude towards me hasn't changed in the past two or three weeks? And if you're honest enough to admit to yourself that it has, is it really so reprehensible of me to think this might be a result of Gaston's effect on you?'

He stood up.

'Anyway,' he added. 'Now that you know the way I feel, I'll leave it at that. Come on, let's go to bed.'

Distraught, and close to tears, she rose to her feet and followed him.

THE HOUSE FINALLY SILENT, Mai stood in front of the kitchen door, staring towards the darkness at the back of the garden, her face anxious.

Where had Vinh been all week, she thought, biting her lower lip. She missed him. Their few minutes together every so often had come to mean so much to her, and now it had been almost a week since she'd seen him, almost a week since she'd felt his arms around her.

On the Monday night, she'd collected a message from the box by the side gate, and hidden it as usual in the tamarind tree. She'd waited a little, but there'd been no sign of Vinh.

The following morning, she'd checked the hollow and, to her surprise, the message was still there. He obviously hadn't gone there the night before.

She'd been tempted to go out again late on the Tuesday night in the hope of catching Vinh, but in the end, she'd decided not to risk it.

With Mme. Delon now knowing what she was doing, she was nervous about going too often to the back of the garden, and without a genuine reason.

On the Wednesday morning, she'd done as she had on the Tuesday and had checked in the tree before the house was awake. The message was still in the tree.

And on the Thursday morning, too.

And also that morning. It was still just that one message. There hadn't been anything else in the week from M. Bouvier.

While it was unusual that Vinh hadn't been to the tree at all in the week, it wasn't the first time it had happened, and she hadn't been concerned—just surprised.

He'd sometimes spend a few days in one of the local villages, offering support to the village's revolutionary group, and when that happened, there'd be no sign of him at all in the week.

But as it was Friday, he might be back in Hanoi by now, and she decided to take a chance and go to the tree that night in the hope of seeing him.

The chance of having a few minutes with him made it worth the tiny risk of being seen by Mme. Delon, and challenged by her.

She checked that her torch was in her pocket, went quietly through the kitchen doorway into the garden, and closed the door behind her.

Reaching the tamarind tree, she switched on the torch and shone the beam into the hollow. The message was still there.

Good, she thought. She hadn't missed him, and she

edged back into the dark shadow thrown by a nearby banyan tree, and started to wait in the hope that Vinh would appear.

But Vinh didn't come.

After waiting for as long as she dared, she turned away in dejection and returned to the house.

If, by any chance, the message was still there the following morning, which was her day off, she'd take it herself to the new headquarters in the native area.

Her spirits lifted. She might see him there.

AT LAST, the operative thought, emerging from his hiding place in the cluster of trees that grew beyond the railings.

He'd begun to fear, with Mai standing there for so long, that the week's efforts were going to be wasted.

With Vinh's time of arrival so unpredictable, the longer that Mai remained there, the greater the risk that Vinh would arrive while Mai was still there.

If that had happened, Vinh would have found the message in the hollow, and his boss's plan would've been thwarted.

It was a miracle that it had worked as well as it had that week, he thought, running swiftly across to the tamarind tree.

Every evening, he'd managed to remove the message she'd placed in the tree, and be safely back in his place of concealment, before Vinh arrived to collect it.

All he'd had to do was wait until Vinh had checked the tree, found nothing and left. And then he'd returned the message to its hiding place, to be there for whenever Mai checked the tree again.

The hollow, therefore, had been empty each night when

Vinh arrived, but it had contained Bouvier's message whenever Mai had peered into the hollow.

Reaching the tree, he swiftly removed the message, and clutching it tightly, ran back to the trees and crouched down.

He'd been back in his position for no more than a minute or two when he heard stealthy footsteps to his left, and a moment later, he saw Vinh walk out from the shadows.

He watched Vinh check the tree and then straighten up, realising that there was nothing for him to collect.

He lingered for a moment or two, glancing towards the Delons' house, clearly hoping to see Mai. And then he turned away and was once again lost in the density of trees.

When he was sure that Vinh had definitely gone, he ran across to the tree, returned the message to the hollow, and then crept alongside the railings to the foliage in which he'd concealed his bicycle.

He walked the bicycle to the road, and then pedalled furiously to the Old Quarter, to the house he shared with the operative who'd need to be outside the Delons' house very early the next day, the day on which Mai was certain to deliver the message to the house that the terrorists were now using.

29

S *aturday*

WEARING an inconspicuous brown tunic top over black trousers, a brown scarf wound around her head, and carrying a basket containing a red silk scarf that she'd grabbed as an afterthought as she was leaving her room, Mai turned on to Avenue Chavassieux.

Her head down, she hurried past the City Hall to Boulevard Francis Garnier, where she crossed over, turned right and followed the path that ran alongside the Petit Lac.

The surface of the dark green lake was sheened with the light of the burgeoning day, but she hardly noticed the beauty of the scene in her anxiety to reach the Old Quarter in safety and unseen.

While she knew that Vinh and his friends changed their headquarters with regularity, the suddenness of the move, and the few words to her from M. Bouvier in which he'd stressed the importance of remaining alert at all times, had left her unusually fearful that someone might be watching her.

When she reached the top of the boulevard, she hesitated.

To her right was Place des Cocotiers, the terminus for the trams. Perhaps she should take the Line 2 tram the short distance north that she needed to go. It could make it more difficult for anyone to follow her.

Not that she thought that anyone was.

In fact, she was sure that they weren't.

But if they were, and if they were close behind, they could get on the tram at the same time as she did. So, in such a circumstance, she'd actually be making it easier for them to follow her.

She decided against taking the tram.

Of course, she could always abandon the idea of seeing if Vinh was at the headquarters, go back to the house and replace the message in the hollow of the tree. Vinh was sure to pick it up within a couple of days.

Going back home should definitely be considered. Vinh had always said that if ever she was in doubt about whether or not she was being followed, she must trust her instinct and go home.

She glanced back along the lakeside path.

There was absolutely nothing suspicious there. No one was taking any interest in her.

She looked back at the road ahead. She was being silly.

She'd been so looking forward to seeing Vinh on her day off that if there was any possible chance of doing so, she ought to take it. And furthermore, M. Bouvier had left the message several days earlier so it really was time it was delivered.

She'd continue to the headquarters, she decided. There was no reason not to.

She turned briskly into Rue du Pont-en-Bois, and headed for the junction with Rue de la Philharmonic.

Chilled by a sudden strange sensation that engulfed her, she stopped abruptly.

Her skin prickling, she looked behind her again.

But still there was nothing to see, nothing out of the ordinary.

She bit her lower lip. Should she go back home, or return to Place des Cocotiers and pick up the tram that would take her up to Rue Jean Dupuis?

No, she wouldn't do either, she resolved. She was better on foot. She knew the Old Quarter very well. There wasn't anyone watching her, but if there were, she was sure she'd be able to lose them.

She glanced across the road, and then again behind her.

There was absolutely nothing she could see to justify her fear.

When she'd first agreed to deliver messages to the revolutionary headquarters, Vinh had shown her the sort of things that would indicate that someone was following her. He'd cautioned her to watch out for them, and had told her the kind of evasive action to take in suspicious circumstances.

But really, there were none of the signs that Vinh had mentioned.

Was she being overly fanciful, she wondered, and seeing what wasn't there, merely because she was aware that Mme. Delon now knew what she was doing, and no matter what Madame had said, she might tell her husband.

She decided that she was.

However, even though no one seemed to be following

her, it would be sensible for her to behave as if they were. You could never be too careful, as both M. Bouvier and Vinh had repeatedly told her.

And if, when she reached the new headquarters, she had any suspicion at all that she was being followed, even if it was no more than an instinctive feeling, she'd continue walking past the house and go back home.

It would be better to return the message to the hollow in the tree rather than risk giving away the location of the headquarters.

As she was going to behave as if she was being followed, she wouldn't go as far as Rue de la Philharmonic, she decided, but would turn off into Rue de la Soie. It was always crowded with those who wanted to buy silk, and with people heading for the market that continued into the night, it would be easy to conceal herself among the crowds.

And also, because the tram went up Rue de la Soie, she'd have an alternative to walking, if she suddenly wanted to get away quickly.

Feeling better in herself, she walked across to Rue de la Soie, and then paused on the corner. Staring up the street, she tried to spot anyone out of place, or anyone who seemed to be lingering deliberately.

But there was nothing.

The road was filled with the usual men on bicycles, with pousse-pousse coolies and cars, and with meandering street sellers.

Whole families had emerged as they always did from the dark, airless confines of the narrow alleys that led to their cramped homes, and were sitting on chairs placed at either side of the entrance to the alley, where they'd stay for the day, watching the people and traffic pass them by, or talking to friends who'd stopped to chat.

On both sides of the road, people were already crouching in the gutters, preparing to sell their fruit and vegetables.

And at intermittent roadside stalls, men in palm-leaf hats were preparing noodles, wanton and chowder, while columns of white steam belched upwards. Gathered around the stalls, the customers ere eating from small hand-held bowls, some using chopsticks, some their fingers.

Lining both sides of the street, in a dazzling panoply of colour, open-fronted stalls were displaying lengths of silk of every hue.

Hovering above the road and the people, the smell of the drains was strong, and of oil and garlic, boiled noodles, spices and dust, and the air resounded with sound: the hooting of traffic; the screeching and squawking of cats, pigs and chickens, some caged, some free; the cries of delight from the small children chasing the animals.

She smiled in relief. The scene, both in front of her and behind, was as it always was at that time of the day. There was nothing at all to cause alarm.

She'd made the right decision to take this street. All she had to do was get from that point to Rue Jean Dupuis, just five or six streets to the north of where she now stood, and she'd have achieved her goal.

Remembering what she'd been told about ensuring that she wasn't being followed, she paused in front of one of the narrow shops, and then went inside, feigning an interest in the bales of silk piled high on stands on both sides of the shop and along the middle of the aisle.

As she rounded the aisle at the far end and started to come back down the other side, she glanced surreptitiously towards the part of the pavement she could see, looking for anyone leaning against an opposite store, or crouching in the gutter while conspicuously covering their face with their hat or a newspaper, or in any way standing out.

Or someone whose shape or stance seemed familiar, as if she'd seen that person earlier on in the day.

But there was no such person.

She hurried out of the shop, and promptly ran across the street to the other side, darting as she did so between a tram and a horse-drawn wagon. A tailor's shop stood in front of her, and she quickly went inside.

At the end of the central aisle, which was lined with wooden mannequins displaying silk garments that could be made by the tailor, she swiftly removed the red silk scarf from her basket, and draped it over her head and around her shoulders.

Then she left the tailor's and turned right, as if to go back the way she'd come.

Moments later, she reached a narrow alley leading off Rue de la Soie, which she knew had a means of exit at the other end.

Members of a family were sitting on either side of the entrance, and she paused and spoke to the oldest woman, asking her if she knew the whereabouts of the friend she was looking for. She came up with a false name for her friend, and described her in an affectionate, but amusing, way.

The old woman laughed, and shook her head.

Having established a degree of familiarity with the family in order to throw off the track anyone who might be wondering if the woman in the red silk scarf was the same as the woman in brown who'd entered the tailor's shop a few moments earlier, she plunged into the alley, and hurried along to the exit.

Coming out of the alley on to a quiet road that paralleled Rue de la Soie, she glanced to her left at the people coming towards her.

There was no one she thought she'd seen before.

Nevertheless, she slipped into the jewellery shop next to her, and lingered there, pretending to look at the jewellery, while all the time watching to see if anyone exited the alley after her.

They didn't.

Feeling much more confident, she left the jeweller's, turned right and hurried northwards. As she walked, she glanced occasionally behind her, but when she'd not seen anyone suspicious—and on a road like that, which was so much quieter than Rue de la Soie, such a person would almost certainly have stood out—she felt sufficiently confident to turn right at the next street she reached.

The short street took her back to Rue de la Soie. She turned left and continued up the street.

She preferred having crowds around her, she decided, as she'd be able to lose herself among people, if necessary.

But it wouldn't be necessary, she was sure. She'd seen nothing untoward.

She decided, however, as she neared Rue Jean Dupuis, that it might be wise to have something less bright over her head, just in case she'd been spotted earlier, and having lost her, they were still looking for her, so she darted into the nearest silk shop.

There she bought a length of dusky blue silk, swapped the red silk for the blue, tucked the red silk low in her basket where it wouldn't be seen, hastened out of the shop and continued to Rue Jean Dupuis.

Even if there *had* been anyone following her, she thought as she neared the revolutionaries' house, and she was certain there hadn't, she was bound to have lost them with the disguises she'd adopted and by doubling back on herself.

Taking such precautions had got her back into the way of being on the alert when going to the headquarters, and that was no bad thing. It would prevent her from ever leading the Sûreté there.

A confident lightness in her steps, she turned into Rue Jean Dupuis.

'THE WHOLE THING set us back a couple of weeks,' Gaston told Emile, 'but now we're on track again. We know the location of the new headquarters, and by tomorrow morning, I'll have teams of operatives watching it, and they'll follow anyone setting out for the villages. As a result, I've been able to relax our vigil on the Delons' house.'

Emile nodded. 'You've done remarkably well, Gaston. I can't imagine how you did it, but you actually got the girl to go to the headquarters today!' He shook his head in wonderment. 'And successfully followed her there.'

'That was down to the operatives. I warned them that she was pretty sure to try some of the usual diversionary tactics, since this was the first time she'd been there, so I put four operatives on to the case.'

Emile nodded. 'Good thinking.'

'I also thought that whatever it was that happened between Lucette and Marc Bouvier, it might have caused the change of headquarters, and put the terrorists on high alert.'

'I doubt that,' Emile said dismissively. 'As you say, terrorists regularly move their headquarters. Doesn't mean a thing.'

'You may be right. But personally, despite what I told you

before, I'm inclined to think that the timing *could* be significant.'

Emile sat back and stared hard at him. 'Are you saying that you think Madame Delon knows what Bouvier's doing, and that, for fear she might report him, he suggested a change of base?'

'No, not at all. I'm sure that if she knew about Bouvier's treason, she'd report it, or her husband would've done—she'd never keep such a thing from her husband. And failing to report Bouvier would make her as guilty as he. But we've heard nothing.'

'Quite so.'

'But even apart from that, she'd never betray her country. She's essentially moral, and loves France. Yes, she deplores the conditions in the Old Quarter, but she's praiseworthy of the improvements that France, through me, is now about to make. She'd never support the terrorists, directly or indirectly.'

Emile stroked his chin. 'I see. Yet you're connecting a conversation she had with Bouvier with the change of headquarters?'

'The timing's a huge coincidence, and I'm no believer in coincidences.'

'So, what next, then?'

'Lucette's coming out with me again on Monday. There's something clearly troubling her. This could be to do with Bouvier, and I intend to find a way of drawing it out of her.'

'I was about to say you'll never be able to do that, Gaston,' Emile said wryly. 'But I know better now than to waste my breath.'

30

M *onday*

GASTON BROUGHT his Citroen to a stop alongside the Jardin
Fleuri Paul Bert, and put on the brake.

Lucette looked at him in questioning surprise.

'We've worked hard all morning,' he told her, 'and we've
seen some fairly ugly sights. I thought we could sit here in
the garden for a while, and restore our spirits in front of the
more beautiful sights of the lake and the flowers.'

'That's a lovely idea,' she said. She paused. 'Do you ever
get angry with France for the way the Vietnamese are forced
to live, Gaston?'

'No, I don't,' he replied without hesitation. 'We've made
mistakes here, yes. But that inevitably happens whenever
one country colonises another—it's not deliberate. The
important thing is to correct those mistakes as far as

possible once they've been identified. Just as you and I are trying to do.'

'But we're so rough in the way we treat the natives. That's not necessary, is it?'

'No, it isn't. And I deplore it. But unfortunately, you'll find brutal people in every walk of life. It's a fact. And in a situation like this, where the French are superior, it can bring out the worst in those with that tendency.'

'Yes, I can see that.'

'Look around you, Lucette. We've made a civilised city out of a place that couldn't even have been called a town. It's not just the French who're benefiting, but the Vietnamese, too.'

'I do hope that's true.'

'When we go for the coffee I hope we'll have before I drop you at your home, you'll see a café which employs a number of people, who, without our intervention, might have been condemned to a hard life in the paddy fields.'

She nodded. 'You're right, of course.'

He hesitated. 'Be careful where you talk about such concerns, Lucette, won't you? You wouldn't want anyone to think you're sympathetic to the terrorists, would you? I'd hate to see the wife of my friend, through casual remarks, get thrown into the prison her husband supervises. It's over-crowded enough as it is,' he said with a laugh.

'I'll be careful, I promise. I wouldn't say anything to anyone but you. And to Philippe, of course. And thank you for thinking of finishing the morning in this lovely garden,' she added with a smile. 'I can't think of anything better than relaxing here for a while, and then having coffee.'

'Let's find a bench, then, shall we?'

They got out of the car and strolled into the small flower garden.

Gaston indicated a wooden bench close to the statue of the former ambassador, Paul Bert, which faced the Petit Lac, and they went across to it and sat down.

Leaning against the back of the bench, they gazed towards the lake that glistened between flamboyant flame trees, on fire with orange-red blossom, and crepe myrtles, which dazzled with a profusion of pink and purple flowers.

'People's attitudes to trees are strange things,' Gaston said reflectively, breaking the companionable silence that had fallen between them. 'Tree worship is said to have arrived with Buddhism. Genies, spirits and wandering souls —all those who didn't have a proper burial—are thought to take shelter in banyan trees. That's why you often see shrines on or near the trees.'

'I didn't know that!' she exclaimed.

'And it's believed that the umbrella created by the trees makes a social space, and that private words whispered by lovers in that space are saved for all eternity.'

He glanced sideways at her. 'I think we're close enough to the trees to be in that social space, and thus able to speak freely to each other, don't you? But as friends, not lovers, of course.'

She blushed. 'What d'you mean?'

He gave her a wry smile. 'I think you know what I mean, Lucette,' he said. 'Our work this morning has prevented any personal discussion, but it hasn't escaped me that you're both worried and, if you'll forgive me for saying so, unhappy. I'd like to help you, if you'd let me.'

Her eyes filled with tears. 'Once again you've shown yourself to be really sensitive and perceptive, Gaston. I'm so glad you're my friend.'

He gave an awkward laugh. 'Now you're embarrassing me. It would be easier if you looked on it as a fair exchange.

You've been helping me with my project, and I'm very grateful. In return, I'd like to help you with whatever's bothering you.'

A tear rolled down her cheek. 'You're right, I *am* a little unhappy. *Very* unhappy, if I'm honest.'

Excitement surged through him.

With difficulty, he quelled it.

'Tell me about it, Lucette. Please, let me help,' he urged, his voice soothing, gentle.

'I've been so happy helping you with your work, Gaston. It's such an important project.' Her voice caught. She wiped her eyes. 'I hate to say this, but I'm going to have to stop coming with you. This must be my last day, and that's making me so very sad.'

His heart gave a dull thud.

He'd no longer be seeing Lucette every day!

'I won't pretend I'm not sorry,' he said, dragging the appropriate words from his throat as he struggled to rise above the wave of disappointment that suddenly engulfed him, 'because I am.'

He struggled to pull himself together.

'You've already been such a help in this short space of time,' he went on. 'But I respect your decision. I was taking up too much of your day. That was unforgivable of me, and I'm so sorry. Please do forgive my thoughtlessness.'

'Oh, no, Gaston,' she said quickly. 'You've done nothing wrong. I was happy to accompany you, to feel I was being useful.' She paused, pulled out her handkerchief and blew her nose. 'It's just that Philippe's not pleased I'm doing this.'

He stared at her in puzzlement. 'But I would've thought he'd be delighted that we're trying to help the natives. I know it's not in his remit to do this, but I thought he'd support any measures to improve their lot. Doesn't he?'

'Yes, he does. It's me being involved that he doesn't like. Basically, he thinks it'll look bad to his colleagues that I'm spending so much time alone with another man. That hadn't occurred to me, but men obviously think in a way that I wouldn't. And he also thought that some women, too, might misconstrue the situation, which would give me a bad reputation.'

He turned to her, an expression of alarm on his face that was easy to assume as he tried to cope with the unexpected emotions within him.

'I'm so sorry, Lucette. It hadn't occurred to me what people might think, and it should have done. Philippe is right.' He put both of his hands to his forehead. 'How can I have been so stupid?'

'Because you don't think like that, Gaston. You're a good man, and you were thinking only of your project. Recognising its urgency, you wanted to complete your report as quickly as possible, and you weren't giving any thought as to what idle gossips might say.'

He nodded. 'It's kind of you to see it like that.'

'As I'm not able to help any more, will it make it much more difficult for you?'

He smiled at her. 'I forbid you to worry about that. I'll manage. It'll take a little longer, but you can be sure that I'll get there.'

'I'm glad,' she said.

They smiled ruefully at each other, and then turned away to look towards the water.

'I think we'll have that coffee now, don't you?' he said after a few minutes. And he stood up.

.   .   .

AT LEAST, now that he was away from Lucette's presence, he'd be able to look at the situation more clearly, he thought as he drove away from the Delons' house and headed for Rue Bonheur and his home.

The morning had been a great disappointment. He was unlikely to get anything more from Lucette, but he was stuck with having to make the project look a genuine one.

He'd still be regularly meeting Marc and Philippe for breakfast before he headed up to the native area, or so they would think, so he'd need to be able to drop in a few casual comments to back up the fictitious project.

And as he had no intention of investigating the waste system himself, he'd have to chase City Hall for the copies of the earlier reports on the sewage system in the Old Quarter that he'd requested, and also any proposals for improvements that had been submitted, filed away and forgotten.

The extra work it would entail, merely to maintain an illusion that he no longer needed, was extremely vexatious.

Having Lucette with him had been the sole purpose of the sewer project.

Anyone would be disappointed that a plan they'd worked hard on had failed. It was no wonder he was in despair.

But it was more than that, he cried out inwardly as he turned into Rue Bonheur. He'd been so blind.

The failure of his plan wasn't the only reason for his dejection.

There was another reason—a very simple one. He liked Lucette enormously, and he'd miss her company.

No. Like wasn't strong enough.

Although he'd moaned to Emile about being encumbered with a woman, he'd actually loved having her at his side for the past week, and he was extremely sorry—no, it was more than that—he was completely distraught that she wouldn't be going out with him again.

Reaching his house, he stopped the car and stared through the windscreen at the road ahead.

Looking back over his adult years, he couldn't recall a single occasion when he'd felt anything at all for a person who was a part of the mission to which he'd been assigned.

In fact, he'd never felt close to anyone since Adèle.

Not until now.

But Lucette seemed to have crept into his affections without him being aware of it.

At least, not until that morning.

Until that morning, he'd thought his affection for her was that of a friend, and nothing more.

He was aware that had it been necessary, he would have attempted to pursue a romantic attachment, but it hadn't. And just as well, he'd told himself more than once, as such a liaison would never have come about.

Lucette wasn't the sort of woman to betray her husband, even when upset with him, as she clearly was—and he was glad of that. It would have diminished her in his eyes. Instead, it made him like and respect her even more.

Like, he used to tell himself, not love.

But now—stunned by the anguish that had swept through him that morning at the thought of no longer spending every day with her—he was being forced to face the truth about the nature of his feelings for her.

He wasn't just losing the companionship of a woman he genuinely liked and whose company he enjoyed, but the companionship of a woman he'd come to love.

Oh, Lucette! He put his head in his hands.

And a pang of desire surged through him.

31

'So I told Gaston this morning that I won't be going out with him again,' Lucette finished. 'I'll revert to being the wife I was before, who goes through the motions of supervising the household, and who has morning coffee and shops for clothes. That sort of thing.'

From his chair on the verandah, Philippe leaned across and took her hand.

'Thank you,' he said quietly. 'I do appreciate what you've done. I know you felt that you were contributing something very important, which would help others, and I'm sure you were.'

He gently squeezed her hand.

'The fact that you're ceasing to do this shows that you've put my feelings, and our status here, above the satisfaction you derived from the work, and I'm more grateful than I can say.'

Lucette looked at him, her eyes unnaturally bright. 'It hurt me to think I was making you unhappy. I love you, Philippe, and there was no other way to show you this.'

'I hope that one day, I, too, will have the chance to show you how very much I love you, because I do,' he said quietly.

'There's no need to feel you have to prove it,' she said. 'I know you do.' She paused. 'I'll see if Simonne wants to go to the café on Wednesday,' she added.

And she turned away so that Philippe wouldn't see the tears falling down her cheeks.

'I CAN SEE you're upset about it,' Simonne said, when on their Wednesday morning together, Lucette finished recounting what she'd told Philippe on the Monday night. 'But I do believe you've made the right decision.'

Lucette glanced around at the waiters tirelessly threading a path between the tables in Café Barnard, at the pousse-pousse coolies, often aged, jogging between the shafts for a handful of coins as they did all day, at the peasants, some barefoot, hurrying along the road in front of the café, many with heavy baskets slung from their shoulder poles.

'How can it be fair that we live so much better than they do?' she said in despair. 'You, yourself, have remarked on how awful the Old Quarter is. So how can I feel comfortable about not helping Gaston, which would have sped things up? Nothing can be done until the report's been handed in and digested.'

'You made your decision because you realised that the needs of the natives weren't the only considerations. The most important thing was what it was doing to you and Philippe.'

Lucette opened her mouth to reply.

Simonne held up her hand to stop her. 'No, don't deny it,' she said quickly. 'On the few occasions I've seen you with

Philippe since Gaston asked for our help, Philippe has seemed unhappy. And it's not just Philippe—neither of you were at ease with the other. If I had to hazard a guess, I'd say you'd been blaming poor Philippe for some of the things you'd been seeing.'

'Of course, I wasn't! Well, not much, anyway. No, I'm upset that Philippe didn't trust me to be alone with Gaston.'

'I'm sure he *did*, Lucette. The people who know you, know you'd never cheat on Philippe. That's the trouble.'

Lucette's brow creased. 'What d'you mean?'

'There are more people here who *don't* know you than do. That may not be true in a year's time, but it's true at the moment. And when people who don't know you, see you out with a man who's not your husband, they're bound to interpret the situation in a way that damages your reputation. That's the way people are. And once you've lost a good reputation, it's extremely hard to get it back.'

'That's what Philippe said. And Gaston agreed with him.'

'And Marc, too, would say the same. He's been unusually on edge during the past couple of weeks, and he's mentioned you and Gaston several times. He asked me what you two talk about, for example.'

Lucette looked at Simonne in surprise. 'Why would he do that.'

'He really likes Philippe, and I could tell he was anxious on Philippe's behalf. You spending so much time with Gaston was bound to reflect badly on Philippe. I'm sure that's the reason for his tetchiness.'

'Well, no one has reason to be anxious any longer. My short stint of work is now over,' she said shortly.

Simonne sat back and smiled. 'You've no idea how delighted I am to hear that. And not just for the sake of the men, but for me, too. I've missed our coffee mornings together.' She took a sip of her coffee. 'So what *did* you and Gaston talk about when you were out?'

Lucette laughed dismissively. 'I've no intention of turning us off our food when we still have cakes to eat, so I won't answer that. Suffice it to say, just be thankful you're French, not Vietnamese.'

She picked up the plate of macarons, and offered it to Simonne.

MAKING as little sound as possible, Mai came down the stairs after her siesta, and went into the kitchen.

As she'd hoped, there was no sign yet of Mme. Fousseret or Cook, nor of Mme. Delon.

Going quickly through the kitchen and scullery, she went out into the garden, and across to the box concealed in the foliage near the side gate.

To her relief, she saw that M. Bouvier had left a message.

Now she had a reason to go to the tree that evening, she thought in glee as she went across to the drying area and started taking down the clothes she'd hung there that morning.

With luck, she'd see Vinh. That moment couldn't come soon enough. Ever since her visit on Saturday to the Old Quarter, she'd been in a state of nervous anticipation, longing to talk to him about what she'd heard at the headquarters.

Vinh was in one of the villages outside Hanoi, she'd been told when she reached the new headquarters that Saturday. Everyone had seemed very busy, and they'd encouraged her to return to her French family, saying that Vinh would have much to do when he got there, and it would be better if she left it until the following week to see him.

But she'd been determined to wait for him, and she'd told them she'd stay there all day if necessary, even if she ended up with no more than a few minutes with him before she had to return to her home.

And she'd sat cross-legged on a bamboo mat in the corner of the crowded room, waiting.

While sitting there, she'd idly listened to what they were saying.

First, they'd talked about an escape plan.

Apparently, a handful of men were planning to escape from Hoa Lo, and there was something about them pretending to have a fatal disease and being taken to the hospital. But that hadn't meant anything much to her, and she'd not paid any real attention to their conversation.

Then they'd said something about the garrison, which hadn't interested her, either.

It was only when they'd started discussing a meeting in the Old Quarter that was soon to take place, to which representatives from the surrounding villages and from every revolutionary group would be coming, that she'd begun to listen more intently.

It sounded, from what she'd heard, as if the revolutionaries were planning to take to the streets at about the same time as the prison escape.

Vinh still hadn't arrived by the time they'd finished their discussions and had started to leave, so she'd had to go home without seeing him. Her disappointment on the way back was so acute that she couldn't think clearly about what she'd heard.

It was only the following morning that she'd realised the significance of the imminent meeting.

The attack on the French must be very soon. And when the French had left Hanoi, the struggle would be over and they'd marry. Vinh had said that again not so long ago.

But such an attack would be dangerous, and she felt a rush of fear for Vinh. Suppose they didn't win. Suppose he was hurt, or even worse.

No, she couldn't think like that. She mustn't.

Not after the hard work and planning for so many months. It couldn't have all been for nothing.

But if they *did* fail in their attempt to get rid of the French, and neither was hurt, they could still marry, even though, as Vinh had told her more than once, in such a circumstance, they'd have to leave Hanoi for their safety.

The first time he'd mentioned them moving away from Hanoi, she'd felt a violent shock at the idea of leaving the city that had been her home for several years, and of going far from the village in which they'd both grown up, and where her mother still lived. But she'd now come to terms with them possibly having to do so.

The most important thing was to be with Vinh, and for them both to be safe.

From the moment she'd realised the implications of what she'd heard, she'd been desperate to see Vinh. And after leaving the message in the tree that evening, she'd wait even longer than usual for him.

And if it became obvious that he wouldn't be coming that evening, she'd go out again the next night, and the next, until she saw him.

MARC SAT at the dinner table opposite Simonne, his gaze fixed on the single lotus blossom arranged in a low flat vase in the centre of the table.

Twirling the brandy in his glass, he listened as Simonne recounted Lucette's news about Gaston, and how she and Lucette had then gone for a stroll around the lake, followed by a quick look inside Les Grands Magasins Réunis.

When she stopped talking, he glanced up at her and smiled. 'Did you manage to ask her what she and Gaston talked about?'

'I did,' she said.

'Well?' he prompted.

'She offered me a cake!' She burst out laughing. 'It was quite funny at the time. But I'm sure she wasn't deliberately avoiding my question. It was just that we'd reached the end of the subject, and I think she wanted to forget about the whole thing, and talk about something else. Also, we'd have hardly enjoyed the macarons if she was telling me about squalor as we swallowed them.'

She laughed again.

He smiled. 'I can see that.'

'But if you're asking, Marc,' she said, her voice taking on a sudden seriousness, 'whether she and Gaston were having an affair, I can assure you they weren't.'

'I wasn't. Unlike Philippe, I don't for one minute think they were.'

She frowned. 'Then I don't understand why you're so keen to know what they talked about.'

'Actually, nor do I,' he said. He put his glass on the table and rested his chin on his hands. 'I won't lie to you, Simonne. There's nothing I can put my finger on, but my instinct tells me to be cautious around Gaston. Think about it. It's only six or seven months since he came into our lives, but now he's at the centre of most of our social activities.'

She frowned more deeply. 'But does that matter?'

'Yes and no. No, because social activities are just that—

people enjoying getting together and having a good time, and he's great company. And, yes, possibly. Philippe and I are high up in the administration. One of our responsibilities is the prison. And I'm an official link with the garrison.'

'I know all that.'

'Well, there are a number of rumours at the moment to the effect that an escape's in the offing, and that it could involve the troops. Obviously, the prison's a hotbed of anti-French activity—you'd expect that. But so, too, is the native quarter, I'm sure. And Gaston spends a lot of time there. That may or may not be significant.'

Simonne put her hand to her throat. 'D'you think he could secretly be a terrorist, then, an enemy of France? Surely not.'

'To be honest, I don't know what to think.'

'But if you're wary of him, why d'you invite him to have breakfast with you and Philippe, and to come to lunch with us, and so on?'

'A wise person keeps a close eye on anyone who could prove to be an enemy.'

She stared at him in open-mouthed amazement.

He cleared his throat. 'I just don't know what to think, Simonne. But if you were able to continue trying to find out what Gaston and Lucette talked about, and exactly what they did in the Old Quarter, it could help. Somehow, I can't see him knee deep in sewage. Can you?' He paused. 'D'you think you could do that?'

'You want me to spy on my friend?'

'It's Gaston, not Lucette, who's the focus on my interest. I want to know exactly what he's up to, if anything.'

'Well, I'll do my best, of course, but I'm sure you're mistaken.' She drummed her nails on the table. 'What makes you think I won't tell Lucette about your suspicions?'

'Because I know you'd never betray France, Simonne. And you might just be doing that if you told Lucette of my probably unfounded concern.'

'What d'you mean?'

'Lucette has no guile to her. If you alerted her, she might mention it in passing to Gaston, and if he *is* a terrorist, he'd promptly disappear and we'd lose a chance of catching the group. I said *if* he is a terrorist. To repeat, I don't know that he is. I'm merely following a hunch. Indulge me, please.'

'If I indulge you, how will you indulge me in return? And I'm not talking about that,' she added with a giggle, pointed up at the bedroom above them.

He assumed an expression of great disappointment. 'Then I suppose it'll have to be the cocktail dress you saw this morning, that you described to me in minute detail over the sole bonne femme, a woeful look on your face as you did so.'

She clapped her hands in glee. 'I think I'll call on Lucette tomorrow,' she said, and she laughed. 'I'll have the dress in cornflower blue, please.'

32

Tuesday

Mai shifted from one foot to the other as she stood in the shadows cast by the dark trunk of the tree that was closest to the tamarind in which the message for Vinh lay hidden.

She'd still been there when Monday had passed, and Tuesday had arrived.

Around her, fern fronds and leaves rustled in the darkness that had crept through the world, bringing with it the screeching of the birds that were ghosting through the night.

Faint sounds from beyond the railings reached her, and her heart leapt.

At last, she thought joyfully as she saw a dark shape emerge from the trees.

Pushing back the cluster of woody vines that blocked

her path, she inched forward, ready to approach the railings as soon as she was certain that it was Vinh.

The shape came closer—it was, indeed, Vinh.

She ran forward, the vines closing in behind her.

Both gripped the iron bars that separated them, and their cheeks touched.

Then Vinh drew back. He put his hand to her cheek, and gazed at her with love.

She covered his hand with hers, and sensed excitement coiled up within him.

'What is it, Vinh?' she asked, holding her breath, hardly daring to hope.

'It's going to happen, Mai.' His voice broke. 'We're rising against the French at midnight on Sunday in two weeks' time. The cells are already bringing the arms they've made to the headquarters.'

'Why a Sunday?'

'Because the French will have been to their church, and will be relaxed.'

'Yes, they will be,' she said in exhilaration. 'It's a good idea.'

'In the evening, the cooks will put something into the food to be given to the garrison troops and to those in the military outposts. And then we'll come out into the streets and take over the buildings used by the French. And there'll be an escape, too, by the prisoners who've managed to have themselves admitted to the hospital.'

His eyes glowed with fervour

'I knew it!' she exclaimed. 'I heard them talking about it last Saturday.'

'They told me I'd missed you. You'll know then that we think it'd be dangerous to wait any longer. Once or twice, our members have wondered if they were being followed.

They decided they weren't, and it's just that everyone's on edge now, but it's given us a greater urgency. And why wait any longer? We're ready. When you come to us on the Sunday, you won't be returning to the French pigs.'

She looked up at him, suddenly worried. 'What excuse will I have? I work on Sundays.'

'Early in the afternoon, instead of going for your siesta, you'll bring a message from Monsieur Bouvier telling us that it's safe to go ahead that night. It's the last thing we're going to ask him to do before he steps back from our cause.'

'He'll know it's safe, will he?'

'He's got a telephone line in his house, and he's the person who'd be contacted by the Sûreté if there were any hint of trouble, and also by the garrison. He'll give you the confirmation, and you'll bring it to us.'

'Oh, Vinh,' she breathed. 'I can't believe we'll soon be free.' She moved closer to him again, slid her arms around his back and pulled him to her.

'And when it's over, Mai, we'll be married,' he whispered into her hair.

They drew back and stared at each other in delight.

Then she sighed. 'I'd better go back in now.'

'Before you go, I've a message for Monsieur Bouvier, telling him what we'd like him to do,' Vinh said. Disentangling his arm, he took a piece of paper from his pocket and gave it to her.

She took it from him. 'I'll find a way of giving it to him.'

'As soon as we hear that it's safe to go ahead, the garrison cooks will move into action, and we'll take up our positions. The confirmation is really important, Mai. Without it, there'll be no attack that day.'

'Will you be waiting for me here?'

He shook his head. 'No. You'll bring it to Garage Boillot. I'll be waiting for you there. And you'll not go back to them.'

'I understand.'

'We've also asked in the note that Monsieur Bouvier arrange it that his wife and the Delons go home after church that day, and stay there for the rest of the day.'

'Why?'

'So that both families are safe. Madame Delon has tried to help us, and we don't wish her or her husband any harm.'

'I'll see that he gets your message tomorrow,' she said. 'I'm not sure how, though. He delivers messages to me, but he doesn't expect me to leave any for him, so he wouldn't look in the box. But I'll think of something.'

He nodded. 'I know you will.' From somewhere in the distance, a solitary dog barked.

'Soon, Mai,' he said, leaning towards her. His cheek touching hers, their breaths mingled. Then he drew back, passion blazing in the depths of his eyes. 'We'll be together very soon. And for always.'

DAWN WAS STREAKING across the sky, leaving a feather-like trail of pink in its wake.

The first in the house to be up, Mai stood in the middle of the kitchen, the message in her pocket, wondering how to get it to M. Bouvier.

He would be up by now, she was sure.

And she could hear M. Delon starting to move around upstairs so he, too, would be down before too long.

Neither of their wives would appear for some time yet.

Next door, Tan would be alone in the scullery or laundry, but it wouldn't be long before Mme. Mercier and their cook appeared, their cook to make the breakfast, and Mme. Mercier to supervise the serving of it.

It wouldn't be easy to get a message to M. Bouvier once their cook and Mme. Mercier had come downstairs.

And it would be even harder to give him a message in the evening, when Mme. Bouvier would be with him.

It meant that if she didn't go across to the Bouviers that instant, it would be too late.

She took a deep breath, slipped out into the garden, closed the door quietly behind her, rushed to the side gate, opened it and went hurriedly through it. Then she ran across the lawn to the Bouvier's kitchen door, and tapped on it.

Tan opened the door. 'Why Mai!' she exclaimed in surprised.

'I'm really sorry to bother you, Tan, but I've got a message from Monsieur Delon for Monsieur Bouvier before he leaves. Could I speak to him, please?'

Tan nodded. 'Of course,' she said. 'Wait here.'

A moment later, M. Bouvier came up to the door, with Tan hovering behind him.

He stared at her in surprise, and then alarm.

'Monsieur Delon asked me to tell you that he won't be able to go with you this morning, after all,' she told M. Bouvier, at the same time slipping the message into his hand.

His face cleared. 'I see. I hope he isn't unwell.'

'He isn't. He just needed to check something before leaving. Thank you.'

And she turned and walked as quickly as she could to the side gate. As she went through the laundry room into the scullery, she saw Mme. Fousseret in the kitchen.

Her heartbeat quickened.

'By mistake, I dropped some pegs in the drying area,' she volunteered. 'I've just put them into the laundry room.'

'THIS REALLY IS the way to start the day,' Marc said, pushing his empty plate away from him, sitting back in the shade of the awning and stretching himself.

'Lucette wouldn't admit it, but I'm sure she's delighted that I come here in the mornings, and that I don't expect her to be up every day, dressed and smiling across the table above a plate of eggs,' Philippe remarked.

'I'm sure that's not so,' Gaston said smoothly.

'Well, perhaps I'm doing her a wrong. She certainly managed to be up early the last couple of weeks.' He glanced at Gaston. 'I'm sorry about Lucette pulling back from your project, Gaston. It's all my fault.'

Gaston shook his head. 'If it's anyone's fault, it's mine,' he said, with a studiedly rueful expression. 'I was so glad of some help that I didn't stop to think how it would look to everyone else.'

'I probably wouldn't have, either, if I'd been in place,' Philippe said.

'That's magnanimous of you, but I should have realised that it wasn't a good idea. Part of the problem was that I'd envisaged Simonne being with me, as well as Lucette. Had that been so, it would've been a very different matter.'

'We'll blame Simonne, then, as she's not here to defend herself,' Marc said cheerfully, and they all laughed.

'How are you managing without any help, or is it too soon to tell?' Philippe asked.

'A little more slowly, I suppose, and I'm slightly hindered by lacking the sensitivity with which Lucette approached the native women. But despite that, I'm confident we'll be able to improve the conditions there.'

Philippe nodded. 'That makes me feel better.'

'There's honestly no need for you to reproach yourself,' Gaston said. 'You jogged me into the reality of the situation, and caused the right thing to happen.'

He glanced at his watch. 'I'm afraid, I'm going to have to get off. Unfortunately, I'll be pretty tied up for the next two or three weeks, looking at waste pipes, drainage plans and so on, and I might not be able to join you as regularly. I'll come when I can, though.'

'Given what you'll be knee deep in all day, it's probably better not to have a full stomach when you start,' Philippe said in amusement. 'Breakfast this morning is on me,' he added. 'And that really will clear my conscience.'

'Thank you,' Gaston said.

He got up, gave them a cheery wave, and headed towards the place where he'd left his car.

'Before we go back to the office,' Marc said, 'Simonne and I would like you and Lucette to come to lunch with us after church a week on Sunday. We're tied up this Sunday, hence suggesting the week after that. Are you free?'

'As far as I know, yes. I'd have to check with Lucette, though, in case she's agreed to something she's not told me about. Are you inviting Gaston, too?'

'Not this time, I don't think. I'll tell Simonne that you think you can come, but that you'll confirm it.'

He leaned across and picked up the cafetière that he'd asked the waiter to leave on the table.

'A final quick coffee before we go back into the fray?' he suggested.

· · ·

LUCETTE GLANCED up from the cup of coffee that Mme. Fousseret had just put on the table next to her.

'Is there anything the matter, Madame?' she asked the housekeeper, who was hovering in front of her.

Mme. Fousseret sniffed, her expression conveying indignation.

'You should know, Madame, that Mai has told me an untruth,' she said, her voice shaking with indignation.

Lucette frowned. 'She has? Well, that does surprise me. I would have thought her to be essentially honest. May I ask what she's lied about?'

'Early this morning, I saw her coming into the house from the garden. She claimed to have gone out to pick up some pegs that she'd dropped in the drying area. But that's not what she'd done.' She paused, as if to let her words sink in.

'How d'you know?'

'Because when I went into the kitchen, I heard the sound of the side gate. Naturally, I looked outside, and I saw her in Monsieur Bouvier's garden, running towards the back of his house.'

A wave of alarm shot though Lucette.

She suddenly felt very cold.

'I see,' she said slowly, trying the still the frantic beating of her heart. 'Why would she go there, do you think?'

'As she's unlikely to have gone to see Monsieur or Madame Bouvier, you can take my word for it, there's a boy involved.' Mme. Fousseret's lips set in a thin, disapproving line. 'She could have gone to see the maid, Tan, about him. Tan and Mai are friendly.'

'I see,' Lucette repeated.

'I have to go out for a short time when I've had my coffee,' she said after a moment or two. 'I'll be back for lunch, and I think the best thing would be that after lunch, you send Mai to me. I think it would be wiser if you didn't tell her that you'd seen where she went this morning,' she added.

'Certainly, Madame,' Mme. Fousseret said, and she turned and left the room.

At least, she'd bought herself some time in which to decide what to do, Lucette thought in despair.

It could be very dangerous if for any reason, romantic or otherwise, Mai were to be linked with Marc Bouvier.

By now, most people would have forgotten, if they'd ever known, that it was Marc who'd placed Mai in their house-hold soon after she and Philippe had arrived.

But if Mai were to be seen to be in contact with Marc, it might remind everyone of the earlier connection, and her household and the Bouviers' might come to be firmly linked in their minds.

If so, should Marc be subject to an investigation or, even worse, be actually caught committing an act of treason, then Mai, too, would almost certainly be taken in for questioning. And the administration might suspect Philippe of being much more than Marc' innocent aide.

She'd have to make absolutely sure that never happened.

She'd realised at once that Mme. Fousseret expected her to interview Mai, and she'd been on the verge of asking for Mai to be sent to her immediately.

Fortunately, in the nick of time she'd refrained from doing so. Mme. Fousseret would have been bound to have had her ear to the keyhole, and what she'd have to say to Mai mustn't be overheard.

And it wouldn't be.

Not now that she'd arranged to speak to Mai at the time

that both Cook and Mme. Fousseret would be in their rooms, asleep.

All she had to do was to come up with somewhere for Tuan to drive her, since she'd now have to be out of the house until it was time for lunch.

SHE STOOD at the salon window, striped in slender bands of gold by the rays from the afternoon sun that streamed through the slatted shutters.

There was a light knock on the door.

'Come in,' she called, and she went across to her chair and sat down.

Mme. Fousseret appeared, with Mai behind her.

'Thank you, Madame Fousseret,' she said. 'I've one or two things to say to Mai, but there's no need for you to delay your siesta. Cook has already gone up, I believe.' And she gave the housekeeper a smile of dismissal.

'As you wish, Madame.' Mme. Fousseret turned and went across to the door. Moments later, they heard her foot-steps going up the stairs, followed by the sound of her bedroom door closing.

Mai stood in front of her, her gaze on the ground.

'I was most disappointed, Mai,' Lucette began coldly, 'to learn that you'd been to Monsieur Bouvier's house this morning.'

Mai glanced at her quickly, and then looked back at the floor.

'I can understand why you needed to lie about it when questioned by Madame Fousseret, but not why you were there in the first place. I thought I'd made myself clear when I spoke to you a few weeks ago, that your role must be limited solely to passing on any message left for you by Monsieur Bouvier. Is that not so?'

'It is, Madame.'

'Yet you deliberately disobeyed me this morning. I assume you thought you wouldn't be seen by anyone. But I also recall telling you that just as *I* had found out what you were doing, others could, too.'

'I'm very sorry, Madame, but it was urgent.'

'There's nothing more urgent to me than the safety of my husband and me. Nothing. Your activities have already put us at risk. And every such act of disobedience puts us in even greater danger. If you disobey me again, and I'm sure I'll find out if you do, then I'll have no choice but to dismiss you at once. Is that clear?'

'Yes, Madame. I'm sorry.'

'You may go.'

Mai turned and walked towards the door, her back straight.

There was a definite hint of defiance in Mai's steps, Lucette noticed in surprise.

And then her surprise gave way to alarm.

From Mai's words and attitude just now, the first time she'd seen a hint of open defiance in her, she was suddenly greatly afraid that Mai had no intention of heeding her warning, and would do whatever she wanted.

The cold hand of fear crept around her heart.

She should have dismissed Mai, and not given her one more chance. That had been a mistake.

But actually, thinking about it, Mai was Marc's responsibility, so he ought to be the one to deal with her.

She'd have to speak to him, and tell him so, and as soon as possible.

33

How could she get to Marc when he was by himself, Lucette had agonised throughout the night.

Philippe had told her the evening before that they'd been invited to dinner with Marc and Simonne a week on Sunday, but the situation with Mai couldn't wait that long.

She needed to ask Marc the questions she'd forgotten to ask him earlier—how long he expected this subterfuge to continue, and what would bring it to an end?

She needed to be reassured that she and Philippe weren't going to tumble over a precipice, on the edge of which she felt they were poised.

If Marc was unwilling to support Mai's instant dismissal, which her every instinct said he'd be against, he must at least impress upon Mai what she had clearly failed to do— namely, that any physical contact between the two of them was forbidden.

Mai must never go to Marc's house.

But she could hardly go across to Marc's before he left for work, as Mai had done, as Mme. Fousseret would be on the alert to catch Mai in another lie, and would very likely see her.

And she couldn't go to his house in the evening as Simonne was sure to be at Marc's side from the moment he returned home.

And going across in the evening and asking for a private word with Marc was completely out of the question, too.

It wouldn't be private, anyway.

Simonne would have thought it strange for her to want to be alone with Marc. And wanting to know why she did, she would have surreptitiously listened in, just as Mme. Fousseret would have done in her house.

Philippe, too, like Simonne, would wonder what she had to say to Marc, and if she went openly to Marc's house, there'd be no way of stopping Philippe from knowing she'd gone there.

Things were better between them now that she'd finished working with Gaston, but they weren't yet back to normal, and she wasn't prepared to take a chance on setting the clock back by seeming to want to be alone with yet another man.

Another possibility was to take advantage of Simonne being out that day, making a duty visit that morning to an elderly friend of her mother's whom she rarely saw, which was why they weren't going to Café Barnard.

As soon as Simonne had left, she could go next door and leave a message for Marc, asking him to call upon her the following morning after Philippe had left for work, as he'd done once before.

But she wouldn't have the freedom to talk that she needed. She could hardly send Mme. Fousseret out of the house again at a moment's notice.

Also, the act of leaving such a message would be so

unusual that it could easily arouse Simonne's suspicions if she came upon the note.

Curiosity about the nature of her relationship with Gaston had probably underpinned Simonne's questions the last time they'd had coffee together, and Simonne must never be put into the position of wondering about her and Marc.

What's more, Simonne would be home before Marc, and she wouldn't put it past Simonne to open any message she'd left for Marc, claiming that she'd misread the name and had thought it was for her.

By the time she'd finished her breakfast, she'd realised that the only way she'd be able to get a note to Marc was to go to the Résidence during the day and give it to him herself.

It wasn't ideal, but she couldn't think of anything else, and it was urgent that she convey to Marc his need to deal with Mai, and that she brought to an end the ever-present feeling of fear that was draining her.

She looked at the clock on the wall. Yes, the timing could work out well.

By the time she got to the Résidence, the men would have returned from their breakfast, assuming they'd gone across the road that morning.

While there was obviously a chance that they'd go straight from their breakfast to the prison or the garrison, for example, Philippe had once told her that they usually went back to the office after breakfast, even if they had to go out later.

If they had already gone out and weren't yet back, she'd have to leave the message for Marc in his office, marked as private.

She went across to her desk, sat down and wrote a brief

note asking Marc to meet her that night by the side gate after Simonne had fallen asleep.

When she'd finished, she tucked it into the pocket of her pink day dress, and rang for Mme. Fousseret.

'I'm going for a walk now,' she told the housekeeper, getting up. 'I won't be needing Tuan today, so perhaps you would set him some tasks to do in the garden.'

'Of course, Madame.'

'I'll be back in time for lunch,' she said.

And she followed Mme. Fousseret out into the front hall, took her pink straw cloche from the stand, and her matching gloves from the table next to Philippe's office, and set off down the drive.

When she reached the Résidence, her steps faltered, and she stopped.

The building beneath the fluttering tricolore looked even larger, more imposing, more official, than ever before.

And she was acutely aware that for a woman to call upon her husband at his place of work wasn't an everyday occurrence.

But she had no choice. She couldn't think what else to do.

Taking a deep breath in an effort to quell her nerves, she went through the wrought-iron gates, up the wide steps that were overhung by an iron-fringed glass canopy, to the arched entrance.

Walking as steadily as she could, she went into the front hall and walked across to the reception desk.

From her chair behind the desk, the receptionist looked up at her in surprise.

With a smile, she identified herself, apologised for interrupting the workday, but asked to be shown to her husband's office.

The receptionist summoned one of the turbaned attendants, and asked that Mme. Delon be taken to M. Delon's office.

Thanking the receptionist, she followed the attendant.

Just as she got there, the door to the office next to Philippe's opened, and Marc came out into the corridor. He stopped abruptly and stared at her in surprise.

She smiled at her guide, said she'd be fine from there on, and thanked him.

The second he'd gone, she thrust the note at Marc.

Taken aback, he glanced at the piece of paper in his hand, and then slipped it unread into his pocket.

'How lovely to see you, Lucette,' he said expansively. 'But I won't flatter myself that it's me you've come to see. Philippe's in there, if you'd like to go straight through to him.' He indicated Philippe's door.

'I'll have to content myself by knowing that I'll be seeing you on Sunday week. But no doubt, you and Simonne will get together before then and sort out the details. Now if you'll excuse me.'

And with a smile, he moved off down the corridor.

She knocked on Philippe's door, heard him call to her to enter, and she stepped inside and closed the door.

'Lucette!' he exclaimed in pleasure, and he stood up.

'I hope I'm not disturbing you. But Simonne's busy, and on the spur of the moment, I thought of going to Les Grands Magasins Réunis, and I wondered if there was anything you'd like me to get you,' she said. 'I hope it was all right to come here and ask,' she added, adopting an apologetic manner.

'I'm sure it won't matter once in a while,' he said, smiling as he came round the desk to her. 'I rather like the idea that you're thinking about me in the day.'

She pulled off her hat, went up to him, and slid her arms around him. 'I often think about you during the day,' she said, resting her head against his chest. 'I love you.'

'Oh, Lucette,' he whispered, and he kissed the top of her head. 'I don't need anything more than to get back to you this evening as soon as I can,' he said, his voice muffled.

'Marc's going to the garrison later on,' he added. 'As soon as he leaves, I'll go home. It won't hurt to finish early for once.'

She looked up at him, and he cupped her face in his hands, and gently kissed her lips.

Impulsively, she pulled him closer and kissed him with a passion intensified by her fear for his safety.

Footsteps sounded in the corridor, and they drew apart.

He took the cloche from her hands, put it on to her head, kissed his index finger, carried the kiss to her lips and left his finger there.

Motionless, they gazed at each other.

At the sound of footsteps just outside the door, he let his hand fall.

Laughing, she gave him a little wave and turned towards the door as Marc came into the office. He gave her an imperceptible nod, opened the door wider, and stood aside to let her through.

With a smile that embraced them both, she went out into the corridor.

FROM HIS POSITION on the opposite side of the road from the Résidence, Gaston waited patiently.

He'd refrained from joining the two men for breakfast that day as he'd told them the day before that he needed to visit City Hall early that morning, and he'd had to allow time for that to have happened before he went to the office.

As he'd approached the Résidence, he'd been greatly surprised to see Lucette a short distance in front of him, going in the same direction. Wives didn't visit their husbands at work, he'd thought, so Philippe couldn't be her destination.

But wherever she was going, he'd been delighted to see her, and had been on the verge of going up to her and saying hello.

Fortunately, he'd managed to pull himself back in time.

He mustn't lose sight of the fact that she almost certainly had information that it would benefit him to know, and he'd swiftly crossed the road, moved into the shadows cast by the trees, and had kept pace with her.

To his amazement, she'd stopped in front of the gates to the Résidence.

So that was where she was going, he thought, and he moved closer to the trunk of the nearest tree, and watched her.

She was clearly nervous, and for a moment, it had looked as if she might be about to turn away, but in the end she hadn't—she'd proceeded into the building.

He'd glanced at his watch as she disappeared from sight. By knowing how long she stayed inside, he'd have an idea of whom she was there to see.

If she'd come to see him, she would leave almost at once.

She'd be told that he wasn't yet in, and as the receptionists knew when he'd arrived and when he left, but no more than that, they wouldn't suggest that she wait for him as they wouldn't know if he'd be in that day.

He looked at his watch again.

Several minutes had passed. If she'd gone there to see

him, she'd have left the building by now. That she hadn't done so, suggested she wanted to speak to Philippe or Marc.

But surely it wouldn't be Philippe.

She'd have seen him that morning before he left the house—she wasn't the sort of woman to spend a large part of the morning in bed. And it was hard to believe that anything could have come up between then and now that necessitated a visit to his office.

So she must be there to see Marc.

It certainly wouldn't be for reasons of romance.

With Marc working next door to Philippe, the two men went in and out of each other's office on a regular basis.

And anyway, he would never believe that of Lucette.

So what could she possibly want to talk to Marc about? And why go to his place of work rather than drop in next door?

He didn't know the answers, but every instinct within him shrieked that he must find out, and he realised that rather than wait until Lucette reappeared, he'd do better to go at once to arrange for the surveillance on the Delons' house to begin again that very evening.

With great reluctance, he turned towards the road, caught the eye of an approaching pousse-pousse puller, and raised his hand to summon him.

EMBRACED by a darkness infused with the perfume of flowers, lemongrass and damp earth, Lucette stood at the side gate and waited for Marc.

After what seemed an age, she heard someone coming towards her. Her heart beat faster. But a moment later, Marc appeared, wearing a silk housecoat, and she felt herself relax.

When he reached the gate, he stopped walking.

She went closer to him, and each stood in their garden, the iron gate between them.

'What is it that couldn't wait?' Marc asked.

'Yesterday morning, Mai came across to your house, and was seen doing so. She lied when challenged about it. The person who saw her knows she lied, and is certain to speculate as to why. No one would think it was for a romantic purpose, not at that hour.'

'I'm sure you're right.'

'There can't be any French person in Hanoi who doesn't know that the natives are desperate to remove us. They may have failed a couple of years ago, but no one can believe they've given up. And Mai is, to all intents and purposes, a Vietnamese woman in a French home.'

'I realise that,' he said quietly.

'So you'll realise that any form of speculation is dangerous as one doesn't know where it'll end. I trusted you to ensure that the contact between you was limited to the messages you leave for her to pass on. By Mai going to your house, she has broken that trust.'

He took a step closer to her.

'It was urgent, Lucette. Mai had no choice. It won't happen again, I promise. But you know how difficult it is to pass on a message that you don't want anyone else to see. After all, I'm sure that's why you came to the Résidence today.'

'Obviously.'

'Well, it's even harder for someone like Mai. Tan doesn't know what Mai's doing, so she couldn't risk trying to reach me through Tan. She couldn't think what else to do.'

'Mai's manner to me when I spoke to her earlier hinted that she would do exactly as she wanted,' Lucette said coldly. 'You got me into this, Marc, and if Mai can't be brought into line, she must leave. She's a good maid, but that counts for nothing compared with Philippe's safety and mine.'

'I understand.'

'I didn't ask you before and I should have done, but when is this going to end? I hadn't realised how afraid I would feel, but I do, all the time, and I can't carry on living like this.'

Hearing the tremor in her last few words, she gave a slight cough.

He took her hands in his. 'I'm so sorry, Lucette. I truly am. You know that I never meant to involve you. It'll soon be over, I promise. I'm stepping back from all this.'

She felt her eyes watering. 'I hope you mean that, Marc, and aren't just saying it. You're meant to be Philippe's friend, and I thought you were mine. A friend wouldn't endanger the life of another friend. This can't happen again.'

Her voice caught in a sob, and she turned and walked back into the house.

For a long moment, Marc stared after her, frowning, and then he, too, turned away.

'And exactly what can't happen again?'

Clad in a negligée thrown on in haste, Simonne stood on the grass in the fresh night air, facing him, her hands on her hips, her eyes shards of ice in a face that was white with accusation.

34

Visibly distraught, Simonne strode back to their house. Pushing the doors aside, she headed straight through the scullery to the kitchen, along the hall and into the salon.

His face ashen, Marc followed her.

Trembling uncontrollably, she turned to face him, her eyes glittering, accusing.

'How could you betray me so?' she said, her voice shaking with anger and distress. 'And with Lucette, too, of all people. I thought she was my friend.'

He went closer, but she jumped back.

'Don't touch me,' she screamed, holding up her hands to ward him off.

He stopped walking. 'You've got this so wrong, Simonne,' he said gently. 'Please hear me out?'

She put her hands to her ears. 'There's nothing you could say that I'd want to hear. I know what I saw. I saw you with her.'

She let out a wail of anguish.

He stepped quickly forward and prised each of her hands from her ears.

'You have to hear me out, Simonne.'

'No,' she cried, shaking her head, and freeing her hands from his grip. 'No, I don't.'

'Ssh,' he said. 'We don't want to wake the household.'

'Of course, we don't,' she snapped, her voice taking on the sharp edge of sarcasm. 'We don't want them knowing you're a lying, cheating bastard, do we?'

She raised her hand to hit him, but he caught her hand, and held it aloft. 'No, Simonne. It's that I don't want to die.'

'Philippe would loathe you with good reason, but he wouldn't kill you.'

'It's not Philippe I'm talking about.'

Her face reflected a sudden confusion and panic.

He lowered his arm and released her hand.

'Then who is it?' she said, rubbing her wrist where his fingers had held her.

'No one in the way that you mean. Quite by chance, Lucette discovered something I've been doing. She was very angry. And very afraid. She thought she could live with it, but has found that she can't. It's why she wanted to see me.'

She inched back, staring at him in alarm, her eyes wide open. 'What're you talking about? Why's Lucette afraid?'

And he told her.

He started with the things he'd seen when based in Saigon, which had upset him so much that he hadn't hesitated when, after his transfer to Hanoi, Simonne's father had asked him if he'd join him in helping the revolutionaries.

And he'd been doing that, he told her, since then.

'I don't know what else I can say,' he said as he came to the end of his explanation. His palms upturned, he gestured his helplessness. 'I'm not sorry for helping the natives, but I *am* sorry that in doing so, I'm acting against our administration. I love my country, but I can't turn a blind eye to what I've seen.'

'And I can't turn a blind eye to an act of treason against France,' she said icily. 'As for my father being engaged in such a deception, I don't believe you. He was proud of being French. He'd never have betrayed his country.'

He shrugged. 'I can't prove it to you, Simonne. I can only tell you that like me, he was unhappy at things he saw when we were based in Saigon.'

'You talk as if they don't benefit from us being here, but they do.'

'We benefit more, and at their expense. The natives used to make their own rice wine and gather their own salt. But now they must buy both through our outlets, at heavily inflated prices. Every year, we produce more opium than the year before. Why? Because the local sales are very profitable, and the addictive nature of opium, and its stupefying effects, are a useful way of controlling the natives. Surely, you can see this is wrong.'

'It's impossible to get everything exactly right when so few people have so much to do,' she said, her voice ice-cold. 'But whatever you say, they're better off having us here than not.'

Marc shook his head. 'I can see it's a waste of time, trying to make you understand. So, what next? Are you going to report me?'

She thought hard for a moment. 'What did Lucette say?' she asked at last. 'She's clearly not reported you or you'd be in prison by now, or dead.'

'I won't lie to you—she's furious that it's happening so close to their home, and involving their maid. But she won't say anything, provided I keep all contact with Mai to a minimum.'

'I see.'

'And I've told her that I'm going to step back from the revolutionary cause.' He paused. 'So are you going to do what Lucette's doing, or are you reporting me?'

'I can't report you, can I? Disgusted though I am, you're my husband. How can I be responsible for you going to prison? But it's got to be stopped. Keeping things to a minimum isn't enough. Mai's got to be reported. Yes, that's right.' She grabbed him by the arm. 'Mai must be reported to the Sûreté, and you have to be the one to tell them.'

He opened his mouth to speak.

'No, don't say you won't,' she went on with a rising sense of urgency. 'It's got to be you. If it isn't, when they take her in for questioning, which one day they will, she'll say that you, too, were involved in the treason.'

'No, Simonne.'

'But if you tell the authorities that Mai's a traitor,' she said, speaking through him, 'and has been trying to black-mail you—saying that if you refuse to help the terrorists, she's going to lie and accuse you of being a part of the group —you'll have covered yourself. That's what you must do. There's a way out of this, you see.' She dropped his arm and stared at him in triumph.

'I'll do no such thing,' he said firmly.

'You've got to,' she cried in panic. 'If you don't, you'll get caught at some point, and you know what'll happen then. You must protect yourself by handing Mai in.'

'And what do you think will happen to her?' he asked quietly.

'The same as would've happened to you, but better it happen to her than to you.'

'I've no intention of handing her in, Simonne.'

'Why not?' She took a step back, and her voice took on a sudden hardness. 'Is it because she's your congaie? That's it, isn't it? You've been bedding her for years. It's why you gave her to Lucette—to have her living next door to you.'

'You're talking rubbish and you know it,' he said in despair. 'Of course, she isn't. I love you, Simonne. I don't need, or want, anyone else.'

'I don't believe you. If you won't report Mai, then I will. I'll go first thing in the morning. I'll tell them that Mai's trying to blackmail you into committing treasonable acts. They'll believe me and you'll be safe, and that's all that matters.'

'You'd be condemning Mai to torture and death. Doesn't that make you think again?'

'When it's between you or some woman who's nothing to us, then no, it doesn't.'

'You're right that she's nothing to me, not in the way that you mean. But she's something to you, Simonne, and she was to your father.'

Simonne stared at him, frowning. 'What d'you mean?'

'Mai is your sister.'

MARC CLOSED the door of the cocktail cabinet, and walked across to the arrangement of sofa and armchairs, carrying a brandy for each of them.

He put Simonne's snifter on the table next to the sofa where she was sitting, and went and sat opposite her.

He took a sip of brandy and waited for her to look up from her hands. She appeared to be studying her nails, but she wasn't actually seeing them, he realised.

Every inch of her cried out her distress, and he longed to

go across to her, take her in his arms and comfort her, but he knew that she needed to think this through on her own, and he waited.

'How long have you known?' she finally asked.

'Your father told me not long before he died. But I'd already guessed. He was always unusually solicitous of her needs, in a way that one normally isn't with staff. When he knew that his health was failing, he wanted to make sure that Mai would have a place to live where she'd be treated well. He guessed your mother would return to France, and Mai would have been cast adrift had someone not helped her.'

'And her mother?' Her voice shook. 'Was she a maid?'

He nodded. 'Yes. She worked for Antoine. That's how they met.'

'I know that not many wives came here with their husbands,' she said, 'which is why so many men have a congaie—a house girl, for example, or the sister of a house-boy, or even the houseboy's wife. It's why we have so many métis. But Father was someone who *did* have his wife with him, so why?'

'Because he fell in love with her. It's as simple as that. I'm afraid your mother wasn't a warm and loving person, but Antoine was. This wasn't a man taking advantage of an employee—he loved Mai's mother, Simonne. And from what he told me, the feeling was reciprocated.'

She shook her head. 'You must be mistaken. If his mistress and bastard child were in the house for any period of time, I would've known. I must've been about six or seven when Mai was born. There was a Vietnamese woman who left when I was quite little, but—'

She stopped abruptly, and her hand flew to her mouth. 'That was her, wasn't it?' she cried wildly.

'Probably. Mai's mother left Hanoi before Mai was born. As soon as Antoine knew of her condition, he sent her back to her village. He visited her, though, before and after Mai was born, and also while Mai was growing up.'

'While she was growing up?' she echoed hollowly.

He nodded. 'It's how he knew that Mai was desperate to leave the village. Rather than see her run away and get sucked into the dark side of the city, he took her to Hanoi to work for him when she was fourteen.'

'And you say he loved her? What about me?' Tears started to stream down her face.

'He loved you very much, Simonne—in your heart you must know that. But he also loved Mai. And if you love your father, you won't do anything to harm his daughter, your sister.'

She wiped her eyes, and was quiet for a moment or two. 'And you say that like you, he was a traitor?' she said at last.

'If you want to put it that way, yes. Some of the Viet-namese must have noticed his frustration at some of the things we were doing, and after he'd settled in Hanoi, he was asked on one or two occasions to pass something on.'

She shook her head. 'He was French. He should have said no.'

'Well, he didn't think so. The occasions increased in number. And when he and I became friends, and he realised we shared the same concerns, he asked me one day if I'd use my access to the prison to help the revolutionaries. I agreed without hesitation.'

'You shouldn't have done,' she said tersely.

'I'm not going to apologise for doing what I believe is right.' He paused. 'I'm sorry, though, that I've involved you and Lucette in this. I never intended that to happen. But as for Mai, when we first met, you used to say that you'd love to have had a sister. Well, now you have one.'

'But not one who looks like me, sounds like me, who shares my educational and cultural background. That's what I wanted. I couldn't care less about Mai.'

'Is that really the truth?' he asked gently.

'Of course, it is,' she said shortly.

'Even though you and she share something that can't be seen—a readiness to stand up for what you think is right, even though it might mean losing your life.'

She glared at him. 'What're you talking about?'

'The fact that you're prepared to go to the police, regardless of the consequences to yourself as well as to me.'

She paled. 'I don't understand.'

'You say that your story would convince the police, but in your heart of hearts you must know that they wouldn't believe you unquestioningly.'

'They might.'

'They wouldn't. The first thing they'd do would be to question Mai in a way that would extract the truth from her. She'd say that I'd willingly helped the revolutionaries, and they'd believe her.'

'You can't be sure of that,' she said, her voice trembling.

'I can. They'll know that material's been getting out of the prison for some time now, and that supports my being involved. Mai couldn't have brought it out.'

Her shoulders slumped.

'And if you think about it, you must also realise that they might believe that you, my wife, knew what I was doing. They'd think you'd suddenly got cold feet, and were trying to extricate us both. And we'd both end up in Hoa Lo.'

The last of Simonne's blood drained from her face.

'So, what are you going to do, Simonne?' he asked at last.

'I won't go to the Sûreté,' she said, shaking. 'But Mai has to be dismissed. The Delons must fire her. This has to end now. I won't have a moment's peace of mind until I know that this whole thing is over, and we're no longer in danger.'

Tears began to trickle again down her cheeks. 'Promise me that you'll stop helping them.'

'I promise I'll stop very soon.'

She wiped her eyes with the back of her hands.

'I want to speak to Mai. You can go across to the Delons before you leave for the office, and tell Mai to come to me. You can say it's to do with Tan, if you like. It shouldn't be a problem—you're good at lying,' she added bitterly.

'I'll do that.'

'We'll sit in the garden so we won't be overheard by the staff. You must make up something to tell Cook and Madame Mercier that'll stop them thinking it strange, me sitting outside, talking to next door's maid.'

'I'll do as you ask.' He hesitated. 'When you talk to Mai, Simonne, try to remember that you're talking to a sister, not a servant.'

'A half-sister,' she snapped.

35

T *he following day*

SIMONNE SAT in the garden at the back of her house on one of the four white wrought-iron chairs that encircled the matching table.

On the table, there was a cup and saucer, a knife, plate and serviette, a cafetière full of coffee, a dish of butter and one of apricot preserves, and a basket of warm croissants.

Marc led Mai up to the table, left her there, and then went back into the house and closed the door behind him.

Mai stood in front of Simonne, her eyes on the grass.

'I won't keep you long,' Simonne said stiffly. 'Monsieur Bouvier is going to occupy my staff while we talk.' She indicated the chair opposite her. 'You may sit down. As you can see, I'm about to have breakfast out here as I sometimes do, but I'm sure you'll appreciate that it wouldn't have been appropriate for me to ask to have a place set for you, too. You do see that, don't you?'

'Yes, Madame.'

'I think it would be all right if you sat down, though.'

Mai remained standing.

'I prefer you to sit, Mai, while we're talking,' she said. Hearing a touch of hysteria in her voice, she coughed. 'Please, sit down,' she said, lowering her tone of voice.

Mai perched herself on the edge of the nearest chair.

Simonne stared hard at Mai's face.

Mai stared back, unflinching.

'Did my husband tell you anything about what he and I said last night?' she asked at last.

Looking away from Mai's face, she reached for a croissant.

Mai nodded. 'He said you know what we've been doing.'

'Is that all he said?' A pink haze spread across her cheeks.

'No, he told me that you know about your father and my mother. You didn't want to believe it, but now you accept that it's the truth.'

'That's right. I've been thinking about this all night, not that there was much of the night left when we'd finished talking.'

Again, she stared hard at Mai, and her brow creased. 'I'm looking for a likeness between us, or for any traces of my father in your face,' she said. 'But I can't see any.'

'I look like my mother.'

Simonne nodded. 'Yes, you must do.' She paused. 'Marc —Monsieur Bouvier—said that my father used to visit you when you were little.'

'That's right. For years, he came to the village to see my mother and me. When I was older, he brought me to Hanoi.'

'Did he ever talk about me?' She gave an embarrassed laugh. 'I'm sorry. What must I sound like, asking such a thing?'

'He talked about you very often, Madame. He always used to begin with the words Your sister.'

'He did?' A lump came to her throat.

Mai nodded. 'Yes, and I was very jealous. It was you he wanted to live with, not me. You had blonde hair and blue eyes, and my mother told me you were very pretty. I could see he loved you. How could he not, I used to think. So how could he love me, too, who looked so different?'

Simonne swallowed hard. 'Oh, Mai. From everything my husband told me last night, my father *did* love you, and he also loved your mother.'

The eyes of both filled with tears.

'I miss him very much,' Simonne blurted out.

'So do I.' Her breath coming heavily, Mai put her hand to her mouth, and stared at the table.

Wiping her eyes, Simonne gave an awkward laugh. 'Marc reminded me last night how often I'd told him I wished I'd had a sister.'

Mai looked up at her. 'But not like me. I think I'm right, aren't I?'

'I said exactly that to him. But now, I don't know.' She stared at Mai in wonderment. 'I didn't expect to feel anything, but I find that I do. I think I could like you very much, grow to love you even,' she said, her voice breaking.

'But I won't have a chance to do so. It's because of the circumstances. Did Marc tell you I've said you must leave?' Her eyes again filled with tears.

'Yes, he did.'

'I'm sorry, but I've no choice. I'm so afraid that Marc will get caught. And you, too, Mai. I never thought I'd say this, but you actually feel as if you're my sister. I know that sounds mad because you *are* my sister, but I don't know how better to express it.'

'I understand. And you've become a real person to me, not just my father's first daughter, or Tan's employer, or Monsieur Bouvier's wife. That also might sound crazy.'

Simonne shook her head. 'It doesn't. And I don't want you to die, or Marc.' Tears ran down her cheeks. 'I would have so liked us to get to know each other. But we can't. It wouldn't be safe. And it would have looked strange to my friends, anyway.'

'I know that.'

'Where will you go? What will you do?'

'I have a beau, and we want to be married,' Mai said. 'He's a good man. I shall go to him. There's one problem, though.' She stopped sharply and bit her lip.

'What is it?'

'He won't be back in Hanoi till the end of next week, so if I leave before then, I won't be able to go to him or let him know where I am. He'll expect me to be here.'

She shook her head dismissively. 'But it doesn't matter. I can go to my mother. When Vinh finds out I'm not here, I'm sure he'll realise I'm with my mother.'

Simonne leaned forward. 'You don't have to leave immediately, Mai. Stay till your beau returns. I'll talk to Madame Delon. A couple of weeks won't matter.' She paused. 'Oh, Mai, what a mess.'

She put her fingers to her eyes and tried to push back the tears.

'SIMONNE!' Lucette exclaimed

She jumped up in surprise, seeing Simonne, her face

pale, behind Mme. Fousseret, who stood at the door to the salon.

Mme. Fousseret cleared her throat. 'I apologise for interrupting you like this, Madame, but Madame Bouvier has just arrived, using the garden gate rather than the front door.'

She glanced disapprovingly over her shoulder at Simonne, and then turned back to Lucette. 'Would you like me to show her in, Madame?'

'Please do,' Lucette said, sitting down again as Simonne pushed past Mme. Fousseret and came into the salon.

'Please, bring us some coffee, Madame Fousseret,' Lucette called as the housekeeper started to close the door. 'Do sit down, Simonne,' she said, indicating the chair opposite her.

'Thank you,' she said.

She glanced at the chair, but went to sit on the sofa, at the end closest to Lucette.

Lucette turned slightly towards her, and gave her a wan smile. 'You look as tired as I feel. We'll talk when we've had a reviving cup of coffee. Did Marc get off all right this morning?'

'He was very tired, but yes. He left a little while after he'd brought Mai across to me.' Simonne leaned forward and lowered her voice. 'Did Madame Fousseret think it very strange, Marc asking Mai to come and speak to me?'

'If she did, she didn't tell me. When I came downstairs, she said it was to do with Tan. There was an increase in her sniffs of disapproval, but I'm now so used to them that I just ignore them.'

The door opened, and they fell silent as Mme. Fousseret entered with the trolley.

'You can leave us to pour our coffees,' Lucette told her.

'Perhaps you'd be kind enough to see that the beds upstairs are changed?'

With a slight inclination of her head, Mme. Fousseret left the room.

Lucette got up, poured them each a coffee and gave one to Simonne.

'I won't have a pastry, thank you, tempting though they look,' Simonne told her. 'I've just forced myself to eat some breakfast.'

'Are you unwell?' Lucette asked as she sat down, holding her coffee. 'You do look rather pale.'

'I'm fine, thank you. I'm just tired. When Marc came across for Mai, did he tell you anything about last night?' Simonne asked.

'What about last night?' she asked warily.

'About me seeing you secretly meeting him in the dead of night? He thought I was asleep, but I saw him leave the house and I followed him.'

Lucette gave a sudden start. Coffee spilt into the saucer, and thence on to her lap. She hastily put the cup on the table next to her, and wiped her skirt with her napkin.

'No, he didn't. And if you've jumped to conclusions, don't. I'm sure he'll have told you that it's not what it might have looked like. I assure you, there's nothing between us, Simonne.'

'I believe you,' Simonne said bitterly. 'That would have almost been better than the truth. At least, he'd have been risking only his marriage, not his life.'

Lucette paused, the napkin in her hand. 'What did he tell you?'

'Everything. How he's helping the terrorists, and that you know about it, but aren't going to report him. By not reporting him, though, it makes you one of the terrorists, too.'

'Of course, it doesn't,' she said impatiently. 'I'm doing this for Philippe. The most important thing to me is his safety. I love him more than anything, and I couldn't live without him. If I have to stay silent in order to keep him safe, then that's what I'll do. But you, too, have obviously decided the same thing. Either that, or you're giving Marc time to get away before reporting him. After all, you're here and not at the Sûreté.'

'I don't know what to do,' Simonne cried. 'I really don't, Lucette.' Her eyes filled with tears. 'I don't want to report him for the same reason as you. And they'd never believe that I didn't know what he was doing. We'd go to prison, or worse.'

She took out a handkerchief, wiped her eyes and blew her nose.

'Marc has promised to stop helping,' she added, 'so hopefully that'll be an end to it. But there's Mai, too. I've told her she can stay on for a couple of weeks, but then she must leave. I know you like her, but I hope you'll agree.'

'I'm afraid there's no alternative. I'd wanted her gone at once, but two more weeks is acceptable. I'll make up a reason for Philippe.'

They heard the sound of the front door bang shut, and Philippe call out to Mme. Fousseret.

'Philippe's home!' Lucette exclaimed in alarm. 'Don't say anything to him, will you?'

They both picked up their coffee cups, and sat back, trying to look relaxed.

The salon door opened, and Philippe entered, smiling.

'Hello, ladies! I'm sorry to disturb your tête à tête, but I knew you didn't sleep well last night, Lucette, so I took the day off. I thought perhaps we could go for a drive.'

Simonne stood up. 'What a lovely thought, Philippe. It'll be especially welcome for poor Lucette as I received a bit of bad news this morning, and I've rather bored her with it. It's nothing to worry about, though,' she added quickly.

She looked down at Lucette. 'I'll be off, then, Lucette. We'll have our usual coffee at Café Barnard next Wednesday, shall we? I've something else to tell you, but it can wait.'

THE LAST LIGHT of day was failing.

Emile sat in the armchair in the corner of his room, his arms folded, his eyes half-closed, while Gaston sat at Emile's desk, working through the reports from his operatives.

Some of the operatives had been keeping an eye on the new headquarters in the Old Quarter, and others had been taking it in turns to watch the Delons' residence since early the previous afternoon.

He'd also had a couple of men watching the garrison after it had been observed that Bouvier had been visiting the barracks more frequently than usual.

Having learnt before he arrived in Hanoi that there'd been an attempt thirty years earlier to poison the garrison troops, which had failed when one of the cooks involved had gone to church for confession, and the priest had reported the matter, he'd started to wonder whether the terrorists might be intending to do something similar.

Whatever they were planning to do, they were going to do it soon, he was sure.

The word from the Old Quarter operatives was that there'd been a noticeable increase in people coming from the outlying villages into Hanoi, and that those they'd been shadowing had frequently looked behind them, a sign of the heightened awareness that prevailed in the last few days before an action was to take place.

And between the Delons and Bouviers, there'd also been some highly unusual activity.

Lucette had been seen going out of her house late at night and having a conversation with Bouvier.

Arranging such a meeting had probably been her purpose in going to the Résidence that morning, but it wouldn't have been a romantic liaison. Of that he was sure. And indeed, that had been confirmed by his operative.

But the fact that Marc Bouvier, known to be aiding the terrorists, was secretly meeting with Lucette, whose maid was part of the terrorist chain, had opened up another line of thought.

It was one that he didn't want to think about. Not for one minute. But one that he had to explore. It was his job to do so.

Could it be possible that Lucette was in some way involved with the terrorists, too?

He felt cold at the very idea.

But she'd shown a great deal of sympathy for the way in which the natives were forced to live, unusually so, and at times had seemed quite critical of the little the French had done to improve their lot.

And what about Simonne Bouvier? Where did she fit in?

The operative who'd seen Lucette meet Bouvier had reported that Mme. Bouvier had approached her husband in the garden just after Lucette had left.

She'd appeared angry, as far as the operative could tell, but he hadn't had a clear view or her, and as the Bouviers had immediately gone back to their house, he couldn't say more.

And then the following morning, Bouvier had gone early to the Delons, and had returned to his house with Mai.

Through the gaps between the bushes, the operative had glimpsed Simonne Bouvier sitting in her garden, talking to Mai. But beyond observing that both had seemed quite upset, especially Mme. Bouvier, he'd had nothing else to report.

Mai had returned to the Delons' house, and Mme. Bouvier had gone indoors.

But not long after that, she'd come out again, crossed her garden to the Delons' house, and had stayed in their house for about an hour.

The operative in front of the Delons' house had reported that Philippe Delon had returned while Simonne must still have been with Lucette.

For a man so intent on sticking to his routine, to see him turn up at his house mid-morning was extremely strange.

And what was even more peculiar was that Philippe had gone into the house, come out a few moments later, stood for a minute or two in front of the door, and had then gone back into the house again.

This wasn't the usual communication between the two families, he thought, frowning. And nor was the time of day at which they'd met.

And the idea of Simonne being emotional, a woman who'd always seemed thoroughly self-composed, and moreover, that she'd actually shown a degree of distress in front of her friend's maid, had taken him quite by surprise.

Something was clearly afoot.

He'd leave operatives watching the back and front of both houses, he decided, and he'd make a point of going to Café Barnard the following Wednesday in the hope that the women would be there.

If they were, he'd do his very best to extract from them exactly what had been going on between the two families.

If they weren't there, he'd have to find a way of getting Lucette on her own, and seeing if he could manipulate her into telling him what had been happening.

Either way, he felt that they were closing in on something significant, and his every instinct cried out that all those random incidents were part of a puzzle that, when fitted together, would lead to Marc Bouvier being arrested for treason.

As he looked down at the reports on the desk in front of him, he felt a sudden urge to shout out in glee.

'They're going to make their move soon, very soon, I suspect,' he told Emile, grinning broadly. 'And when they do, we'll be ready and waiting.'

36

*Café Barnard
The following Wednesday*

FROM HIS POSITION between the lake and a huge pile of panniers filled with flowers, Gaston watched Lucette and Simonne sit down at their usual table.

So they *had* come that morning, he thought in relief. He was ready with his excuse for joining them, so he just had to wait for the right moment to cross the road to the café.

His gaze focused upon Lucette, and he watched her stir her coffee.

Then he glanced at Simonne.

Her body, like Lucette's, was unusually tense, he noticed, and both were strangely quiet. Normally they were very talkative, but neither had spoken to the other since they'd sat down.

He frowned thoughtfully.

Could he have been wrong in dismissing an affair

between Lucette and Marc, merely because he couldn't bear to think that it might be true? And could Simonne have found out about their closeness?

He felt a sharp momentary pain. Surely it couldn't be that.

But given the tension between the women, he'd need to pick his time with care. There was clearly something bothering them, and it would be better for them to get it out of the way before he turned up at their table.

If he went across before they'd cleared the air, it could stultify the conversation, and he'd have had a wasted morning.

On the other hand, if he left it too long, they might decide that they weren't in the mood for chatting, and leave before he'd even stepped out from behind the flower seller.

What best to do, he wondered.

'THE TREES LOOK glorious in their autumnal colours,' Lucette remarked, breaking the silence.

Simonne nodded. 'I suppose so.' She paused. 'I suggested coming here today as having coffee here on a Wednesday has rather become a habit. And if we're going to get back to normal, which I really hope we are, we ought to return to our routine as soon as possible.'

Lucette looked up from her drink and gave Simonne a half-smile. 'But you're not as relaxed as you usually are. Doesn't that defeat the purpose?'

Simonne gave a mirthless laugh. 'Maybe.'

'What is it, Simonne?' Lucette asked. 'Last week, you said there was something else you wanted to say. But Philippe had arrived, and you couldn't tell me.'

'That's right.' She cleared her throat. 'Did Marc say anything to you about Mai last week?'

Lucette frowned in puzzlement. 'Not really. He just said you wanted to ask her something about Tan. And later that you wanted her to stay for two more weeks. That's all.'

'If not last week, then, did he at any other time tell you anything at all about Mai?'

'What sort of thing?' she asked, perplexed.

Simonne shrugged. 'I don't know. Maybe that she was my sister.'

Lucette gasped. She stared at Simonne, her mouth falling open. 'Your sister?'

Simonne nodded. 'That's right. We share a father.'

'He never told me that, Simonne, I promise you. But how? I don't understand.'

'The usual way,' Simonne said bitterly. 'He and a maid who worked for him.' Her eyes glistened. 'No, I'm being mean. It wasn't the usual way—he obviously loved Mai's mother, and also Mai. He used to visit Mai when she was growing up. And I can't entirely blame him for betraying Maman—she wasn't a very warm person, but Papa was.'

'I don't know what to say,' Lucette said helplessly. 'We know this happens. But that he cared for Mai's mother must mean something, and that he acted honourably. Lots of men would have instantly discarded a native woman carrying his child.'

'I know. I wanted to hate Papa for the fact that I'd had only a share of his love, and for not letting me know that I had a sister. But I can't.'

'But would you have wanted a Vietnamese sister?' Lucette asked. 'I'm thinking of all the things I've heard you say against the natives in the short amount of time I've been here. Your father probably thought he was doing the best thing by not telling you.'

'I'm sure he did. It doesn't make it right, though.'

Also,' Lucette continued, 'it would have forced you to keep a secret from your mother, which would have been wrong.'

'I hadn't thought about that, but I suppose it's true.' She fell silent, and bit her lower lip.

'And Mai?' Lucette asked gently. 'How d'you feel about her now that you know the truth?'

Simonne's shoulders slumped. 'I've surprised myself, but I think I could actually come to like her very much, and to feel sisterly about her.'

Lucette smiled at her. 'I'm not surprised. Mai's a very sweet girl.'

'But there isn't time for that. She's leaving at the end of the week, and I won't see her again. If Marc's going to get out of the mess he's in, which he's promised to do, he won't be able to do so if Mai' is still close at hand. So she must go.'

'I'm afraid you're right about that. Oh, Simonne, I'm so sorry.'

A SHADOW FELL across the table.

'Gaston!' Lucette exclaimed.

'Well, well,' he said cheerfully. 'I had a hunch that I might find you here, and indeed I was right. May I join you?'

He sat down.

'It's nice to see you, Gaston,' Lucette said. 'It feels quite a while since we've had that pleasure.'

'I've been busy,' he said. 'Dealing with sewers. No, please, don't ask for the details.' He held up his hand in feigned horror.

Both of them smiled.

Just two thin smiles. No laughter.

They obviously weren't in the mood for his customary banter, he instantly realised. Whatever had been bothering them, it clearly still was.

He'd just have to accept that he wouldn't get anything helpful out of that morning, and the sooner he extricated himself, the better.

The waiter put a coffee in front of him. He signalled for the waiter to stay a moment, took some piastres from his pocket and put them on the waiter's tray.

'Thank you,' he told the waiter, his tone dismissing him.

'You shouldn't have paid for us,' Lucette admonished. 'That was naughty of you.'

'It was a pleasure. And as I can't stay long, it was easier to settle up now.'

'What was it you wanted to talk to us about?' Simonne asked bluntly.

Ouch, he thought.

Most definitely, neither was in the mood for him. A sudden feeling of hurt engulfed him, but he forcibly brushed it aside.

'I was wondering if you'd all like to go to the Métropole on Sunday afternoon,' he said. 'They're showing one of my favourite Charlie Chaplin films, *The Gold Rush*. It's an American comedy. I'd like to see it again, and I thought you might enjoy it, too. I know it's the ladies who decide the social calendar, so I decided to suggest it to you rather than to your husbands.'

Lucette and Simonne exchanged glances.

Simonne coughed. 'We can't make it next Sunday, I'm afraid,' she said with a trace of awkwardness. 'I wish we could. We don't seem to be doing an awful lot that's cultural at the moment. Lucette hasn't even been to the Opera House yet.'

'It's early days yet,' he said with a smile.

'But on Sunday,' Simonne went on, 'Lucette and Philippe will be lunching with us after church. The men have some work they'd rather discuss away from the office, and they think Lucette and I will be company for each other, and not realise we're being ignored.'

Her smile didn't quite reach her eyes, he noticed.

A surge of excitement ran through him, pushing away the last of the hurt.

That wasn't the whole story, he was sure, but it was a start. Perhaps he could retrieve something from the morning, after all.

'That's a shame,' he said ruefully. 'It's an amusing film and I thought it might cheer you up. You both look a little downhearted, if you don't mind me saying so.'

Again, they exchanged glances.

'It's just that Mai's leaving,' Lucette ventured. 'I'm not looking forward to finding a replacement for her.'

He pulled a sympathetic face. 'I'm so sorry about that, Lucette. I know how much you like her. But I'm sure she'll give you plenty of time to find someone who's closer to her in age than to Madame Fousseret.' He laughed.

Both smiled weakly.

'She's leaving next weekend—she's getting married,' Lucette volunteered, her face wan.

Now he had the whole story, he thought in triumph.

What had looked only moments ago as if he'd wasted his morning, had yielded gold!

Next weekend, the terrorists would be taking action. He'd never been more certain of anything than that.

It made sense of everything his men had observed, not

least of which was the influx of peasants in the last few days. And Mai's work would be done so she'd no reason to stay on.

Now to take his leave of them as quickly as he could.

He finished his coffee and stood up. 'I really ought to get off now. I think I'll go to the film myself on Sunday, and when I'm there, I'll find out what they're showing in the next month or two. I'll let you know, and perhaps we can go to one of their other programmes.'

'Thank you. That's a good idea,' Lucette said.

She and Simonne smiled up at him in gratitude.

As he walked away from the table, he sensed their relief that he was leaving. It was almost as if his presence had been rejected by Lucette—and by Simonne, too, of course—and that really hurt.

He mentally shook himself. He mustn't let himself think like that. There was work to be done.

There were only three full days to Sunday, but that was long enough for him to make the necessary arrangements and to get his operatives in place.

As for him, he'd be at the back of the Bouviers' house on Sunday as he wanted to be the person to make the arrests.

This was between him, alone, and the two families. His operatives would be deployed elsewhere, at strategic parts of the town.

But he wouldn't be hiding behind the metal railings at the rear, his access to their garden slowed, or even crucially delayed, by the impossibility of stepping forward on to their lawn.

Rather, as soon as he was sure that Mme. Mercier and Tan had gone up for their siesta, he'd be going through the wrought-iron gates in front of the Bouvier house, and up the side of their garden, keeping close to the railings so as not to be noticed by anyone inside the house.

When he reached the end of the garden, he'd hide in the foliage there. There were fewer plants and trees than at the end of the Delons' garden, but there was more than enough for his purpose.

And once there, he'd wait for the crucial moment.

And Mai, whom they no longer needed to follow, wouldn't be celebrating a wedding in two weeks' time, or at any time at all. On Sunday night, she'd be in Hoa Lo, along with all the other terrorists.

STANDING in the small room at the top of the house, Mai stared at the clothes in her wardrobe.

There weren't many, but even so, she was going to have to leave some behind. She wouldn't be able to move easily if she were overloaded, and as Vinh had stressed, with the outcome of their plans uncertain, she needed to be prepared for every eventuality.

That outcome would remain uncertain until the end of Sunday. By which time, she'd be long gone from the house.

She would've liked to have been able to get to know Mme. Bouvier—although she'd known all her life that Madame was her sister, she'd never thought about her in such a way, and it was too late to begin—but there just wasn't time.

On Sunday, the revolutionary fighters were going to come out on the streets and, with the troops in a drug-induced torpor, they'd take over the administration buildings.

In order for that to happen, she'd be going early in the

afternoon to M. Bouvier's house and collecting from him a note saying that it was safe for the revolution to proceed.

The uprising would only go ahead if they received M. Bouvier's confirmation that the authorities didn't suspect a thing. Without that assurance, everything would have to wait for another day.

Once she'd collected the message from M. Bouvier, she'd go back to the house, get her bag and, unseen by the Delons, who were going to be having lunch with the Bouviers, or by Cook or Mme. Fousseret, who'd be upstairs in their rooms, she would leave.

She'd take the confirmation to Vinh, who'd be waiting for her at Garage Boillot, and together they'd go to the headquarters.

And she wouldn't be returning.

So she wouldn't see Mme. Bouvier—her sister—again, and that made her extremely sad.

But she mustn't think like that, she chivvied herself—she'd be with Vinh.

She picked up two calico tunics, one dark brown and one white, and two pairs of trousers, one black and one white. She'd take those, plus a few personal items, and one pair of wooden sandals. With what she'd be wearing, that would be sufficient.

And she'd take her bright red silk *ao dai*, of course.

That was what she'd wear for her wedding.

Vinh was born in the year of the dragon, so she'd sewn a line of small golden dragons into the neckline of the *ao dai,* and these would bring them happiness, luck and prosperity.

Smiling happily, she started to put her clothes into her bag.

37

S *unday morning*

DESPITE THE TURBULENCE of her life in the past couple of weeks, to Lucette, as she stood at the top of the steps leading down from St. Joseph's Cathedral, beneath the clear blue sky of a lovely September morning, the world appeared to be revolving as it always had.

It was just that she seemed to be standing on the outside, looking fearfully in on something of which she was no longer a part.

She glanced back at Simonne.

Although pale, Simonne was smiling as she stood with Marc in front of the high-arched entrance, talking to a group of friends. Philippe was on the other side of Marc.

She turned back to the view.

White-suited Frenchmen in solar *topis* or panama hats, with silk-clad wives on their arms, wearing sun hats or carrying white parasols to protect complexions that were never meant for such a land, were strolling down the steps and away from the church.

Some were heading further into the town, others towards the crowds that thronged the promenade encircling the Petit Lac, which was red-gold in the reflected blaze from the flame trees.

In the cafés beyond the copper statue of Mother Maria that stood at the foot of the cathedral steps, she could see white-turbaned waiters in long white tunics moving deferentially between marble-topped tables as they served aperitifs to customers who scarcely deigned to glance at them.

Occasionally, glimpses of Vietnamese life broke into the scene in the shape of a peasant in black, brown or white calico, in a conical straw hat and wooden sandals, or a pousse-pousse being pulled by a coolie hunched between the shafts, or a graceful golden-skinned native woman clad in a silken *ao dai* in one of the many bright colours that she so admired every time she saw them.

'What're you thinking about?' Philippe asked, coming up and standing beside her.

'Nothing in particular,' she said with a smile. 'Just what a lovely scene it is. And how gorgeous the clothes of the native women.'

He looked around. 'It *is* beautiful, and yes, they are.'

She glanced at him. 'D'you ever think about returning to France?'

'That's a strange question,' he remarked. 'As we haven't even been here for a year, the answer's probably no. Placements like mine are usually for at least two years, and maybe for as many as five. We knew that when we came.'

He paused. 'But it doesn't mean to say that we couldn't

leave if we wanted to. Are you nostalgic for France, and wanting to go back?'

'There's hardly any need to do so,' she said with an attempt at lightness. 'Living here's about as close as you can get to living in France. Everything around us is French. We only realise we're not in France when we step into the Old Quarter.'

'You say that, but I'm not sure I believe you. I won't pretend that I haven't noticed you've not been yourself for the past couple of weeks.'

He paused, hesitating. 'You know, if you wanted to go back to France, Lucette, even though it's less than a year since we got here, I'd ask for a transfer. I can only be happy if you're happy.'

She took his arm. 'You're right that I've not been quite my usual self. But don't ask me why as I couldn't tell you. It's not because I want to leave Hanoi, though.' She forced a reassuring smile.

'Please let me in on what's worrying you?' he said, his voice suddenly very serious. 'You mustn't keep anything from me. Whatever it is, if I know about it, we can work it out together.'

She looked up at him, at the warmth and love in his eyes, and at the concern for her.

The temptation to tell him what she knew was suddenly overwhelming. She started to open her mouth, and then stopped.

If he knew what Marc was doing, a man he genuinely liked, it would put him in a terrible position, a dangerous position, and the uncertainty about what to do could tear him apart. She couldn't do that to him. For his sake, she had to keep her knowledge to herself.

'It's just that I'm not sure how safe I feel,' she said, and she gave a short laugh. 'I know that sounds mad. We control everything here, and the Sûreté is second to none. And we've highly trained troops stationed around the town.' She bit her lip. 'Maybe it's knowing that we need troops and police to guard us that's unsettling.'

'But the situation's no different from when we arrived.'

She turned to him, her eyes watering. 'But *I* am,' she said. 'I've seen now how the natives live, everything we've taken from them, the poverty of their lives compared with ours. They must hate us. It's only a couple of years since that hatred broke out and we were attacked. We may have won then, but they're bound to try it again one day.'

He was quiet for a moment.

'I think you're trying to tell me something, Lucette,' he said slowly. 'I need you to be more specific.'

A weighty silence hung in the air between them.

Then she shook her head and laughed dismissively. 'Of course, I'm not. I'm just being silly. Ignore me.'

'Why should Philippe ignore you?' Simonne asked coming up to them.

'We're joking,' Philippe said. 'No one could ignore Lucette, least of all me—she's beautiful.'

'How very romantic, Philippe,' Simonne said with a smile. 'I order you to instruct Marc as to how it's done.'

All three laughed.

Marc came across to them. 'If everyone's ready, shall we set off? There's a call I need to make from the house before we eat.'

'Not another one!' Simonne exclaimed. 'You made two before we came out.'

'We're in the middle of a project, that's why,' Marc said quickly.

'Which project?' Philippe asked in surprise.

'It's to do with the garrison. Don't worry, Philippe. You've not been involved in that,' he said, and he smiled at Philippe.

Lucette glanced at Marc. His smile was strained.

He was afraid, she realised in alarm.

She looked quickly at Simonne. From the expression on Simonne's face, she, too, had picked up on the fear that emanated from Marc.

Despite the heat of the day, she felt cold.

J'AI deux amours was playing softly on the gramophone.

'Marc ordered this from Paris,' Simonne told Lucette. 'He knows I love Josephine Baker's voice. He thinks it's too light and fluffy, but I think it's soothing jazz at its best.'

'Sorry, Marc, but I agree with Simonne,' Lucette said with an apologetic smile.

'I'm prepared to forgive that,' Marc said, 'and to offer you a cognac, nevertheless. You haven't had anything at all to drink today. Can I tempt you?' He raised the decanter of cognac and angled it in her direction.

Smiling, she shook her head. 'No, thank you. It was a lovely meal, but I've had sufficient. I wouldn't say no to a coffee, though.'

'Would anyone else, apart from me, like another cognac?' Marc asked.

Both Philippe and Simonne declined, but asked for a coffee.

'I'll have to drink alone in that case,' Marc said, and he poured some cognac into the snifter next to him.

Then he pressed the bell for Mme. Mercier, and asked her to bring coffee for them all.

'Which reminds me, Lucette,' Simonne said. 'Shall we go to Club French and then Café Barnard on Wednesday?'

Lucette nodded. 'I'd like that. And I hope Gaston decides to pop in, too. I feel a bit guilty about making it clear last week that we didn't want to talk to him.'

Marc paused in lifting the snifter to his lips. 'You didn't mention seeing Gaston, Simonne. Or say that you'd effectively given him the brush-off. It's unlike you not to be pleased to see him.'

Simonne glanced at Lucette, and then back at Marc. 'I didn't realise I hadn't told you we'd seen him. Lucette and I were talking, and I suppose we weren't really in a Gaston mood. That's right, isn't it, Lucette?'

Lucette nodded, and pulled a face. 'I feel a bit bad at how obvious we were. Poor Gaston couldn't get away fast enough.'

'What did he want?' Marc asked, swirling his brandy around the glass.

'For us all to go to Hôtel Métropole this afternoon to see a Charlie Chaplin film,' Lucette told him. 'It was a bit embarrassing as I had to tell him that we couldn't as we were coming to you.'

'What did he say to that?' Marc asked.

Lucette shrugged. 'Just that he'd go by himself. What else could he say? I think we both felt a little awkward, though.'

'I almost asked him to join us,' Simonne volunteered. 'But I remembered you saying you wanted it to be just the four of us today.'

'That's right. I've nothing against Gaston—he's charm itself, very good company and generous to a fault. But Philippe and I see him almost every day, and I rather liked the idea of a social occasion when he wasn't with us.'

The door opened and Mme. Mercier came in with a hostess trolley, followed by Tan, who was carrying a large cafetière.

Mme. Mercier put the milk and sugar on the table, gave each of them a demi-tasse cup and saucer, and put a silver stand in the centre of the table, on which there was a selection of petits fours.

'You can leave the cafetière, Tan. We'll pour the coffee when it's ready. There's no need for either of you to delay your siesta further,' Marc told them with a slight nod. 'Tell Cook he can go up, too.'

'Thank you, Monsieur,' the housekeeper said, and she and Tan left the room.

Simonne waited for a moment or two, and then pressed down the cafetière plunger, and filled each small cup with coffee.

'Help yourself to petits fours,' she said, and she picked up her cup and sat back. 'The record seems to have finished, Marc. Would you put on another, please? You can choose this time.'

Marc picked up his cup, drank his coffee and stood up. 'If you'll excuse me a moment, there's something I have to do. I'll put on another record when I come back, Simonne.'

With a brief smile, he went across to the gramophone, removed the stylus from the record, and then left the dining room. A moment later, they heard the office door close behind him.

'Marc slept badly last night, and he's been restless since he got up,' Simonne told them.

'Why d'you think that is?' Lucette asked.

Simonne shrugged. 'I don't know.'

The two women stared at each other. Fear flickered in the eyes of both.

'It's a busy time at work, and he might be feeling the pressure,' Philippe suggested.

'Well, if he is, it's the first time he's made it so obvious,' Simonne snapped.

Her face anxious, Lucette turned to Philippe. 'Are you having a difficult time of it, too, Philippe? You *would* tell me if you were, wouldn't you?'

'I'm fine,' he assured her. 'And, yes, I would.'

'My apologies,' Marc said, coming back into the dining room, tucking a small piece of white paper into his trouser pocket. 'It's turned out to be one of those days. I wouldn't mind some more coffee, Simonne.'

As she picked up the cafetière, there was a knock on the back door.

No one moved.

The clock sounded loud in the silence that fell on the room.

'I'll get it,' Marc said. 'Just as well I've not yet sat down again.' He went out of the room and they heard him go into the kitchen. A few minutes later, he returned, smiling.

'It was Mai,' he said, sitting down. 'She wanted to speak to Tan, but I told her she was too late—that Tan was upstairs.'

The sense of relief around the table was palpable.

'Who else would like more coffee?' Simonne asked, filling Marc's cup.

Before anyone could reply, there was another knock on the kitchen door.

Motionless, they all stared at the dining room door.

Then Simonne put the cafetière back on the table and stood up.

'It'll be Mai again. It really is too bad of her. You stay

sitting, Marc. Would it be all right with you if Tan goes across to her later, Lucette?'

'Of course, it would.'

Simonne went briskly out of the room, and moments later, they heard indistinct sounds in the kitchen.

All eyes were on Simonne as she came back in. Her face was chalk-white. Just behind her came Mai, who was visibly trembling.

And behind them both was Gaston.

In his hand, he was holding a small piece of white paper.

38

His face ashen, Marc rose slowly to his feet, and stared wordlessly across the room at Gaston.

Philippe glanced swiftly at Lucette, and then at Marc, and he, too, stood up. Pushing back his chair, he moved to Lucette's side, and placed his hand lightly on her shoulder.

Gaston waved the small piece of paper. 'This originated with you, I believe, Marc.'

'You know it did,' Marc said quietly.

Simonne jumped up, ran to Marc and clutched his arm, facing Gaston with a mixture of fear and defiance.

Gaston nodded. 'You're right, I *did* know that.'

Lucette looked up at Philippe, deathly white. Her gaze lingered a moment on his face, and then she turned back to Gaston.

'How long have you known?' Marc asked, grasping Simonne's hand.

'We've known what you've been doing for months.'

Marc nodded slowly.

He released Simonne's hand, and tried to push her away

from him, but she grabbed his hand again, and stood as close to him as she could.

'And we were pretty sure what would be happening this afternoon,' Gaston went on. 'You were going to make sure that no one in the Résidence or garrison had any idea of the planned uprising, and then you were going to let the terrorists know they could go ahead.'

He held up the paper again. 'No piece of paper, no uprising.' He lowered his hand. 'But you were wrong, Marc, I'm afraid. *We* were aware of the terrorists' plans.'

'Who's the we?' Marc asked.

'Why, the Sûreté, of course.'

There was a collective intake of breath in the room.

'I knew it!' Marc exclaimed. 'All along, I've felt there was something about you that didn't ring true. I as good as told Simonne that. One minute we didn't know you, and the next, you were with us in everything we did.'

'Oh dear, Marc,' he said soothingly. 'The first thing we're taught is always to trust our instinct. It's a pity you didn't have the same instructor.'

Marc freed himself from Simonne, and took a step forward. 'So what are you going to do?'

'Well, for a start, there'll be no uprising. We don't need the terrorists to identify themselves in such a way as we already know who they are and where they come from. We can arrest them whenever we want.'

Marc frowned. 'Why let everything get as far as it has, then?'

Gaston shrugged. 'I needed sufficient evidence before accusing someone of your seniority. And also,' he added with a dry smile, 'I've been letting you to do some of the work for us. With most of the terrorists now in Hanoi, along with the bombs they made and the arms they intended to use, it'll be easy to take them in. Plus, although we knew the locations of some of the caches of arms, we didn't know them all. Now we'll get the lot.'

'You won't put an end to this,' Marc said defiantly. 'For every person you catch, there'll be double the number the following day.'

Gaston nodded. 'I'm sure you're right. And in the fulness of time, they, too, will be captured. In the meantime.'

Holding the piece of paper aloft, he very slowly tore it into little pieces.

Rooted to the spot in fear, they watched as the scraps of paper floated to the floor.

'No confirmation, no uprising,' Gaston said. 'Just five people in this room, who either plotted to overthrow the administration, or who knew about the plot and chose not to report it, which makes them just as guilty.'

Marc shook his head vigorously. 'You're wrong about that. I'm the only one involved. The others don't know a thing.'

'Now that's not true, Marc, is it?' Gaston said, wagging his index finger admonishingly. 'For a start, Mai is clearly guilty.'

He glanced at Mai, who stood a little way to the side of him, her head bowed.

Her trembling increased.

Then he looked back at Marc.

'And we both know that Lucette and Simonne were aware of what you were doing.'

Simonne's hand flew to her throat. She stared at Gaston in panic.

Marc went white. He went back to Simonne and put his arm around her shoulders. 'I'm so sorry,' he mouthed.

'As did Philippe,' Gaston added.

'No!' Lucette cried. Jumping up, she caught hold of Philippe's hand. 'No, he didn't. You're wrong, Gaston. He didn't know anything. He's completely innocent. Please, let him go.'

Gaston looked at her, the expression in his eyes softening. 'I'm afraid that it's you who's wrong, Lucette. Philippe knew exactly what was going on.'

'No, he didn't!' She spun round to face Philippe, and tried to pull him forward. 'Tell him, Philippe.'

'Gaston's right, Lucette—I *did* know.'

Marc gave an exclamation of surprise.

'Oh, Philippe, no.' She let out a loud sob.

'How did you find out, Gaston?' Philippe asked. 'I've not said a word to anyone, not even to Lucette.'

'Your face confirmed what I'd suspected. When I came into the room, Marc and Lucette looked at me. But not you. You looked at Lucette, and there was fear in your eyes, but fear for Lucette, not for yourself.'

Philippe put his arm around Lucette's shoulders. 'Of course, I'd be afraid for her. I love her with all my heart.'

Lucette slid her arm around Philippe's back, and edged closer to him.

'It took me a while to work it out, Philippe, I must admit,' Gaston said. 'I don't like loose ends, and it had been bothering me that a week or so ago, when Simonne was in your house talking to Lucette, you returned home, went inside, but came out moments later. You hung around a bit and then went in again.'

Lucette glanced at Philippe in surprise, and then back at Gaston. 'I don't understand,' she said, frowning in bewilderment.

Gaston smiled. 'Correct me if I'm wrong, Philippe, but I'm surmising that the first time you went in, you heard

Lucette and Simonne talking about Marc's nefarious activities.'

Lucette's heart gave a sudden jolt.

'You didn't want them to know you'd heard them,' he continued, 'so you went out, and then came in again, this time making enough noise for them to hear you and end their conversation. He was thinking of you, Lucette. He thought it'd be less fretful for you if you didn't know he'd overheard you.'

He felt an acute pang as he saw Lucette's expression as she looked up into Philippe's face.

'Oh, Philippe,' she whispered, her words weighted by love.

He turned to Simonne. 'As for you, Simonne, like Lucette, you were caught up in something you'd rather not have known about. I imagine you thought a wife would be presumed to know what a husband was doing, and decided that your only option was to say nothing.'

Simonne nodded. 'That's right. I didn't have a choice. But Mai was in an even harder position,' she added, looking across at Mai. 'She was obliged to help Marc because he'd found work for her. It's not her fault. You must let her go.'

'On the contrary,' Gaston said, 'she's been deeply involved for a long time, and willingly so. The instructions she followed came not from Marc, but from her terrorist friend, Vinh.'

Mai gasped. Her hand flew to her mouth. She looked at Gaston in panic.

'But what's interesting about your defence of Mai, Simonne,' Gaston went on, ignoring Mai's silent plea, 'is that it came from *you*. I've lost count of the number of times you've made disparaging remarks about the natives. So just now, you managed to surprise me, which I don't often say.'

Simonne glanced across at Mai. Their eyes met.

'Mai's my sister,' she said quietly.

'What!' Philippe exclaimed.

'Well, well. I certainly missed that,' Gaston said ruefully. 'You, too, Philippe, judging by the look on your face. So, Mai.'

He turned to Mai.

'You left your bag in the kitchen. Get it and go to Vinh as you planned. No one will stop you. My operatives are in the Old Quarter. But when you've met him, don't try to get word to the terrorists. You'll immediately head south and leave Hanoi. If you make any attempt to do otherwise, you and Vinh will be arrested.'

'I can go?' Mai asked tremulously. 'I can really go.'

'That's what I said.'

Her eyes brimming with tears, she looked up at him with gratitude. 'Thank you, Monsieur.'

'You realise, don't you,' he told her, 'that if you're ever seen in Hanoi again, either you or Vinh, you'll be captured and taken to Hoa Lo. I'm sure I don't need to tell you what that means.'

'I understand,' Mai said, her hand on her heart. 'Thank you.'

'Oh, thank you, Gaston,' Simonne cried, and she ran across to Mai, put her arms around her and hugged her.

Then with tears in her eyes, she released Mai and stepped back.

Mai stared intently at Simonne, as if memorising her features. 'My sister,' she said, her voice shaking with love. 'Thank you.'

She glanced across the room to Lucette and Philippe. 'I'm sorry, Monsieur et Madame. You are good people and I deceived you.'

Then with a wan smile that embraced them all, she turned and ran from the room.

A moment later, they heard the kitchen door close behind her.

Simonne moved back to Marc's side, but gesturing to her to stay away from him, he went a few steps closer to Gaston.

'I'm very relieved and very grateful that you've let Mai go, Gaston,' Marc said. 'Will you now let the others leave? None of them deserves to be punished—only me.'

Gaston looked slowly around the room.

His gaze moved from Simonne, whose face was devoid of colour, to Lucette. He lingered a few moments on her terrified face as she clung to Philippe. Then he encountered Philippe's defiance and, finally, he looked back at Marc.

'*I'm* doing nothing,' he said. 'But *you* are.'

'And what exactly does that mean?' Marc said angrily. 'Stop playing around with us, man.'

'You, Marc, are going to resign immediately from your post, and you and Simonne will leave Vietnam this week. Blame an illness in your family, if you like. You can go wherever you want, and do whatever you want, except that you're never again to work for the French Government. Not in any country, not in any capacity. I shall see that your name's blacklisted.'

Simonne moved to Marc's side.

He glanced at her, questioning, and then looked back at Gaston. 'I don't understand,' he said in bewilderment.

Gaston shrugged. 'You probably hadn't thought as far ahead as to what you would do after the terrorists' revolution, had it succeeded. Had you done so, you'd realise that I'm putting you in the position you would have been, had that happened.'

'What about Marc's work?' Philippe intervened. 'He can't just walk away from it.'

'He can if there's someone to take it over. And there is— *you'll* step into his shoes.'

'Me?' Philippe exclaimed.

'It'll take a good year for them to find a replacement for Marc. In that time, you'll be able to decide if you want to apply for the position permanently, or if you'd rather move somewhere else. You'll have done two years here so you could ask for a transfer if you wanted.'

Weakened by the surge of relief that flooded through them, Philippe and Lucette tightened their hold on each other.

'Thank you, Gaston,' Lucette said, her voice shaking. 'Thank you so very much.'

'Is that why you let Mai go free?' Marc asked. 'So she couldn't be forcibly persuaded to tell the truth?'

Gaston nodded. 'Well reasoned, Marc.'

'But why, Gaston?' Marc asked, putting his arm around Simonne's shoulders. 'You've put a huge amount of effort into your operation, and it's obviously involved a number of people, and a substantial sum of money. After all that, why would you let us walk away?'

'It's a good question,' Gaston said with a wry smile. 'And one I'll be asking myself in the weeks ahead. When I came here today, I intended to take you all into custody. But when I saw you in front of me, I knew I couldn't.' He gave an awkward laugh. 'I can't really give you a good reason why.'

'I can, dear Gaston,' Lucette said, moving across to him. 'On one of the days we were in the Old Quarter, I happened to glance at your face and I saw your genuine horror. It was as if you were seeing for the first time—truly seeing—the appalling conditions there, and you were as shocked as I.'

'Is that so?'

She smiled up at him. 'Yes. You're essentially a good man, and I think that in that moment you understood why so many natives are risking their lives by fighting us, and why Marc decided to help them.'

He shrugged. 'Maybe there's something in that,' he said. 'But maybe it's simply that, without intending to, I came to like you all. I've always relied on myself, and have never felt the need of friends. But as I wormed my way into your lives, I found that I actually liked being there.'

'And we liked having you with us,' she said warmly.

He gave a short laugh. 'Not always! I don't think I realised quite how much I enjoyed being a part of your group until you and Simonne ousted me from Café Barnard that day.'

'I'm sorry we hurt you, Gaston,' Lucette said. 'But Simonne was telling me about Mai being her sister.'

'Whatever the reason, it made me stop and think about you as people. I believe you're sincere, Marc. You're not betraying France for personal profit—you're doing it because you think we're acting wrongly. And you, Philippe, you'd do anything to protect Lucette. And you'd go a long way to support Marc, too. He's your friend and you're loyal to him.'

Philippe nodded. 'Yes, he is.'

'And Simonne would never report Marc, the man she loves, even though she must've been horrified that he was helping the natives. I can respect that. As for Lucette.'

His gaze settled on Lucette with deep affection, and he took a step towards her.

'I came to like Lucette very much,' he said, his eyes on her face. 'You'll note I said *like*, Philippe,' he said with a wry smile at Philippe. His gaze returned to Lucette's face.

'It was never more than that. But it so very easily could have been.'

'Oh, Gaston,' she whispered.

'You're a lovely person, Lucette. You're kind and gentle, and you genuinely care about those who are less fortunate. That's a very rare quality. I could never do anything that might hurt you, which arresting Marc would have done. I just couldn't. So I had no choice but to let you all stay free. Do as I suggest, and you will.'

Lucette's eyes filled with tears. 'Thank you, Gaston,' she said, and she put her hand gently on his arm. 'You've been a true friend. I do hope we won't be the last friends you make —you have so much to give.'

He nodded in acknowledgement.

'For someone who's not used to having friends, you're remarkably good company,' Marc said drily. 'And as one of the few friends you've got, I'm anxious about what's going to happen to you. How will you account for not arresting us?'

'I'll blind them with the numbers of those we do arrest, and with the mountain of arms we've seized, and with the fact that I've broken the delivery chain that began with you. In that respect, I've done as I was asked.'

'I can see you could get away with that for the others, but you said the Sûreté knows the extent of my involvement,' Marc said anxiously. 'They'll want to know why you didn't bring me in.'

'There's knowing and proving. I'll say that a thorough search of your house and office in the Résidence failed to reveal any evidence of your involvement in terrorism. To throw someone of your status into prison without any proof would be frowned upon by Paris. The administration here knows that, and they'll have to accept my report.'

Marc's shoulders relaxed. 'I won't pretend that I'm not

more grateful than I can say, Gaston, because I am. We all are.'

'What will you do next, Gaston? Will you stay in Hanoi?' Lucette asked.

He shook his head. 'I don't think so. There's one person who won't believe my account, and that's the man I answer to in the Sûreté. Emile will never trust me again, and I doubt he'll buy my story. But provided that Marc leaves Hanoi as soon as possible, there's nothing he can do about it.' He forced a grin. 'Maybe I'll ask to be sent to Africa. I've read enough about it.'

'You mean, you've never been there?' Simonne exclaimed in surprise.

'No. But maybe I should go.'

'You could always be a tour guide here while you're waiting to hear the result of your application for a transfer,' Marc suggested with a slight smile.

Gaston laughed. 'So I could.'

He gave a deep sigh, and looked slowly around the room. 'Well, then,' he said, his words tinged with deep regret. 'It's goodbye, my friends, and good luck for the future. I shall remember you, and I hope you'll sometimes think of me.'

'We will, Gaston,' Lucette said, her voice choked off by tears. 'We often will.'

He gave her a regretful smile, and then turned and walked out of the room.

And out of their lives—out of Lucette's life.

And into emptiness, and the unknown.

But one thing he now knew for certain, that his love for Lucette, and the unexpected feelings of friendship that he'd developed for the others, had shown—he couldn't go back to what he'd been, a loner who had no need of anyone else.

He *did* need friends in his life.

And as he left the Bouviers' house, he resolved that wherever he ended up, he'd leave the door open for friendship, and perhaps for even more than that.

Yes, definitely, for even more than that.

THEY HEARD the back door close behind him.

Relief, tinged with sadness, crept though the room.

But no one moved, no one spoke.

39

L *ater*

WITH HER ARM tucked into his, Lucette sat with Philippe on a bench next to the Petit Lac, listening to the gentle lapping of the water.

The air around them was bitter-sweet fragrant with the lingering aromas from the many flowers that had lined the lakeside path throughout the day, and with the scent from the reeds that grew at the water's edge and from the pink and white lotus flowers that floated on the surface of the lake.

As they sat there, the red-orange hues of the sunset sky melded into the indigo blue of night. And a crescent moon slipped from behind the clouds, and lit a shining path across the expanse of black-green water.

'I haven't forgotten,' Lucette said quietly, breaking into the companionable silence. 'And I'll ever be grateful to you.'

'Forgotten what?' Philippe asked, glancing down at her with a smile.

'That you kept what you heard about Marc to yourself. You didn't want to add to my anxiety, even though it must have been burdensome for you not to have been able to talk about it.' She looked up at him, her eyes watering. 'I can't thank you enough.'

'I don't need any thanks, Lucette. I couldn't do anything else. I love you, and I'm so proud of you. Whatever Gaston may have said about us all, I truly believe that were it not for the fact that he came to see and admire the genuine person you are, we would now be in prison.'

'I think he came to like us all. And why not? Take you for a start. I couldn't have a more lovely, likeable husband,' she said snuggling up to him.

He smiled down at her, and then rested his cheek on the top of her head.

'It's going to be very strange not having Simonne and Marc next door,' she said after a few minutes. 'I liked Simonne very much, and I'm really going to miss her. Every Wednesday I'll think of her. And I'll miss Marc, too. And also Gaston. Nothing's going to be the same again.'

Her eyes watered.

'We'll both miss them. It's impossible to believe that after tomorrow, we'll probably never see them again. Marc's going to use Gaston's family illness idea. He'll say that whatever the outcome, he'll be needed at home, and he won't be back. He'll leave his letter of resignation at the Résidence tomorrow morning, empty his desk and then go home and finish packing.'

'So soon!' she exclaimed.

'For everyone's safety, it has to be. He can't risk Gaston's boss issuing orders to bring him in. They'll be leaving for the port at Saigon the following morning before we're even up.'

She gave a sigh of acceptance. 'It's really sad, but I can see that he has a choice. Perhaps they'll end up in Paris. Simonne would like that.'

She nestled closer to Philippe. 'I wonder who'll move into their house,' she said after a moment or two. 'I hope they're nice.'

'We'll soon find out. I doubt it'll be empty for long. I imagine their servants will be taken on by the new people.'

'I'm glad Tan's coming to us. If she ever hears anything about Mai, I'm sure she'll tell us.'

'From what I've heard about Vinh, he's committed to the revolutionary cause, and won't be abandoning it. Marc told me that Tan refused to be involved in terrorism, and I'm sure she'll keep away from them. I doubt we'll hear anything more about them. And for the sake of our safety, it's better that we don't.'

'Then we'll just have to hope that Mai stays safe,' Lucette said. 'I liked her, and I want you to be wrong about Vinh.'

He raised his head, glanced down at her face and saw her anxiety.

He tightened his hold on her. 'When I've completed a couple of years here, we'll ask to be transferred back to France, or to another country.'

She felt her heart leap in relief. Then she steadied herself.

'It'll be up to you, Philippe, to choose whether we stay or go. Whatever's best for you, is best for me, too.'

'What I'm thinking is, our eyes have been opened to situations around us that could be hard to live with for long. We'll do our best to help the natives whenever we can, but I can see occasions when we might feel less than comfortable.'

She nodded'. Me, too.'

'Of course, everything might look different in a year's time,' he continued. 'But as I see it today, I think it'd be wise to start afresh somewhere new when we're able to do so.'

'I think so, too,' she said quietly.

She felt him plant a kiss on the top of her head.

'Nothing matters to me as much as you, my lovely Lucette,' he said, his voice thick with emotion. 'I want you to have peace of mind.'

She gazed up him. 'And I have it when I'm with you, because I'm with you. I love you with all my heart, Philippe, and I always will.'

And closing her eyes, she leaned against his shoulder.

The last of her anxiety faded, and for the first time in what felt a very long time, her smile came from deep within.

IF YOU ENJOYED HANOI SPRING

It would be really kind if you would take a few minutes to leave a review of the book.

Reviews give welcome feedback to the author, and they help to make the novel visible to other readers, both through the review itself and because many promotional platforms today require a minimum number of reviews before they'll accept any publicity for a book.

Your words, therefore, really do matter.

Thank you!

LIZ'S NEWSLETTER

You might be interested in signing up for Liz's newsletter.

Every month, Liz sends out a newsletter with updates on her writing, what she's been doing, where she's been travelling, and an interesting fact she's learned. Subscribers also hear of promotions and special offers.

Rest assured, Liz would never pass on your email address to anyone else.

As a thank you for signing up to Liz's newsletter, you'll get a free full length novel.

To sign up and get a free book, go to:

www.lizharrisauthor.com

ACKNOWLEDGMENTS

As always, I shall begin by thanking my brilliant cover designer, Jane Dixon-Smith, for another really striking cover, which captures the tone of *Hanoi Spring*, and my superb editor Jane Eastgate, whose advice was invaluable.

Also, a huge thank you to my Friend in the North, Stella, who sees every completed manuscript before anyone else, and who never fails to give me much-welcome constructive criticism.

Highlights of the year are my regular lunches, and occasional writing retreats, with my writer friends. A thank you to the many writer friends I've made over the years—too many to mention. You help to make the writing process such an enjoyable one, and far from a lonely one.

In writing *Hanoi Spring,* I drew upon many different sources, including my own experience during my visit to wonderful Vietnam. It would be impossible to list them all, but I must mention S*aigon,* by Anthony Green, *Dumb Luck*, by Vu Trong Phung, and *Dragons on the Roof,* by Carol Howland. Invaluable also were the books published by the Thê Giói Publishers, which I bought in Vietnam.

I should like to thank also Linda Mazur, the author of *Hidden Hanoi Houses.* During my research, I encountered praise for talks she'd given, and for her guided tours of Hanoi. I was unable to buy her book as it was available only in Vietnam, but when I made contact with her, she was kind enough to send me the notes for one of her walking tours.

I'm extremely grateful to her for her kindness. If I've made any mistakes, the faults will be mine alone.

A note about France. I love France, and I love French, in which I used to be fluent. I still have some very good friends in France, and I'm hoping that they won't be upset by aspects of this novel. I've been true to what I found during my research, but as with Marc Bouvier, it doesn't mean that I don't still love France, because I do.

Finally, a heartfelt thank you to my husband, Richard, who keeps the real world at bay while my characters and I live in my fictional world.

INTRODUCING 'DARJEELING INHERITANCE'

Although part of a series called The Colonials, *Hanoi Spring, Darjeeling Inheritance* and *Cochin Fall* are all standalone novels. They are set in different years, in different locations, and with different characters.

If you enjoyed *Hanoi Spring* – and I hope you did – and haven't yet read *Darjeeling Inheritance*, set in 1930, the first book in the series to be published, I thought you might enjoy reading its Prologue, which you'll find in the next few pages.

DARJEELING INHERITANCE: THE PROLOGUE

In the foothills of the Himalayas,
  Darjeeling, April, 1919

The early spring sun beat down on the back of the seven-year old girl as she struggled to keep up with the man in a worn safari suit who was striding ahead of her up the steep path.

Every so often, the girl slipped and fell on the red earth, picked herself up, brushed the dirt from her dress and hurried more quickly after the man.

But Charles Edwin Lawrence, lines of grief etched deep into his sun-browned face, neither turned to his daughter nor paused to wait for her. His eyes fixed in front of him, he continued resolutely up the narrow path that led between the tiered rows of tea bushes, the tender young leaves of which shone brilliant green in the light of the sun.

When he arrived at the summit, he stood in the cool breeze and stared down at the neat rows of terraces that fell away beneath his feet.

His vision blurred with unshed tears, he turned to face

the mass of dark green forested slopes that rose in layers beneath the clear blue sky, and the range of mountains behind them, their gold-tipped peaks linked in a chain of gold above the snow-covered slopes, as if suspended in nothingness.

The girl reached the place where her father stood, slid her arm round his leg and put her thumb in her mouth.

He glanced down at her, bent slightly and gently pushed her thumb away from her mouth. 'Only babies do that, Charlie. You're not a baby any longer.'

'I'm seven now.'

He nodded. 'That's right. So you're not a baby any longer, are you? You're a big girl, who'll soon be off to school.'

Biting her lower lip, she stared at the ground and nodded.

She sensed him smile his approval.

Glancing up, she saw tears on his cheeks, and she frowned. 'You're crying. You've got a wet face.'

He shrugged his shoulders dismissively. 'It'll just be perspiration. I suggest you look at the view instead of looking at me.'

Picking her up under her arms, he swung her high up above his head, and slid her on to his shoulders. Her legs hung down in front of him on either side of his face, and he took hold of each foot.

Clutching his forehead with one hand, she ran her other hand down the side of his cheek.

'You *are* crying, Papa,' she said, her voice accusing, and she wiped her wet hand on the skirt of her dress. She pulled the *topi* from his head, let it fall to the ground, wrapped her arms around his chin, leaned forward, and rested her cheek against the back of his head. 'Is Eddie ill again? I haven't seen him today.'

She felt him tighten.

He pulled one of her feet closer to the other so that he could hold them both with one hand, and she wobbled as he swiftly ran his free hand across his face. Then once more, he held a foot in each hand.

'Yes, he's been ill again,' he said after a short pause.

Her forehead wrinkled with puzzlement at the strange note she heard in his voice. She inclined herself sideways in an attempt to see his face.

'But not any longer,' he added quietly. 'He's gone to join your brothers.'

She straightened up and let out a wail of misery. 'I don't want him to go. I want him to play with me.' A sob rose in her throat, and she screwed up her face, ready to cry.

'You're not going to cry, are you, Charlie? Remember what we said about you being a big girl. Well, I need you to be big. Kick your foot against me if you're going to be big.'

She swallowed her sob, and with his hand still tightly holding her leg, kicked his chest with her right foot.

'Good girl,' he said. 'You see, it's just you and me now. And all of this.' Slowly he turned in a full circle, with Charlie sitting high on his shoulders. 'Just look at it all. Sundar is Hindi for beautiful. You can see why my father called it Sundar. We love it here; it's where we want to be. My grandfather and father both loved Sundar, and so do we, you and me. Isn't that so?'

She nodded.

'Say it, Charlie. Say, It's where I want to be.'

'It's where I want to be,' she echoed.

'Good girl. Look around you. I bet you've never noticed that tea bushes don't grow all year round—they're asleep from late November to early March. They won't wake up and start growing again until the first rains of spring have fallen and the sun has warmed the air. But then they'll grow so quickly that they'll need to be plucked every four to five days. Did you know that?'

She shifted her position.

'Hold tight,' he said, 'and I'll get you down.' He raised his arms, lifted her up over his head and stood her on the ground next to him.

Then he knelt down beside her and stared into her face. 'There's only you left now, Charlie. There won't be any more.'

She felt a momentary fear at his serious expression, and put her thumb back into her mouth.

'But I know that Sundar's in your heart, just as it's in mine, and when the time comes I'll do my very best to make sure you have a husband who'll be able to run the garden when I've gone, and who'll continue to grow the very best tea that Darjeeling can produce. There'll always be a Lawrence at Sundar. That's what we both want, isn't it?'

She could tell that he wanted her to nod, so she did.

He gave a dry laugh, and stood up. 'You've no idea what I'm talking about, have you?' he said, his voice relaxing. 'But one day you will.' He gave a playful tug on the long auburn hair that hung from under her *topi*.

She stared up at his face, and saw that his eyes were red and he still looked sad, even though his mouth was shaped into a smile.

'It's where I want to be,' she repeated.

His smiled broadened, and this time his eyes smiled, too, and she felt a glow of happiness spread through her.

She was very sad that Eddie had gone to join the two older brothers she'd never met. She'd loved Eddie and had been looking forward to him being old enough to play with her, and now she was left with only the servants' children to play with and her *ayah*.

But she was happy that her father thought that she and he were alike. She wouldn't have wanted to be like her mother, who always seemed angry.

'I want to grow tea, too, Papa,' she said.

Her father laughed. 'Like I said, you're a Lawrence through and through, Charlie.' He leaned down and hugged her. Then he straightened up and stared again at the terraces that lay below them and on either side.

His gaze drifted across the verdant bushes to the house where the last of his sons lay, silent ever more, and his smile faded.

ABOUT THE AUTHOR

Born in London, Liz Harris graduated from university with a Law degree, and then moved to California, where she led a varied life, from waitressing on Sunset Strip to working as secretary to the CEO of a large Japanese trading company.

Six years later, she returned to London and completed a degree in English, after which she taught secondary school pupils, first in Berkshire, and then in Cheshire.

In addition to the fourteen novels she's had published to date, she's had several short stories in anthologies and magazines.

Liz now lives in Oxfordshire. An active member of the Romantic Novelists' Association and the Historical Novel Society, her interests are travel, the theatre, reading and cryptic crosswords.

To find out more about Liz, visit her website at: www. lizharrisauthor.com

ALSO BY LIZ HARRIS

HISTORICAL NOVELS

The Colonials

Darjeeling Inheritance

Cochin Fall

Hanoi Spring

The Linford Series

A sweeping saga set between the wars

The Dark Horizon

The Flame Within

The Lengthening Shadow

General Historical Novels

The Road Back

A Bargain Struck

The Lost Girl (To be republished in 2023 under the title 'Golden Tiger')

A Western Heart

CONTEMPORARY NOVELS

The Best Friend

Word Perfect

Contemporary novels set in Umbria

Evie Undercover

The Art of Deception

Printed in Great Britain
by Amazon

32150919R00209